PURGATORY'S
REVENGE

OTHER BOOKS BY J. B. SISAM

FICTION

Divine Providence

King Lyle and the Purple Dragon

Vengeance at Purgatory | Jacob Creek Book 1

NON-FICTION

Grace: What's So Amazing About It?

Thinking Forward Journal

Focus Up, In, and Out

You can purchase any of Jason's books on his website or at your favorite retailer!

JBSISAM.COM

A Jacob Creek Novel | BOOK 2

PURGATORY'S
REVENGE

J. B. SISAM

LIVING LIGHTS
PUBLISHING

MINNEAPOLIS, MINNESOTA

For more information visit…
JBSISAM.COM

Published by Living Lights Publishing / Sisam Enterprise
P. O. Box 43732
Minneapolis, MN 55443

Scripture quotations taken from the New King James Version®. Copyright © 1982 by Thomas Nelson. Used by permission. All rights reserved.

Scripture quotations are taken from King James Version (Public Domain)

ISBN: 979-8-9856493-0-7 (*print edition*)

Printed in the United States of America
10 9 8 7 6 5 4 3 2 1

IN LOVING MEMORY OF UNCLE VICTOR

A true Texan and cowboy at heart, and he gave me my first belt buckle.
You are forever in my heart, and I miss you every day.
I love you!

PURGATORY'S
REVENGE

PROLOGUE

For from within, out of people's hearts, come evil thoughts, sexual immoralities, thefts, and murder.

— JESUS

ONE

I t didn't take long to escape that house, and away from his father's watchful eye. He walked around the front of the house to avoid his father's staff, and found his way to the kitchen's back door. His next move was to check the kitchen for a knife.

He tiptoed toward the door, peeked inside, and scanned the room. No one was there. He slipped in and grabbed the nearest knife off the counter, then bolted out. Nobody saw him. He smiled and ran into the woodlands behind his family home.

He raced through the woods as several branches and twigs slapped him in the face. A few nicks and scratches didn't bother him. Joy flooded his mind. His eyes darted back and forth, searching for any sign of a small animal he desired, no, needed, to kill.

Home, not a place he enjoyed and hated. Father punished him for any slight wrongdoing. His parents weren't saints. They always fought. So, today seemed fitting because Mother was mad at Father and took to the cottage just outside of town, leaving him alone with his ruthless father. A rustle of leaves caught his ear. He crouched in search of what made the sound.

The boy sighed. The rustling continued, and he glimpsed grey fur poking out from behind a fallen branch.

Gotcha!

The leaves crunched under his weight. He slid out the kitchen knife. Sure, he'd get in trouble for sneaking away from the residence and into the woods, but this grand adventure was far better than lying in an enormous mansion with nothing to do but smash floor crawling bugs.

He heard several gunshots echo from near the estate, and he figured some of his father's men were goofing around. No doubt sitting around bored them. Let them have their fun and he'd have his own kind of fun. He peeked at the fallen branch and crouched down. A rabbit munched on a few loose berries, unsuspecting that he'd soon be dead. In one swift motion, he grabbed the creature by the fur, yanking it up and away from its snack. He looked into the hare's eyes, and a grin crawled its way across his lips. This rabbit wasn't anyone's dinner and in fact, all he wanted to do was slice its throat and dismember the animal limb by limb. He would watch it bleed out.

The rabbit squealed and kicked its long paddle like feet, desperately trying to escape the boy's death clutch. Grasping the knife, he positioned the steel on the animal's throat. No one was coming, no one would care. This was his catch. This was his kill.

Just as his hand arched downward toward the creature's neck, a cry cut through the wooded area.

"Felix!"

Felix's hand froze mid slice. He focused on the intruding sound. Had someone seen him run away from the kitchen holding the food weapon? Was his father rampaging about because his son was not at home?

The animal continued its screaming and twirling in his grip. And that's when he remembered why he came. Felix wished to kill. He needed to feel the life drain out of a living animal. Without hesitation, Felix drew the sharp blade across the rabbit's throat. Blood spilled from the neck and snaked down his fingers before dripping off his elbows. He held the animal close to his face and looked into its lifeless eyes. Like two black orbs, unseeing, unmoving, sitting neatly in their sockets.

Felix smiled.

TWO

Somehow, looking into the two black holes, Felix felt this animal could fill in for his father. Because Felix was only 10 years old, he didn't have the strength to kill his father. Maybe one day, and maybe when his mother had enough of Gabriel Grant ruining her life, could he do something about his father.

Felix tossed the animal aside and washed his hands in a nearby stream. The chilly water rushed over his bloodied hands, and he watched in amazement at the swirling red plumes that floated downstream.

"Felix!"

There it was again. The same voice, the same urgency. Having no clue what time of day it was, he wondered if Mother was home and came looking for him. Mother was the only saving grace Felix had at home. Nothing Felix did pleased his father. If he wasn't doing as his father wished of him, he'd receive a whipping.

"Felix!"

This time the voice drew closer. Time to go home. He

shoved the knife into his back pocket and tromped back through the woods, finding his way back to the house. The mansion rose through the tree line like a giant monument, gaudy, impressive, and too much for this rathole of a town. It reminded him of the colossal buildings in Washington. Two years prior, his father took him on a business trip with the Wyoming Governor to visit the White House. Just like those buildings, his father's mansion was showy and imposing.

Though it was a memorable trip, it reminded Felix of how much money couldn't buy; love. It's all he wanted from his father. Just one brief acknowledgement. But Felix knew better, and so did Mother. One day Felix would be the one to teach him a lesson he'd never forget, make him pay.

As he crossed onto the green lawn, a staff member rushed up to Felix. "Felix, you've got to get home." She grabbed his hand and led him up the hill.

"Why?"

"It's your mother... quick. Your father's study!"

The staff remained calm at all times, but the closer they got to the house, several bodies littered the ground. He assumed they were dead. Upon closer examination, he saw a bullet wound in the chest of one of them.

That must have been the gunshots he heard. Only one thought echoed through his mind. *Who shot them?*

She saw he was staring and sought to cover his eyes from seeing the lifeless bodies, but that's all he wished to look at; the blood, the violence, and the gun fight carnage.

"Felix, your father demands to see you. He's in the study. It's about your mother."

The boy ran into the home. Upon arriving, he dashed past the grand staircase as he whirled into the hallway. Darting left, he enters the study and saw Mother laying in a pool of her own blood. It halted him in his steps.

So much blood. Her grey skin and lifeless eyes caused him to turn away and spit vomit. *Who did this to Mother?*

"Mother?"

He dropped and cradled her cold, clay-like hand in his. A lone tear slipped from his eye and dripped onto her pallid skin. He tried rocking her awake.

Nothing.

Like the rabbit he killed earlier, his mother lay dead and nobody would bring her back. Felix's throat tightened as he struggled to maintain control of his emotions. His father wouldn't appreciate the display of frailty. A flutter of heat cascaded behind his eyes and tears streamed down his cheeks.

"Mother—"

The simple term of endearment slipped from his quivering lip, and this time Felix didn't hold back the tears. His mother was dead. Someone had murdered her.

No more birthday wishes. No more dinner. No more spending the day with her. She was dead. That's when he remembered. The staff said his father called for him.

Felix walked out of the study door and asked the butler, who remained pale-faced in the corridor, "Where's Father?"

From the smoking room's entrance across the hallway, Gabriel Grant opened his arms to receive Felix's embrace. Felix collapsed into his father's arms and wept.

"Shhhh…. It's okay," Gabriel said. "He can't hurt you."

Felix pulls back and wipes his tears. "Who?"

"The Preacher." He knelt down. "I'm sorry, I have some sad news for you."

"Worse than Mother dying?"

"Yes." Father took off his hat, "The man who killed your mother is the Preacher."

Felix pushed away from his father and shook his head.

"No!"

"I'm afraid so, son. Jacob Creek caused your mother's death."

Felix remembered the knife in his back pocket. "I want to kill him."

Father pulled closer. "We'll talk later about what needs to happen next."

GOOD TO BE HOME

Behold, the former things have come to pass,
    And new things I declare; Before they spring forth I tell you
of them.

— ISAIAH

CHAPTER ONE

TEN YEARS LATER...

S TORMS APPROACH fast and without warning, striking terror, and often leave a path of destruction in their wake. Jake Callihan surveyed the sky and saw ominous inky clouds swirling and growing. The uneasy feeling of being caught in the open during a thunderstorm made him pause.

A gust of wind blew against his coat. Jake called to Freddy, his foreman, "Let's keep this herd moving. This storm's coming in fast."

The cracking of the leather woven whip exploded above the moaning sound of the cattle. Black clouds gathered above, and heavy rain greyed the fast approaching horizon. Jake and his crew had been on the trail for a month and the journey from Atlantic City, Wyoming to the Callihan-Heller Ranch, located 10 miles outside Cedar Grove, was long and arduous. Storms, mishaps, and sick men made travel harder.

This storm would make getting everyone back to Cedar Grove a fun adventure.

Without another word, they pressed forward until small droplets of rain pelted the ground. The storm arrived and it would take everyone working together to tighten things down. They would have to move fast.

The wind almost flipped Jake's hat off his head. "We need to break for camp before things get worse. Tell everyone we're breaking. I'll head back and tell Ted," Jake said to Freddy before he kicked his animal hard against the side and rode back to the chuck wagon.

"What's up, Boss?" Ted "Wide-Eye" Jeffries asked as Jake rode up alongside the wagon.

"We're breaking for camp. This storm's gonna hit hard." Jake had to yell through the howling wind.

"Sounds good to me." He pulled back hard on the reins, yelling, "Whoa!" and the team of horses slowed to a stop.

The rain had stopped as lightning and thunder rippled through the evening sky. With each thunderous boom, the horses and cattle jolted. Things were getting set for the evening. Jake had placed Freddy as the night herder and watched as his friend rode around the herd, keeping them in place.

Jake was hungry, so he headed back to the chuck wagon.

"Wide-Eye, what do we get for grub tonight?" Ted Jefferies, a skinny black man who had crossed eyes, making it difficult to look at both eyes at once. So, they gave him the name *Wide-Eye*, and it stuck.

"Not much." He hopped down from the wagon. "Oh, just a few cans of beans, coffee, and a few slices of dried beef." His grin was as white as snow against his black features. "Thought I'd save that for you, Boss."

Jake shook his head and returned the smile. "Ted, what would I do without you?"

"You'd starve, that's fershor," the boney man said.

Jake listened to him whistle away as he cooked up some beans and the rest of the dried beef. Ted's cooking was terrible, and Jake didn't have the heart to tell him as much. The old man could drive a chuck wagon like no one else in Cedar Grove. Jake paid him well for his time—fifty and found. Nothing was impossible for Wide-Eye. Jake always had faith in him.

"Food's ready boys!" he said, ringing the dinner triangle.

"Wha'dya got, Wide-Eye? How about a big juicy steak?" Cory Jackson, the drag rider, inquired.

"Not even close." He pulled the spoon out of the boiling pot of beans, pointing it at Cory. "Mock my cooking again, and I'll shove this spoon up yer backside."

There was a ripple of laughter.

Wide-Eye cussed. "Bunch of idiots don't like my cook'n, Boss."

"I'm sure they're grateful, Wide-Eye," Jake said, then grabbed a plate, "and don't cuss."

"Yeah, Wide-Eye, don't ya realize the Boss don't like no cuss'n." Cory tapped his plate on the Cook's head.

"Why I oughta!" He grabbed the spoon again.

"Settle down, old man." Freddy snatched the spoon from Wide-Eye's hand and filled his own plate full of beef and beans.

"Guess this ain't your night, Wide-Eye?" Jake laughed.

Jake rarely ate with the boys, always liked to eat alone and think. He watched as they gathered around the fire, then dug into his own plate next to his horse, Tucker. He wanted to hunker down early.

After dinner, the storm moved in fast. Jake was glad they tied the horses up, or they'd have run clear to the other end of

Wyoming. A few days of travel remained. They would stretch for the food. Sure, they had stocked up in Atlantic City, but the train was late getting fresh supplies into town. He heard that a group of train robbers held up the train and killed the conductor, slicing his throat before tossing him overboard. Once the train arrived, Jake bought all he could without cleaning the General Store out.

It was a freeing feeling to be on the range, moving cattle from one town to another or to his ranch in Cedar Grove. The dust, the smell, everything about it made life enjoyable. Jake had lived a simple life in Cedar Grove for the past ten years, with no desire to move. It took significant amounts of money and loans to maintain his ranch—yet now he was turning a profit with a few small loans.

With these 300 cattle, he would have 1,800 head on the ranch. Not bad. Each animal would still have plenty of acres to roam.

Wide-Eye asked Jake for help. Because the wind kicked up so much dust, he worried sand would fill the water barrels. If that happened, they wouldn't have water to finish the trip, save for each canteen carried.

Jake helped heave a fifty-gallon water barrel into the wagon.

It would be a slow night. "Try to get some sleep, Wide-Eye. This storm won't quit anytime soon. There's nothing else we can do. And in the morning, you'll still have your wagon to pilot."

"Not funny Boss, not funny at all." The bony black man crawled inside the wagon and hunkered down.

"All right boys get some shut-eye, we'll need all the rest we can get. Tomorrow's gonna come fast."

The small tent Jake set up didn't matter, the force of the

wind kept knocking it over. He'd have to tough it out and sleep under the elements of the storm. Some ranch hands loved storms. It gave a sense of being alive. Jake hated them.

He was glad it wasn't raining any longer.

A crack of thunder roared overhead. The heavens lit up like a stick of dynamite. With each lightning finger that snaked across the sky, Jake noticed the dark, rolling clouds. He was sure it would happen, and when it did, it would strike without warning. He pulled on his rain slicker.

Within seconds, rain pelted hard against the ground, creating small pools where they fell. Jake pulled the tent over his head to block most of the water, which soaked his wool blanket. Relentless amounts of rain bombarded the ground, creating lakes and rivers, which became a slippery mud bath.

So much for sleeping.

He heard Freddy calling through the howling wind, "CALLIHAN! We've lost a calf."

CHAPTER TWO

J AKE GRABBED his hat. "I need a horse."

"It's already saddled up," Freddy said, leading the powerful animal to Jake.

He pulled into the saddle. "How long ago did he go missing?"

"Not sure. I figure we'll head toward the canyon. That's the logical guess so he could get away from the storm."

Jake agreed, and he kicked Tucker hard in the side.

Freddy and Jake rode side by side in the downpour of rain before splitting off. Jake took the high road, while Freddy took the lower road. It was amazing how much water could escape the heavens and encroach upon the earth in a torrential deluge. The heavy liquid fell off the brim of Jake's hat in a solid sheet. It was hard to see the road, let alone find a small calf.

"Find anything?" he heard Freddy yell up between thunderclaps.

Jake cleared the water from his face. "No, nothing yet." He looked around for any sign. "He couldn't have gone far."

Freddy suddenly disappeared below. Jake pulled his horse higher up the bluff, looking for any sign of the lost animal. His clothing hung heavy and stuck to his body. He glanced up above at the ominous clouds. The poor animal was probably dead, if he came this way.

Jake was grateful for Freddy. The man meant more to him than anyone else on the ranch. Following the deaths of his wife and daughter, Sarah and Virginia, Freddy joined him in Cedar Grove. The memory of their deaths flashed through his mind like the current deluge.

Both he and his late friend, Bill Erickson, arrived at the burning schoolhouse to arrest the Mayor of Purgatory, Gabriel Grant, for the murder of the town Sheriff, breaking out of prison, and the murder of his lawyer, Clyde Heller. Gabriel Grant threatened Jake's wife and to his horror, Virginia ran into the burning building to fetch her dolly. Sarah ran in after her, and that's when the building erupted into flames.

It had been months since he'd thought of their deaths, and he missed them more than life. That day Jacob Creek died. He took his wife's maiden name as his own and became Jake Callihan. It was his way to honor Sarah's death. He hoped this calf wouldn't die...

He felt the horse's hoof slip.

Not good.

The animal fell sidelong into the mud, pinning Jake's leg momentarily before the animal found its footing and stood up.

Great!

He peeled himself off the ground and cleared the thick mud from his eyes. Once Jake could see again, movement caught his eye, and that's when he noticed Freddy's horse was tied up.

"Freddy——"

Where could he be?

A crack of thunder roared overhead. Jake slid his .45 Colt revolver from the holster. He stared at the blue, casehardened steel and pulled back the hammer. It felt good to hold the cold steel in his grip. He continued forward.

Jake normally didn't wear a gun unless he was out on the range and only used it to defend himself as a last resort. A few years back, he tried stopping someone accusing him of being a horse thief. He confronted an eighteen-year-old kid who tried to settle the score with his pistol.

"That is my horse, I want him back, mister."

Jake fingered the hammer. "I don't have a quarrel with you, son. See this brand? That's my brand on this horse." He motioned toward the scarred CHR monogram on the animal's right side.

"That is my horse. I've already told the Sheriff you're a hustler."

Jake flipped off the leather thong that held the gun in place. "The Sheriff is on my side, son. He knows this is my horse, saw me ride into town on it."

The boy went for his gun.

Jake's gun fired one shot before the boy cleared his holster.

"Why d'you have to be so stupid?"

A rifle blast interrupted his thoughts. He hit the ground, ducking for cover.

CHAPTER THREE

THE RIFLE SHOT echoed off the rocks as Jake took to the mud again. When no other shot came, Jake peeled himself off the ground, grabbed the reins, and pulled into the saddle. Circling his horse for a moment, he galloped toward the sound. When he arrived at the bottom of the bluff, Freddy was replacing his Winchester back into its scabbard.

"Sorry, Jake, he wasn't going anywhere. Found him pert near dead under this bush. Looks like he broke a leg. Could've fallen from the bluff. Wouldn't have survived much longer."

With a hand to his friend's shoulder he said, "It's alright. Do another count when we return; make sure we have the others accounted for. We can't lose any more, ya hear?"

"Yes, sir."

Jake pulled a large Bowie knife from his belt to cut branches from around the animal. They had no choice but to gut, tie, and haul the carcass back to camp. Seemed like the Lord had been looking out for the crew after all. Not that he believed much any longer. But Wide-Eye had mentioned they had but a few days of rations until returning to Cheyenne before they could stock up and let the boys get some needed rest along with something to drink at the local Saloon.

After building a makeshift sled, they gutted the animal, tied its hooves, and heaved it onto the sled. Freddy pulled himself onto his Appaloosa and Jake followed suit. "Seems like we'll eat well tomorrow."

"I think the boys will be happy. We won't get more than a meal out of this one, no way to preserve the meat. Wide-Eye will have to cook what he can and discard the rest."

"Jake, God's been good." He held up a hand. "I know you're still not talking to the Lord, but you have to consider that this is God's provision."

Not wanting to get into a theological discussion with the former blacksmith, Jake kept his eyes focused on the road ahead and thought about his clouded past. When he and Sarah arrived in Purgatory, they took over the local congregation. It wasn't a large congregation, but enough to feel that God called them to continue the work of the Gospel. All that changed when they died.

His lawyer, Clyde Heller, owned the CHR. He offered to help Jacob bring Gabriel Grant to justice. Once Clyde was killed by Grant, Jake found the deed and a bank note worth seventy-five thousand dollars. Jake considered himself a good man, but one night he allowed himself to feel pure rage. That night he had one motivation, putting a bullet in Gabriel Grant's head for killing Clyde and his family. But Grant's wife, Moira, got caught in the crosshairs and was killed.

After her death, Jake ran and never looked back. He left everything behind and started his new life in Cedar Grove.

They rode in silence for several minutes before deciding he shouldn't ignore his friend. "I get that God does things. But I don't think he listens to me any longer. That part of my life is dead, buried, and gone."

"Jake, you do realize that God has not left you nor has he abandoned you."

He could feel Freddy's eyes burrow into his neck and that same guilt washed over him. "I'm done talking about this," Jake shot back. "God's done with me."

"Jacob—"

"ENOUGH!" Jake turned his head around and glared at Freddy.

They rode in silence again, and Jake felt bad for snapping at his friend. But what more could he say? God quit speaking to Jake and Jake quite speaking to God. The equation was simple, and the only thing that mattered to him was the here and now. No sense in rehashing the past or reliving something as painful as losing your wife and child. That, he could not do, would not do.

The storm had nearly stopped when they arrived back at camp, and several of the men were trying to dry their blankets and shirts over fires. The sight brought about a smile as the previous conversation faded from his mind.

After dismounting, Freddy walked up to Jake and placed a hand on his shoulder. "I'm sorry, Jacob. I shouldn't have pressed the topic."

"It's okay. I need to go check in with Ted, let him know we'll be having some meat in the morning for breakfast."

When he found Ted Jeffries, the man busied himself drying off the wagon and his bedding. Everything was soaked, and Jake hoped his men didn't become ill because of the storm. He couldn't help but smile as the skinny man danced around in his undergarments, singing some tune that could only have come from somewhere deep south.

Ted was not a quiet man. After being freed during the Civil War, Ted Jeffries walked west from Alabama with nothing but a small bag and the clothes on his back. When he made it to Wyoming, he settled in Cedar Grove, looking for work. He didn't want to be known as a vagabond. He wanted to do his part as a *free* man, or so he told Jake.

After taking ownership of Heller Ranch, Jake kept Ted on as the cook.

"Ted," Jake finally said after watching him work.

He stopped and dropped a wet blanket over a simple line he ran from the wagon to a nearby tree. "Boss, what can this old cook do for you?"

"We lost a cow and had to kill it."

"Shame. I take it you need it cut up and prepared before it goes bad."

"I'd appreciate that. The boys will be grateful for some good beef in the morning."

"I'm on it, Boss."

"Get some sleep, we have a long ride to Cheyenne tomorrow."

CHAPTER FOUR

F ELIX GRANT kicked a pile of dust over the burning coals. It was enough to snuff out the remaining flame. The sun poked its shards of light through several pine trees that pointed their tops toward heaven. Heaven, one place that would elude him if he were to die on his quest of hunting the man who killed his mother. Over the years, he often thought of Jacob Creek, wondering if the Preacher would wind up in some cow-poke town he fixed to rob. Nonetheless, it seemed like a fruitless quest. Jacob probably moved back to Utah or down into Colorado, or even further south toward New Mexico. He'd probably never hear or see Jacob Creek again.

Or would he?

Then a couple weeks ago, a woman named Diamond Rose showed up claiming she knew where the Preacher was hiding and wanted to help him in his quest for revenge.

All traces of the night's cool vaporized with the rising of the sun. Sweat trickled down his rough, unshaven face before dripping off of his chin. He wasn't a tall man, about five-five, but he figured he was good looking, rugged even with a short beard. His hair was long and pulled back in a pony that flapped across his shoulders as he walked. He grabbed his hat and pushed it onto his already soaked head, covering the sandy blond of his hair.

They camped for the night and then the plan was to head toward Fillmore; a small community just on the southern border of Wyoming.

Word got around that a large sum of cash, from the Governor's office, was being held at the local bank and to end up on the next train to Cheyenne. Before any Pinkertons showed up, Felix wanted to make sure to grab the cash.

"Frank, get up. Time to saddle. We're off to Fillmore."

The rough looking man named Frank, a gun hawk who went by the name Desperado Slinger, leaned against a tree branch, sat up and scratched his bearded face. "Hey Felix, isn't it a little early to be headed out? Haven't even finished my breakfast."

Annoyed, Felix snapped, "Early is best. Get moving. I don't want Diamond to be upset that we failed to scope out the town before she arrives."

A dark fear crossed Frank's eyes at the mention of Diamond Rose. Even Felix was slightly afraid of what she was capable of. It wouldn't take long to break for camp and get moving. If all went well, she'd meet them after the job in Fillmore. And Felix didn't want to be late.

Slinger tossed his tin plate. "Okay, you heard the boss. He wants us up and moving." Frank kicked Jared Kidd's boot. He was a young gun from Purgatory. "You too, Kidd!"

"Who made you the boss, Frank?"

"Felix."

Kidd laughed, "And I bet you a silver dollar that Felix is trying hard not to put a bullet in your brain."

Frank twisted on his heel and popped Jared Kidd right in the jaw. His head snapped back before he grunted against the pain. Kidd shoved his fists into Frank's chest, tackling him to the ground. The two men rolled, cussed, and knocked each other in the face, head, ribs, and back. They crashed into a pile of saddle bags and knocked over a couple rifles that were leaning against a rock.

Felix watched amused by the scuffle, pulled his gun, and fired one shot into the air. "Enough!"

The two men stopped, both heaving hard, trying to gain some much-needed air into their lungs. The look in their eyes told him enough, they didn't want to die by Felix's hand.

Some said he was crazy, ruthless, and a vile man. He had no idea if they were right. He did like his six-shooter but favored his knife. Its simple edge was clean and made a job quick.

"He started it—" Kidd exclaimed.

"I's don't care who threw the first punch, if we don't get moving, one of you will be left for the wild dogs. Do I make myself clear?"

They both nodded. The other two men just stood there, not wanting to get involved. Wise choice. There were five men in all. Each had unique skills and talents that proved useful for robbing a bank or stagecoach. But with each passing day, little rest, and hot tempers, small fights like this were a dime a dozen and if Felix didn't gain some composure, they'd tear each other apart. He holstered the weapon, then rolled his blanket and secured his saddle for the ride to Fillmore.

Pulling up into the saddle, Felix circled his horse around the now broken camp. "We're headed to Fillmore. If we make haste, we'll arrive just as the town is starting her day. The bank should be open, but not busy. Kidd, you'll stand guard outside the bank doors. If you spot any trouble, like the law, I want you to calmly walk into the bank and let me know."

Felix pointed to two others. "Lenny and Fin, I want ya to ride through the street, keeping an eye fer the law. If you see 'em, fire a warning shot into the air to draw their attention away from the bank. Frank, you're with me inside." He pulled hard on the reins to steady his horse. "I want this quick. I expect us to ride out of town with five-thousand dollars of the Governor's money."

Satisfied they all had their assignments, he kicked the animal hard and shot toward Fillmore.

CHAPTER FIVE

WHEN DAY BROKE, the ground was moist from the night's storm. Wide-Eye busied himself cooking biscuits, coffee, and the rest of the beans. Jake couldn't wait for the newly cut beef. They still had a few days of travel left and Jake knew everyone would be glad to get back to the ranch and get some of Loretta Lynn's good cooking.

Loretta Lynn. The woman was more like Momma than Jake realized at first. After he took ownership of the CHR, she welcomed him with open arms. Loretta really became family and was a good friend. He couldn't wait to get back home to some of her good fried chicken and bear sign.

There was something about the smell of fried chicken that made Jake feel at home. Maybe because his late wife, Sarah, always made it. No getting it here.

Jake was hungry and needed a good plate of food. He needed the strength to carry on toward Cheyenne. The goal was to hit town before nightfall.

Several of the men gathered around the coffee and started gobbling down Wide-Eye's terrible cooking. He shuddered, then his mouth started watering at the sight of a large steak being added to a plate.

Jake was given a plate of food and a nicely cooked steak. It sure was good to eat some good food. He thought of the calf as he chewed. They were lucky to not have lost any more cattle during the course of the night. The calf would provide enough for the day and he knew the men were grateful they had some fresh beef to eat and Jake relished that he had a nice cut of steak. Shame he lost it.

He started sweating under the hot sun. Even though it was still early, this would be a scorcher of a day. Sweat dribbled down his sideburns and he quickly poured some water on his head.

Focusing back on his plate, he shoved another mouthful of steak. Glancing around, he saw that Freddy sat by a fallen tree, eating his breakfast and sipping on some coffee. Jake had distanced himself from the man this morning. It's not that he didn't want to talk; he didn't want to broach the topic of God with his friend. The prior evening hung in his mind like fog and it wasn't fair that he gave Freddy the cold shoulder.

Laughter rippled the air as he looked at each man who risked their lives to help Callihan/Heller Ranch be successful. They weren't the largest ranch, but they made a decent profit from the cattle sitting on the land's pastures. Jake had big plans for the ranch. In time, he wanted to start a meat packing facility and begin the production of food products to serve the growing Wyoming Territory. It seemed to be the wave of the future, but with everything in life, having enough capital was always an issue when starting a new business venture.

Still, Freddy stood by his side and made sure Jake had a right-hand man, even on his worst days.

He finished his plate and tossed it to Ted. "Boys, time to

saddle up. We're headed to Cheyenne. I want to be there by nightfall, if at all possible."

No sooner than he finished speaking, Cory Jackson called out, "Hey boss, someone's dust'n up yonder."

Jake grabbed his spyglass and spotted a lone rider headed their direction. He put away the spyglass and pulled his revolver, checked the cylinder. "Looks like we have some company. Freddy, stand at the ready, don't know what he wants. I'm riding out there." Jake pulled on his hat, mounted his horse, and took off toward the rider.

As the two men met, the lone rider lifted his hands at the sight of Jake's short gun. "I come in peace."

"Who are you?"

"Can you at least put the gun away?"

"I asked you a question, mister."

The rider kept his hands raised. "I'm Deputy Marshal Drake from Cheyenne. I have a message from Marshal Bennington."

What was a Deputy Marshal doing all the way out here? And what would be so pressing that Bennington would send someone out here just to meet with him? Jake holstered his Colt.

"What's so urgent that the Marshal couldn't come out this way himself?"

"He wouldn't say. Says it's real important that you meet him in Cheyenne as you pass through."

Jake nodded. It was time to see what the U. S. Marshal's office wanted.

CHAPTER SIX

B Y THE TIME Felix and his gang reached Fillmore, several shop owners milled around their tiny establishments, to set up and wait for their regulars to buy as buggies, wagons, and other vehicles littered the main street. Fillmore was busier than Felix originally imagined. The town was also smaller than most in the lower portion of Laramie County; ten to twelve buildings in all. One of which was the Sheriff's office. This would complicate matters.

Felix gritted his teeth until each popped against the other like rocks scraping under his boot. "Lenny, we're going to make this quick; we'll draw even more attention to ourselves the longer we linger in town. Don't like that the Sheriff's office is sit'n next door."

"Want me to cause a distraction—I can take the Kidd with me."

"No, I want this quick, quiet, and easy." He turned to Kidd. "You and Frank are with me. Let's go."

The three men secured their animals. Kidd sat down outside while Felix and Frank dismounted and pulled their

32

bandanas up, concealing their faces. Felix flung the bank door open, gun drawn, approached the counter and said, "This is a withdrawal!"

A stifled cry escaped a woman's lips and everyone else raised their hands like they were praising God or singing hallelujah. Felix grabbed the nearest man and shoved the barrel of his gun against his neck. He dragged the poor soul to the counter, the banker stood frozen by fear of death, and Felix pushed the man's face into the teller's bars. "Now, I'm here to withdraw some money. I don't want any funny business. If anyone tries to be a hero, this nice-look'n fella will get a new hole in the head. Do I make myself clear?"

The banker nodded his head. "Y... y... yes si...rrr."

"Good." Felix leaned in close. "The Governor has nearly five thousand dollars held in that safe of yours." He waved his gun. "Would you be so kind as to open that safe and retrieve the cash?"

Again, the banker stood frozen. He didn't move, and Felix grew tired of waiting. The Sheriff wouldn't be long with new riders in town. "Frank...?"

Frank walked over to an elderly man who shook against the far wall and buried his gun into the man's skull. A sickening thump filled the small room. A woman cried out, "Jeremiah?"

Frank shoved his gun against the woman's shoulder. "I wouldn't worry about the old man, he'll be fine. Now be a good girl and sit down."

She did and whimpered.

The banker got the message and opened the safe. "There's not much here."

"I want it all," Felix said.

A moment later he brought out a small bag of money and

handed it to Felix. He took the money and opened the sack. Inside the safe was a small bundle of cash, a few coins, and a small bag of gold. He tossed the bag to Frank.

"Where's the rest of the cash?" Frank asked.

"That's it… someone picked it up yesterday."

Felix trained his gun on the banker. "Who?"

"I d… don't know… I think someone from the Marshal's office."

He squeezed the trigger. The gun roared, and the bullet hit the banker's chest. The man Felix held begged for his life, but he turned the gun and fired against the hostage's skull. The man crumpled.

Felix turned to Frank. "Kill them all, but leave the woman for me." He holstered the gun and drew a large Bowie knife from his belt.

He heard Frank's gun bark a couple times. As he approached the woman, she started scream. "Shhhh. It will be okay. It'll be over really quick."

She tried to crawl away as he grabbed her by the hair and pushed her to her knees.

"Please—"

"Since you asked so nicely. Okay, I'll do it quick." Then Felix slid the knife through her neck.

CHAPTER SEVEN

A FTER SEVERAL grueling hours of travel, they strode into the bustling city of Cheyenne. The amount of traffic astounded Jake. Unlike the small town of Cedar Grove, Cheyenne held not only Laramie County seat and territory government, but also its sprawling streets and lavish buildings. With the cattle fenced off outside the city, Jake stationed three of his men to keep watch while he attended to business in town.

Riding through the winding streets, Jake came across a large, impressive building. Its tall gable and impressive pillars stood proudly on the corner. His guess, The Cheyenne Club: a swanky place for men to socialize, smoke, drink, and do business—where Tan Bennington said to meet him. If he'd known better, Jake would have cleaned up before heading to the club. His dusty clothes, gun belt, chaps, and overcoat didn't fit in with suits and neckties.

A large man stood with his back against one of the white pillars that faced the street, smoking a cigarette, his long coat draped like a curtain down his tall frame before stopping just behind his calves. Tan flicked his cigarette into the street and repositioned his hat before taking the steps. Jake rode up and dismounted.

"Jake, good to see you."

They embraced.

"How've ya been? Bet it's been what, six months since returning from Arizona?"

"Sounds about right. Is this where we're meeting?" Jake said, pointing.

Tan smiled. "Don't think they'll let you in. Let's head down to my office, then we'll grab a drink."

They walked down the street, deeper into the city of Cheyenne. Each building they passed reminded Jake of Salt Lake City. Twenty years prior, he and Sarah moved there to attend a small Methodist seminary.

After Sarah and Virginia's deaths at the hand of Gabriel Grant, he'd chased the man's ghost ever since.

Jake guessed the reason Tan Bennington called him back to Cheyenne involved wearing a badge. Helping Bennington down in Arizona was one thing, but having him as his boss? Jake pushed the thought aside.

"So, Jake, how was the drive? Where d'you buy?"

"Acquired these from a guy near Atlantic City. Been a long journey, but almost home. Another two days to Cedar Grove and some of Loretta's good fried chicken."

"Atlantic City? Rough place. Any trouble with the local Indians?"

"They left us alone. Saw one scout before leaving the reservation."

"Must have wanted you to know he saw you."

"Suppose so."

Minutes later they walked into the United States Marshal's

office building. Connected to the Sheriff's office, the building was small, enough office space for maybe four marshals. This is where his friend worked.

Bennington rounded the desk and sat.

"Nice place," Jake said. He tossed his hat onto a hook before taking his own seat. Leaning forward, Jake rested his elbows on the desk. "What did you want to talk with me about, since you sent your man out to fetch me?"

Bennington's eyes narrowed, "I want to talk about your vendetta against Gabriel Grant."

Right to business then.

"I've been doing a lot of thinking about him lately. It's been six months since any news. You must have something new."

Tan leaned back against his chair and sighed. "Jake, I'm going to put this as plain as I can. Governor Warren has asked me to assist Marshal Wellman in apprehending a gang called, *The Knife Gang*. They've been terrorizing some lower towns. The Judge has issued warrants for their arrests."

"Gabriel's running a gang?" Seemed an odd profession for the former Purgatory proprietor.

"They have instructed me to stop my search for Gabriel Grant."

Air sucked from Jake's lungs. "What? Why?"

The man killed his family. After everything they'd been through these past ten years, to give up like this.

Tan had become a good friend over the years. They'd worked together. Ridden together. And now to give up? Stop looking?

If Jake had his way, and Gabriel Grant showed his face in Lower Wyoming, Jake wouldn't hesitate to put a bullet in the man's chest.

"Tan, I'm at a loss for words—"

"Jake, I know how much finding Grant would mean to you and I honestly wish there was another option. We have to face reality; Gabriel Grant hasn't made a move in ten years. The trail has gone cold. I'm grateful for your friendship and your willingness to help me and Marshal Earp track down John Ringo, but I have to move on…you have to move on."

Jake buried his head into his hands. Maybe he'd known all along that nothing would ever turn up regarding Gabriel Grant. The man was a ghost.

"Jake, maybe you should focus all of your attention on Callihan Ranch and to marry Charlotte Jennings. She's a respectable gal. You can put this all behind you and live a happy life."

The Marshall was right. He lifted his head, wiping away the tears. Tears that somehow pulled at his heart. So many days had gone by where he wished for Sarah. He longed for her warm embrace, to kiss his face, and to tell him that everything would be okay. But that would never happen. He had Charlotte, and that washed away any sadness, and offered hope.

He pressed his back against the chair, stretching away the long ride. "Tan, I appreciate all you've done for me over the years. It's not been an easy road. I've been contemplating the facts as well. If we've not found Gabriel by now, we probably won't ever find him." He hated every word.

"I'm sorry, Jake. I really am."

Jake sighed. "I know."

"There's another question I've been meaning to ask you."

"Shoot."

"Have you thought about my offer in joining the United States Marshal's service?"

CHAPTER EIGHT

T AN ASKED if he wanted a drink. Jake quickly grabbed his hat and they walked back down the street to one of the local drinking establishments. As they sat in the Saloon, Jake contemplated the question. How could he be a government agent? Being more than a rancher felt suffocating. If he couldn't even catch his family's killer, how could he do the job Tan was asking him to do?

Tan Bennington sat across from Jake and fingered for a refill of whiskey. "Jake, this knife gang has been ravaging lower Wyoming. We don't know who they are. We just know that they have left several dead in their wake."

"Why call them the knife gang?" Jake asked.

"Because apparently one of the men likes to slit the throats of women and children. It's a sick game to him. I could really use your help to find these outlaws before they claim any more lives. It's the Governor's top priority."

Tan threw back another shot of whiskey.

"If I were, not saying yes, what would be expected?"

"You would report directly with me and Deputy Drake. By

taking a badge, you would be given your own jurisdiction. Heck, I'd give you Cedar Grove. Something the Governor's been wanting, being how fast the town's growing."

Jake ran his fingers through his hair and puffed out a blast of air from his lips, causing them the flap. "Tan, I just don't think I'm ready."

"Will you at least think about it?"

"Yes, I will think about it."

Marshall Tan Bennington stood and extended his hand to Jake. "Well, then I will give you my blessing to continue home. I'm sorry to have wasted your time." With that, the Marshal gathered his hat and securely placed it onto his head, then walked out of the Saloon.

Jake sat for another minute, contemplating Tan's request. He was fast enough with his six guns to take on gangs and murderers and psychopaths. Putting himself in harm's way seemed a reckless Fool's errand. Maybe it was, but the idea of putting on a badge would leave him little time to keep building what he had at the CHR. He'd built a good life in Cedar Grove. Everyone knew him by the name.

Jake popped his hat onto his head and strolled through the double doors that flapped closed behind him. It was time to see how the boys were doing across town, check in with Freddy to make sure all of the cattle were ready to be counted, so they could push off towards Cedar Grove at first light.

As he walked through the town, thoughts of every decision he'd made fluttered through his mind like bumblebees. Life was rarely ever fair, and Jake wondered when his moment would arrive.

He passed by a few locals gathering food and essentials. Probably lived in town, being that they were nicely dressed. A few buggies darted around the corner and Jake wondered what living in a town like this was like. Give up the CHR, move into the bustling city of Cheyenne, and then live a quiet life with Charlotte.

Not a chance! He loved the land, cattle, and life he'd built as Jake Callihan.

There were the scars very few knew about: Tan Bennington was one and Freddy was the other individual who knew his former minister life. As he pushed further into town, his thoughts wandered to Momma. How long had it been since he stepped foot in Purgatory to even say hello? Jake honestly couldn't think of the last time he graced the town with his presence.

The thoughts evaporated when he saw Freddy off in the distance, sitting on a post, waving at him. Jake averted his eyes, wishing he didn't have to talk with Freddy. The idea of broaching the conversation they had earlier that day beat down on his face like the afternoon sun.

He strode up and leaned against the pole next to Freddy. "How are things over here?"

"Going well. Sent the boys to the saloon. Told them to have a good time while I sit here twiddling my thumbs watching the occasional tumbleweed." Freddy smiled. "But it's not like I had anything else to do."

Jake chuckled. "I thought you were going to hire one of the locals to take a watch over the cattle, that way you can get some much-needed R&R?"

"Well, I figured it best if I were the one to stay here, rather have somebody I trust watching the cattle than some random local."

Jake looked the cattle over. "I want you to grab a local and I want you to rest. I will meet you over at the saloon in ten minutes." He patted Freddy on the back. "Ten minutes, Freddy."

Freddy's squeezed has eyebrows and hopped to the ground. "Alrighty, Boss, have it your way."

Jake turned in mid-stride. "Oh and tell the boys we're leaving at first light. I don't want them up too late. We have a long day's journey ahead of us," It was time for a much-needed drink.

Back down the street, he found another saloon. Seemed quieter. As he walked up the steps to the saloon, he stopped with his hand on the double doors. The man sitting to his right tipped his hat, spit some tobacco, and said, "Howdy, Mister."

Jake did a double take. The man looked like Joe, the man who betrayed him in Cedar Grove ten years ago. They had run 250 cattle to the CHR in exchange for Clyde's legal services. Joe was offered an ultimatum by Gabriel Grant to swindle the land out from underneath Clyde Heller. By the time Joe realized his mistake, Gabriel had him and his family murdered.

Jake squeezed his eyes and then pushed through the doors without saying a word. He needed that drink.

CHAPTER NINE

I T'S ONE THING to strike gold, it's another to leave empty-handed. That safe should have had five thousand dollars. Felix walked away with was a measly thousand dollars. He needed a drink. They'd spent all day riding hard for Cheyenne. After arriving, he told his men to enjoy the pleasures of life. He said to not bother him until morning. He needed a few hours alone. Find one of those painted doves and have his way.

He placed his hands on the double batwing doors and pushed through. Several men sat at nearby tables laughing, playing games, or just doing some business. The dank room had a sour tobacco odor that turned his stomach, but getting some needed spirits into his gut might help the foul stench offending his nose. Strolling up to the counter, he tapped a coin against the hard maple top.

"What'll it be, sir?"

Felix thought for a moment. "Got any tequila?"

"Fresh in from New Mexico yesterday." He poured a drink as the room grew quiet.

Felix turned as a large man who stood six foot five strolled through the doors. His cut cheeks accentuated a trimmed Vandyke. He almost reminded Felix of pictures of Bat Masterson or Wyatt Earp, but without a badge. Good. He didn't need the law sniffing around his business or men. The man wore a long brown oiled canvas coat that swung like a flag swaying in the wind. Felix glimpsed the man's short gun strapped to his hips. His brown eyes set deep into their sockets sent a chill down Felix's neck.

He tapped his glass for more. "Who's that?"

The barkeep refilled, then wiped the counter. "That's Jake Callihan. The fastest gun in these parts. He comes into town every so often. On some sort of business with cattle or to see our Marshal. Excuse me," he said before helping another cowboy.

A law friendly type, someone Felix didn't want around. Grabbing his tequila, he made his way to this Jake Callihan.

Jake looked at him. "Nice day, isn't it."

"Shor is. Haven't seen ya 'round these parts before, mister."

Jake raised an eyebrow. "Just passing through. You?"

"Same. Where ya from?" he asked. The gunslinger's voice sounded familiar.

"Cedar Grove. Taking some cattle there," he said, swallowing a drink.

"I grew up in Purgatory. Ever hear of the place?"

A wave of recognition, or was it something else, crawled across Jake's face but faded as quick. "Listen, kid, I'm not much of a talker. If you'll excuse me." Felix watched as Jake found a lone table near the back of the room.

Few cowboys stood this tall. Last man he remembered being this tall was the Preacher, Jacob Creek, from Purgatory.

His father promised vengeance on the Creek family, but abandoned Felix to some old couple.

He wondered if their corpses were still laying in that abandoned home, deep in the mountains. He didn't blame them for trying to raise him as a good Christian boy.

The old hag often said, "Out of the mouths of babes and infants bring perfected praise. You'll learn how to love God, Felix, it'll just take some time." Effectively saying some good old fashioned religion would make a saint out of him.

The old man tried to whip repentance with a belt and demand that the devil leave the boy's soul. Did Felix have a devil inside of him? Hard to say. What does the devil even look like?

One night, Felix grabbed the old man's knife and a rope. He tied him to a bed post before beating him senseless. "Now, you're going to watch how easy it is for the devil to kill your wife." Felix drew the knife across the woman's throat, to the old man's horror. He watched her choke against her own blood, and then pulled out the old man's .44 and shot him through the head.

He tapped the .44 still strapped to his waist, and then poured another shot, allowing the liquid to shove the memory aside, and focused instead on Jake Callihan, who sat at the far end of the room, drinking his whiskey.

Felix knew where they were headed next. If Callihan was a rancher, he'd have money and it sat inside the Cedar Grove bank vault. Another thought punctured his brain. Diamond Rose said she knew of a rancher in Cedar Grove, loaded with cash, and living a life he didn't deserve. The thought rattled around in his mind as he looked at Jake Callihan. That rancher looked like Jacob Creek. Was Diamond right after all?

Grabbing his hat, he left the saloon and found Frank

sitting, smoking a cigarette. "Tell the boys we're riding out toward Cedar Grove at first light."

"Cedar Grove?"

"We're hitting the bank there. Met a rancher we're going to take care of."

Frank lifted an eyebrow. "What are you talking about? What rancher?"

Felix pointed through the door. "See that fellow at the far end?"

"Yeah?"

"That there is Jake Callihan."

"I've heard the name. Some kind of gunslinger or rancher?"

"He's not who he appears to be. He's running some cattle to Cedar Grove. I saw those cows when we arrived, big ranch. Jake Callihan is loaded."

Frank started walking away. "I don't know, seems risky being the fact we just hit Fillmore. No doubt the law is already on to us for the job."

Felix grabbed Frank by the shoulder and shoved him against the building. "We're hitting Cedar Grove's bank tomorrow. Tell the boys." He slid his .44 from his holster and shoved it up Frank's nose. "I won't ask again."

CHAPTER TEN

A S MORNING BROKE, Jake sat up and clawed the night's sleep from his eyes. He peeled back the covers and stretched. A basin of water sat on the dresser. Jake splashed the cool water on his weathered face. He gazed into the looking glass. He looked so ragged and old. When did that happen? Dark circles hung below his eyes, puffy. Crow's feet hugged each eye. Ten years since leaving Purgatory, but having some cow slicker remind him of the town brought the night of his family's murder to the forefront of this mind. He splashed some more water onto his face and shook the awful memories.

With a new herd to take home, he pulled on his pants, shoved in the shirt-tail, and pulled on his boots. Jake grabbed his spurs and fixed them to each heel, then strapped the hostler to his waist. One last glance in the mirror. "Okay," he said, then slipped in his .45 Colt Peacemaker.

When he stepped onto the front porch of the hotel, Freddy sat smoking a cigarette, waiting for him.

"Boss."

"Are the boys ready to push off?"

Freddy stood and pulled on his hat. "I told them to be ready to go the moment you showed. Figured you wouldn't be long, so I sent them to move the cattle out of town a couple hours ago."

Jake smiled, "Thanks. I take it no one ran into trouble?"

"None that I can think of. Why?"

"Ran into someone from Purgatory. Wouldn't give me a name, 'course I didn't ask."

"Purgatory? Haven't checked into that place in a few months."

Jake saw Freddy's tomahawk strapped to his waist. "Keep that handy, don't know what kind of trouble we're going to run into."

Jake had a sixth sense about trusting his gut. The stranger bothered him, and he didn't know why.

Freddy flicked the cigarette and watched it tumble. He grabbed the reins of his horse and swung into the saddle.

"Let's ride." Jake pulled into his own saddle and reined the horse toward the edge of Cheyenne.

The crew was already well outside the city limits. A couple hours of hard riding and they caught up in no time. The cows moaned and kicked up dust as they moved east toward Cedar Grove. He figured it'd take a good day's journey to finish the trek before arriving in town. Hungry, Jake pulled out some dried beef and gnawed off a chunk.

The saddle creaked under his weight as Tan Bennington's conversation weighed on his mind. If he were to take up the U. S. Marshal's badge, he'd have less time at the ranch and the idea of always wearing his Colt seemed foreign. Always felt like a different man with it tugging against his pants.

He fingered the leather's ridges before stopping his finger on the hammer. There was dust on the horizon.

"Freddy, you see that?"

He nodded.

"I'm heading out, keep this herd moving."

"You think'n it's that cowboy from last night?"

"Dunno, checking it out."

"Want company?"

Jake shook his head before gently tapping the horse with his spurs. The approaching rider kicked up dust just to the south. Jake pulled his horse away from the herd and Freddy. Thoughts rifled through his mind like a bullet. He pulled his pistol and kicked harder. The closer he rode to the approaching rider, Jake disarmed and holstered the gun.

Tan Bennington pulled to a stop and dismounted. He patted the horse. "Jake."

"Marshal? What are you doing out this way?"

Jake plopped to the ground with a jingle as his spurs spun against the dirt. "Must be important since you personally came all this way for a little chat."

"Remember that Knife Gang?"

"Yup."

"They struck again. This time, Fillmore. My guess is they're headed this way. Took a thousand dollars from the bank and killed five. Shot the banker and a few others and slit the woman's throat."

Jake grimaced. "Jeez...You think they're head'n this way?"

"Someone spotted a disreputable character in or around the Cheyenne area."

"That's right." Jake spit. "Ran into a curious fella at the saloon. Too many questions about me and Purgatory, if ya know what I mean."

"Figure they're headed—"

"—to Cedar Grove," Jake interrupted.

Tan pulled into his saddle. "Need your gun on this one, Jake. I'm heading back, but keep your head up and gun strapped. Make sure the Sheriff knows trouble could be head'n his way."

"Will do. Thanks, Tan." Jake grabbed the horn and swung into the saddle. He kicked the animal hard and rode for the herd.

CHAPTER ELEVEN

THE TOWN of Cedar Grove rose in the distance. It wasn't like the sprawling city of Cheyenne, but it was home and that's what made Jake smile. The cattle moaned as they moved in a tight group up the hillside into the town limits. A new town sign posted read, "Welcome to Cedar Grove. No unruly behavior allowed." Jake loved familiar territory—the air was cleaner, and the people were friendlier.

As expected, many stopped all activity to watch as Jake and the crew moved the cattle through the dusty streets. Over a month on the trail and they were finally home.

The Livery Stable was the first building one encountered upon entering Cedar Grove. A small saloon sat across the street where the whiskey flowed daily along with gambling and prostitution. You'd see a handful of passers in there. Most, however, minded their business and being a Christian town, few locals frequented the establishment. Cedar Grove was a friendly town with little trouble.

The man Jake ran into in Cheyenne was nowhere. That was good. Jake didn't want any trouble.

The shopkeepers gazed on to watch the cattle and crew move through. Everyone would stay on the wooded walkways or in the stores as Jake or as other ranchers moved their cattle. They were used to ranchers and cattle. Cedar Grove was, by all intents, a rancher town.

Slim's Meat Market was the next business up. Slim was a loyal man. One could find Slim in the saloon getting drunk off the tequila imported from Mexico. It was amazing that Slim retained all ten fingers.

Living in a place for ten years earned you a certain respect you couldn't gain elsewhere. Especially if you helped local businesses.

"*Hola, Señor* Jake," Slim said with a smile as wide as the Grand Canyon.

The corner of Jake's lip curled upward at his friend. "Slim, got ya a good cow here if ya want it."

"Want to bring her by tomorrow and I'll give you some *dinero* for her?"

"Sure thing *señor*, see ya men-ana." Jake was sure he just butchered the butcher's native language.

"*Jefe*, it's *hasta mañana.*"

Jake just waved at him as they pushed through town toward home. They had 10 miles left before reaching CHR land. Thoughts of Sarah tumbled through his mind like a dried tumbleweed. She would have loved this crew and what God had provided. Jake thanked God for this herd and crew and ranch. Jake honored his late wife by renaming the ranch from Clyde Heller Ranch to Callihan/Heller Ranch.

He pulled at a chain wrapped around his neck and looked at the wedding ring he'd given Sarah. It wasn't a large ring, and he could just fit it over the tip of his pinky finger. Kissing the ring, Jake put it back under his shirt and continued toward home.

CHAPTER TWELVE

IT WAS ALWAYS a welcome sight to see Callihan Ranch open up like clouds parting the sun. The ranch was his shining light and often considered it his redemption from the sins of the past that haunted him. Jake longed for his own bed and a warm bath. His mouth already watered for the feast Loretta no doubt planned the moment they crested the hill.

Several dogs greeted them, barking at the herd to keep moving. Jake and Freddy trained them to start the herd separation. The calves, and bulls and heifers were split into two separate pastures. This would allow them to prepare them for branding. He'd head into town to fetch Sheriff Whalen to sign off on the purchase.

"Freddy, let's move the fifty into the holding area. Can't have them roaming with another's man's brand." These he'd have to prove ownership.

"Alright, boys, you heard the boss. Let's round 'em up." Freddy let out a loud *yip-yip,* and the cattle began their tight squeeze into the fenced off area.

All went well until a steer rubbed against Cory Jackson's

leg, pinning it between it and horse. He reached down with his leather prod and struck the animal.

In an instant, the cow threw its head into the rider's horse and tossed the boy to the ground.

"Freddy!" Jake yelled.

Freddy turned just as the horse's hoof found the inside of Jackson's leg. It snapped like a twig and flopped on the ground like a dying fish.

Jake kicked his horse and shot toward Jackson's horse and pulled at its reins.

"My leg!"

Keeping his horse in a tight circle, Jake looked down and saw the twisted mess that used to be Jackson's leg. It lay contorted and bent against his upper thigh. It looked as if his lower leg had separated from the rest. Jackson screamed against the obvious pain.

"Keep the herd moving," Jake said to the other wranglers. He turned to Freddy. "Help me get him up."

Jake dismounted. "Cory, I've got ya. Try not to move."

"I'll fetch a board," Freddy said then ran toward the barn.

"It's bad, isn't it?" Cory said.

Jake looked at the leg again. "It could've been worse," he lied. They had to get the boy to safety.

Freddy ran up with a short board and some kerosene rope. "This will have to do. I'll fetch Loretta after we—" Freddy shot forward as a cow knocked him over and onto Jackson, who now screamed against the new intrusion.

"You okay?"

"Fine," Freddy said.

Jackson moaned.

Jake said, "No time to set his leg. Let's move him, now."

Freddy peeled himself up and held the boy's legs and Jake

reached under his pits and together they pulled him away from the moving herd.

Jackson collapsed against Jake's lap in a sobbing groan as Freddy placed the board under his leg, tying it down.

"Get him to the house. That rope should hold long enough."

At this point, Loretta showed up. "Dear Lord. Let's get him into the house. I'll fetch a pot of water to clean the cuts."

They did their best to slide the boy onto a long board, and it took four men to carry the boy to the house. Loretta already had a table ready with towels and an apron. She technically was the resident doctor, although she had no professional medical training—more like on-the-job training. Jake had had his fair share of injuries working on the ranch. This injury was the worst he'd seen in a long time.

THERE WAS no saving Cory's leg. He would live his days stuck in some blasted wheeled chair. Jake stood in the room's doorway while Loretta cleaned everything up and watched the boy sleep off his missing leg. Shame. His gut knotted tight, and he wanted to vomit. After all they'd been through over the last month, ended with Jake gaining more cattle and the boy losing his leg for his own profits.

He walked down the steps and sat in his favorite chair by the fireplace. Loretta handed him a cup of hot tea.

"He'll be just fine. We'll take care of him. He's family."

"Shame he lost that leg."

Loretta placed a hand on his shoulder. "But God spared that boy's life. He has you to thank for not being trampled to death out there."

Jake looked up at her and smiled. "I suppose so."

The door opened and Freddy stepped through. He removed his hat and tossed it onto a waiting hook, something Loretta always required upon entering the home.

"Cattle is all squared away. Separated them like you wanted."

"I want you to get things ready while I'm in town. Fetch me a good steer for me to take to Slim. He asked I bring one for him. Need to fetch the Sheriff for proof of ownership."

Freddy nodded before heading to his own room.

"Thank, Loretta."

She squeezed his arm. "You're welcome. Now, go clean up, I'm making fried chicken."

CHAPTER THIRTEEN

IT DIDN'T TAKE long before Jake cleaned, shaved, and was ready to eat, and boy was he hungry. He'd waited a long month for her good cooking. Loretta's attention to detail, and the way she made fried chicken, reminded him so much of growing up under Momma's roof. She wasn't like quite like Momma. Loretta was stubborn, angered easily, but Jake could always count on her when he needed a helping hand.

Jake combed his Vandyke and looked at himself over in the mirror. Good enough for dinner. He walked down the hallway and stopped at the room where Cory Jackson lay. Poor lad had everything, and now he'd have to send for the boy's folks to tend to his care.

When Jake walked into the dining room, it was already tidy, clean, and ready for dinner. He admired at how easily Loretta turned it into a surgery room and back again for dinner.

"I see you're all cleaned up and respectable. Good, I'll go fetch your dinner. I have it in the warming oven for you."

"Thank you, Loretta."

The dining room was large enough to hold twelve guests around the table, though these days, Jake ate alone after everyone else. He preferred it that way. Mahogany wood lined the walls and a silver candelabrum adorned the fireplace. A large china hutch and another candelabrum hung from the ceiling, bathing the room in its golden glow. He had four other staff members that tended to the care of the home, Clyde Heller employed all of which before Gabriel killed him in cold blood.

Loretta brought in a plate of warm fried chicken—his favorite dish—and set it before him. She was a tall woman who commanded respect. Her near black hair sat perched up in a tidy bun on her head. Her rosy cheeks and warm smile reminded Jake how much he appreciated her.

"Thank you, Loretta."

"You're very welcome. Now tell me, how was your trip?"

He pulled apart a leg and allowed the food to fill his growling stomach. "It was good. Marshal wants me to take a deputy's position."

"Is that right?"

He smiled. "Loretta, the problem is, I like what I've got going here. Besides, tomorrow, I've got to fill the sheriff in on a disreputable character headed toward Cedar Grove. Killed a woman in Fillmore, slit her throat really good."

She wrinkled her nose. "Oh my."

"I'm sorry, Loretta. Shouldn't drag you into all this talk."

She patted his arm. "I'll be cleaning up in the kitchen if you need me."

After she left, he pulled apart another leg. A nearby pitcher filled with water beckoned him to fill his glass. He grabbed the pitcher, poured a glass, and drank deep. The cool liquid hit his stomach, and he welcomed the refreshing relief it provided.

A few minutes later, Jake retreated to his study. He sat down in an oversized chair and breathed deep. Looking out the window, he could see that Freddy made sure the cattle were ready for branding in a couple of days by keeping them separated. It always took two days. Since Callihan Ranch sat ten miles outside of town, Jake made it a two-day trip to fetch the Sheriff out to prove the sale of cattle.

He opened a drawer and pulled out a tin image of him, Sarah, and Virginia. Sarah wanted an image of their time in Utah as a reminder of God's goodness in their lives.

He lightly kissed his fingers and pressed them to the image. "I miss you something terrible. I know I've not been back to Purgatory to talk to you and visit your graves. It's been hard, but God's been good. Though I'm not sure I would consider myself a man of God. Not anymore."

A single tear formed and slid down his cheek. "Did I tell you I have met someone? She's real nice like and an excellent schoolteacher… reminds me a lot of you, in fact. Not sure how to tell you this… but I've fallen for this one. I know you'd want me happy and to move on. Guess it's taken me ten years to do just that. I hope you can forgive me for not keeping my promise of being married to you, even though you're gone."

He wiped his eyes and cleared his throat. "God, if you're listening, I know I've been a little distant, but it seems as if my past is trying to remind me of all the things that have happened to me in Purgatory. Guess I could have been better at all that and then some. But I know you're watch'n over them. Give Virginia a hug for me and let her know that her daddy misses her something terrible."

Despite it all, Jake saw the future as something to run

towards. He had Charlotte to think about now. The girl he loved, respected, and admired. Never thought that he'd fall in love all over again, with a schoolteacher nonetheless. Notwithstanding, she was a wonderful cook too.

He'd stop by the schoolhouse, just outside of town tomorrow, and visit with Charlotte while the children worked on their studies. He'd have to figure out a way to gather her attention without distracting them.

Glancing at the photograph again, he fumbled with the drawer and put it away. Jake pulled out a small leather pouch and poured its contents out into his palm. Staring back up at him—a glint of gold sparkled against the lantern lighting the room—was a wedding ring he'd picked out for Charlotte six months earlier in Tucson.

CHAPTER FOURTEEN

L IGHT SHIMMERED through branches as the sun peaked over the ridge at the far end of his place. Jake stood on the front lawn looking at his new herd. They were a good purchase. Steam rose from his coffee cup and tickled his nose. The moaning of the cattle blended with warbler's calls as his dog pulled up and sat at his heels. Jake reached down and pet the animal's head before taking another drink.

"How are ya, Dog?" He couldn't find a better name for the mutt, so Dog became its name. Seemed fitting, considering.

Dog lifted his head and pushed against Jake's hand, demanding some more attention.

"Guess you've been lonely," he said. Jake looked at the barn that needed some attention. "Sorry. I've not been around much."

Dog whined a bit.

"Yep. I suppose you want someone to paint the old building, eh?" He looked down at Dog, who panted his non-understanding.

"Suppose you don't know what I'm talking about. Bennington wants me to take the Marshal's job in Cedar Grove. Seems like the Governor has signed off on it. Just a formality."

Dog barked and took off running.

"Bye." That's when Freddy walked up.

"Morn'n, Boss."

"You've got to stop calling me that."

"Sorry, Jake. Kind of a habit."

Jake smiled. Freddy was a good friend. "Headed to town. Need you to fetch me a good heifer for Slim."

"Already done. She's already tied up. Just need to saddle your horse."

That got another smile from Jake. "Thanks. I'll head out soon. Get everything ready for the Sheriff's arrival. I'll be back sometime tomorrow."

After finishing up his coffee and with Freddy, Jake mounted his horse, attached the heifer's rope to the saddle horn, and set off toward Cedar Grove.

The ride to town was not fun. Rain pelted the ground for the last couple of hours. The farms needed it. Jake didn't mind a little downpour on his way into town. The trench coat helped. Its weight fell hard against his shoulders.

After a few hours trekking through the plains and wooded pines, Jake strolled into town. Cedar Grove, the town where most stayed dry from alcohol—the sheriff wanted the tavern gone, but the die-hard out-of-town folks and some locals found it enjoyable.

As usual, the town buzzed with activity in the late morning. Though Cedar Grove wasn't the largest town in Wyoming, it met the needs of the locals.

A few young children ran past, spooking his horse. He

patted Tucker's side to calm him down. Clicking his tongue, he rode his way to Slim's Meat Market. It was the last business on the main street and sat next to the sheriff's office. He tied the heifer in the back of the shop then rounded the building. The place reeked of rotten entrails and dried blood. Slim had the best cuts of meat in all of Cedar Grove.

The Mexican busied himself hacking away at a set of ribs on a chopping block. His nearly black hair sat greasy against his otherwise bushy face. It was the most terrible display of a beard Jake ever saw; it needed a good trimming.

"*Hola, Señor* Jake, how's it going on this *mojado* day?" he said in a thick accent.

"Hey Slim. Looks like it'll be slow for ya with all the rain." The sight of his overweight friend made him chuckle.

"Eh, not too bad, just sold a good quarter to some folks." His eyes lit up as he chopped his cleaver into a rack of ribs. "Did you bring that *vaca marrón grande* you were talking about?"

"I've got her tied out back."

"Jake, let's go see this *vaca* before I give you any *dinero*." He wiped his bloodied hands on his apron.

"You don't trust me? I've always been a man of my word. Maybe I should just sell her to someone else."

Both men laughed. They rounded the back corner of his shop and there she was. "Oh, she's a real *bonita, Señor.*"

Jake fell in behind his friend. "I told ya," he said with a smile.

"How much you want for her?"

"How about seventy-five?" Normally, he charged fifty for a prime heifer, but this one was different. This one was born from two of his prime long horns. This was a prize. The best of the best. So, Jake didn't think seventy-five was asking too much.

"Wow, *intentas llevarme por todo lo que valgo?*"

Jake had no clue what Slim just said.

Slim's fist connected hard with Jake's right shoulder, "I'm just messing ya. *Vamos al Banco por el dinero.*"

"No *problema*," Jake answered, still trying to figure out what his friend said.

"*Señor*, it would be, *no hay problema*," he said with a wide golden grin. Jake figured there'd be more gold in his mouth than in a single vein on a boom town.

"You saw *Señorita* Charlotte yet?"

"Was fix'n to after we've finished up."

Slim ran bloody fingers through his greasy hair. "She missed ya something *malo*."

Jake smiled. He missed her just as much and couldn't wait to embrace her, kiss her, and see her beautiful smile. The ring he kept in the desk drawer at home flashed through his mind.

"Are you planning on, *que es la palabra…matrimonio* anytime soon?"

There it was. "Marriage?"

"*Si, Señor* Jake."

Slim couldn't help himself. Both he and Charlotte grew up together. He married her sister and had been fixing to find a suitable suitor for his sister-in-law.

Friendly gesture. Course he wanted to marry her, but was Charlotte ready?

The two men quietly walked down the street, and Jake's boots kicked up pockets of dust and tossed them into the air.

At thirty-eight, Jake wanted to examine his life before getting back in the marriage saddle. Sarah would approve of marriage. And the ring in his desk drawer told him it was time to ask.

"I've been thinking about a lot of things, Slim."

"No *matrimonio?* Going to be hard to have many *niños* much longer."

"What's that got to do with anything?"

"Ain'tsay'n any *mas*. But you'd be happy with her. I'm happy with Regina. Happiness runs in the *familia*."

Jake said little more. It was time to kill off their confabbing.

CHAPTER FIFTEEN

F ELIX GRANT walked into Cedar Grove's only saloon. For a town with one drinking establishment, it was depressing. Who didn't drink? Town seemed more dry and good for noth'n do-gooders abounded; at least that's what he'd heard. He tossed a four-bit coin onto the rough counter. "Barkeep, whiskey."

"Whole bottle?"

Felix drew his gun, pulling back the hammer. "I said, whiskey." Several at the counter pushed away and vacated, not knowing if he'd pull that trigger.

"Easy there, Fella," he said, and poured a short glass and left the bottle.

Holstering the short gun, Felix picked up the wet glass. He threw back a long gulp and its fire burned all the way to his stomach. It was a simple plan. Send two riders through the street, shooting. The goal, to create a lot of chaos as he and Frank slipped into the bank. There should be several thousand dollars in the safe. This was a major ranch town.

He poured another round and watched the amber liquid

swirl inside the glass. He laughed. "Great to be alive. And good to have a drink." He tossed it down his throat. Felix hated drinking with anyone else, always alone.

"Barkeep, you ever heard of a Jake Callihan around these parts?"

The man smiled and finished pouring a glass of cheap beer for another customer before turning his attention to Felix. "Sure do. Jake's a regular. You know 'im?"

The whiskey now lulling his senses fogged his mind for a moment. What was in this stuff? "Yeah. Old ranch hand from years ago. Passing through, thought I'd say a little howdy."

"That right? Heard he's in town this morning, dropping a heifer for good'ol Slim. Possibly be by before long. Then to the CHR."

"CHR?"

"Callihan/Heller Ranch. Course most just say Callihan Ranch, or I like to use, the CHR."

"Oh Right, CHR. I forgot, he used to run another ranch years ago." Felix smiled with a slight chuckle. *Stupid hick.*

"You want to wait around for Jake? I won't mind. Most avoid this place. Good Christian town, in all."

A tall and slender woman sat next to Felix. "Hi, Diamond."

She always showed up when he least expected and he hated having to talk when he was trying to have a drink. At least he wouldn't have to talk with the dumb *hick* any longer.

"Ma'am, don't think I've seen you come through these doors before. Can I get you anything?" the barkeep asked.

"No, thank you. Very kind of you to ask. Few men treat a lady with respect in these parts."

"Ain't that the truth. You two know each other?"

"He's a...friend." Diamond Rose said. Waiting until the

barkeep helped another cowboy, she turned to Felix, "Is the plan on and moving forward? Frank filled me in on what you're thinking."

"Yep, should draw him out."

"It's all on you, Felix. He can't know I'm in town. You know who he is?"

"Pretty sure. Saw him in Cheyenne. Same voice, as I me'ber."

"Will this work?"

"Don't worry, Jacob Creek will die."

"Don't get cocky. He's the best gunslinger in these parts. Been getting trained by Marshal Tan Bennington. He even helped the Earp brothers a month or so back."

Felix slammed back another drink. "Why ya care so much what happens to 'im?"

"I have my reasons."

"And what would those be?"

"None of yours."

He laughed and set the glass down. Pushing back from the stool, he pulled her close and kissed her deeply. Her lips were moist and ready for him.

When they parted, she ran her finger across the top of his mustache and then sucked on the end of her finger. "You left some whiskey on your lip."

Felix didn't care that she was older than him. "How about we go upstairs?"

"How about," she said.

Felix pulled out a sliver eagle and tapped it on the counter. "Need a room."

CHAPTER SIXTEEN

Jake and Slim stepped onto the bank's boardwalk as a woman's voice caught his attention. "Alright, John, thanks for holding these for me. When do you expect the next shipment to roll into town?"

Jake couldn't hear the owner's response, but he glimpsed Miss Charlotte Jennings' long strawberry hair and long powder blue dress as she backed out of Jim Bowie's General Store.

"Slim, I'll be right back."

"*Si, Señor* Jake. I'll settle with the bank."

Jake nodded but kept his eyes on Charlotte. Her frame was slender with a beautiful long neck that helped the look of her high cheekbones. He loved her rosy cheeks, soft lips, and porcelain skin. He caught her smile and sauntered up to her.

She wasn't paying attention.

Jake lowered his voice. "Excuse me, Miss, isn't the schoolhouse on the other side of town?"

"Um, yes. Can I—" she finally looked up. "*Jacob!* When

did you…? I didn't think you were back. I hadn't heard from Loretta in weeks."

Jake smiled. He loved that his sudden appearance surprised her. Her cinnamon eyes sparkled.

She blushed. "Why, Mr. Callihan, I'm not headed to the schoolhouse right now."

"Isn't school in session right now? Why are you not with the children?"

She pushed the hair away from her eyes and smiled. "I'm getting a special treat for the children. They came in yesterday from Atlantic City." She showed him a flour sack that held several new books for the children.

"Why, that's a mighty fine gift for the children," he said.

"Would you like to accompany a lady to her class? We're out by the old large oak behind the church building."

"I'd be obliged." Jake offered his arm and together they strode through the dusty street without saying much. Jake was never this comfortable with a woman, except Sarah. Figured he fall for a schoolteacher again.

Tomorrow's branding weighed on his mind, and he realized he'd not spoken with Roy Whalen regarding the purchase of his cattle.

"You're awfully quiet, Jake."

That made him smile. "Sorry. A lot on the brain. Had an accident yesterday with one of my boys."

She stopped walking. "Who?"

"Cory Jackson."

"What happened?"

Jake recounted the heifer rubbing against Cory's leg, pinning him between the horse and cow. "He went to prod the animal away and fell. The horse came down clean on his leg. Broke it really good."

Charlotte's hand went to her lips, "Oh, Jacob, I'm so sorry."

"Worst part, Loretta had to cut off the boy's leg."

She had no response.

"I need to tell the boy's father."

She placed a loving hand on his arm. "Don't you go worrying about it. The Lord will give you the right words to say when they're needed."

"He's still at the ranch. You can see him tomorrow if ya like. Having a branding party tomorrow out at the ranch. I'm wondering if you'd accompany me at the CHR tomorrow?"

She smiled and blushed again. "I would love to join you, Mr. Callihan."

"You don't have to call me that."

"It's respectable for a man of your stature."

"I don't even know what that means?"

"It means, since I'm a southern belle, it's only right and fit that I call you by a respectable name. And Mr. Callihan is respectable."

"Fair enough, Miss. Jennings."

She nodded. "It suits you."

They arrived at the large oak tree behind the church building. The children were playing kickball, reading, talking, and several boys were trying to climb the old tree. One girl in a pink and blue flowered dress waltzed past them, and Jake's heart lodged itself in his throat. He swallowed over the lump forming and watched as she giggled and ran after a butterfly dancing about the purple crocus patch. She looked just like...

"Children, come gather around," Charlotte said.

They stopped whatever it was they were doing and walked up to Charlotte and stood at attention. Each child stood with hands behind their backs, boys behind the girls, and the younger ones up front. They impressed Jake.

"What do you see in my hand?"

One boy with sandy-blond hair belted, "A flour sack. But I'ma guess'n not much ado 'bout flour."

"You're correct. But use proper grammar, Billy."

"Yes, um…I mean, yes, ma'am."

"Better. Anyone else want a guess…Stacy?"

A small girl who looked like Virginia stepped forward. "Yes'um. It looks like you might have a bit of candy. Or another sort of treat for us to enjoy?"

Charlotte smiled. "You're very close." She reached into the bag and pulled out a small handful of books. Each with their own adventure.

"These are for you all to share—"

The children gathered around, nearly knocking Charlotte over. "Now, wait a minute. One at a time. There are not enough for everyone. But we all can share."

Several girls grabbed a book and took off to sit under the old tree. After all seven books were carted them away, she folded the bag and sat down in a heap.

Jake smiled at her and knelt next to her. He couldn't help himself and leaned in for a kiss. She did not pull away as he wrapped his arms around her. "I'm so grateful for you."

A sly smile formed and begged for another passionate kiss. He did, of course, give her another kiss. She bit her lower lip and pushed up onto her knees.

"Why, Mr. Callihan? That was truly unexpected."

His face warmed. "I'm going to tell the world about our love. But for now, I'll see you tomorrow. I'd hate to make a respectable woman like yourself town talk."

She tossed a handful of grass at him.

"You missed. Now, Ma'am, if you'll excuse me, I have business at the bank to attend to."

Jake pressed his hat back onto his head and headed back toward the bank.

CHAPTER SEVENTEEN

A s Jake walked toward the bank, his mind rested on the kiss he gave Charlotte by that old oak. She was good with the children. They seemed well behaved and enjoyed her lessons. Walking up the steps, he could hear Slim's boisterous laugh. He opened the door and made his way inside the bank. Besides Slim, Alex, and the bank manager, there was a woman and her girl being helped by the other bank-teller.

"I figure he was as big as a buffalo, *Señor!*"

"Horsefeathers."

"*Sí*, he couldn't have been more than *doscientas libras*."

"You're telling me, the man who tried to seduce your wife was two hundred pounds?" Alex turned around to put some papers down. "I don't believe a word of it."

Seeing Jake walk in, Slim continued, "Tell *Señor* Alex it's true. You saw the *jefa* sneaking around my shop, making *ojos-saltones* at *mi mujer*?"

Jake shook his head. "Slim…yes, he was a very large man ogling for your wife."

Slim slapped the counter. "See, I told you, Alex."

Jake chuckled, "And why are we talking about that old codger anyway?"

"Slim was telling me since I have a beautiful woman, I have to watch her like a hawk, or some fat *jefe* will try to *robar* her from me."

Jake raised an eyebrow. "And Slim, did he seduce your woman?"

"No *Señor,* he didn't get far with *mi señora*, she's a crazy one, but knows I take good car'n her *needs*."

"So, Slim tells me you're here for some cash?" Alex said, changing the subject.

"I saw you bring'n that heifer into town. I'm first to see what ya got, front business in all." Alex was already into the safe by the time he'd finished talking, "Jake, seems like you've not deposited in a while?" Back out, he added, "Here's the seventy-five, and Jake, you owe me fifty for the rest of the loan you took out for that new horse rig of yours."

Jake had forgotten about that. "Alex, why don't you take it out of that seventy-five and we'll call it even." Jake knew fifty dollars was a lot of money. Even if he paid it all back at once, Alex would protest.

Alex hesitated. "You sure you want to do that, Jake?"

"I'd rather have it off my conscience so we're still good with each other, and you won't give me another loan until I pay this one off." Jake grinned. "Not that I couldn't go to any other bank I have cash stored up in."

Alex's finger scratched through the matted beard, making a terrible sound. "I'd rather you do yer business with me, and you're right." He handed Jake the twenty-five to pocket. "There ya go."

"Say, Slim, Alex…having a shindig out at the CHR, we're

branding the new bunch I just bought near Atlantic City. Extending an invitation."

Alex jumped at the chance. He always wanted to be a rancher.

"Count me in. I'll bring Annabel and the girls with me, if that's alright with ya?"

Before Jake could answer, several shots rang out down the street. He slipped the thong off his short gun as the Savings and Loan door hissed open and two armed men plodded in. One robber had his face obscured by a bandana. His voice was low and raspy. "Alright folks, this here is a hold-up." He slid the Colt out of the holster with one smooth motion, pulling back the hammer.

Sonofagun... Jake covered his gun with his coat and secured his hat low over his brow, then moved to the side of the counter, hoping it might conceal his holster.

Alex's voice shook with each syllable. "Mister, I don't know what yerthink'n but the Sheriff's coming."

The second robber looked at Alex, "Ah ahah!"

Great sarcastic bad guy. Jake held his hand against the hilt of the gun and moved farther out of position, not giving away his gun. He believed he recognized the voice of robber number one. Almost sounded like the Desperado Slinger, or otherwise known as Frank Gallaway. Not good, if that's who this was.

"Now, all you other cowboys sit still. I don't want no heroes here. This will all be over very soon," he said, waving his gun around.

Jake noticed the shorter robber peek out the window before drawing the shades.

The robber turned to Alex. "Mr. Bank Man, I want you to give me what you've got in the safe there."

"I don't have the vault combination."

Jake knew that Alex just lied. His friend looked for consolation and Jake mouthed, "Be careful."

The man who sounded like The Desperado Slinger reached down and picked up the little girl and shoved his gun's barrel against her neck. "I doubt that. Now, if I shoot her, I'm sure you'll give me that combo." He re-cocked his gun. "Don't make me kill a little girl."

CHAPTER EIGHTEEN

GUNS BLAZED outside the bank, and Jake figured the sheriff had his hands full trying to stop the other outlaws wreaking havoc around town. He had to decide his next move as the bank robber held the little girl in his grasp with a gun to her neck. His heart pounded inside his chest like a sledgehammer nailing railroad ties together. Jake was fast enough and figured he could kill the man with one bullet. But was it worth missing and killing the little girl by mistake? But he wouldn't miss. He couldn't miss.

"Mommy!" The girl's tears streamed across her face.

The girl's mother pleaded to Jake with her eyes. Her eyes were wide. Her little girl was about to die. If God had any mercy at all, he'd spare her life. Jake would have to spare her life.

"I don't have all day, open the safe," Slinger growled through gritted teeth.

"Alright, just don't hurt the girl. She's just a customer," Alex pleaded.

"Not my problem now, is it, Mr. Bank Man?" He dug the

gun deeper into her neck, leaving a small impression of the barrel as a souvenir.

Alex moved toward the safe and Slim skirted around the counter to hide. Jake knew the man reckoned bullets would soon start flying.

"Move it, Mr. Bank Man!"

The girl wept.

The mother sobbed. Pleading.

It was now or never. The man threatened the child's life. He wondered why the gunfighter didn't shoot him first. Probably too caught up in what he was doing. That was a good thing and would be Slinger's undoing.

The moment arrived. Jake Callihan slid his fingers against his coat, pulling it back as a curtain showing the newest show on stage, his Colt .45.

"Boys, I don't think you want to do this."

"I said no one move! Who are you?" Slinger said. He pointed the gun at Jake.

"Name's Jake Callihan. I don't want to kill either of you, but I will if you don't leave this bank, now."

The bank robber laughed. "Guess you don't know who I am." He puffed out his chest, tossed the girl to the ground, and holstered his gun. "I'm the Desperato Slinger."

Jake smiled. "I figured, by your foul stench. And I bet you think you're faster than me?"

"Darn right I am."

"Frank, let's go. It's not worth it. We'll get him later. Didn't know he was armed. He's supposed to be fast."

"Shut up, Felix."

"I'd listen to your *compadré*, Slinger," Jake said.

Slinger laughed. "I thought you'd be older, considering the stories I've heard about you."

"Walk out now, and I'll let you live. The Sheriff's coming, boys, and if you don't want the end of noose, I'd leave."

The one called Felix pulled his hand away from his gun. "It's not the right time for this! I'm not fast enough. Dy'n isn't in my cards today."

"Felix, there's two'vus, we can take'm." Desperado Slinger grabbed at his gun.

Jake glided his palm on the hilt and drew fast and accurate. His gun barked fire as the bullet left the end of the gun in a puff of smoke.

Slinger developed a third eye in a spray of pink mist as his body slumped, dead hand still on the grip. He barely cleared the leather.

"You killed him! Why I ought to…" Felix's hand inched for his gun.

"If you want to end up like your friend, I'd drop your gun."

Felix slowly pulled out his gun and let it fall to the floor.

Jake bent down and picked it up. He slid it into his own belt.

"You alright there, miss?" Jake asked the frightened girl.

"Yes, sir," she said through sobs.

He watched as the mother mouthed the words. "Thank you."

Jake heard the door to the bank open.

"Don't move, Felix," Jake said with his gun still pointed at the outlaw.

Felix's feet danced against the wooden plank floor as he turned into the chest of Cedar Grove's Lawman, Roy Whalen.

"Get over there." Whalen shoved the man against the door jamb with a sickening thud. He eyed the situation and saw the Desperado Slinger laying in his gore. "Looks like I missed all the fun. I took out two riders before the rest rode south of town."

"Cowards," Felix said.

"Shut-up," Whalen said, shoving his elbow into the man's neck.

Jake stepped over the dead man. "Well, it was one of those days."

"I'm assuming this is your work, Jake?"

"Yup, not proud of it, but it's my gun that killed him. Would've killed that girl over there. Guess I didn't get the chance to tell you trouble was coming."

"Thanks for the heads up," the sheriff joked.

Alex and Slim stood up from behind the counter.

"*Señor,* some fancy shoot'n, I've ever seen," Slim said in his thick Mexican accent.

Jake smiled at his friend. "Guess I'll go get the mortician."

CHAPTER NINETEEN

ROY PULLED a pair of iron cuffs from his belt and fastened them around Felix's hands before he shoved the man to his seat. "Sit there, or I'll put a bullet in your head."

Jake looked at the gory mess that was the Desperado Slinger. He hated killing the man, but it happened. In his previous life as a minister, he'd prayed with a few folks who'd died by gunshot. Jake punched out the empty cartridge and stuck in a fresh round from his belt. He holstered the gun and secured it, then stepped onto the boardwalk as Charlotte came running up. "*Jacob!* Are you alright? I heard all the shooting. Took the children inside the church for safekeeping until things quiet down."

She saw the blood on his shirt. "You're shot!"

He looked down and wiped it with his hand. "Sorry, it's his blood. Not mine. I'm fine."

"I was so worried."

Charlotte's eyes wandered toward the bank's door, and he

gently led her away from the dead soul on the bank floor. "You don't need to see that."

"Did you kill him?"

"I did."

"They could have shot you, Jacob." Her hands were shaking.

He grabbed them and held her close enough to smell her hair. "I'm fine. Saw trouble coming before they entered the bank."

She nodded against his chest. "What if he would have killed you?"

Jake lifted her chin and kissed her lips, light and tender. "I was faster."

They walked back toward the church, where the children played quietly inside. He let a lull settle as they walked up the church steps. Holding her waist, he reassured her he really was okay.

"That's not what's upsetting me."

"What is it?"

A tear snaked down her delicate face. "Dan Baley's boy was shot and killed."

Jake's mind went numb. Dan Baley's boy? Baley was one of the few farmers in the area. They had a hundred head of cattle and several horses. Most of the ranchers couldn't care less for the farmers, since they brought so little business. Baley was different; a proper Christian man who lent a helping hand. Jake felt responsible for the boy's death. He knew he wasn't. If he hadn't waited so long at the bank, maybe he could have helped the sheriff?

Kissing her on the forehead, he took her hand and reassured her that it would all be okay. "I need to go get the undertaker. Suppose he must build a box for the poor soul."

"What about the other robber you stopped?"

"I reckon he'll stand trial and be hanged. They've killed several women and children. I'll have to send word to the Marshal in Cheyenne and let him know we caught one of the bad guys."

As he walked back toward the bank, he realized the girl could have died if he wasn't fast enough.

That notion stopped him cold. One thing most gunslingers have to live with, the words of Jesus: *if you live by the sword, you die by that sword.* He noticed that the mortician was already at the bank. Guess he had a box. They perched the Desperado Slinger up in the coffin, and folks were lining up to have their picture in the *Cedar Times* paper. One young man pulled out his short gun and posed, acting as if he slew the outlaw with his own pistol.

Jake shook his head. *No good idiots.*

"Jake!"

It was Randal, the newspaperman.

"Care to have you picture next to the outlaw? Let everyone know you're the one who killed him and saved the town from a terrible tragedy. You saved the girl's life, and the town deserves to hear your side of the story."

Jake's stomach churned. He hated the attention and hated it even more when newspaper men tried to take an exposure of him for the paper.

A little boy, hardly ten years old, came up to him. "Mister Callihan?" he said, grinning ear to ear.

Jake knelt down. "What can I do for you, young man?"

The boy held out a small dime novel with a smile. He

looked at the title: *Callihan and the Earp Brothers*. Great, now they were making dime novels of his escapades?

"My Pa says yer the fastest gun in the west. Isa wondering if you'd sign my book."

Impressed the boy could read, Jake grabbed a pencil from his belt and scribbled his name across the cover's front.

Handing it back, he said, "There ya go. What's your name?"

"Jacob."

He smiled at that. "That's a good name. Now, don't do any dangerous things written in that book."

The boy smiled. "Thanks, Mister! I promise, I won't." He ran off toward his mother. "Ma! Did you see, Mister Callihan signed my novel."

He looked up at Randal, still standing there with all his camera equipment. "Better get this over with."

Randal smiled, "No need. I took one of you signing that young man's dime novel. What a treat to see."

Jake hated those blasted books. All hornswoggle and humbug.

CHAPTER TWENTY

A FTER FOLKS had their fill of the dead man, the mortician removed the body. Roy had already taken the outlaw over to the jailhouse for holding. He walked over to the telegraph office and sent word to Cheyenne recounting the events, and then headed over to the Sheriff's office. Several nodded in his passing by, and others thanked him for killing the bank robber. His spurs jangled on the boardwalk as he stepped into Roy Whalen's office.

Roy sat behind a small desk with his feet propped on top of it while he read a newspaper. He noticed Jake step into the office and neatly folded the paper into his lap.

"Jake, thanks for stopping by. I'm so glad you were inside the bank. Could have been much worse."

"Thank God it wasn't," Jake said as he tossed his hat onto a nearby hook.

"Take a seat."

Jake grabbed the chair across from Roy and sat. "You hear about the Baley kid?"

Roy's countenance faded as he lowered his legs to the

ground and leaned forward on his elbows. "Damn shame, too. Wish I was faster."

"But you killed two."

"I did. Don't make it any better, knowing young Billy is now dead. You realize he was only twelve years old?"

Jake rubbed his forehead. "No…I didn't realize that."

"Had his entire life ahead of him. The only boy the Baley family had. Now it's up to the girls, but girls can't run no farm. He'll run it until he dies and then the family will have to sell."

"Well, we'll see how we can help them. I could use another man in my employ. Down a man. Maybe I'll go see him later."

Changing the topic, "Sent word to Bennington. Figured he'd know what to do with the fellow you've got caged."

"Appreciate that. I saw his likeness on the poster over there. We just had a first name—Felix the Knife. Sides that, no one knows who he is, and I don't reckon that he'd get a fair trial being that he's killed several in nearby towns."

"Suppose you're right. Quite resourceful to use a distraction like this to rob a bank. Don't think I've witnessed something like that before."

Roy agreed, and they talked about the similarities between this robbery and what he'd read about what the James/Younger Gang tried to do in Northfield, Minnesota. They tried to tree the town but didn't count on the locals all being armed and returning fire.

Jake figured these outlaws tried their own version and didn't have enough firepower to scare the town of Cedar Grove. They didn't count on Jake being armed in the bank. A little relief washed over his parched soul that it was him facing the robber instead of Slim.

"Jake, been meaning to ask you a question."

"Shoot."

"I could use a man like you on my team. I'll deputize ya right here and right now. What say you?"

There it was again. First Tan Bennington asking him to join up with the Marshal's service, now Roy wanting him to be a deputy.

"Roy, I'm flattered you're thinking of me. I don't think now's the right time for me to strap on a gun and badge."

"You've already got the gun. Just need a badge is all."

"I've got Charlotte to think about and don't need her worrying on my account."

Roy stood and put out his hand. "I understand. But do me this...do some think'n on it. Let me know."

"I'll tell you the same I told Bennington. I'll think about it."

"It's all I can ask."

Jake's stomach protested as he exited the office. He glanced at his pocket watch. It was already half-past two in the afternoon.

Jake strolled across the street to the cafe to grab a bite to eat.

Pushing through the door forced his eyes had to adjust to the low light. The owner, Beatrice Burns, stood as if waiting for Jake to meander on in.

"How's my Sugar?" she said, pulling him into a warm embrace.

Beatrice was a black large woman who ate too many of her own pies. Her wide frame and small head seemed dispro-portionate. Her silver hair was pulled into a tight bun, red apron hugged her large frame, and her hands could crush a grown man's.

"I'm doing fine," Jake said.

"Take a seat. Since you kept us safe, I'm giv'n you my special sweet potato pie. What else you want, Sugar?"

He smiled. "I think I'll have a piece of your fried chicken, that sweet potato pie you were talking about, and—" A small bowl on the table caught his attention. He pulled it closer and examined its contents. Inside sat peanuts, sunflower seeds, raisins, and some strange curved looking nut. Pouring some into his hand, he threw a handful into his mouth.

He rather liked the crunch and sweetness combined with the salt she had added. "What is this?"

"Why, Sugar, that's my special trail mix."

"Trail what?" he said between bites.

"Trail mix. Being that most come through town have never been on the range, I thought I'd bring the range to the table. I call it trail mix."

"The trail doesn't taste this good."

She threw her head back and laughed. "Anything else you want?"

"How about some bear sign?"

"Funny you mention, I just whipped up a small batch of bear sign before you walked on in."

Of all the food she made, he loved her bear sign. Charlotte called them doughnuts, but to Jake, who grew up on the range with his father, it was bear sign.

She brought out a plate of chicken and beans. He ate, drank some coffee, and by the time he finished the last bite of sweet potato pie, she brought out the bear sign.

Each bite stuffed Jake as a pig. Peeling out of the chair, he grabbed his hat and headed for his horse. A minute later, he stood in front of the bank and mounted Tucker for the long ride back to the CHR.

CHAPTER TWENTY-ONE

F IVE RIDERS sat perched at the top of the ridge, looking into a ravine that stretched for miles. A two-horse team wagon rolled along below, and the sounds of *Amazing Grace* pierced the otherwise quiet morning. A cool fog covered the valley which carried the hymn up and over the ridge.

How long had it been since Diamond Rose sang a song she believed in? Too long, by her recollection.

Scanning the horizon, she couldn't detect any other riders. That was acceptable. It meant the traveling wagon was all alone, with no one to protect their valuables. By the looks of the loaded down wagon, they were making a dangerous trek across Wyoming toward Cedar Grove. That was also good. Too bad they wouldn't make the trip. It was rough living in the west, and things could get rough if you go traveling alone in the wide-open spaces of Wyoming. Indians, outlaws, and wild animals could all threaten the livelihood of a simple family trekking to a new home.

"It's like shoot'n ducks in a pond. Isn't dat right, Diamond?" Joe Kidd said.

Diamond Rose swallowed her tongue, then cussed. "Quiet, Kidd. You screwed up earlier today. I can't afford any more mistakes. Felix is in Whalen's jail and Slinger is dead. You've done enough." She stopped talking. No need to explain to someone like Kidd her plans.

She wanted to leave a single message and tell Jacob Creek that she was coming for him.

Course, it didn't help matters that Felix had failed. They planned every detail the night before. Felix told her he wanted to get even with Jacob Creek and watch the man bleed, but cold feet and Jacob gunning down Desperado Slinger seemed enough for him to yellow. Felix was weak, but Diamond still needed Felix. Once he served his purpose of drawing out Jacob, she could dispose of him. Time to execute the second part of her plan.

The little family continued their singing.

"Alright, boys. Felix needs our help."

"What's the plan, boss?"

"Since that pesky sheriff and Callihan stopped us in town, we're going to do things a little different."

"I spect it's getting hard to be robbing banks and such. But why a family?" Kidd said.

Diamond's throat burned. She pulled her .44, eased back the hammer, and aimed at Joe Kidd's head. "You're young and rightly don't understand. But your sorry excuse for a face will get a bullet if you question me again. Do you hear me, boy?"

She watched him swallow, then nod.

"Good." She eased back the hammer and holstered the weapon.

Diamond Rose tugged on the sleeve to cover her scarred

arm and remembered the events which lead to her scarring. She killed a man in cold blood—a man who allowed certain events to go unanswered in her husband's murder. She snuck into his hotel room, tossed the whore he was with aside, and slit his throat. Before she could get the knife to his neck, he bit her arm.

Those scars reminded her of the night Gabriel Grant fought with Jacob in the street. She hated the scars and detested Jacob for killing her friend, Moira. He got away with it all. The money, not avenging her Jamison's death, and allowing her friend, Moira, to be murdered. She wanted Jacob to pay.

If Jacob hadn't interfered at the bank, they would have been able to walk away with several thousand dollars.

She looked at each man. They had lost three by the sheriff's hand. Diamond needed more men, but these four would have to do.

"Are you boys ready?"

They each nodded an emphatic 'yes.'

"Good, let's go get their strongbox."

Diamond Rose lifted her Colt .44 and opened fire into the air. At once, they all rode down the ridge shouting and shooting. A smile crawled across her lips. This would be fun, and Jacob Creek would get the message loud and clear.

The small traveling family started moving faster as the man slapped the reins hard against the team pulling the wagon. She heard him yell something but couldn't make it out. He reached down and pulled out a rifle. That could pose a problem if he could shoot.

She looked over at one of her men when pink mist popped out from his head just as the sound of rifle fire reached her ears. Diamond returned fire and hit the gun toting preacher in the shoulder. The man fell off the wagon and the team of horses slowed to a soft canter.

She pulled up next to the wagon and said, "You killed my man."

Hopping down, she kicked his Remington away, then clobbered the preacher over the head with the butt of her gun.

DIAMOND ROSE STOOD over the family, gun pointed at the man, telling him to make no sudden movements or he'd receive a bullet to the brain. For now, they sat and obeyed, biding their time before the horror ended. She'd have some mercy; after all, she wasn't out to kill for the sake of killing. It was all to send a very specific message and to create a distraction for the sheriff.

It took a couple of days to figure out how she'd pull it off, but it wouldn't be long before the sheriff caught wind of the family's demise.

The man drooped his head and fell asleep again. Must have hit him too hard, she thought. Snapping her fingers, the man woke from his braining. Her boys had already tied the woman and child, but she needed him awake.

"Good morning, sunshine," she said.

The man grunted and horror marched into his eyes upon seeing his wife and daughter tied up to the wagon wheels.

"What do you want? We're headed to Cedar Grove to start a new church. We don't mean any trouble."

Yak yak. She snapped her fingers and Kidd brought over the strongbox. "Open it."

"There's not much there."

She pulled her pistol, armed it, and pointed it at his wife. "I said, open the box."

The minister's hands shook as he fumbled with the lock. "I need my keys. They're tied inside the wagon."

Kidd got up and climbed into the wagon. After fumbling around a bit, he reappeared with a small skeleton key. He handed it to the man.

"Thank you," he said, opening the box.

Diamond watched as he peeled open the lid. He was right, not much of the content that occupied the chest was worth all the fuss. But that didn't matter. She leaned down and whispered into his ear, as if to seduce him, then in a quick motion, she sliced his neck.

The wound opened, and she watched the dark blood soak into his white collar, coloring it red before staining his black shirt.

His wife screamed behind her gag and the little girl wept uncontrollably.

"Take the box. Shoot the woman. Leave the kid." She reached into her man britches and pulled out a note. Rereading the note, she then stuffed it into the dead man's mouth. "Let's see them figure this one out."

Mounting her horse, she said, "Let's go, Kidd." She turned to her other rider, Beau Jackson, and said, "Take care of the woman, but leave the girl alive."

Beau pulled his gun and put a single bullet into the woman's head. He reached down and patted the girl's head, cut the bonds, and handed her the dead man's gun before mounting his own horse.

Diamond departed as a wave of nausea knotted her gut. Their deaths had to happen. Jake saved the girl's life in the bank, Diamond repaid the same favor, but now the girl will live knowing that life isn't fair. Life is hard, choked with chaos and fear, and death is a beautiful finality that leads to everlasting life.

TRUTH ABOUT THE PAST

The pangs of death surrounded me, and the floods of ungodliness made me afraid. The sorrows of Sheol surrounded me; The snares of death confronted me.

— KING DAVID

CHAPTER TWENTY-TWO

J AKE AWOKE to sparkling light reddening his closed eyes. Popping them open, he squinted against the ray of light peeking through the curtains. He took a moment to clear his brain of cobwebs. He stood and threw open the curtains. Now, the early sun flooded the room in golden hues. A basin of water sat on a small tiled table. Jake splashed water on his face and the cool water refreshed his senses.

A smile crossed his lips.

Today was the day.

Throwing on some pants, boots, and a fresh shirt, Jake made his way into the hallway. He should check on Cory. In the dark room, Cory snored away, like a lumberjack sawing down a pine. Too bad he lost his leg.

When he stepped off the stairwell, Loretta greeted him with a smile. "Good morning, Jake. I have a breakfast plate already for you. Brought back some bear sign from my run into town yesterday. Stopped by Beatrice's cafe. Grabbed a few to bring for the boys today." She smiled again. "After they complete their chores."

Jake grinned. It would be a good day. "Thanks, Loretta," he said before kissing her on the cheek.

"Why, Mister Callihan, I'd swear to the good Lord that you've got something on your mind. And I hope it's not the awful shooting that happened yesterday. I was at the general store when the gunfight started. Horrible thing to happen to the Baley kid. But glad you were there."

He sat down and shoved a doughnut deep into his mouth and bit. The warm, sweet bread tasted good. A good way to start the day.

"Loretta, I didn't know you were in town," he said between bites.

"I was. Had some supplies to replenish. Now, you didn't answer my question."

"I don't have any idea what you're talking about, Loretta." A beat. "I'm picking up Charlotte in just a little while. Would you mind showing her how to make some bear sign? I'm sure she'd appreciate some fine cooking."

"It's called baking. I'm not the best at it, but I will show her." She wiped her hands on the apron and hummed a tune as she turned back toward the kitchen, "Mm-hmm, now I know what's on Jake Callihan's mind."

Jake felt his cheeks flush. "I'm going outside now."

"Okay. Take some with you. Bought plenty to go around."

After eating a hearty breakfast of eggs, bacon, and bear sign, Jake headed outside to check in with Freddy.

The moment he stepped onto the home's porch, he breathed deep and sent one boy to hook up the wagon for his ride to pick up Charlotte. She lived six miles to the west in a small shack, on the edge of CHR land. Gravel crunched under his boots as he saw Freddy tending to a fire. The man shoved a branding iron in and busied himself chopping some wood.

"How close we ready?"

The axe arched over Freddy's head and slammed into a waiting chuck of wood. The wood split down the middle and he propped up half to repeat the process. He set down the axe. Pulling a bandana from his pocket, he wiped his sweaty brow.

"Should be ready, once Roy gives the sign off. You headed out to get Charlotte?"

"Shortly, waiting for Roy. Said he'd be here when the birds started their song."

Freddy grabbed the axe again and chopped the second half. The wood lay in several pieces. "Heard about what happened in town yesterday."

Jake grabbed a piece of wood and set it up for his friend. "Yep, didn't give me a choice. He grabbed for his gun. Gave him a way out, but Slinger decided the grave sounded better than liv'n life, I guess."

"I heard about the guy. Seems you ran into him a few years back. Wasn't he a hired gun for ranch owners in the norther part of Wyoming?"

"A couple. I don't remember. Just his voice, is all. Killed a few farmers who wouldn't give up their land. Governor had a five-thousand-dollar reward for his capture, dead or alive."

"Guess that business all but dried up. Robbing banks, a better payoff?"

They both laughed as the axe split another log.

Freddy set the axe down. "Rider's coming."

Jake turned to the sound of hooves hitting gravel. "Well, I'll be, it's the Sheriff."

A minute later, Sheriff Roy Whalen rode up and dismounted. After shaking hands, he said, "Jacob, let's go see that cattle of yours."

CHAPTER TWENTY-THREE

JACOB WALKED Roy over to the holding area where his purchase sat. The moaning of the cattle brought a smile to his face. No matter how many times he saw his cattle, they reminded him of God's favor.

"How many beeves did you buy in Atlantic City? And I'maguess'n that they're all unbranded?"

"Got me around three hundred of them. Lost one. Freddy took his Henry to it. Made for some mighty fine breakfast the next morning."

"Noth'n better than fresh beef."

Roy walked up to the fence and asked one of Jacob's hands to fetch one and bring it closer for inspection. The boy led a dark brown cow over to the sheriff and pointed to its rump that no other man's mark lay burned into its hide.

"I know and trust ya, Jake. This is just a formality. Let me see a few more cows and then we'll take care of the paperwork."

With the Sherriff pleased with the cattle, Jacob had another five brought out.

"Got that paperwork and sale of purchase?"

Peeling open his vest, Jacob pulled out a trifold piece of paper. It bore the Lazy River Ranch logo at the top with the sale amount in the respective columns.

"Looks to be in order."

"Thanks for coming. I have a bunk bed set up for ya, if you want to stay. Loretta is making some great food, and I'd love for ya to stick around."

"I rightly appreciate that, Jake. I've always wanted to brand some cattle; it's been a long time since I've stayed long enough. Some idiot is usually stirring up trouble. So, I don't make too many branding parties."

"Can't disagree there. But nice that Cedar Grove is a relatively quiet."

Roy couldn't argue with that. Roy kept to himself, but the people loved him. They elected him seven times, and he did his job well. Quick with the gun, too.

Roy's head was bald and his sixty-nine-year-old body was hunched from saddle slouching. Jake never mistook the deep blue eyes as anything but serious. The town needed someone serious to run the law, and he'd kept them safe.

"Do you have an answer for me?"

Jake didn't know when he'd give Roy a yes or no concerning the job.

"It's okay. I can wait."

Jake pulled out his pocket watch and realized the time. Time to go to the other side of the CHR to get Charlotte.

"Sheriff, I need to head out and pick up Miss Jennings. She's joining us today for the festivities."

"Well, I won't keep you from getting a beautiful woman." He scratched his face. "I 'member the time when Saribel and

I were married. She was the most kind and respectable woman I ever knew. Though I disremember what young love feels like. Enjoy it while it lasts."

Jacob smiled at Roy. "I'll do my best."

"Before you ride out, I want to thank you for stepping in to help out when those pesky outlaws who tried to knock over our bank."

"Sure, ended bloody. Glad that little girl didn't get injured or something worse. Don't know if I'd seen them before."

Roy thought about that for a moment. "Don't reckon I know them either. My guess'n they're pass'n through and stopped to deposit something before heading out. My understanding is they be some minister family headed out to start up a church."

"We could always use another good Christian folk around these parts. Seems the west has gotten tougher and rowdier the more come traveling this way."

"Don't I know it. Again, thanks for be'n quick on the draw." He pulled out some cash. "Before I forget, this is the reward for killing Slinger. Recognized him from the poster on my wall."

Jake didn't know if he should keep the money or not. He took the cash and tapped it. "Thank you. Who's this fella you've got locked up right now?"

"Don't know. Hope the Marshal will tell me something about him."

"Let me know when Tan arrives. I want to speak with him regarding something we'd talked about before I left Cheyenne a week ago."

"Will do. And I want an answer regarding the job. I won't be Sheriff forever, ya know."

"Roy, not ready yet."

He waved it off. "You best be off. Don't want to keep a pretty woman waiting."

Frustrated in Roy's persistence, he hopped up into the buggy, released the brake, and set off for Charlotte's cottage.

CHAPTER TWENTY-FOUR

J ACOB LOVED the simple beauty of all he owned. Never in his wildest dreams would he imagine he'd have everything he could ask for in this life. It all felt meaningless without his family. Sarah would have loved this land. Creek Ranch in Purgatory was more like a glorified farm. He didn't mind. After the fallout from Gabriel Grant, Jake desired to get away, change his name, and forge a new life. Which is what he'd done. It took him ten years to rebrand.

The buggy bumped along as he looked out over the horizon. A few meandering beeves picked at the grass in a nearby clearing. Several others nosed at the spring that trickled through the southern edge of his property. He'd have to remember to get Freddy and the boys to round them up soon. When Clyde left the deed to his ranch, there were three thousand acres. Since then, Jake purchased another fifteen hundred.

Now being able to share the land and blessings with Charlotte excited him. Jacob didn't remember the last time he felt butterflies fluttering in his heart. He tapped his trousers. The ring burned a hole inside his pocket. He felt like that kid again. Kinda like when he asked Sarah for her hand.

"What would ya say if a guy like me asked a girl like you to marry him?"

"I would depend on the guy——"

"What if me'sask'nya?"

The memory evaporated as a gunshot rang out.

Reaching behind, Jacob grabbed his Henry .44 and levered a round. Sounded like the shot came from Charlotte's cabin.

"Heya!" Jacob slapped the reins. The horse and buggy sped up. The vehicle bounced along. It took every ounce to keep in the bench. Head on a swivel, looking for riders, outlaws, or hustlers; he could just make out the cabin's smoke rising above the tree line. The closer he got, a second shot echoed off the trees.

Jake pulled back on the reins. "Ho." And before the wagon stopped, he jumped down and ran toward her cabin.

"Charlotte!"

Twigs slapped against his face. His hat flipped off his head. He'd find it later. Pressing through the trees, the cabin came into full view. Jake readied the rifle to his shoulder and placed a finger on the trigger to…

Charlotte whirled around and fired.

Ducking for cover, the bullet whistled by. He said, "Charlotte, it's me…Jacob!"

"Jacob Callihan!" she said, holding a six-gun and a dead rabbit. "What are you doing sneaking up on a woman with a gun? I could have shot and killed you."

Dusting himself off, he disarmed the rifle and lowered it to the ground. "I'd appreciate it if you'd set that pistol down."

She stuffed it into the apron that draped around her neck.

She dropped a dead rabbit at the door and wiped her hands on the apron and walked inside.

"What are you doing out here? Don't you have a ranch to run?"

She forgot, he thought as he stepped into the cottage. How did she forget that he was coming for her?

"My dear Charlotte. You didn't remember that I was coming for you?"

Charlotte's hand flew to her mouth and she let out a quick gasp of air. "Oh my. I did. Forgot to pick up supplies at Slim's, so thought I'd try my hand at some hunting." She plopped into a chair. "I'm so embarrassed." She smiled. "But I shot myself a nice rabbit."

"And you call yourself a southern belle?"

Blushing cheeks and all fidgety, she smiled. "I never said I couldn't handle a gun."

"That was supposed to be for emergencies."

Looking at the dead rabbit, she frowned. "It was. I was hungry."

Jacob threw his head back and laughed. A laugh that would make a man pee. He doubled over and slapped his knee.

"What's so funny?"

"Glad I didn't get a bullet to the head."

"And that's funny?"

"Shor is."

She stood, then picked up the dead animal. "You going to show me how to prepare this?"

As Jake dressed the rabbit, Charlotte readied herself. A few minutes later, she took his arm as they strolled back to where he left the buggy and horse.

"I am sorry for shooting at you. Few come out this way."

He smiled. "I'm fine. Are you ready for some fun?"

"Why, yes I am, Mister Callihan."

"Really, we've been courting for a year. Call me Jake."

A small giggle escaped her lips, and he smiled at how beautiful she was against the sun. It illuminated her red hair and caused her skin to glow. She was radiant in the blue flowered dress. Hanging around her neck was a gold necklace with an ivory camee broche. Looked like it came from France, though he'd never know, since he'd never stepped foot on a boat.

Her hand slid over his and Jacob's heart raced like a horse headed for the win.

"So, what happens at a branding party?"

"Before we get into that, I have something to ask you."

"Okay."

Even though the ring burned a hole in his pocket, he had to tell her about the two job offers. He wasn't sure how she'd take the news but figured it's worth the try. "Before coming into town with the cattle, I stopped in Cheyenne to see Tan."

She smiled at his name. "How is the Marshal?"

"He's good. Wants me to take a job with the marshal's office."

Things were quiet, and Jake wondered what thoughts she had. "And what did you say?"

"Well, he's not the only one."

"Roy asked you to take his job, didn't he?"

Jake popped out a laugh. How did she know? Of all the women in Jake's life, Charlotte knew him the best. Swallowing hard, "Maybe."

"And you said, *no*, right?"

"Right," he lied. Jake's heart thumped against his ribs and feared it might actually pop right out and tell something different. It wasn't a lie, per se, he told himself; more of a fabricated truth. Jake told both Roy and Tan that he'd think about it.

"Good," she said. "I'm glad. Don't want to worry about you more than I already do."

Jake said little as the buggy bounced along the road to the CHR homestead. The stupid ring still burned a hole in his pocket.

CHAPTER TWENTY-FIVE

O THER THAN CHARLOTTE trying to shoot Jacob dead, their ride to the CHR was pleasant. The buggy bounced along the road as Jake looked over at Charlotte. Her soft skin glowed in the morning sun and he was thankful for her company. They met after he arrived in Cedar Grove. He figured eight years' difference sat between them. Not that it mattered, but with him nearing his late thirties, child-bearing years could be numbered.

Children? He wondered if that would happen. Supposed she said yes. But then there was the offer of taking a badge. As the buggy bounced along, they talked about life, the robbery, and the stupid job kept pricking at his mind.

A quiet settled between them and he tried to push aside all thoughts regarding the jobs from both Tan Bennington and Sheriff Whalen aside.

"Jacob, I am sorry about firing that gun in your direction," she said, pulling him from his musings.

"You can stop apologizing. You didn't kill me."

His smile seemed to calm her down.

"Now, I do believe you're in for some real fun."

She blushed and Jacob noted the soft smile playing the corner of her lips. Her beauty radiated like the early sun, just as it crested the mountains and sent sparkling ripples of color across a quiet lake. It'd been a long time since his heart raced like a thoroughbred. Each moment he spent alone with Charlotte, he felt like a wild stallion again.

He loved this woman more than life and would do anything to protect her. Jacob skimmed his hand over the side of his pocket and felt for the ring. His fingers brushed against a round object poking through. *Phew!* The ring was still there. He stole another glance as she smiled.

It would be a fun day.

"I'm looking forward to this. How long has it been since you've invited me to one of your extravagant parties, Mister Callihan?"

A beat. "I'd say it's been a while."

Charlotte leaned over and wrapped her arms around his. She laid her head on his shoulder and the smell of her perfume washed over his mind like one of the doctor's numbing drugs.

"Well, we're having...we're having some of...Loretta's fried chicken." What else? Yes, he remembered, "She's also going to show you how to cook up some bear sign."

That got her attention. "Seriously? You're not joshing me, now are you?"

He smiled. "Now why would I do a thing like that, Miss Jennings."

"I'm not really sure. But I'm think I'm going to like this adventure today."

Feeling for the ring again, he said, "You have no idea."

Their conversation lulled until the Callihan/Heller Ranch

came into full view. He stopped atop a bluff that overlooked the valley. The homestead sat about a mile away, and Jacob loved this view. It reminded him of the view overlooking Creek Ranch in Purgatory.

A wave of sadness slithered into his mind like a rattler. Momma had to sell some land just to make payments on her lodge. Enough grief happened over failure to pay that she didn't want history to repeat itself. Jacob was certain it wouldn't, because Gabriel Grant had disappeared.

Despite all that happened ten years prior, Charlotte helped him heal. Trusting God again would be hard. It was a big deal for Charlotte. "Trust in the Lord with all thine heart." The good book made that clear enough.

She reminded him often that life didn't work when you relied on your strength, that's when bad things happen, and he knew that. When he tried taking matters into his own hands, his family died—something he'd never forgive himself for. But in it all, Charlotte gave Jacob purpose again. He was thankful and eager to share life with her as husband and wife. It was time to move forward and stop looking backward.

"You okay?" she asked.

"Just remembering." He pointed to the view below. "This looks similar to the view I had growing up in Purgatory. Leonard, my father, started a small ranch-farm. I had a bluff like this overlooking the property."

"I'm sure it was nice."

He smiled at the memory of proposing to Sarah there. "It was."

Charlotte's eyes brightened and he wondered if he should propose.

"But I was talking about the robbery. You had to kill a man, Jacob. I'm worried about you."

So much for proposing. Slinger didn't give him much of a choice. It was him or the girl. Jacob chose Slinger and put a bullet in his skull. He shuddered at the memory. Hated it when he had to kill another man. Each death haunted him and rattled inside his thoughts.

"I'm fine," he lied.

She pulled at his hands. "You know you can talk to me about it, right?"

Jacob didn't want to talk. "I know, but not now. I have a ranch to think about, a boy who's figuring out his new life, a marshal who wants me to take up a job, and a sheriff who wants to deputize me. I can't think about what happened at the bank."

"I understand. You're not taking either job, are you?" She squeezed his hands. "I'm not saying it's bad, but I also want you around. I've grown quite fond of you. It just… Jacob, it scares me to think you might be shot or worse if you take either man up on their offer."

He smiled and avoided eye contact. "I was just an offer. Not saying I'm going to take either of them up. But they did ask."

Jake didn't blame her to have more questions regarding becoming a lawman. The look in her eye told him she wouldn't press for more information. She always knew when to talk and when to let him be.

Charlotte placed a small kiss on his cheek, then eased back against the bench. "I'll leave the subject alone," she said. "Now tell me what else can I expect, Mister Callihan."

CHAPTER TWENTY-SIX

WHEN THEY pulled up with the buggy, Freddy was hard at work. Several ranch hands busied themselves moving cattle, castrating the bulls, and branding. The thing Jacob loved about trusting Freddy as his foreman, he didn't hesitate to start early and keep moving, even if Jacob had other things on his mind.

That's why he hired the man.

It was a beautiful day. The sun crested over the distant hills as birds chirped their morning tune, mixing with several moaning cows. So many things to do. But after he connected Charlotte with Loretta, he'd stop by Cory's room, check in on the lad, see how he was doing. Jake told Loretta to give Cory a wheeled chair so he could get around.

Freddy tossed a branding iron into the fire before acknowledging Jacob and Charlotte's presence.

"Looks like you've got everything under control," Jake said walking up. He propped a leg onto the fence and pulled down his hat.

"We just started. Don't worry, I'll put ya to work." Turning to Charlotte, "Howdy, Miss Jennings."

"Good to see you again, Freddy."

He took off his gloves and lifted her hand to his lips. "Ma'am."

"That's very kind of you."

Jake told Freddy he'd be out soon after checking in with the house staff. Then Jake offered his arm to Charlotte; she obliged. Together they walked toward the house and he helped her get settled into Loretta's kitchen before heading up the stairs to check in on the lad.

The door creaked as he stepped into the dark room. A sliver of light peeked out from the drawn red drapes into the room. A simple dresser sat to against the wall, perpendicular to the window and Cory's bed perched against the wall to Jake's right. The boy lay weeping.

"Cory?"

The boy wiped his eyes and stifled his cry. "Mr. Callihan, I didn't hear ya check'n on me."

"After what's happened to you, call me Jake." He walked into the room and sat on the bed, admiring the empty place where the lad's leg should have been.

"How are you doing?"

"Hurts like hell. Loretta got me some special tea to help the pain—said it was magic leaves. Helps a little. But boy does it make my head all dusty in such."

Jacob couldn't remember the name of the leaf. Margewanna or marjiwana…something or another. Not sure how to pronounce it. Supposedly Loretta learned of it from some Indians. Probably some spooky shaman stuff, he didn't know.

"I'm sorry this happened to you."

"I don't know how I'ma supposed to live without a leg. Gonna be some kinda invalid no good sonofagun."

Jake's words halted in his mind. If only he hadn't hired the lad to work on his ranch. Shame really, Cory Jackson was a good cowboy. He could handle and wrangle with the best of 'em. Now, here he laid in one of Jacob's beds, wishing he were dead.

"Listen to me, I'm going to help you get on your feet—" he noticed the leg, "I'm sorry, poor choice of words."

"Thank you, Jake." He stretched against the headboard. "Do you think you could send Phillip in to see me? He's my best friend here and not seen me since the accident."

Jacob patted the boy's arm. "I'll see what I can do."

After talking with Cory, they worked hard to get the new herd ready for pasture. Cows cried against the intrusive brand on their hindquarters. A few hours later, the smoke-filled air cleared. Satisfied with his crews work, it was time to eat.

Boy, did they eat. Loretta had quite the spread. The women worked hard to prepare a feast for Jake's men. After they had eaten, Jake walked back inside to find Charlotte walking out of the kitchen with a wide smile on her face.

"Why, if it isn't my handsome man."

"You did great! Thanks for helping Loretta. She needed all the help she could get."

Charlotte kissed his cheek. "My pleasure."

He noticed she carried a cloth bag. "What's in the sack?"

She smiled. "If I told you that, it wouldn't be a surprise."

"I was thinking about a quite spot I'd like to take you to. The boys are finishing up the cleaning and I'm free to spend time with you."

She took his arm, and the strolled out of his large house and climbed into the waiting wagon he had Phillip prepare before sending him in to see Cory.

Slapping the reins, the wagon jolted forward and off they

went to Jacob's secret place. It wasn't far, a mile or so from the homestead. He pulled the team to a halt. Hopping down, Jacob offered a hand to Charlotte, and they walked hand in hand.

They walked into a clearing that overlooked a small lake. The emerald water butted against the edge of the bluff that reached high and met the clouds. A few deer sauntered in the distance, unaware of their presence. He found a fallen tree and sat down on the makeshift bench.

She pulled in beside him and tucked her arms around his bicep. Leaning her head against his arm, the sense of completeness filled his mind. The serenity of this spot was perfect. Everything inside wanted to burst like a July firework.

After one year of courtship, folks asked when they were to wed—a topic he avoided. If Charlotte said yes to marriage, he would effectively be saying goodbye to Sarah forever. He would make room for Charlotte and Sarah to occupy the same heart.

"You alright? You're normally not this quiet."

She must have noticed his thoughts. He smiled. "For the first time in years, I feel like I can live again. It's like my heart is telling me one thing and my mind is telling me another." He faced her, "You know the past ten years have been difficult for me. I've had to readjust to a new life in Cedar Grove. I left everything behind in Purgatory.

"Coming here was a new chapter for me. The day I left town, Momma made a wonderful dinner. I ate, packed, and left. I'm not sure what the future holds—"

She played with his hands and his thoughts jumbled about and spill out of his head. Jake stuffed his hand deep into his pocket and fingered the ring. Clasping it, he said, "Charlotte, I've got a question for you."

CHAPTER TWENTY-SEVEN

J ACOB HELD the ring tight against his palm. He swallowed hard and prayed for the right words. The last time he asked for someone's hand, his words fell out funny. Jake planned to ask the proper way—all romantic and such. Something he wasn't particularly good at. He grew up with Sarah, and after she moved in with the Creeks following her parents' deaths, they formed a fast friendship. After a short courtship, Jacob asked for her hand in marriage.

His life changed. Soon after, they had Virginia, and it was off to Seminary in Utah. Things moved fast and when he learned that his father died, they took up the call and returned to Purgatory to take over the community church and Sarah the school.

Funny enough, since meeting Charlotte, he learned that she was the teacher Gabriel Creek ran out of town before Sarah took over. Fate has a funny way of showing up when you least expect. Now here he sits, ten years later, staring at a beautiful lake, on a fallen tree with the woman of his dreams.

How could tenderness come from a past filled with anger, failure, and death? Sarah wasn't coming back, and if she still lived, she would have approved of Charlotte. She'd want him happy, to move on and enjoy his life—something he'd fixed to do just now.

Fingering the ring he asked, "Where do you see our relationship headed in the next year?"

Thinking for a moment and letting a serious smile cross her rosy lips, she said, "Well, I'd say that we'd be pretty serious."

He smiled. "How serious?"

"I think we might head toward a future that leads toward marriage."

"You're saying you'd be open to the discussion for marriage?"

"I'm saying that we'd be very serious." She shifted. "Where do you see us in the next year?"

An arrow lodged deep into his heart. One of those cupid types from those Greek books Sarah used to read. "Um, well —" He let his eyes wander to the green lake in front of them, figuring on the right words to say. The sun sparkled across the water like hundreds of shiny emeralds refracting its light. "Do you see that water?"

"Yes."

"See how green it is against the otherwise blue sky?"

"I do."

"It's an illusion. If we were to walk down to the water, we'd see it's a bluish grey. Life often gives these illusions. We think everything looks great, but deep down it's empty, grey, and dark.

"Charlotte, my life has been complicated and lonely the

past ten years. When I lost Sarah and Virginia, I lost my entire world. They meant everything to me. I fear that in my search for vengeance, I've lost a part of my soul that I can never get back."

Sitting closer, Charlotte wrapped her arms around his shoulders and kissed his lips. He turned and faced her. She wiped the tear that slipped down his cheek. Jacob wished he wasn't so emotional, but that's how God built him.

Her lips pressed against his again, and he welcomed the embrace and warmth of her touch. Their arms wrapped around each other and he kissed her deeply.

She caught her breath as he pulled away. "Did you just see how I kissed you and showed you my love?"

"Yes."

"Never forget that." She pulled at his hands. "Jacob, I understand that Sarah will always be a part of your heart. I know the deep wounds caused by Gabriel Grant. Trust me, I know how vindictive he was. Ran me clear out of Purgatory. I don't want to make light of it, ever, but look at all of this—" she said, spreading her arms wide. "God has been good to you, never forget that."

She was right. Each word she spoke was beauty wrapped in grace. If he were to describe Charlotte to anyone, it'd be velvet and iron. Compassionate and strong at the same time. His fingers reminded him of the ring in his grip. "Charlotte, I love you more than I can place into words. More than songs I could sing. More than anything, this world offers. I. Love. You."

As he was about to kneel, a twig cracked behind them. Jacob reached for his gun and realized he left it sitting on the wagon bench. He did, however, have a knife in his belt. Slowly, he pulled the blade from its sheath and stood.

"Stay here." He gently crept toward the thickness of the woods as Sheriff Roy Whalen popped into view. "There you are, Jacob, could I have a word with you?"

CHAPTER TWENTY-EIGHT

WHAT WAS Sheriff Whalen doing wandering around the spread looking for him? He was certain no one would disturb them, but here the sheriff was, messing up his proposal to Charlotte. Jacob shoved the ring deep into his pocket before setting the knife back in place.

"What can I do for you, Sheriff?"

The lawman's eyes were tired and weathered from years of hard work. "I'm about to head back to town and thought we could talk about what happened. If that's alright with the lady?"

Did Jacob have a choice? He'd rather the sheriff leave and get back to more important conversations. He hated this. Jacob mouthed a quick sorry to Charlotte, and she placed a knowing hand on his arm and nodded her approval. Not that he needed her to approve, but he was thankful that she cared enough to say it was okay for him to postpone their alone time.

"I'll take you back and then," he turned to Roy, "we can have a chat in my study."

"I'd be obliged, Jake."

They piled into the wagon and Jacob headed back toward the homestead. Once Charlotte was chatting with Loretta, Jacob showed Roy to his study. When they walked in, Roy's eyes widened at the space. Cherry wood lined the walls with four bookshelves built into them. To the right sat a fireplace with a lovely green tile with bits of silver and gold outlining each tile. A burgundy leather chair adorned the space near the fireplace. His favorite spot to sit and read.

It had been ten years since he first sat in this room with Clyde Heller. The short man tried to help Jacob to get rid of Gabriel. Clyde also introduced him to Tan Bennington, who'd become a trusted friend. No doubt he'd take a bullet for the man. It'd never come down to that.

Jacob's desk sat in the middle of the room and looked toward the door. In front sat two wingback chairs. He offered one to Roy, who sat down and removed his hat, then placed it onto his knee.

Rounding the desk, Jacob sat in his own velvet red chair. "What can I do for you, Roy?"

The man closed his eyes and breathed deep. "I talked with Dan Baley before coming down here. His spread is just west of yours. Anyway, Isa talkin' to him and realized that he has no one left to care for his land. Told him about yer offering to give him a job."

Not knowing what to say, Jacob rubbed his face. Baley was a good man and could be trusted, but with the death of his son, no telling what a man's capable of doing, if he's not thinking. It's the least he could do. The man needed some work, caring for his wife and daughters. A farm was no place for a woman's hand. Though he didn't mind, it just wasn't proper to most folks.

"I'ma taking yer silence is a withdraw of your offer."

Jacob held up his hand. "Not so fast. I said that I would talk with him. Hasn't happened yet. Been a little busy."

"You reckon you could help him out? The wife and girls need someone to help their Pa. No girl can run a spread like he's got."

"Suppose you're right. I'll head over there and have a chat this evening."

Roy rose from the seat and started for the door before stopping. "Thank you, Jake, you're a good man. I appreciate all you've done and what you did at the bank."

"What's going on? Something's bothering you."

He shuffled back to the chair and plopped down. Jacob pulled a bottle of scotch from the drawer and poured them a drink. Roy took the glass and downed the amber liquid. He wiped his mouth. "That's good stuff."

Jacob smiled. "Clyde left an original bottle, liked it so much I bought more. I only pull it out when I'm feeling down. You seem to need it more than me."

"Tell you the truth, I'm getting old. I can't do this anymore."

It didn't take a genius to figure out that the Sheriff wanted to retire. Life was hard in the west and even harder being a lawman. Jacob knew what was coming next and what the sheriff said didn't disappoint.

Roy leaned back and huffed. A blast of air sent his mustache in many directions before settling back into place. "Jake, I'm stepping down as sheriff of Cedar Grove. I've had a good run, but with my age and all that's happened, I can't do this any longer. I'm tired of the fighting, the bloodshed, the keeping folks in line, and just don't have it in me any longer."

Jacob hated it when he was right. And he was apprehensive the day would come—he just didn't expect it to be days after being asked to be a deputy. "When are you planning?"

"Two weeks. I've already wired Tan Bennington. We both know he wants a U. S. Marshal's office working with local law. I know it's a tall favor to ask, and there'd be a special election, but I want you to take my badge and be the lawman the Grove needs."

"Roy, I—"

The elder sheriff held up his hand. "Just think about it. You can give me an answer in a few days when you come to town for supplies."

Not what Jake expected, but it didn't surprise him either. He had a choice to make, but which choice would be the right one? Should he continue to build his ranch, take up Marshal Bennington on his offer, or become Cedar Grove's new sheriff?

He didn't know.

CHAPTER TWENTY-NINE

I T HAD BEEN a long day. They branded the cattle and ready for the pasture. He'd have to remember and thank Freddy for all his work. Freddy had made it a successful day. The ride back to Charlotte's place was quiet. They spoke seldom, and Jacob's mind had clouded from his earlier conversation with Roy.

Charlotte said her vote didn't matter and realized it was a good idea for Jake to take Whalen up on his offer to become the next sheriff. He was glad he didn't wait to share the news. Not wanting that conversation, the ring still burned in his pocket. But everything would have to wait.

Jake glanced at the horizon as the orange glow of the falling sun painted the clouds a deep purple. Trees dotted the space with their dark silhouettes. A few stars pricked the greyish sky with their light and reminded him of the time he tried to put on a star-shaped badge the night his family died.

Could he do the job? He didn't like being associated as a gunfighter. The town folks would probably be okay with him as their new lawman, but giving up ranching? Could he do both? So many questions rattled his brain as the buggy bounced along the rough ground.

Charlotte interrupted his thoughts. "Jake, it's not like you have to give up ranching anytime soon. Sure, it's a public office. But you could do a lot for the town folks. And most respect you. I know they'd vote for you in the special elections."

"Not just up to them. The Governor's office would have to sign off on the election. I'd only be acting sheriff until he could send in his own men to assess whether I'm up to the task. Roy's leaving some mighty big shoes to fill."

She rested her hand on his shoulder. "Be that as it may, you'd make one handsome sheriff." It seemed as if she chewed on the handsome part for a bit.

"Sheriff Jake Callihan." Jacob smiled at the name, "Guess it has a mighty fine ring to it."

She wrapped her arm around his and they settled in for the last mile to her place.

When Jake arrived back home an hour later, he couldn't find sleep, or maybe it eluded him for torture. It even eluded his weary eyes. Was he meant for more than just cattle ranching? What did God want? Being sheriff wouldn't be an awful job. Lord knew he was fast enough and had the wits about him to make Cedar Grove safe. Should he consider taking Whalen's job?

He took time to comb Tucker and offer some fresh hay as a midnight snack. He was a wonderful horse. The lantern lit the stall as memories of his barn in Purgatory burned to the ground. He almost lost his previous horse, Gypsy, that night. Grabbing the lantern, Jake headed inside for bed.

Jake pulled the ring from his pocket and let it stare up at him. Guess that picnic was a waste. He kissed the gold, then tossed it into the drawer and shoved it closed. He tossed and turned. Flopped and flipped. No amount of sleep could quell his mind. Tossing the covers aside, Jake pulled on his pants and boots, then made his way downstairs.

Jake signaled for someone to bring a horse to the house, then pulled his coat on. He climbed up and shoved his boots into the stirrups. Time to pay Dan Baley a visit. It was late, but he should get it done, anyway. He couldn't sleep and needed to clear his mind. More than likely Dan would be up. Jake knew what Dan was going through.

Shame it happened to such a nice boy. Awfully young to die with too much life to live. Now he's six feet under. Like Virginia. Like Sarah. Like Jake's very soul.

When he arrived, he found Dan sitting on the porch, smoking a pipe.

He nodded at Jake as he dismounted. "Jake, what brings you out to my spread this late at night?"

Walking up the steps, he found a seat next to Dan. "I'm sorry for what happened to your boy." The words seemed to fall flat. There was nothing he could say to quell Dan's sadness.

Dan's eyes pulled away and look ahead. "Not right, ya know. Raised my children to be good Christian folk. They don't cheat, steal, or run around like headless chickens. Always minded their manners." He dumped out the ash and set the pipe down and tried to hide that he wiped tears which began their fall. "I just don't know why the good Lord took'im from me. He was such a good lad. Had his full life ahead of 'im. Ya know what I mean?"

Not much that Jake could say. He knew full well how Dan Baley felt. "A child's death leaves an awful taste in the mouth. I know, lost my own Virginia ten years ago this fall." The church fire flashed through his mind. Sarah bloodied. His ribs cracking under torturous kicks. The screams of his family caught in the blaze, unable to escape. He shuddered at the memory. "My Momma told me once that we have to trust in the Lord. Only he'll be able to pull us through life's tragedies. Don't know if that helps. But I know it's coming from the Good Book."

"You sure sound like a preacher. Bet you were one in a previous life, not that I believe in that stuff."

"In another life—" Jake let the thought trail away. "Listen, I know it'd be hard to run a place without your boy to help ya out. Fall's coming and you'll need all the help you can get."

Dan squeezed his eyes closed. "Not sure what I'mago'n to do. Billy was all I had. No girl can run a place this size. I know my girls will want to try'n all, but I still need some men. You don't know anyone, doosya?"

Jake smiled. It wouldn't fix needing someone to help his spread, but it would help. "I've got a proposition for ya. I'm down a man at the CHR, and I know it's not your spread. But I could use you for some mending and fixing things."

"I'ma good at that stuff. Maybe not farm'n but I can fix a good plow if need be."

"That's what I like to hear. I'll pay you fifty and found. If you decide to keep your spread, that's fine. But I still want you found when needed."

Dan Baley seemed to chew on the thought for a moment, spit into his palm, and stuck out his hand. "Sounds favorable to me. You got yourself a deal."

They shook hands.

CHAPTER THIRTY

THE NEXT MORNING came fast after Jake tossed and turned in bed all night. Thoughts of taking Roy Whalen's position as sheriff weighed on his mind like iron. It's not that he couldn't do the job, he could. Based on years of working alongside Tan, it seemed a natural fit. His mind drifted toward the ring that should be on Charlotte's finger but occupied the upper drawer of his dresser. He should have just told Whalen to bug off and leave them alone.

The night before, he'd never seen another man look so forlorn and down in his mind than Dan Baley. He guessed that's what he looked like all those years ago, except he didn't have anyone to keep him busy on a ranch. It was the right thing to do. He pulled out of bed, splashed some water on his face, and pulled on his clothes.

By the time he got downstairs, Loretta already had a substantial breakfast prepared and warming for him. He ate, grabbed his hat, and headed out to mend the south fence. Freddy mentioned something about it being broken and instead of sending one man, Jake fixed it himself.

The day was already humid, and Jake dipped his bandana into a bucket of water before wrapping over his head. He secured the cloth with his hat and continued mending the south pasture's fence.

Hammering new wire into the fence, his thoughts gravitated toward Bennington's and Whalen's offers. How could two lawmen want his services in serving and protecting the community? One wanted him to take over his job, and the other wanted him to become a territorial lawman. He pounded against a nail's head and the darn thing bent. What was he supposed to do, take both men up on their offer? Pulling the nail out, he tried it again, and after his second attempt failed, he cursed and stuck the hammer's claw into the post, pulled off his hat, wiped his brow, then untied Tucker from the post.

He needed to ride to Cheyenne to see Tan Bennington. Maybe he'd head into town first and grab a few supplies for the trek. He'd need coffee, dried beef, and some beans. Grabbing the reins of his horse, Jake pulled into the saddle.

After arriving back at the homestead, he told Dan Baley to finish the fence in the south pasture, then he set off toward Cedar Grove for some supplies.

After arriving in town to gather a few supplies, Jake inquired of Sheriff Whalen when the Marshall would arrive in Cedar Grove to take Felix to Cheyenne to stand trial. He wanted to make sure they didn't miss each other. If Tan was coming today or tomorrow, he'd wait.

"Not for a couple of days yet. Why?"

"Headed to Cheyenne to talk with the Marshal about his job offer."

Whalen understood that he'd have to find someone else to

replace his role as sheriff. Jake offered to help find the right man.

The ride was long, and he stopped only for meals and breaks for Tucker to rest and drink. By the time he arrived in Cheyenne the next day, the sun had already dipped behind the horizon. He'd find the marshal in one of the saloons. The question was; which saloon?

Deciding to try the saloon from a few weeks prior when he met with Tan, he tied off his horse and pushed his way through the batwing doors. They flapped closed behind him as his spurs jangled against the hardwood floor.

The barkeep yelled at him to take them off and hang them at the door. Jake complied and tossed them onto a nearby hook. Gazing around the room, he spotted Tan Bennington at a table at the rear. The man always sat with his back against the wall and his eyes on the door.

Smart man, Jake thought.

Tan noticed Jake's entrance and waved him over.

"Didn't know you'd be coming to town, would have ordered ya a drink." He leaned back against the wall and sipped on his beer. "What brings you to Cheyenne, Jake?"

Jake tossed his hat onto a vacant chair and sat in his own. "Wanted to talk about your offer."

"Have everything drafted back at the federal building. Care to join me on a stroll?"

Jake told him to lead the way and the two men got up and made their way out of the building and walked down the street toward the federal building. The town was quiet, except a few shouts and some ladies looking for an easy man. They ignored the prostitutes and kept moving toward the federal building, which sat two blocks from the saloon.

Tan lit a lantern after they walked into the dark building.

Once they entered the office, which sat near the front door, he asked, "So, are you talking me upon my offer?"

Jake smiled, "Not quite so fast. I need to know what I'm signing up for and how often I'd be away from Charlotte."

Tan plopped into his chair and leaned back. "You two ever going to get hitched?"

"I'm working on it."

"In what, a few years. What's it been, a year since you've courted her?"

"Like I said, I'm working on it. Quite pushing me, alright?"

Tan pushed some papers forward, ignoring the comment. "These are the papers. I've gotten the Governor to sign off on you coming aboard as a Deputy Marshal. You'd report to me and I report to the Governor's office."

Looking the papers over, Jake figured it all looked good.

"I hear you stopped a bank robbery in Cedar Grove?"

"Guess you heard what I did."

"Shor did. Not every day someone stops a robbery. Heard ya killed Frank Galliger, the Desperado Slinger."

Jake frowned. "Not what I meant to happen, but he was about to kill a little girl. I couldn't let that happen."

"Well, since you've been busy killing, I've been tracking Felix for quite some time. Now that you've captured him, I can bring him to justice."

That got Jake's attention. That was excellent news. Tan knew who the robber was. It might just put an end to the terror the Knife Gang had been causing in the lower part of Wyoming.

"On top of all of that, Felix has been killing a lot of folks with a large knife to the neck. They bleed out and he watches them gasp for their last breath."

Jake's stomach churned and the thought of that happening to anyone in Cedar Grove made his decision that much easier. It was time. "I'm interested in taking you up on your offer. Talked with Whalen, he's stepping down as sheriff, asked if I'd take his job. I told him I'd help appoint someone and would do my part until that happens."

"Good, then we can have you take the oath of office, first thing tomorrow, in front of a judge. That way you're already set as a lawman before heading home. After you've got your shiny new badge, we'll ride to Cedar Grove with my partner Alan Drake and bring Felix back here to stand trial."

It was happening, he was about to become a lawman. Maybe it was best to wait to ask for Charlotte's hand in marriage after all. Would she really want to marry a busy lawman? He'd be chasing bad guys and murderers, but somewhere deep inside he knew it was best and now was the time. Yes, he loved her more than life itself, but this just felt right.

Freddy could take care of the CHR and he had more than enough manpower to keep things going, something he didn't have while in Purgatory as a minister. He thanked God every day for Clyde Heller's generosity.

"Anyone know who Felix is? Whalen didn't seem to know, other than his nickname."

Tan breathed deep and looked toward the wanted posters that littered his bulletin board.

"What are you not telling me, Tan?"

He crossed his large fingers and stood, facing the window. Tan Bennington was a very tall man, large in the shoulders, and his hands looked like they could crush a man's skull. His muscular form hunched before turning to face Jake.

"He's from Purgatory."

"Purgatory?"

"His name's Felix Grant."

All air escaped the room and Jake's head spun for a moment and then flashed hot, boiling his blood like a pot of coffee about to spill out onto the stove.

Felix Grant? That *Grant?*

"How is that possible?" How could Gabriel's offspring be the weasel of a man he stopped at the bank?

"I've been tracking him for some time. Once I heard about the robberies, the killings, I did some digging and asking a bunch of questions. Turns out some girl knew him from their time in school and identified him in Fillmore."

Something snapped in his mind. "How could you keep this information from me? You know he could very well lead me to his father?" Jake shoved the chair back and stood. He pointed his finger at Tan's face. "I trusted you."

"Jake, please…understand—"

"*Understand!*" Jake yelled, "I am trying to understand how you could keep this from me. I'm done." He headed toward the door. "You should have trusted me with this and told me who Felix was when you figured it out. Yet, you sat there a couple of weeks ago and told me to give up the search for my family's killer? How dare you!"

Tan's face didn't twitch, and he remained still. Jake knew he shouldn't blow up at his friend, but the dynamite detonated, and the damage was done.

"I still need you to take the oath of office."

He offered no explanation. Just *take me up on my offer, Jake, and it'll all work out.* Not this time. Jake was done.

"No!" he said, then stormed out of the building.

CHAPTER THIRTY-ONE

AFTER LEAVING Cheyenne, Jake set up a small camp for the night. He lit a fire and cooked up a hearty meal of beans and dried beef. Inside the satchel was the bag of bear sign Charlotte had made with Loretta. They never got around to opening the sack she brought on their journey to his favorite lookout on the night he was going to propose. Loretta said he should take the sack and eat the special treat Charlotte had made.

He pulled out a doughnut and shoved one in his mouth before chewing. Teeth ground against the sugar and he needed a drink. He grabbed at the canteen only to find it empty. Jake threw it against a rock and screamed as it bounced harmlessly to the ground.

Why did Tan keep the information about Felix, from him? Felix, the boy who kicked Virginia in the face on Sarah's first day at school. The two children fought over a piece of bread Virginia had for lunch and then Felix kicked her. He knew nothing about the boy and that made Felix Grant more dangerous. Good thing he's locked up in Roy Whalen's jail, Jake thought.

Knowing he had to get a grip, he swallowed the doughnut and found his second canteen filled with water. He drank deep, allowing the liquid to wash his senses and calm his anger. Tossing dirt to put out the fire, he crawled under a blanket and leaned against his saddle and stared up at the stars that pierced the heavens above. Guilt washed over him as the evening's chill wrapped around his body. He shouldn't have blown up at Tan. His friend was just doing his job.

God, I don't understand. Why is the Grant family back in my life? Why haven't I dealt with this anger?

The stars twinkled at him, as if God were whispering a cruel joke only he understood, leaving Jake to guess at the good Lord's intentions. He closed his eyes for some much needed sleep and dreamed of Gabriel Grant setting the CHR on fire and killing Freddy, Loretta, and Charlotte, filling his mind with unspeakable horrors and evil.

He turned his head to see Sarah standing next to his horse, Tucker. Her body erupted into flames and terror filled his eyes as her body melted against the heat. A laugh caught his attention and he turned to see Gabriel Grant pointing his crooked finger at Jake as he said, "You're next, Preacher! I'm coming for you. I promised I'd kill you and I'll make good on that claim."

JAKE'S EYES OPENED WIDE. He stared up as sunlight filtered through the trees. It was morning. Sitting up, he wiped his brow and splashed cool water onto his face from the canteen. Thank God it was only a dream.

Still tied, Tucker stood, and snorted his *good morning*.

"I see you had a better night's sleep than I did."

The horse snorted again, and his head bobbed up and down.

After some breakfast and coffee, Jake started off toward Cedar Grove. He rode and stopped, then rode some more, all the while thinking about how he'd get Felix to admit to Gabriel's whereabouts. He'd do whatever it took to make him squeal like a pig. It's all he thought about until his pulled his horse up to Charlotte's cottage.

Her light was on and Jake knew he shouldn't bother her this late into the day, but he needed to see her, touch her, kiss her. He had to be near her and hear her soft voice. Dismounting, Jake tied off Tucker's lead rope to the porch banister. Before he could knock, the door opened and there stood Charlotte Jennings, still in her day dress with her hair let down.

"Jacob? What are you doing here so late?"

"I know it isn't proper, but I had to see you. It's been a long couple of days."

She opened the door wide and offered him some tea as he stepped through the threshold. Within a few minutes, she was boiling some water on the stove and setting teacups on the small dining table by the picture window.

"Freddy told me you were off to Cheyenne. Wasn't sure, but since I hadn't seen you around, I figured he was right." She set a cup of hot tea next to his hands. "I'm guessing you took the marshal up on his offer." It was a statement, not a question.

Jake let the tea warm his hands. He didn't even have the words to say; and how could he tell her that the man he stopped was his family's killer's son? He stared at tea swirling in the cup, not really in the mood to talk about…

She pulled at his hands. "Whatever it is, you can tell me."

His lips flapped a sigh. "The man sitting in Sheriff Whalen's jail…is Felix Grant."

"The same Grant, as in Gabriel Grant?"

The tea wasn't doing his emotions justice. He pushed it aside. "The same one."

Charlotte's hands up flew to her lips. He didn't blame her; it was a natural reaction to shocking news. "How did you figure that out?"

Now Jake was up and pacing like a caged animal, "Charlotte, Tan knew who Felix was. He knew and he didn't tell me."

"I'm sure he had a good reason."

He stopped pacing and slammed his hand against the table. The teacups rattled their objection, spilling their contents. "I can't even fathom what that might be. He knows that Gabriel killed Sarah and my little Virginia. He knows I've been searching for Grant for ten years with nothing to show for it."

Jake plopped into a chair and buried his face into his hands. Heat rose through his face and fresh tears formed and dripped off his palms.

He felt Charlotte's arm reach around and hold him tight. He wept against her shoulder. She said nothing and he was thankful for her silence. It had been a long ten years and somehow, he thought those emotions of anger were long buried and dead. But when Tan said who Felix was, those feelings and emotions washed over him like an April storm.

"Jacob, I love you. It hurts me to see you in pain. I know Gabriel Grant took something precious from you. It's horrible the way your family died and I can't imagine what you're feeling." She pulled at his chin so he could look her in the eyes.

"But I'm here for you. I hope I'm not overstepping but try and see things from Tan's perspective. He was right to keep this from you, judging by your reaction."

He sniffed something thick into his throat and swallowed hard. Charlotte was right. That's why he loved her. The wisdom and grace she exhibited reminded him of his late wife. Sarah always knew what to say and could make him calm down. Kind of like the day he wrapped his Colt .45 around his waist with full intention of killing Gabriel Grant. Sarah reminded him to let God fight the battle, to be strong and courageous, trusting God in all things.

"Talk it over with Tan and try to see it from his vantage point," she said again.

"I love you, you know that? And you're right. He was doing me a favor."

She kissed his lips. "That's why I love you. You're a stubborn man, Jacob, but you also do a lot for those in your life. And though they can never be replaced, he's given you me, and I love you, Jacob Callihan."

"I love you, too." And then they kissed.

CHAPTER THIRTY-TWO

O NE THING worried Tan Bennington the entire ride to Cedar Grove. What would Jake Callihan do now that he knew about Felix Grant? The very question rattled his brain, and he feared his friend would do something rash, or maybe stupid. He hoped Jake wouldn't be as stupid as to stop him from taking Felix back to Cheyenne. He didn't want to clean up this mess. He let the thought slide away and glanced to his right. Deputy Marshal Alan Drake rode next to him as they neared the town limits. A few tattered signs advertised the local saloon and Mamma Bear's Café. The last time he ate there was six months ago. She sure had good food. His favorite there was, of course, her famous trail mix.

As they pushed into town, several cowboys and cattle pokes stopped what they were doing and eyed the two men. Most towns didn't like federal marshals sauntering into town, but as they passed, several said a hearty, "thank you." He didn't know why they thanked them, maybe because they were hauling a hardened criminal back to the capital. Felix wouldn't stand a chance in this town. If the sheriff didn't do something, they would hang Felix before they could hold a trial. Tan wouldn't blame them; the Baley boy was dead because of the Knife Gang antics earlier in the week.

They tied off their horses outside the Sheriff's Office. The door was open, and he figured the sheriff was here. Their boots clacked on the aged wood as they stepped into the dank room. Tan let his eyes adjust and didn't see Roy Whalen at his desk.

"Marshal, good to see you," came the sheriff's voice from behind.

Tan turned around as the old cowboy walked into his office. "Sheriff."

"Wasn't expecting you for a few days from now," Roy said as he tossed his hat onto a nearby hook.

"Thought we'd get this over with and get Felix out your hair. I'm sure you'd rather be at home with your wife."

The older sheriff nodded and grinned. "Want some coffee? Just whipped up a batch. It'll grow hair on yer chest, and who's this?" he asked, speaking of Marshal Drake.

Drake stuck out his hand. "Alan Drake, I work with Mr. Bennington."

"OK, great!" Roy walked over and grabbed three cups and poured drinks for everyone. Then he pulled out a small flask and poured some amber liquid into his own cup. He held it out to Tan and Drake and they both declined. "OK, suit yourself." He took a swig before replacing the cap. "Helps take the edge off the coffee."

Alan grabbed a cup and took a drink. "Good stuff, Sheriff."

The elder lawman smiled before taking a drink of his own.

Tan pulled out some transfer papers to make their taking legal custody of Felix Grant official. "You'll find all the paperwork in order. Had a judge sign off on the prisoner transfer just yesterday, before speaking with Jake."

"Perfect." Roy took the paperwork and looked it over then said, "Seems in order. Don't think I need anything else. I'll have Judge Roberts look it over, but we should be able to hand 'im over to ya right quick." He tossed the papers on the desk and contemplated something. "Yeah, Jake stopped by before heading your way. Said he's taking you up on your offer of being a marshal?"

Tan figured the conversation would come up. If Jake was unnerved to take up the marshal's job, he certainly wouldn't relieve Roy of his offer of being town sheriff. "Drake, wait outside for a bit. I need to speak with the sheriff."

Alan Drake nodded and stepped out of the building, coffee in hand, leaving the sheriff and marshal alone. Roy took a seat at his desk and offered the chair across to Tan, which he took and sat down. He would not like this conversation. Especially since the man wanted to retire. If he were in the elder's position, he'd be looking forward to stepping down and handing the jail keys over to a younger man who could handle the job.

"Roy, the thing is, Jake may have changed his mind about the job."

"How ya figure? Seemed determined a few days ago."

Tan took off his hat and ruffled his hair to the side. "I discovered some information regarding your prisoner."

Felix spoke, "Yeah, what's that, marshal?"

"Shut up, Felix," Roy called out, "before I come over there and knock ya on yer rear."

Felix just cackled.

"Let him be."

Roy relaxed. "What did ya find out?"

"Felix is the son of the man who killed Jake's family."

A heavy blanket covered the air like iron. Roy leaned back and pondered what he'd just heard. He folded his hands in front of his face as if ready to pray, the exhaled. "So, this is Felix Grant. Nice to put a name to our resident prisoner."

"You know noth'n about me, marshal," Felix said. "I have more connections than you know, and this whole thing is just getting started. I'm not done with the Preacher yet. He's going to die, and I know who's going to kill him."

Tan Bennington stood, walked to the jail cell, and rapped the bars. "Did I ask you to speak?"

The bank robber leaned in close, pushing his nose through bars. "Oh, the fun's about to start, and you don't even know what's at stake here, do ya?"

"Why don't you try me?"

He whistled a Dixie tune and sat down on the cot. A darkness crept into his eyes, something that made Tan shiver. Felix Grant was as evil a man as he'd ever seen. The man was hell-bent on taking out his revenge on Jake for the death of Moira. He was certain of that fact.

"I'll tell you this, Felix, I've been looking for you for a very long time, and now, you're going to Cheyenne to hang for your crimes. I promise you that your neck is what's at stake here." He turned back toward the sheriff. "We'll get him out of your hair."

Roy nodded. "What are you going to do about Jake Callihan? I still need someone to take my job when I retire. I'm getting too old for this crap."

"Leave Callihan to me. He'll take the job, but I may need help to convince him to reconsider."

When they finished, the sheriff took the paperwork over to Judge Roberts, who signed off on the prisoner transfer. A few more rounds of talking before Tan ushered Felix Grant out of his cell, cuffed and chained him, then helped him get on the back of Alan Drake's horse. He instructed Drake to head toward Cheyenne and that he'd meet up later.

After Drake set off, Tan said his goodbye to Roy and headed out toward the CHR to speak with Jake. He had to help his friend understand why he kept the information a secret. Maybe he shouldn't have, and now he feared Jake might do something rash.

CHAPTER THIRTY-THREE

MARSHAL ALAN DRAKE sat high in the saddle. Following behind was Felix Grant, who not more than a week prior held up the Savings and Loan in Cedar Grove. Not the smartest idea a bad-guy had—with Jake Callihan standing near the counter; how dumb could a man get? If the stories about how quick Jake Callihan pulled a gun were true, it'd taken less than a second to pull, aim, and fire his gun. Slinger didn't stand a chance and Felix, who sat behind him, was stupid enough to rob a bank with a gun hawk like Callihan in town.

He'd only met Jake once, but on that one occasion the legend became a real person. Drake figured Callihan was six foot, two inches and weighed around two hundred pounds— all muscle. Callihan's set jaw and large neckline made the most hardened man cringe. Alan was awestruck when he met the man. He also knew Jake carried a .45 caliber gun. He hoped that Jake would join them at the U. S. Marshal's office. By all intents and purposes, Jake Callihan was a lawman, just without the badge. One thing Alan hated it was this, men who took the law into their own hands by wielding their own iron like they were Bat Masterson or Wyatt Earp. But Jake always stayed away from trouble, unless they forced him to draw.

"Marshall, I need a drink," the outlaw said.

"You'll get a drink when I say you get a drink; do you understand me?"

Felix cussed. "Don't suppose you'll be granting my request anytime soon then?"

Drake's hand slapped the outlaw hard, cutting him in the mouth.

Felix spit what he guessed was blood, then leaned in close. Alan felt the outlaw's hot breath on his cheek. "If I weren't cuffed, I'd slit your throat." His smile cut a feline-like flair across his face.

"It's a good thing you don't have a—"

His stomach blew open like someone put a stick of dynamite inside his gut. Alan Drake glanced down at the gaping, bloody hole ripped in his abdomen as two riders approached; one of the two, a woman, slid her scattergun into its scabbard.

Drake fell off his horse and plopped to the ground. His body went numb.

"Good afternoon, Marshal," she said.

"Come on—cut me loose," Felix barked.

The woman walked over and took the cuffs off. "There you go Felix, free as a blue jay."

Felix, now free to move about, knelt next to Drake. "Oh, now that looks real bad, Marshal. Does it hurt?" he cackled.

Drake tried to speak, however, with the blood filling his lungs, it became a futile effort—no way he would he be able to speak. He tried to get the words, "go to hell" out; yet only air escaped the hole as blood oozed out the side of his mouth.

"What was that? You want water?" Felix slapped him hard

and raised his voice, "YOU'LL GET A DRINK WHEN I SAY YOU GET A DRINK." His cackling laugh echoed off the canyon walls. "Hey boys, did you hear him speak?"

"Com'on Felix, we have to go. Let the poor man rot in his own sticky blood."

"NO!" Felix cussed.

Alan Drake felt Felix reach into his belt and pull out the large Bowie knife he always carried.

"This oughta do the trick." Felix held up the blade. "Ooowee, a pretty blade at that!"

As he leaned in close, Alan could smell his hot, moist breath. The marshal stared at his own shining blade in Felix's hand. He was about to die, and no one was coming to his rescue. "Go...to...hell," he finally choked out through a blood-filled throat.

"You first." His cackling stopped as rage ignited in his eyes. Felix let a crooked smile play at the corners of his lips. "I told you I'd be cutting your throat, if I weren't cuffed." He looked at his right hand waving the Bowie knife through the air, stopped to consider for a moment, then said, "Let's give it a test run, see if I want to keep it."

The blade slid through Alan Drake's neck like butter.

CHAPTER THIRTY-FOUR

I T WAS LATE afternoon as the sun began its descent when Tan rode up to the CHR homestead. He hitched the horse to the post and walked up the porch to join Jake, who sat, leaning back on his chair. It was a warm day and sweat dripped down his neck. Though the sun had lowered some, its heat forced him to take his time riding out to meet with Jake. Part of him wanted to avoid the conversation because of earlier in the week when he revealed that Felix Grant was the man sitting in Sheriff Whalen's jail. The other part of him knew that if Jake didn't take the job, the town would not have any law until they found a suitable replacement. For Tan Bennington, having Jake Callihan with a silver marshal's badge fixed to his lapel would solve a lot of problems and the area should have a marshal regardless.

"Howdy, Jake," he said, then sat down on an adjacent chair.

"Marshal. Guess you figured to talk me out of my decision of not joining up with you."

That didn't surprise the lawman one bit. Jake made that

clear when he left Cheyenne a few days prior. Now that Felix was on his way to prison, Tan figured now would be a good time to rein Jake into the fold. With Felix out of the way, Jake wouldn't be so defiant as to circumvent the law on the matter. That at least brought a sigh of relief.

"Jake, listen...I'm really sorry for what happened. I should have been more up front with you about Felix. It's just—" Tan looked at the ground, weighing how to word his feelings. "I have had nothing for years in our search for Gabriel Grant. Like you've said, the man's a ghost. It wasn't until I learned of Felix's name."

Jake set the chair on all fours and leaned forward. Tan could see the confusion and frustration written across his face. He felt bad and wished he would have done things. But the past was over and all he needed was to do everything in his power to salvage their relationship.

"Jake, I'm sorry. I should have told you."

His friend pursed his lips and then spoke slow, "Tan, I know you were just trying to save me from doing anything rash. Lord knows I would have; Charlotte made that clear to me last night. I needed to sit and listen to your perspective and all." He closed his eyes as if to think of something else to add, but Jake just waited for Tan.

Tan didn't expect that level of depth to come from Jake, who was stoic and quiet. "I appreciate that, Jake, I do. Truth is, I wanted this one time to be different. I wanted to be the one to bring Gabriel Grant to justice. I wanted to do that for ya, I wanted to bring both Felix and his father to justice because you're my friend." He wanted to add, "And because of all the pain you've been through and turmoil over the past several years, this time had to be different—better." But he chose not to add that bit.

The silence of the early evening seemed loud and the crickets' chorus screamed their song. Tan wished they'd quiet down so he could think, or so Jake would say something. Yet, the man sat there quiet as a church mouse. He didn't move, didn't blink, just sat there unmoving. What was going through Jake's mind?

"Tan, I'm going to say this once. You should have told me who Felix was. It wasn't your call to keep it from me."

Tan stood. "Jake, that's where you're wrong. I had every right to keep this from you. It's my duty to uphold the law. It was an active investigation. Things may run differently out here in the west, but I'm not local law. I have to keep things close to the chest, otherwise it could very well get me shot and killed."

Jake seemed to soften his approach. "Sit down, Tan. Charlotte told me to see things from your perspective, and I'm trying my best to do just that. When did you find out?"

That was one response Tan didn't figure on, and he appreciated Jake's willingness to listen. He pulled the black Stetson Yancy off his head and leaned forward. "Found out a day before you arrived. There was a family headed toward Cedar Grove. Seems as if the Knife Gang struck and killed the husband and wife and spared their young girl."

Now it was Jake's turn to stand and pace. "Who were they?"

"Not sure. Wanted to see if you knew of anyone coming to town."

"Why?"

"We found your name at the murder scene."

Jake stopped pacing. "My name?"

"Jake, they slit their throats. Nearly decapitating the man's head. Stuck inside his mouth was this note." Tan pulled a folded piece of paper out of his vest and handed it to Jake.

Sitting in silence, except the crickets who continued their singing, Jake read the note and his eyes grew wide, then read the note out loud, "*I know who you are, Jake Callihan. I know you had a life outside Cedar Grove in Purgatory, and that Felix Grant wants you dead for killing his mother, Moira. I also believe you killed our partner, Desperado Slinger. Also, I'm coming for you, and you can't stop what's going to happen next. See you in hell, Jacob Creek!*" He set the note down on a small table. "Who knows about me?"

That's something Tan had been trying to figure out. Since discovering the note, he wanted to see if Jake knew the family. "You have no idea who was coming to town?"

"The only people I knew coming to town were a preacher and his wife. They were going to take over the recently vacated church. But what's this have to do with me?"

Tan sat forward again on his elbows. "Think about it, Jake. You were a preacher. You lived in Purgatory. Your actions resulted in Moira's death, and you changed your name from Creek to Callihan."

Jake stood and scratched his head. "I guess we must stop whoever this guy is and before he kills someone else."

CHAPTER THIRTY-FIVE

AFTER LEAVING Jake alone with his thoughts, Tan decided it best to head out and catch up with Marshal Alan Drake. His partner had a good day's ride ahead of him, but with a good night's ride, a quick rest in the morning, he'd be able to catch up with Drake by mid-day. If only he'd let Jake in on his findings, the moment he knew, maybe things would have turned out differently. Albeit, Jake offered a bit of hope. He will help stop the man pulling Felix's strings. Maybe it was the least Jake could do, given the circumstances. Tan wasn't sure what he'd find in his search for Felix's accomplices, but truth to tell, he wasn't too sure where to look. If he could catch up with Alan Drake, maybe he'd be able to get Felix to talk.

He bounced along in the saddle, shifted his weight, and thought of Jake. As frustrated as he was, he didn't fault his friend for getting upset for his holding back information. Next time he'd be more mindful, get someone to take the oath of office first, then divulge information.

He continued pressing his horse forward through the

night. The moon sat high in the sky with several owls hooting off in the distance, searching for their next meal. Hungry, Tan pulled out some jerky and munched down on the dried meat.

Jake wouldn't disappoint him. He had offered to help Tan hunt down these killers and bring them to justice. It didn't matter if it were at the end of a noose or by a bullet, made no difference to him, he would hunt every one of those pigs down. They were killing folks for sport and Tan hated each one; Felix for killing that woman and child. Above it all, he was thankful Jake had made a life for himself in Cedar Grove, found a kind woman, forgetting about the past just to move forward. The only hang up, his quest for Gabriel's arrest, or death. Tan wasn't sure. He hoped Jake would make the right choice when that moment ever arrived. That was his hope, anyway.

When the moon descended and the sun cracked the sky, he figured it best to take a rest. His backside burned, and he needed to stop. A few minutes later, he came across a simple outcropping that opened up into a small clearing. After stopping, Tan unsaddled the horse and rubbed the animal down. No doubt if his quarter horse could talk, she'd tell him to slow down and rest more often. Grateful for the clearing, he made a small camp, then gathered some tall grass so his horse could have a late meal. The evening air felt damp and chilled his bones. Looking around, he gathered a few twigs, leaves, and branches to build a small cooking fire. He opened his knapsack and pulled out some potatoes, carrots, and an onion. He chopped them up, added a little salt, and made a small bowl of stew.

Tan figured he'd catch up to Drake before nightfall. When that didn't happen, he ate then fell back against his saddle and slept.

The following morning, he whipped up a batch of black coffee and pulled out a sack of bear sign that he'd purchased over at Mama Bear's and thoughtfully chewed over his next steps. So far, he'd taken the same route both he and Drake took coming to Cedar Grove. As he bit into one doughnut, movement caught his eye. Peeling off the thong to his gun, Tan yanked the cold steel out of its leather and swallowed the drying bear sign.

"Alan? Is that you?" Not sure why he thought it was his partner, he should have been halfway to Cheyenne by now. Tan pressed forward.

A bolt of brown flew past and forced him to jump back and land on his rump. Standing next to his horse stood a tan colored quarter horse, Drake's horse. It still sported the black saddle and U. S. Marshal's badge attaching the tie strap to its buckle.

"Easy, girl," he said, getting up and dusting off his slacks.

The animal, spooked, snorted and bobbed her head up and down. Putting the gun away, he gingerly approached the frightened animal. His own horse yanked at her lead rope, neighing and trying to move aside. Nothing scarier than a panicked horse. Get on the wrong side and she'd clock you clean in the head. Couldn't afford to let that happen.

"Easy, girl," he said again as he reached for the bridle. "Where's Drake?" The horse jerked as he held firm. Not letting go, he ran his fingers across her smooth snout.

Sure, it looked like Alan Drake's horse, but where was the other horse, and where was his partner? Tan had a bad feeling about this as his stomach twisted into a knot. What if his friend was dead? Was Felix free? The note from earlier flashed through his mind. *I know who you are, Jake Callihan. I know that*

Felix Grant wants you dead...I'm coming for you, and you can't stop what's going to happen next. See you in hell, Jacob Creek!

"Drake? Answer me?" It had to be a cruel joke. His partner was still alive. They were just resting before pressing onward, and he happened across the same campsite. Maybe Alan didn't want to go it alone with Felix and waited it out until Tan arrived. He had a nagging feeling that something was wrong and worried for Alan's safety.

That's when he spotted a boot sticking out from behind a bush. His heart stopped beating for a moment and his gut fell to the earth. He rounded the bush and there lay in a pool of sticky blood, his partner and friend, Alan Drake.

Drake's shredded stomach had flies and maggots making their home. His throat had a deep slice, nearly decapitated his partner's head. Reaching down, Tan checked for a pulse, useless, but he had to check.

Cold.

Tan searched his partner and noticed the missing Bowie knife. A barbarous thing to do to a man. Felix Grant had no soul, and Tan was now certain of that fact. The question lingering in his mind was, why didn't Felix make his move in town? What stopped him from finishing the job?

Turning away from the grisly scene, Tan Bennington vomited into the bush. He pulled off his hat and slapped it against the ground, then walked back to his camp and gathered his wool blanket to cover his friend.

What was he going to do now?

Felix Grant was in the wind!

CHAPTER THIRTY-SIX

S UN RAYS PEEKED through the clouds long after Jake was
up and feeding the horses. The CHR was a busy place
most days as his crew tended to the day-to-day care of
running the place. He now had the largest ranch in Cedar
Grove. That made him smile.

Several chickens clucked as he threw some grain into their
trough. He refilled their water and gathered a dozen eggs for
Loretta. As he put the last egg into the basket, one popped out
and cracked against the ground. Jake picked it up and figured
it'd be alright for breakfast.

Staring at the cracked egg reminded him of the crack that
formed between both him and Tan Bennington. It's not he
didn't trust his friend, he did, but Jake wished the man hadn't
been so blinded.

Sure, it was a noble effort to keep information regarding
Felix Grant a secret so that Tan could take credit for finding
Gabriel. But it was stupid and reckless. Tan didn't know how
dangerous the Grant family was. Gabriel Grant knew no
bounds and showed as much when Sarah died. He pulled the

egg out and tossed it against the far wall and walked toward the house.

Thoughts continued their scrambling as he gave the eggs to Loretta to make something for breakfast. He changed, shaved, and by the time he arrived to the dining room, Loretta had made a steaming plate of bacon, scrambled eggs, and toast with apricot jam. He hungrily ate and left for Charlotte's place.

He loved the ride to her shack. The trees lifted to a small bluff that overlooked the pasture he rode. Golden sunlight sparkled through the pine trees and reminded Jake of thanking God for the small things in life. If it weren't for Charlotte, he wouldn't give God the time of day, but now, she's showing him how to trust once again.

And maybe trust is what he needed to give Tan Bennington. Maybe the time had come to put a badge back on. Ten years ago, he tried, but after ten years of practice with the United States' Marshal's service, he could do the job. Tan had full faith and trust that Jake would make a good marshal. One thing he prided himself on was being a man of his word. It was time to become a marshal and help bring The Knife Gang to justice.

The note still bothered him. Was Gabriel behind the murders of that poor preacher family? Made sense because of the man's disdain toward Jake, who once was a preacher himself. But it didn't seem like a move Gabriel would make. Why would someone leave a note?

Charlotte's cottage sat in a clearing nestled against a few white pines and birch trees. A small clearing of green grass with several sunflowers and orange daisies planted next to the small home, welcomed him with their smiling petals. Tying off

Tucker, Jake picked a handful of flowers, then knocked on the door.

"Jake," she said, opening the door. "What brings you out so early on a Saturday?"

He handed her the flowers. "Can't a man come and see his girl before riding to town?"

Her radiant smile and blushing cheeks melted his heart like butter. He loved her to death. If his heart stopped beating at this moment, he'd die happy.

"I take it you're on your way to see the sheriff?"

"Actually, I'm on my way to find Marshal Bennington."

Her smile faded, and she hung her head. Her hands played at the corner of her apron before walking toward the table to put the flowers in a vase that sat on its wooden top. "I know it's the right thing to do, but you have to promise me you'll be careful while wearing that badge?"

He didn't enjoy seeing her uncertain and worried. There was no guarantee he'd be safe out on the range, hunting bad guys, and keeping the people of Cedar Grove safe.

Jake pulled at her hands and ran his thumbs against her palms. They were smooth, and he loved her touch. "I promise I'll be safe. I worry more about the other guy than myself."

Her lip quivered and curled. "I don't want to lose you. It makes me nervous each time you venture out with Tan Bennington."

"He's got my back." He pulled at her hands and wrapped his arms around her waist.

"I know that, I just…never mind."

"Never mind, what?" Jake asked.

"Just promise me again."

He reassured her he'd be safe. God had his back, or so he

told her. Sure, he began trusting God a little more, but did God trust him? That was the real question.

Knowing he'd never receive an answer to that question, he kissed Charlotte goodbye and headed off toward Cedar Grove for some supplies.

CHAPTER THIRTY-SEVEN

T HOUGHTS OF CHARLOTTE lingered in his mind as he pressed out of Cedar Grove. She deserved to have happiness and to have a man unconditionally love her. Jake felt that being away on federal business wouldn't help calm her mind. At least with cattle ranching, he was home more than gone. Being a federal marshal would change all of that. Not that Jake planned on dying soon. But he understood why Charlotte had those thoughts.

When he got back, his first order of business would be to ask Charlotte for her hand in marriage. That ring would burn a hole in his dresser drawer if he waited any longer.

Then there was Tan Bennington. Maybe it was time to let bygones be bygones. Tan had good intentions, and it wasn't fair to hold him accountable for keeping Jake in the dark.

He'd been riding for several hours and wished he could turn off his thoughts. They annoyed him. But that's how he was, he thought, and his mind always replayed the same thing repeatedly. A trait he hated about himself.

In the distance, a small cloud of dust rose. Looked to be

two riders coming his direction. His stomach twisted into a knot. Bracing for trouble, Jake flipped the thong off his gun, ready to pull his weapon at any moment.

A few minutes later, it looked to be a lone rider pulling along another horse. It didn't look good. Someone hauling a dead man back to Cedar Grove. Sunlight glinted off something metal on the rider's chest, and Jake figured it might be law.

"Tan? Is that you?" he called out.

"Jake?" came the reply.

Jake kicked his horse and let the reins out. Tucker responded with a snort and nod and moved from a canter to a soft gallop. Tan Bennington rose into full view, no longer darkened by the sun.

"Jake, it's Alan Drake. He's dead."

"Dead?" It had to be Felix Grant.

"Found him about a half day's ride east of here. It was brutal. Blew open his gut and nearly took off his head."

Jake's gut twisted again as bile rose. He swallowed it back. "Oh man, that's awful," Jake said, steadying his horse. "Was it Felix?" asking and knowing the answer.

"That's my guess. He's gone and with the wind."

The two said little more until they eased back toward Cedar Grove. The sheriff went and found the mortician to prepare Drake's body for burial. Shame, Alan Drake was a good man who had his entire life ahead of him.

Jake didn't know the deputy marshal that well, but he took a liking to the kid. Alan Drake was only twenty-four years old. Far too young to have your life snuffed out in such a brutal way. But that was the way of the west and what you signed on for as a lawman. You could die at any moment. That's what worried Charlotte Jennings. The difference between Jake and

Drake was his six gun. He could draw, fire, and holster long before any other man could clear leather. Though he tried to avoid those circumstances at all costs.

Once the mortician arrived with a pine box, they took Drake's body to the church's cemetery. The only problem, the town didn't have a reverend and their new reverend had been killed by the person who knew he was Jacob Creek. The same one who killed Drake and freed Felix.

"Jake, would you do the honors? You used to be a man of the cloth," Tan asked.

Jake shot Tan a look. Most in town didn't know that he used to be a reverend, something he wanted to keep secret. Only Freddy, Tan, and Charlotte knew the truth. But now that the cat was out of the…

"You were a preacher?" Whalen asked.

"In another life. Gave that up to be a rancher." Which was true.

Jake entered the church to find a Bible, something he hadn't opened in years. It almost felt foreign to him. He still had the one his wife gave him when he went into the ministry. That copy sat in a chest back at the CHR.

He found the passage he needed in John's gospel. "John chapter eleven says, '*I am the resurrection, and the life: he that believeth in me, though he were dead, yet shall he live: And whosoever liveth and believeth in me shall never die. Believest thou this?*'" He closed the Bible. "I didn't know Alan Drake for long, but I saw he had a keen eye and a good heart. It's a shame what happened to him, but as Jesus says, he is the resurrection and the life. I don't know if Drake was a religious man, but I know that God loved him and maybe in those last moments on earth, he cried out for Christ's salvation."

Jake picked up a fistful of dirt after praying. "So, we

commit to the ground, our friend, Alan Richards Drake. For dust we are, and dust we shall return. Amen."

"Amen," the others responded.

Jake dropped the dirt on to the coffin and watched it dance about before settling in place. Tan and Roy did the same. Jake clenched his fists. Before they could bring Felix to justice, how many more would die?

Sheriff Roy Whalen then shook Jake's hand. "By cracky, I guess ya were a real preacher. Did a mighty fine job of committing our friend to God's hands."

Jake smiled at his friend. "Thank you."

"Let's go back to your office, sheriff, and discuss our next steps to find the sonofagun that murdered my friend," Bennington said.

CHAPTER THIRTY-EIGHT

AFTER THE QUICK funeral for Alan Drake, Jake followed Roy back to the jail to talk through next steps to capture Felix, dead or alive. If he had the chance, he'd put a bullet in the boy's skull for killing all those people, especially Alan.

The town sat quietly as they walked up the steps into the Sheriff's Office. Maybe word about Felix's escape made its rounds with townsfolk hunkering down in their homes. He picked up the local paper. Nothing yet about Felix's escape. He slapped the paper down. "Roy, what's next? How do we stop this maniac?"

The sheriff poured himself a cup of coffee and leaned against the center post. "I rightly don't know. We'll wait until Tan receives word back from Cheyenne."

The whole thing was maddening. Who knew that his proper name was Jacob Creek? It didn't matter what he called himself. He ran across several gun hawks who changed their names to avoid recognition from their past. But few knew his past and he feared it might be someone he knew, someone from Purgatory.

"Boys, I just sent word to the Governor's office. He had a quick reply and is issuing a warrant for the capture of Felix Grant, either dead or alive," Tan Bennington said, walking into the dank room.

That put a smile on Jake's face. Felix was a dead man and Jake would pull the trigger. "I think it's high time you pin a badge on my chest."

Both the marshal and sheriff smiled.

Tan asked to see the Roy's Bible. He pulled out a piece of paper and a round silver badge with a five-pointed star affixed inside the ring. The top of the ring read, *U. S. Marshal*, and the bottom read, *Wyoming Territory*.

"Guess you figured I'd say something," Jake said.

Tan smiled. "Sure did. Now, Jake Callihan, raise your right hand and place your left on the Bible."

Jake did as he was told.

"Repeat these words after me… I, Jake Callihan, do so solemnly swear that I will uphold, protect, and preserve the people of the greater territory of Wyoming. I will execute the duties and responsibilities to the office I am about to enter, according to the law and constitution of the United States and the territory of Wyoming. So help me God."

Jake repeated each word, and he meant everyone. He would bring justice to his family, and all the other families who'd suffered at the hands of the Grant family.

"Jake, I hereby solemnly authorize you to execute the duties of the office of United States Deputy Marshal, according to the law, with all the powers, privilege, and emoluments. I have the privilege to subject you to the conditions prescribed by the Governor's office and by the law."

Tan picked up the badge and fixed it to Jake's left lapel of his overcoat. He signed the document and handed him the piece of paper. "Congratulations, you are now an employee of the United States' Marshal's office."

Roy clapped and sighed what seemed to be relief. He could now retire in peace until Jake and Tan found another sheriff to take his place.

Jake stared at the shiny badge. Last time he'd worn a lawman's badge was the night his family died. He had taken it off after leaving Purgatory. The funny thing about life, it seemed to go in circles. "Thank you, Tan. I will honor this badge and the office you've assigned to me. Now, let's go get Felix Grant and bring him to—"

"SHERIFF!!"

The guttural scream came from outside. Who was yelling? Couldn't be Felix, could it?

The three lawmen walked out of the office and stepped onto the boardwalk. Standing in the street was Dan Baley. Dan was not a large man but built for hard labor. His sandy blond hair poked out from under his wide-brimmed hat. His eyes set and Jake figured trouble peeked around the corner.

"What do you want, Dan?" Roy asked.

"I want to know why Felix isn't in your jailhouse, Sheriff?"

Roy spoke, but Jake put his hand out, stopping him. "Dan, what are you doing? You should be out at the CHR working with Freddy. We have a lot of work to get done before we do a round up."

"Stay out of this, Jake! This is between me and that no good, lazy sheriff." He saw Jake's badge. "You law now, Jake?"

Jake noticed Dan's tied down guns, and the thongs were off each hammer. He didn't think the man usually wore two guns. Dan Baley was fixing for a fight. Jake stepped off the porch and gravel crunched under his boots. His spurs jangled as he steadied his breathing. He flipped the thong off his own gun and placed his palm on the weapon's hilt.

"Dan, I don't want any trouble."

"Is it true you buried a deputy marshal?"

"It is," Tan said. "Go home before I authorize Jake to arrest you for disturbing the peace."

"Stay out of this, marshal!" Dan bellowed.

Jake felt his chest tighten as Dan's hands moved toward each gun. His world stilled. "Dan, let the law handle this."

"I tried, there's no other way. I need to go find Felix. Either you're going to help me or I'm going to do this my own way. Law or no law, Felix is mine."

"Stand down, secure your guns before things get ugly."

"He killed my boy, Jake!" he started sobbing. "My boy's not coming back."

"You still have your family. Think about them. Let us handle the outlaw."

Dan didn't say another word. His hand reached for his left gun.

The world stopped spinning and Jake's hand wrapped around the hilt of his .45 Colt Peacemaker. The gun cleared the holster smooth and fast. His gun barked and spit fire. The bullet punctured a hole in Dan Baley's forehead. The cowboy stood there for a moment before crumpling to the ground, dead.

Jake noticed the gun in Baley's left hand as sweat dripped off his brow. Dan had cleared the leather and by some miracle Jake pulled his trigger first.

CHAPTER THIRTY-NINE

JAKE DIDN'T move for several minutes. Dan Baley was dead. He lay in his own gore in the middle of the street. People started milling around the area and Jake's throat tightened. His stomach churned and he walked away. What did he just do? Finding a post near the rear of the Sheriff's Office, Jake gripped the wood, collapsed to his knees, and vomited.

He wiped his mouth, squeezed his forehead, and cried. His bullet made Dan's wife a widow and his daughter, fatherless. A footfall behind him caught his attention. He looked up at Tan Bennington's tired eyes.

"It wasn't your fault, Jake," Tan said. "No way you could have known."

Jake shook his head. "How could I not have? I've been in his boots. I know the kind of people the Grants are. They're ruthless, cowards, and killers. That's who they are. I've had Dan's rage, the only difference, I had Sarah there to stop me before I did something rash."

"Like putting a bullet in Gabriel Grant's skull?"

"Something like that." Jake spit the sour taste from his mouth and stood to face Tan. "I know it was within my legal right to defend my honor. Dan made a move for his gun; I had no choice. Don't make me feel any better knowing that, is all."

Tan put his large hand on Jake's shoulder. "Jake, trust me. We'll find Felix, you have my word. Besides, you should go tell his wife she's a widow. Roy has gone for the undertaker."

Jake nodded. Time to clear his head of the cobwebs. He walked around the building and mounted his horse. Tucker snorted and bobbed his head. Jake steadied the animal with a pat to the neck. "Guess you didn't get too spooked with all the gunfire."

Tucker was a good horse, and Jake treasured his loyalty. Too bad Dan wasn't as loyal, and it got him shot. Why did he have to be so stupid? "I'll be back after talking with Mrs. Baley, and then I'm going to find Felix."

Just then, Roy walked up with the undertaker. "Jake, wait, Derick has something for you."

"What is it?"

Derick, probably the oldest person in the Grove. He stood only five feet, five inches. He stood hunched. How could he still build pine boxes and prepare a body? The elderly man handed him a dried, blood coated folded note. He took it from Derick's boney fingers, opened it and read:

I'M COMING FOR YOU, PREACHER, AND THERE'S NOT A THING YOU CAN DO. WATCH YOUR BACK AND EVERYONE YOU LOVE, ESPE-CIALLY THAT SCHOOL TEACHER.

Something like dynamite ignited against his skull. This was the second note found on a dead body. One thought rushed through his mind, Charlotte. He had to keep her safe. He had to make sure nothing bad happened to her. Every time the

Grants got involved in his life, the people he loved were in danger.

"I'm heading out to find Felix." He tossed the note to his partner.

Tan snatched it from the air and read. He folded the paper. "Jake, do nothing stupid. You go for Charlotte; we'll ride out for Felix Grant. We'll put a posse together. We'll find him. Let me handle this."

"I told you—"

"I know what you told me. Let me handle this, Jake!"

Jake pulled his gun and leveled it at his friend.

The sheriff pulled his gun. "Jake, think this through."

"Stand down, Roy! This is between me and Felix."

Roy cocked his gun. "Don't end up like Dan. We'll take it from here."

Jake fired one warning shot at Roy's feet. The elder sheriff backed off and holstered his weapon.

"I said, I'm going after Felix. If you don't want me to kill you, I'd advise you to not follow me. This is *my* fight, he called *me* out, and Grant is mine!"

Neither Tan nor Roy said or did anything to follow Jake. He took off to the south of town and rode out toward the CHR. He had to warn Charlotte. She needed protection and needed to stay where Freddy could look after her.

He already lost Sarah; he wasn't about to lose Charlotte on account of another Grant. As he rode, one thought rifled through his mind: Purgatory wants its revenge and its eyes set on Jacob Creek.

The newly polished badge pinned on his left lapel shone in the sun. This time, he had the law on his side, and he was about to extend the full arm of his rights as a United States Marshal.

CHAPTER FORTY

J AKE MADE out Charlotte's shack just at the bottom of the bluff. This was Callihan land. He took a different way out of town than normal to mask his tracks. He didn't need Felix, or anyone else, following him. Taking a different route helped him double back and continue out of Cedar Grove.

Smoke emitting from the single chimney told him that Charlotte was home. The sun sat mid-sky and Jake had little time to explain the situation to Charlotte. Would she agree to stay at his place? If not, he'd help by dragging her if need be. Not that he expected it to go that far. Charlotte would understand.

He rode up to her place fast. Tucker hardly stopped by the time Jake dismounted and ran up the steps of the cottage and threw open the door. He pulled his gun and scanned the room, half expecting to find Felix or one of his outlaws holding Charlotte hostage.

Charlotte screamed when she saw Jake with his six-gun

out. "Jacob Callihan, what are you doing ramming through my door like that?"

Charlotte's already porcelain complexion paled as he holstered his gun. Maybe barging in gun drawn wasn't the best idea, but her life depended on their moving fast. He needed her at the CHR.

"I'm—"

"What were you thinking, barging in here like that?" she asked again.

"It's Felix. He's at large. Killed a deputy marshal. He knows about you. I have to get you safe."

She breathed in deep, her breasts rose and fell with each breath. "I thought you locked him up in Roy Whalen's jail?"

"We transferred him to Cheyenne when someone killed the marshal and then Felix left a note saying he's coming for you and I can't stop it. The only safe place for you right now is at my homestead. Freddy's there and he'll keep you safe."

Charlotte reached for his hands and said, "Jake, it'll be okay. No one knows I'm out here. And besides, I'm protected on all sides by the bluff. I can see who's coming a mile away. I have a gun, you know."

He looked at the rifle mounted above the davenport. It didn't reassure him. It made him more nervous. No way would he leave the love of his life stuck out here, alone.

"Sorry, not going to happen. We're leaving, now."

"Let me gather a few things, first."

Jake watched as she gathered her items and a primer for her class. He was about to say she should let it alone but thought better of it. Jake pulled her small two-person wagon and hitched it to Tucker. They set off toward the CHR. Toward safety.

The sun set high and its heat pounded the air. Turning to Charlotte he asked, "You okay?"

She'd been quiet with her face set and jaw clenched tight. No doubt she worried for her safety, but it there seemed to be more. One of her fingers flicked at the silver circular badge affixed to his coat.

"When were you going to tell me about the badge?"

He'd nearly forgotten about it. "I was going to tell you."

"After you got shot and killed?"

"That's not fair, and you know it." Just yesterday she seemed okay with his decision.

Charlotte looked forward again, contemplating what to say next.

A huff of air escaped his lips. "I'm sorry—"

"Jake, I'm not mad that you didn't tell me, I'm upset that you're already planning to run headlong into danger without even considering who you'd be leaving behind."

He pulled the horse to a halt and turned to face her. "You don't think that I'm not thinking about you? You're all I think about. You're all that matters. Why do you think I'm taking you to my home?" He raised his voice, not meaning to, but he couldn't stop. Not waiting for an answer, Jake said, "To keep you safe! That's why. I want you safe. I don't want another Grant to take someone I care about."

A hand landed on top of his, and that's when his heart broke into a thousand pieces. He loved her. If only he could take back his tone.

"Okay, Jake. Take me to the ranch. I'm sorry. I know how much the Grants have hurt you, and I won't get in your way of stopping this evil man."

After a long while of silence he breathed out, "Okay, good."

When they arrived, all looked to calm and pristine on the ranch. No one seemed to be around. Maybe Freddy had the boys out in the southern pasture fixing the fence. Dan Baley should have been the one to fix that fence, but Jake shot and killed him hours ago in town.

The door to Jake's home opened and Freddy walked out, shaking his head before plopping down on a bench. Something was wrong, and Jake feared it was Grant.

"Freddy?" he said, jumping down then helping Charlotte climb down.

Freddy looked up at the two of them and stood, putting his hat on. "Ma'am," he said, tipping his hat in her direction. "Jake, it's Cory."

A vice gripped his heart. "What happened?"

"It's really bad, Jake. Shot himself about fifteen minutes ago. Loretta heard it happen as she was taking up some soup."

Cory was dead? The boy could've lived without a leg, but to shoot himself. "How'd he get a gun?"

Freddy pulled a Colt .44 from his belt. "Don't know," he said, then handed over the gun.

Taking the weapon, Jake inspected it and found Phillip's initials (a young cowboy Jake hired six months ago) etched into the hilt. He purchased and gave each ranch hand a gun. He etched everyone's initials next to the CHR monogram into their gun before sending them off to work. That way, any nefarious thing happened, he could talk to the right person.

It was a habit. He didn't want anyone having their own gun while in his employ. "Find Phillip and bring him to me."

CHAPTER FORTY-ONE

W HAT WAS Phillip Jones thinking, taking a gun into Cory's room? Jake was nearly beside himself and could just about smack the boy for it. He paced his study, weighing the right words to say when the cowboy came walking into his office. Not wanting to deal with this, Jake ran his fingers through his hair and sat behind the desk.

The curtain moved and in walked Phillip. "You wanted to see me, sir?"

Slamming the gun onto the desk, several graphite sticks rattled about and fell onto the floor. "See this gun, we found it in Cory Jackson's room…next to his dead body!"

At seventeen, Phillip's ruddy look and boyish blond hair made him seem far from the man that Jake knew he could be. His body stiffened, and he kept his mouth closed, not saying a word.

"What were you thinking? I have half a mind to arrest you right now for murder."

The boy's dark brown eyes saw the badge and welled with

tears. Several snaked their way down his cheeks. "Mr. Calli-han, I didn't mean—"

"You didn't mean to what? See to his death? What were you thinking?"

By this point, Phillip hyperventilated. His sobs came hard and with each breath he sucked his lower lip into his whimpering mouth.

"You're fired. I never want to see you around the CHR again. I hired you because you were good and could ride almost better than any man I've seen. But now..." Jake inhaled a quick breath. "...you've wasted your potential on my ranch. Get out of my sight."

He turned to leave. "Mr. Callihan? I'm really sorry fergiv'en 'im my gun. But he axed me to do that fer him. Couldn't live without just one leg to get by on."

Jake didn't say another word but started writing anything to keep his mind clear of all that happened and was happening.

After Phillip left, Freddy walked into the study. "Guess we gotta hire another man?"

"Can't think about that right now. I have pressing matters. It's about Charlotte."

Freddy sat down and placed his hat onto his knee. "Saw her come in with ya. What's up, boss?"

Jake tossed the pen and puffed some air, rolled his neck to help relieve some building tension. "Someone knows my proper is Creek, and they know that I'm seeing Charlotte."

That caused his friend to cross his arms. "Who?"

Freddy was a good man, fifty years old. He combed his jet-black hair to the side, waiting for Jake's answer. He first met Freddy ten years prior, the day he arrived in Purgatory. He was wiry and strong as an ox, though one wouldn't be able to tell. Jake didn't know anyone as loyal and fair as Freddy.

"Felix Grant."

"Is that who's been sit'n in Roy's jail?"

"He was."

"Boy, didn't see that coming. That why yer wearing that badge?"

Astute thought from the former blacksmith. "I need you to keep Charlotte safe. Give her a gun, have someone on watch at all times of the day. Trouble's coming and I'm afraid that when this thing explodes, things'll get bloody and I don't want Charlotte caught in the middle of a gunfight."

Freddy rose. "I'll keep her safe."

Jake plopped his hat on and stood, "One more thing, make sure Phillip doesn't come around again. I don't trust him, and I don't want that kind of man on my ranch."

"Consider it done."

After Freddy left, Jake found Charlotte and Loretta sitting at the dining room table talking about the differences of childhood years. Loretta was perfect for Charlotte. If anyone, a capable woman like Loretta could help ease Charlotte's fears. The story went that her late husband got in with the wrong person. He tried to stop the man from taking their land. He was tragically killed. She never told Jake how he died, only that revenge filled her mind.

Loretta hunted down and killed the man who caused her husband's death. Afraid of being arrested for murder, she told Jake to keep it quiet and let it be. He respected her and couldn't blame her for wanting revenge.

Green carpet adorned the dining room, a large mahogany table sat under a silver candelabrum, and a fireplace warmed the room. He watched them laugh and talk for a bit then looked at his pocket watch; time to go. Closing the watch, he slipped it back into his pocket and walked up to the table.

"Ladies, sorry to interrupt. I'm riding out for a few days. Don't know when I'll be back."

Charlotte's eyes flashed with concern. "Promise me you'll be safe?"

He kissed her lips. "I promise, I'll be fine. But I need you to stay here. Freddy's going to give you a gun. I want you to wear it at all times. Loretta, make sure you give her some man britches to wear. It'll be easier with a gun belt."

"Expecting trouble, Jake?" Loretta asked.

"It's bound to happen. I know you can use a gun, find one and strap it on yourself too." Turning back to Charlotte, "I love you. You're safe here. If you need anything, ask Loretta or Freddy, but under no circumstances are you to leave the ranch. It's too dangerous."

Jake kissed her one more time, then he walked out of the house, mounted his horse, and set off to find Felix Grant.

He rode for several hours and found the spot where he met up with Tan the previous day. As the sun dipped behind the horizon, Jake broke for camp.

He ate a healthy meal, snuffed out the fire, and leaned against Tucker's saddle. It took a matter of minutes and Jake's eyes closed, praying he'd find Felix Grant before he found Charlotte, then he slept.

CHAPTER FORTY-TWO

As THE SUN crested the horizon, Jake ate some dried beef and brewed a small pot of coffee. Not allowing himself a full night's sleep, he needed to press on and catch up to the outlaws. He swallowed the last drop of coffee and tossed the rest. He kicked some dirt over the fire and pressed forward for several hours.

A few tracks marked the earth to his left. He dismounted and felt the impressions. Hours old. They couldn't be far at this point. Somewhere inside, he wondered why they took their time, and tried to push the thought aside. That's when rifle fire grabbed his ears. It came from the east. He nudged Tucker toward the gunfire.

Dismounting, Callihan grabbed his rifle and headed across the ridge. Even though it had rained two days prior, the bone-dry ground cracked under the weight of his boot. The sun began its slow climb across the pale blue sky. He wiped the now dripping sweat off his brow, wishing he'd left the long trench coat with the horse.

He peered over the edge. Falling would be a bad idea—no

one would ever find him. Twenty-four hours passed since Marshall Bennington found Alan Drake's body with no sign of the prisoner. Jacob watched as two jackrabbits ran below. He stared at the animals again as they ran from something.

The sound of popping cracked through the canyon again, and Jake perked his ears toward the sound. He levered the rifle and ran back to his horse. He remounted, kicked the animal in the side, and carefully headed down the ridge. The gunfire could be for several reasons, and he didn't want to take any chances—his rifle ready to fire at a moment's notice. He sat high on the mount, eyes alert.

He heard several voices echoing off the canyon walls.

CRACK!

Another gunshot and now laughter thundered through the chasm. Dismounting again, Jake tied off Tucker to a nearby tree. He proceeded down the steep embankment toward the voices. The sound came from his left. Carefully, he set the rifle down and peered through the bushes, hoping they'd hide his figure from sight.

"Felix, you realize we need to get back to Purgatory?" The tall one said. He wore a tan, wide-brimmed hat and a brown high-button coat.

"What and get back to the old man? He's a bastard, and everyone in town knows it. I long for the day when I can put the old codger in the ground."

Jake figured that must be Felix. He picked up his rifle and aimed at Felix's head. One perfect shot is all he needed to end the man's life. After all, he killed a deputy marshal. Time to take matters into his own hands. Jake slowly rose into view, keeping his sight on Felix.

"Felix, this is Jake Callihan, I'm a federal marshal. I'd

advise you to remove your gun belt and toss it to the side. Tell your buddies to do the same."

The sudden extra voice in the gorge startled the three men. All of whom drew their weapons.

"And if we don't?" Felix said. It wasn't a question.

Not taking any chances, Jacob fired one round from his Henry .45 repeating rifle. The bullet hit soft leather and Felix's gun belt fell to the ground. "I won't ask you again. Take off your belts and toss them to the side."

The robber next to Felix fired a single bullet that slapped into the rock next to Jake.

Chambering another round, the gun bucked his shoulder as he returned fire. The slug struck the man standing next to Felix, and he dropped to the canyon floor writhing in pain.

"Now, I'd advise you all to drop your weapons."

Felix dove for his gun and rolled out of the way of Jake's next shot. Felix returned fire.

The bullet pinged off a rock to his right. He crouched down, took aim, and fired. The man running after Felix tumbled to the ground, dead. "I gave you one chance! Now Felix, stop your running or I'll shoot you as well."

Felix stood and dropped his gun. "Now, I have a good explanation for all this."

Jake slid down the ridge and leveled his rifle at the outlaw. "I'm sure you do. Now, stay put." He kicked the gun aside, twisted the rifle, and smacked Felix in the jaw. "You killed a marshal!"

He yelped in pain as blood dripped out his nose. "You broke my nose," he spat.

"I'll break more than that."

Felix cracked a smile. "I'll slit your throat like I did that marshal." He spat blood. "I used his own knife, too."

Jake hit him again. This time, Felix dropped to the ground, laughing hysterically.

"Get up," he said, kicking the son of his family's killer. "I know who you are, Felix Grant. What do you want from me?"

Felix smiled a golden grin. "Dead."

That's when a bullet ripped into Jacob's shoulder. He looked at the hole as blood dripped out of the fresh wound. Where did that come from? A dark shadow crept into his vision as a second bullet slammed into his gut like a locomotive. Felix cackled a laugh somewhere as Jacob fell backward.

"You got 'im, Diamond!"

"I did," a voice said that sounded soft and female.

His vision blurred. Hard to breathe with blood choking out the air as if someone squeezed the very life from his chest. And just before the light blinked out of his eyes, he saw Gabriel Grant's visage.

"I've got you now."

Then Jacob Creek died.

ALL PATHS LEAD TO PURGATORY

In my distress I called upon the Lord, and cried out to my God; He heard my voice from His temple, and my cry came before Him, even to His ears.

— KING DAVID

CHAPTER FORTY-THREE

I T WAS A beautiful day. The birds chirped their songs, cattle moaned in the distance, and the sound of hammers brought a smile to Freddy's ears. Most called him by that name, but his proper name was Franklin Pierce. For years he was made fun of for his skinny stature, but sitting next to Ted Jefferies, Freddy felt like a big man.

They continued the work on the southern fence since Dan went and got himself killed. What was Dan Baley thinking? Going up against Jake? Dumb move for a cowboy to make. Freddy swung his hammer and shoved a nail deep into the wood, securing some wire. He still didn't get the whole using wire bit, he grew up using wood as a fence, but Jake wanted to be innovative.

"Hey Freddy," Wide-Eye said.

He looked at the old skinny black man working hard and twisting wire around a nail. "What's up?"

"Any news of when Jake will be returning?"

"Sorry, he didn't say."

Wide-Eye worked on moving wire further down the fence

line. Though he was skinny as a railroad tie, Ted "Wide-Eye" Jeffries was as loyal and hardworking as any man Freddy had the privilege to know. The man, however, had a knack for exaggerating stories and getting on his nerves.

"Wide-Eye, remember the time you shot yourself in the foot?"

"Did not," he said.

Freddy popped the hammer's hook onto the post and turned to face Wide-Eye. "You did. Shot yourself clean through the foot."

"How yafigger since I was aiming at that coyote…he bit my foot."

Freddy chuckled at the absurdity. "Bit by a coyote, my butt. You tried to clear the leather and put yer finger in the trigger hole and the gun fired."

Wide-Eye laughed. "Oh yea, I's didat some point. Wasn't the time the coyote bit me." His grin was wide and nearly toothless, except for the visible canines. "That time, I'd be working in the pasture over east here. That was the time Clyde ran things. I got lost and dis big coyote comes from nowhere. Swears he's snarl'n, snapp'n and foam'n at the mouth n'all. Pulled my pistol and shot into the air. The bugger didn't move. Then came and bit my foot."

Freddy shook his head. Wide-Eye was an idiot, but Freddy liked the skinny black man. "Prove it."

"Rights now, sir?"

"Show me the bite."

Wide-eye sat down and pulled off his boot and then started on the nasty looking sock.

Freddy stopped him. "Okay, I believe ya."

Wide-Eye grinned. "See, I's told ya I'd got bit by a coyote."

Freddy turned away. Something in the distance caught his attention.

"Boss?"

He held up a hand. "I hear something,"

When nothing happened, he turned back to his fence. For days, Jake's actions worried him before he left to find Felix. He even asked that Charlotte wear a gun and man britches. He'd never seen a woman in man britches before, but she wore them well. It took a bit, but Freddy gave her some shooting lessons with a six-gun. She took to it well enough, but didn't like the short gun, and preferred a rifle or scattergun.

"Boss! Rider."

Being pulled from his thoughts, he looked up as a rider cleared the tree line a quarter mile out. It didn't look good. He pulled his tomahawk and told Wide-Eye to be ready and not shoot himself in the foot. That's when he saw how slumped over the rider appeared.

"Boss?"

Freddy ignored the elderly man and turned his attention toward the rider.

Jacob Creek.

He recognized Tucker, but Jake didn't look so good.

"Freddy…he…help…me."

No sooner than Jake spoke, he fell off his horse and disappeared in the tall grasses.

The two men ran toward their boss. Freddy pulled up at the sight of Tucker covered in blood. He pulled the animal to the side as Ted called out, "He's over here!"

The amount of blood that soaked into Jacob's clothing was enough to wonder how he survived at all. His skin was pale and translucent. He needed treatment, or he'd be dead before long.

"Ted, go get Loretta. Tell her to bring the wagon."

Wide-Eye didn't move.

"Ted, look at me."

He did.

"Jacob needs our help; he'll die without help. Now, go get Loretta."

Wide-Eye grabbed his horse and galloped toward the ranch.

Turning his attention back to his boss, Freddy said, "Jake, stay with me. Help's coming." There was no movement, no sound, nothing. Jacob lay still and Freddy feared the worst; someone just killed Jake Callihan.

CHAPTER FORTY-FOUR

CHARLOTTE'S HANDS were knuckle deep into dough when Ted Jefferies ran in screaming about something. She tried to wipe the flour from her sticky fingers, but Loretta told her to continue with the dough. "I don't want it to become too elastic, otherwise the bear sign won't turn out soft and chewy."

"Help!"

"Ted? What is it?" Loretta asked as she vacated the kitchen.

"It's Mr. Callihan—"

She heard no more. Charlotte wiped her hands and joined them in the hallway. "What about Jacob?"

Ted looked pale and out of breath. His hands dug into his kneecaps. "Ms. Jennings, It's Jake. They have shot him really good."

Charlotte shook her head. "*Shot?*" How? Who? Why? All these questions fluttered through her mind like oak leaves in the fall. Her knees buckled and her head spun with the news. "Is he—" she stuttered to get the words out, "...dead?"

Ted shook his head. "No, ma'am. He'd not dead. But I fear the worse for him." Turning toward Loretta, "Mr. Franklin asks for the wagon, we'd best get to him."

Loretta was already out the door, Charlotte close behind. The two women worked hard to hitch up a horse to the wagon. Ted was most helpful, since he was the one usually doing the work. Loretta climbed up next to Ted and Charlotte hopped onto the back.

"Honey, I don't think it'd be good for you to see what you're about to see. I need you to stay behind and boil some water. Sterilize a couple of knives. We're going to need all the help we can get to keep Jake alive." She turned to Ted. "How bad is it, Ted?"

"Real bad, Ms. Lynn."

Charlotte couldn't move. Wouldn't move. How could she let them go out there to fetch Jacob when she's stuck here?

"Charlotte, look at me," Loretta said.

She did.

"I need you to boil some water. Get Cory's room ready. It's the easiest room to take him to. It must be ready when we're done pulling the bullets from his body."

Every part of Charlotte's body demanded that she yell at Loretta, tell her to get out of the way, that there's no way she was going without her. Yet, she knew better than to argue and to start getting things ready would be a help. And she knew nothing about removing bullets from people. That's something Loretta has done a few times.

She climbed out of the wagon and watched them leave. A tear slipped down her cheek and she stifled a cry that begged to become a wail. They hurt her Jacob. If only she never let him leave. She knew better than to tell him it was okay for him to take the job and hunt the bad guys. How could a girl be so stupid as to let her man strap on a gun and fight?

She stood there until the dust settled. Ted told them Jacob rode into the southern pasture as he and Freddy were mending the fence. It would be a couple of hours before they returned.

Her feet stood on the driveway as if someone nailed them to a board. Pulling up whatever reserve of strength she could muster, Charlotte turned and ran into the house. The stove was hot, but not hot enough. She threw a few logs into the fire and tossed a kettle of water onto the stove to boil.

While she waited for the water, she stripped the sheets on Cory's bed and moved the furniture out of the way as best as she could. Loretta would need the place as clean as possible. She knew that much from teaching science. The human body could withstand so much, but anything unclean would infect a wound and cause...oh, what was that...something green.

Gangrene.

Tears filled her eyes. Her mind flooded with all the possibilities of Jacob not making it. Would he die? Would she be alone? She needed him. Everything was a blur.

Back downstairs, she checked the now boiling pot of water, then covered the kitchen table with towels and a pillow. She searched the kitchen over for some knives and pliers. Finding a few, she tossed them into an open flame to sterilize them. Not knowing what to do, she did what she could with the little knowledge she had. They glowed red hot. Using towels wrapped around her hands, she pulled them from the flame and tossed them into a bucket of cold water. The water spat and jumped from the extreme heat.

One of the house maids told Charlotte that the wagon arrived. She straightened her apron and willed her mind to be ready for the sight she was about to witness. Her Jacob was shot and dying coming through those doors. She glanced around the room one last time. Everything was ready for Loretta.

They opened the door as Freddy and Ted carried her beloved inside.

So much blood. It was hard for Charlotte to tell exactly where Jacob's wounds were. Too much commotion and Freddy was talking, but she couldn't make out his words.

"What?" she finally managed. She couldn't keep her eyes off Jacob.

"Charlotte, where should we go?"

Loretta didn't hesitate. "She has the kitchen set up." She touched Charlotte's arm. "It's okay, dear. I need your help. Jacob needs your help."

Something deep inside her soul welled up. Charlotte wiped her tears and followed Loretta into the kitchen to save Jacob's life.

CHAPTER FORTY-FIVE

T HEY LAID Jacob on the makeshift bed that Charlotte made from the kitchen table. The amount of blood soaking into his clothes led to her to wonder how much he'd lost and if he'd make it through the night. A tear slipped down her cheek as Loretta used a large knife to cut off Jacob's shirt. She noticed two holes: one in his shoulder and the other just below his stomach, above the right hip. Her lover moaned, tried to sit up, but was forced back down by Freddy. "Easy now, let Loretta help you."

Jacob's eyes rolled back into his head and his hand fell limp off the side of the table. She rushed forward and grabbed his hand, holding it against her cheek before kissing his calloused fingers. How could this have happened? Loretta started washing Jacob down to expose the gunshot wounds. "Can't we call for the doctor? He's at his home," Charlotte asked.

Loretta stopped washing the blood off Jacob's chest. "Honey, we can't wait. If we send for Doc Williams, Jacob will die. I can't have that happen on my account. And not on my table."

Charlotte grabbed at Loretta's hands and held them tight. "Save my Jacob."

"You have to let go of my hands for that to happen." Loretta turned and continued cleaning the blood and prepping Jacob for surgery.

It all seemed so fast. Her heart raced and felt like it was about to escape her throat. It took every ounce of energy to not burst into tears. Each heartbeat sent waves of heat to her eyes and a dry burn in her throat. She couldn't take it any longer and Charlotte wept. Water marred by blood dripped off the table, splashing to the ground in a continual *drip, drip, drip*. Each time a water or blood droplet splashed onto the tiled floor, felt like a knife to the heart which caused her own tears to fill her vision, blurring everything out.

Freddy steadied Charlotte as her knees buckled.

"Get her out of here."

He guided her to the door. "I'll find you later. Just let Loretta work her magic."

Charlotte nodded, then walked down the hallway to the room she'd been staying in while Jacob was away. Her room wasn't large, but enough for a bed, dresser, and a small writing desk. Never making it onto the bed, her legs gave out, and she collapsed next to the mattress. Pulling the blanket down, she wrapped it around her back, trying to find some comfort in the pain.

A good cry was all she needed right now. And cry she did. A long, guttural cry. She felt she'd have to move out, leave the county, and find another new teaching position in a new town. All because Jacob would die today. That alone brought on more tears. She loved him, and her heart prayed to God that he would find mercy and save her lover. If anything, the Lord would hear her cry, maybe he'd bring Jacob around to preaching again, telling folks of God's goodness.

She knew that deep down Jacob never wanted to give up his life as a minister. It took the loss of his wife and child to push him over the edge and start over with a new life in Cedar Grove. Wiping the tears from her eyes, she willed herself to sit on the bed and pray. Talking with God was hard right now— and seeking a miracle, felt impossible—but she cried out, anyway.

"God, if you're listening to my heart's cry, you know that I love Jacob. He's the one I've been searching for all these years. Please, please, don't let him die; not today. I need him—"

The door creaked open and Ted Jefferies poked his head in. The small black man bowed his head slightly. "I'm sorry ma'am, didn't know you'd be praying n'such."

Pulling out a hanky, she blew her nose. "It's okay, Mr. Jeffries. Come in."

"Freddy wanted me to check in on ya, see how you were fair'n."

His white eyes popped against his dark features. Ted's hands fiddled with his brown open-crown hat before forcing a smile in her direction.

"That's awfully nice of you." She patted the bed. "Care to keep a lady company?"

He bowed his head. "I don't reckon that'd be right proper, ma'am. What would the others think…you alone with a negro like me?"

It took all but a breath for Charlotte to stand and pull at the man's hands. "Mr. Jeffries. You are every bit as valuable as the next man on this ranch. I don't want to hear you talking like that again. You're a free man, Mr. Jeffries and Jacob and the boys have treated you. Don't go forgetting that."

"Yes'um," he said.

They sat in silence for a while before he turned and looked her in the eye. "Ma'am, thank you for not call'n me *Wide-Eye*, I don't care for that name. But I can't argue with a white man."

"Why don't you tell Jacob?"

"He's the boss. Can't seem to find the right words to say. But I's likes the way you treat me, Miss Jennings. You're a right kind woman." He looked at his lap. "Can I's axe you a question?"

"Sure."

"I's never told this to no one's before. I always wanted to be the boss, ya know, owning a spread of my own. I'sa wondering if Mr. Callihan would let me find my own way, be my own man and not be work'n for no one else? Following God's Divine plan in my own way."

She landed her hand on Ted's bony back. "You'd make a wonderful ranch owner." Just then Freddy walked in. His eyes saw her hand on Ted's back, and she slipped it back into her own lap. "How's Jacob?"

His frown faded to a faint smile. "I think he'll be just fine. Loretta and I found both bullets. Someone patched him up a bit, and I reckon that's what saved his life. Would've died otherwise."

A wave of relief washed over her mind like springtime flowers. The weight of not knowing if he'd die fell from her shoulders. "Can I see him?"

"You sure can."

She turned to Ted. "Mr. Jeffries, keep that dream alive and when Jacob's feeling better, you ask him your question."

Freddy stopped in the hallway. "What question is that, Wide-Eye?"

"Not tell'n you. Between me and Miss Jennings."

"Enough yammering on about your dream, you old coot, we've got to move Jacob to Cory's room."

Ted, Freddy, and Charlotte help move Jacob to the room she'd prepared earlier in the day. If he had died, her life would have changed and been empty, but thanks to Loretta's quick thinking he'd be okay, and for that, Charlotte was indebted.

"He's a fighter," Loretta said as she covered Jacob to the neck. "He'll sleep for a while, but he'll wake up. We just trust the good Lord that he'll gain his strength and pull through."

Charlotte hugged the large boned woman. For a woman, Loretta was more man than woman. She still wore a dress, but if she cut her hair and wore man britches, she'd pass for a man. It was a strange thought, but if it weren't for Loretta, Jacob would be dead. "Thank you, Loretta."

"You're welcome, my dear. I try and take care of problems when they arise. Now, you sit, I'll bring you some tea."

Finally left alone, she could cry joyful tears. Jacob would be just fine. He'd sleep and when he wakes, her prayer would be for him to ask for her hand in marriage.

Why was he waiting?

It didn't matter. Thinking about it wouldn't make it happen any sooner. She let him sleep. Several hours slipped by and when she opened her eyes, the sun peeked out from behind the trees. She grabbed at the tea for a sip and found it cold.

Did she sleep all night in the chair?

The rooster crowed.

Guess so, she thought.

The bed creaked and Jacob stirred. His brown eyes

opened in her direction. He tried to speak, but his lips looked dry and cracked. "Where…am I?"

She kissed his cheeks and hugged him. He groaned. "I'm sorry." She touched his face. "My sweet Jacob." Standing, she raced to the steps and called down for Loretta. "Jacob's awake!"

CHAPTER FORTY-SIX

D ARKNESS BECAME fuzzy light, almost as if someone had placed a sheet or blanket over his head, obscuring the color and contrast of the world. How long had he been out and how long had he been lying on the ground? He didn't know. His mind cleared enough to remember that someone shot him, twice.

There were two things Jacob knew the moment he started opening his eyes: one, he wasn't dead, at least he didn't think so, and two, he didn't hear the birds or anything else, which meant he was lying in a bed. The clouds that filled his vision began their slow drifting and he realized he wasn't alone.

His mouth felt like someone shoved sand down his throat and without even trying to speak, his Adam's apple tried to bob up and down, begging for something wet.

"Where...am I?" Each word split another part of his lips and he could taste the coppery blood on his tongue.

"Oh, my sweet, Jacob!"

The sound of Charlotte's voice pulled him out of the fog and into the bedroom. She sat holding a cup of tea and quickly placed it on the bedside table. He tried to move his head as she glided toward the door.

"Jacob's awake!"

Just as quickly as she left, she was back, cradling his hand in hers. She kissed his fingers, then arm until she reached his cheek and chin, before landing on his cracking lips. She wiped the blood.

"Don't try to move. You've been through a lot."

"Where, am I?"

She shushed him with a finger to his lips. "Save your strength. You're home. The CHR. You're in Cory's room."

"Cory?"

Everything seemed jumbled and foggy. Cory. Wasn't he the boy who killed himself in this room? How'd he get here? How'd he get home?

His head ached and felt as if someone took an ice pick to his skull and hammered away until the bone shattered into a thousand little pieces. "Can I get a drink?"

She jumped up and grabbed a glass that sat nearby. "Loretta had brought it up several hours ago to help me wash the tea down."

It was wet, and Jacob felt as if he'd forgotten how to drink. Some made its way down the desert lodged in his throat and most dribbled out the side of his mouth, wetting the pillow and his neck. It seemed as if several minutes went by, but the fog faded, and he knew where he was. He was home. He was with Charlotte.

Another thing he knew in that moment, someone shot him while attempting to bring Felix Grant in. It didn't turn out the way he planned. There were at least two others in the moments before he lost consciousness. But he couldn't quite remember who they…

"Jake, it's good to see you in the land of the living," Loretta Lynn said as she came into the room.

He tried to speak, but again found that his throat closed off and the sand was back. How much sand was in his throat?

"Here, let me give you some more water."

Charlotte tipped the glass again, and the water wet the sand and he could talk. "Thank you."

"What happened, Jacob?"

Loretta stepped in. "Before we get to that...How are you feeling? I have a bit of opium from the doctor. He said it should help with the pain. I'll go fetch you a glass."

Jacob managed a, "Thanks."

Once they were alone, he turned his head to look at Charlotte. She was beautiful. It didn't matter if she had matted hair, or she hadn't presented herself. For all he knew, she sat in the chair all night.

"Hi." He wanted to say he was thirsty for more water, but *hi* came out instead.

"Hi," she said.

"How long have I been here?"

"Ted and Freddy were out when you rode up. Said you looked nearly dead. You've been out for a day, now." She grabbed at his hand. "Jacob, I thought I was going to lose you. You put me through quite the scare."

Jacob frowned. "All was going well until someone shot me. Came out of nowhere."

"Was it Felix?"

He shook his head; and he shouldn't have. That hurt. "No. I disarmed Felix. I think a girl shot me."

Charlotte raised an eyebrow. "A girl?"

"I think Felix is riding with a woman. Maybe his lover?

And then—" A sharp pain shot through his stomach, probably from where the bullet knocked him off his horse.

"You okay?"

He winced. "I'm fine. Hurts is all." It took a moment to catch his breath and to allow the pain to subside. And then he said the thing which scared him the most. "Charlotte, I think Gabriel Grant was there."

CHAPTER FORTY-SEVEN

L YING IN BED HURT. It wasn't so much the bullet wounds; it was the not being able to move much. And yes, the bullet wounds hurt. Each time Jake tried to move, it was like someone took a hot knife and sliced away at his stomach and shoulder. The pain would race through his body and force him to reposition, but it was of no use and there he sat, useless.

Jake had been shot before, but nothing this serious. And what frustrated him the most, he should have seen it coming. He was fast enough and could take any man who drew and opened fire. Yet, this time, someone got the drop on him. Jake chewed the inside of his cheek and wished to God he could get up and start moving.

Laying in this blasted bed for two days with Loretta saying she'd deem it necessary if he could come crawling out and join the land of the living.

"Loretta, I need to be up and moving," he said as she walked into the room with a tray.

She said, "Now Jacob, you'd be dead if I didn't step in to

fix you up. Now, I think I have the right to say what you can or cannot do. Now, you and Ms. Charlotte catch up and I'll set your lunch right here."

A bowl of something that resembled chicken soup sat on a tray. After Loretta left, Charlotte handed him the bowl. He tried a few spoonfuls and spit the stuff out.

"I'm so tired of this stuff," he said.

She handed him a napkin. "It's what the doctor ordered."

"The Doc or Loretta? She's like a slave master; always telling me what to do and what I can and cannot eat. I'm sick of sitting in this bed. I'm sick of being in pain. Felix is in the open. I want to know who it was that shot me. And—"

"Did you see Gabriel Grant," Charlotte said, finishing his question.

"Did I see Gabriel Grant?"

She seemed to think about that for a moment. "Jacob, why would Gabriel let you live? It seems illogical that he'd disappear all this time just to help patch you up?"

The thought had occurred to Jake. Loretta mentioned the other day that when she cut open his shirt, there was some kind of packing stuffed into each would. She figured it was a combination of pine needles, cloth, and clay. Maybe that's what kept him alive. He still didn't know how he got back to the CHR.

If Gabriel patched him up, then who shot him? He closed his eyes as the room spun. Stomach acid rose and his mouth watered. He breathed deep and prayed the dizziness would subside. Charlotte's image blurred as the walls marched toward him, closing in. The room was already small and shrinking by the second. He needed out of this room. No wonder Cory shot himself.

"Jacob, are you alright?"

He barely heard her and shoved the blankets off his legs. Perspiration dripped from his calves. The cool air prickled his skin, and he regretted the decision. If he'd just stayed, he wouldn't be this bad and Charlotte wouldn't have needed to worry.

"I'm so sorry."

She touched his arm. "For what?"

The spinning subsided. "For going out there alone. It was reckless and stupid. But after I killed Dan Baley, I felt I didn't have a choice. Someone had to go after Felix."

She said nothing for a moment and they just sat in the room's silence. That was okay. He didn't want to talk, anyway.

Jake knew she worried and the fact he came back shot to heck was proof enough to warrant her hesitation of him being a United States Marshal. What struck Jake the most was Sarah would have had the same reaction. Why did it always come down to the women in his life keeping him levelheaded or stopping him from making a stupid decision?

Charlotte was a good woman. Strong. She stayed by his side and hardly left. They'd talked for hours and he'd gotten to know her better in two days than in the last several months. Except, she knew full well that the moment he was well enough to travel, he'd head back out to hunt down Felix Grant. Jake wouldn't rest until they brought him to justice. It was something they'd have to talk about, and they both avoided the topic.

The room returned to its normal state, and Jake swallowed his bile. Time to see if he could stand and walk. Loretta would scold him, and Charlotte would disapprove.

Charlotte tried putting the blankets back on him and he placed a hand on top of hers. "Don't. I need to try."

"You can't be serious, Jacob?"

He didn't respond. Swinging his legs over to the side of the bed proved harder than he thought. They felt like lead weights. Charlotte was up in an instant and helped bring his knees to the edge of the bed. His toes touched the floor, and he rested his hands on top of his knees.

"Jacob, please be careful."

He smiled. "I'll be just fine."

"You don't look all that fine."

"You don't think I know how to walk? I've been doing this for thirty-eight years."

Trying to settle some more weight, his feet dug into the rug and he grabbed at Charlotte's hands to steady his balance. Each leg felt like someone had filled them with water. They wiggled and wobbled. One knee buckled, and the bullet wound to his gut burned with raw fire and he screamed.

"Jacob...?" She grabbed at his arm.

"Just give me a minute," he bit off.

"Lands, Jake, what are you attempting to do?" Loretta said, waltzing into the room with a glass of water. Setting it down, she walked over and held the other arm.

Sweat rolled off his brow and dripped onto the floor. This was harder than he thought it'd be, and his side continued its burning sensation. It felt as if someone was ripping the wound open or poking a firestick into it. "I'm wanting to get rid of this blasted bed."

He stood for a moment, then sank back into the mattress. The pain waned. The women helped him lift his legs onto the bed and Charlotte covered him back up.

"Well, that was fun," Jake said.

Loretta shook her head. "If that's what you call fun. Tell you what, Jake, I'll go grab a cane and once you gain some more strength, you'll be able to use that around the house."

"Thank you."

"But remember, take it slow. You were shot pretty bad. It's not like the one time in the other shoulder. That time, you just needed a sling, and you were good as new. Jake, you lost a lot of blood. It'll take time to regain your strength. I'm going to say it again, take it slow and stop forcing it. You'll heal in time." She reached for the glass. "I've mixed some opium in the water, take it, it'll take away some pain."

He did as he was told and drank the mixture, then prayed that he'd be up and moving before long.

Charlotte kissed his cheek. "I love you, stubbornness and all."

Jake laughed and returned the kiss. "I love you too. Thank you for taking care of me. I should be dead, but I'm grateful that God has protected my life."

She sat next to him on the bed, leaned down, and kissed his lips. He welcomed the sweetness of each kiss, then wrapped his arms around her and pulled her close.

CHAPTER FORTY-EIGHT

J ACOB HELD onto the cane and ambled into his study. It felt good to be up and moving the past week, albeit slow like a turtle. His first attempt at getting out of bed this morning didn't work so well, but with some persistence and the help of Charlotte, he was up and moving. As each day passed, his side felt better and he could move his arm higher than the previous day.

Good news.

Freddy, as foreman of the CHR, took over the day-to-day duties of running the place, and for that, Jacob was grateful. Things had been relatively quiet and he had no news of Felix or his gang's whereabouts. That bothered him. You always knew a storm was brewing, it was a way of life in Wyoming. Before a major storm, things calmed and cooled off. Something big was about to happen. He could feel it, almost like the changing wind.

Charlotte had sent word to Cheyenne that he was up and moving, so Tan Bennington was waiting for him to have a chat about what happened; that's why he was on his way to the study that afternoon. Jacob knew what was coming and shuddered at the thought of Tan pulling his badge or grilling him on the proper protocol for a law enforcement officer.

Tan was already sitting in the green chair waiting for Jacob. The large lawman stood when he heard Jacob enter the room.

"Jacob. Good to see you up and moving."

Tan's massive hands swallowed Jake's hand. Jacob felt small next to Tan Bennington, who stood at a staggering six-foot- six. Not that Jacob was small by any means, Tan was just bigger and broader.

"Tan, it's good to see you again. Thanks for coming by."

He back down after Jacob rounded the desk and sat.

"You have a wonderful woman there, Jake." He leaned forward. "So, when's the big day, that way I know not to be out chasing some outlaw?"

"No wedding yet."

They both laughed and let the topic die.

"So, tell me Jake, what happened?"

For the first time in the week since arriving pert near dead at the CHR, Jacob remembered with clarity what happened the day someone shot him. He recounted what happened after leaving both Tan and the sheriff behind to go find Felix.

"It was strange, Tan. One minute I've got the drop on Felix and his men. Shot one of his men, even killed one. The funny thing, I had him. I hesitated just long enough for someone to shoot me." Jacob never let someone else get the drop on him. He was quick enough to spot danger. "Guess my judgment's been a little clouded."

Tan rubbed his soul patch. "Jake, I know you're upset, and all, but I'm glad you're okay. I know about the man you shot; he'll live. Roy and I found him suck'n on a cactus. We brought him back to Cedar Grove. Wouldn't tell me what happened to you. Now I know."

"I shouldn't have gone out alone. Was a stupid mistake."

"Probably would've done it myself. The thing is, Jake, you have a choice to make; either learn from your mistakes or die trying to prove you know better than anyone else. Jake, only a fool ignores sage advice and sound wisdom. It gets a man killed or in trouble. It's like my Pa used to tell me, knowledge is knowing a tomato is a fruit, but wisdom is knowing to not cut it up and add it with apples. Something like that. What I'm trying to say is, trust your men. You're part of a great team of lawmen. Let us help you bring Felix to justice. Don't go off trying to be a hero, you'll only wind up dead. Let's build a posse of lawmen aimed at one thing, bringing the outlaw in, dead or alive."

"Thanks, Tan. That means a lot." Jacob leaned back into his chair. He had to tell his friend about seeing Gabriel Grant. They'd been searching for ten years and then he saw the man before he passed out. Could it be Gabriel Grant returning? But one question still plagued his mind, why didn't Gabriel kill him when he had the chance?

"There's something else. I think I saw Gabriel Grant."

That caused the large lawman to lean forward again. "Are you sure?"

"Can't reckon for sure, but he said something as I blacked out. He said, *I've got you now.* Way I figure it, Gabriel patched me up. Saved my life."

"Or it could be a ploy to mess with your head. For all you know, he's the one who shot you."

"Suppose, so, or had me shot."

"How ya figure?"

"One thing I know. I heard a woman's voice after hitting the ground. Don't know if she was with father or son."

"Think they're working together?"

"Rightly so."

Tan Bennington stood up. "Jake, this gives me some new leads. I can piece together who Felix is riding with. I'll find them and I'll find Gabriel. If they are working together, Felix knows where his father is at. If so, they're up to no good. And if a woman's ridden with them, can't be too many outlaw women roaming around. Should be able to figure who it is."

Jacob smiled. "Find the son, find Gabriel."

"That's the plan. I'll see you later." And Tan Bennington walked out, leaving Jacob alone.

CHAPTER FORTY-NINE

A WEEK LATER, Jacob did his best to be useful. Not back to what he was, but the wounds were healing, and he was regaining some of that lost strength. He tried to lift some bales of hay and had to set them back down. Way too much pressure on the one bullet wound to his abdomen. Freddy was having none of Jacob's tries at work. After convincing him to regain his strength, Jacob relegated himself to his study.

His vision blurred as he attempted to read a book by some guy named Lew Wallace. Jacob fancied a pleasant story, and this story of a Roman turned slave was good. A knock at the door caught his attention and he placed the book down and rubbed at his tired eyes.

"Hello, my dear," Charlotte said, walking into his study. Her red and white flowered dress sashayed around her waist as she walked around his desk and kissed his cheek.

She must have just come from teaching out at the school. He didn't care for her insistence to return to teaching, not with Felix and his gang still at large, but one thing he quickly learned, don't argue with a woman who's decided—and with no sign of Felix or his gang, she assured him she would be safe. He still insisted she carry a gun.

"What are you reading?"

Picking up the book, he showed her the cover. "*Ben-Hur.* Fascinating tale of a Roman slave in search of his identity. It says on the cover that Christ is in the book, though I've not gotten to that part yet."

A simple, knowing smile crossed her lips. "Sounds like a good read."

"You've read it, haven't you?"

"About two years ago. A friend of mine from Boston sent me a copy. Somehow she knew the publisher."

He smiled and placed the book back down onto the desk. "Don't spoil the ending. Have nothing to do but to sit and read. Frankly, I'm tired of it all, my dear. Not something a man likes to do, sit and do nothing while the women folk in my life do all the work."

Charlotte crossed her arms and scowled at him. "Doing nothing? You're getting better, and I'd say you're healing up nice. Now, you read, and I'll go fetch you some soup."

After Charlotte left Jacob to his thoughts, he tossed the book back onto the shelf and walked over to a mirror that hung on the wall. Lifting his shirt, he stared at the two scars. One on his shoulder and the other on his stomach. There they sat, reminding him of his failure to bring Felix to justice. The pain had subsided and didn't bother him all that much, but he knew something lingered in the darkness of his heart. There sat scars that never seemed to heal, scars that if he were to reveal them, would rip wide open and he'd bleed a river of blood filled with past pain and regret.

With nothing to do but sit and think, consistently reminded of his failure to save his family and keep them from being killed in that fire. Now another Grant threatened everything he'd worked hard to build, and he hated them both.

Two Grants, two sets of scars, and they both hurt. The first set just stung deeper.

When Charlotte returned with the soup in hand, he pulled his shirt down, hiding the scars so she couldn't see how deeply wounded his soul felt.

"Those are healing." She set the soup on his desk and walked over to him.

"I suppose."

"You're not so sure, are you?"

He could see the sadness and questions in her eyes. They were dark with a desire to please him and to help make him whole. They both also instinctively knew that wouldn't ever happen. He was too wounded to escape ten years of pain.

"Not really, no."

She placed a hand onto his shoulder. "Jacob, you'll get back onto your feet and you'll get out there and find Felix, then bring him to justice."

He fought to keep the tears from welling up and slipping out of his eyes. They burned and his nose clogged up. Jacob lifted his hands and slapped them against his waist. "I feel so lost. I feel like it doesn't matter what I do, how much I build, how much passion I have for the work that I do, I can't escape the fact that no matter what I touch, it fails or dies."

The tears began slipping down his face as he slid into a chair. "Charlotte, I lost everyone and everything. I had to give up my life, the only life I knew. I walked away a failure. My wife is dead. My daughter is dead. My best friend…all dead! I lost everything. I only knew the ministry and loved to serve God's people. I just couldn't anymore, gave up, and I walked away from God."

She knelt down next to him and placed her head on his knee. That's when he cried. The sobs came deep and guttural. He couldn't breathe.

"I'm so scared, Charlotte. Scared of failing again. Especially scared that everything I've built here will leave, wither, or die. I'm afraid that you won't love me or the man that I'm becoming. There's no redemption for a man who let his family die. No going back, no reclaiming the lost. I can't lose you too. I just don't know what to do anymore. I'm at a loss and that loss is catching up with me. All I've ever done is be the guy who said yes. I tried to please everyone and fix everyone's problems except my own. My heart's breaking and there's nothing I can do to stop what's going to happen. If I lose everything again, I fear I'm but an empty shell with nothing to offer this world."

Charlotte sat quiet for a long time. In part, Jacob was glad she let him cry it out and let the emotions he'd been bottling up spill out. He was bitter, frustrated, and crushed. It was like a giant white pine crashed upon the ground of his heart and shattered what little faith he had left in God and life.

She hugged him and kissed his forehead. "I know that Sarah and Virginia will always be a part of you, part of your life, and I can't imagine the pain and frustration you feel. You're carrying the weight of the world on your shoulders, and I hate seeing this weigh you down. I want you to remember this, God will restore the years the locusts have eaten. You have to go through the valley times of life before you get your mountain top moment. Trust God. He'll bring you the breakthrough you desire. When you allow him to become the center place in your life, he takes those desires and makes a miracle happen."

She placed her hand on his heart. "It takes faith to see

God move. We first have to wait on him with our hearts and hands lifted high in praise. Remember, it's only God who carries the burden of your soul. Your faith is the substance of things hoped for, the evidence of things not seen. Look beyond the pain and circumstance and focus on the truths of the Bible. Allow God to heal you and you will find your life restored. If you want to sing your halleluiah, come to the end of your rope and let God do the rest. It's like the story of Ben-Hur. His life was broken, lost, and he felt worthless. But then he meets Jesus, his life is changed. Let Jesus back into your life and watch him change you from the inside out. Only then will you be able to sing in the middle of your storm."

It had been years since he allowed God to truly work in his life. Clyde Heller gave him a new start, everything he had. Never once did he thank God for any of it. Maybe that needed to change, maybe it was time to stop wallowing in self-pity and start putting more faith and trust in God. Above it all, Charlotte was the person he needed. Without her consistent faith, he'd have lost his years ago.

"Charlotte, I've not been a good Christian man. I've not allowed God center place in my heart. Will you pray with me? Will you pray that God will direct me and guide me in this new journey? I can't do this without you. I love you, and God has blessed me with you. I need you."

She smiled and pulled at his hands. "I thought you'd never ask."

CHAPTER FIFTY

F ELIX WARMED his hands above the crackling fire. As the wind sliced through his bones, the fire felt nice against his hands, causing steam to roll off his knuckles and escape into the cool morning air. It had been four weeks since Diamond came to his rescue. Jacob had gotten the drop on him and he felt stupid for allowing two of his men to be killed. If Diamond wasn't there, he no doubt would've been taken to Cheyenne to stand trial.

His face burned as he leaned closer to the crackling flames. Orange, red, and blue swirled around a charred log. He gently blew on the log and watched as red sparks shot upward before a blast of smoke enveloped him. If only he hadn't done that. Stupid.

The other stupid thing, chickening out when the moment came for him to kill Jacob Creek. And that was the moment Frank got himself killed. Stupid.

How did the Preacher get so fast with that six-gun? Sure, it'd been ten years, but what in the tarnation had he been thinking to go up against someone with that kind of speed?

That's when he turned tail and ran into the chest of another lawman. Another stupid mistake.

Diamond Rose sat at the far end of the camp chewing on some dried scones. He wasn't sure how he felt about her right now. Rumor had it she used to be a cook, but the way he figured, she was cold, heartless, and ruthless as they come. Showed when she pulled that trigger on the Preacher and shot him good as dead. And he loved her for it. Didn't really matter that she was a mite older than him, but she sure could please a man and he didn't mind one bit.

A smile played on his lips and he wondered why she was so taken with Jacob Creek. What part of her past was tangled up with the Preacher to shoot him and know he'd be left alive long enough to reach home? Felix tried to remember when he first met her. It wasn't until he came back to Purgatory, long after his father disappeared. She was down and out on her luck, a prostitute who had nothing going for her and recently set free by a fat judge who was on his death bed. What was his name? Talbert, Judge Rex Talbert. One of the most loathed men in the lower territory of Wyoming and in his father's back pocket.

That was two years ago. He told her about an opportunity to make something of her life and help right the wrongs done to her by life, just as he had and would continue to do. The problem he faced, she was poising herself to take over the gang, as if she owned each man. Felix hated her for it, and having someone else call the shots could get them...

"Felix, what are you doing? We're to be packing and headed out. We're going back to Purgatory."

Purgatory. He hated that place, especially now that his father had returned to the estate. If he had a chance, he'd put the old man down for abandoning him the day his mother died. "Let me ask you a question, Rose. What's your beef with the Preacher? Why'd we let him go like that? We couldn't take him? I know my reasons for what happened at the bank, but what's yours?"

She looked up from rolling her blanket. "I've got my reasons."

"Alls the same with ya. No reason, just doing your own thing. This is my gang. I brought you in, I can ask you to leave."

That's when she pulled her pistol and eased back the hammer. "Question me like that again, and I'll kill you."

Felix put his hands up into the air. "Sorry, Rose. But it'd be nice if you fill me in on what you're plannin' is all."

Joe Kidd walked up and placed a hand on Felix's arm. "You okay, boss?"

Felix smiled then rolled a cigarette. "I'll be fine, don't like someone else calling the shots, is all." He pointed his finger at Rose's back. "When I get the chance, Diamond's good as dead."

"Just be careful, boss. She can be scary when she's hotter than a disturbed hornet's nest."

Felix patted his friend on the back. "Don't worry about me. You take care of the horses, I've got to find some more men."

CHAPTER FIFTY-ONE

F OR THE FIRST TIME in weeks, Jake felt alive and back to full strength, at least that's what he kept telling himself. Work around the ranch hadn't slowed since he'd left to go find Felix. But one thing bothered Jake, why hadn't Felix made a move in the days following his shooting? All had been quiet, almost too quiet.

Birds tweeted their songs as he made his way from the house to the barn for some much-needed work. Even with Freddy running things, he still had a lot of work to catch up on with all the bed rest he'd endured. Pulling down several bales of hay made the already dust filled air become a throat choking cloud. He coughed and grabbed at his side. Still hurt like a rattler bite. He wiped the sweat beading on his brow and climbed down. A pitchfork sat perched near the barn's entrance and after pulling on a pair of gloves, Jacob grabbed the tool and began shoveling hay into the stalls for each horse.

The sun was already high in the sky when he finished with the barn. Charlotte was already outside with a pail of water and a scoop.

"Need a drink?" she asked, pulling out some water.

Jacob took a drink from the scoop and let the water dribble off his beard. He hadn't shaved since returning home and he rather like the mountain man scruff forming across his features. Grabbing the scoop from her hand, Jacob plunged it into the water and then poured it over his head. The water snaked down his near shoulder length hair and soaked into his shirt. He poured another round into his hat, then took a second drink.

"Thanks. I needed that."

She smiled and kissed his lips. "I thought you might. Say, tomorrow is Sunday. I know I've asked you a few times, but I figured since you've been of a fresh mind as of late, would you mind accompanying a lady to church tomorrow?"

The question lingered in the air, and Jacob hesitated. He hadn't been in church since Sarah died. Ten years of ignoring God and living your own life made one not desire to go back. Besides, what would the town folk think of Jacob Callihan, feared gun and now lawman coming to church?

"Charlotte, I—"

"If you don't want to, I will understand."

Her countenance faded and the strength she had approaching the question waned, and Jacob instantly felt bad for even hesitating. He had to go. It was the right thing to do, even if he had to put aside his feelings and frustrations of being a Christian. He still believed, and knew that God had blessed him, but attending a service seemed out of the normalcy of life.

"Okay."

"Okay?"

He tugged at her hands. "Okay, I'll go with you. I'll have Loretta iron my suit."

She blushed, turned, and walked back into the house.

THE NEXT DAY, Jacob had it all planned out. He'd pick Charlotte up, go to church, then take her back to his favorite spot on the ranch for a picnic—just the two of them, then would ask for her hand in marriage. It was decided, and he'd have to remember to grab the ring before leaving the house. Except, now sitting in a pew at Reverend Johnson's church located just three miles outside of Cedar Grove, he'd forgotten the ring and each moment of sitting and listening to the hymns and message caused his mind to wonder how he could be so stupid.

"Let's open to the gospel of Matthew." Reverend Johnson began. "We find the story of the thief on the cross, next to our Savior. He was a wretched man, full of sin, sorrow, and loneliness. But that day, he found himself next to Jesus. He was paying for his sins, and Jesus was paying the price because he was God's son.

"Let's think about this. It doesn't matter what you've done in your past. Maybe you've cheated, swindled, or killed someone. Maybe you've been a rotten father or horrible mother and you wish you could take back the things you said to your kids. It doesn't matter. Today, you're sitting next to Jesus. Your mind is troubling you and you feel as if your past has come home to roost. Don't fret and be dismayed, because today your salvation is nigh. Today is the day that God has forgiven you. Today is the day you get to move forward into the future you're destined to walk in."

All thoughts of the ring slipped from his mind. He knew Charlotte was sitting next to him. He knew several townsfolks surrounded him. But Jacob felt alone. The Reverend Johnson was talking straight to him.

One question kept spinning around his mind; *what is my legacy?*

Ten years ago, his heart burned in an all-consuming fire—he threw it all into the fire. He walked away from God, walked away from the ministry. Sure, he told Momma that God pulled him back from the brink, and maybe so, but Jacob walked away. Jacob sought vengeance for all that happened in Purgatory. How much like the thief on the cross was he? Could God truly forgive his past?

In seeking to bring in Gabriel's son, he was shot and left for dead. The notes left in the two dead bodies swirled around his mind like pesky gnats. Who was it that knew who he was? Who was this woman he heard after getting shot? And how did Gabriel Grant fit into all of this?

"...If you don't allow God to come into your life and forgive your past, you'll continue how you've always been; broken, alone, and afraid of the future."

Reverend Johnson was right, and Jacob knew what he needed to do. He needed to confront his past. He needed to look deep at the charred remains of his heart and see if there was anything left for God to save. Like the day Gabriel burned down his barn, Jacob entered the fire and saved his friend Bill from a falling beam and pulled a horse to safety. Maybe God could let Jacob enter the fire one last time and save his own soul.

"Remember to trust God in all circumstances and allow him to be your constant strength and guiding hand. Amen."

After service, Jacob brought Charlotte back to her place. Rain pelted against the ground, and Jacob remained quiet most of the trip. He was glad Charlotte remained quiet so he could process what he heard. As the rain continued, they pulled up to her place and Jacob helped her down from the wagon. They made their way inside to dry off. So much for their picnic.

While Jacob peeled off his slicker, Charlotte added a few logs to rekindle the fire and then put a pot of water onto the stove. He tossed his rain slicker onto a nearby hook, then set the wicker food basket onto the table. A small dripping caught his attention and Jacob saw a small leak in the roof. Several drops of water dripped from a broken shingle and made its way to a small pool of water that collected on the wooden floor.

"How long has your roof been in disrepair?"

She stopped what she was doing. "I'm not sure. I usually put a bucket down when the rains come." Then she continued fixing something for them to eat.

Why didn't she tell him? He had nothing going on tomorrow and it would be a good day to fix the hole, so long as it didn't rain. Just like the hole in his own heart that God was showing him, Jacob said, "Let me fix that for you."

CHAPTER FIFTY-TWO

THE PREVIOUS day's message by Reverend Johnson lingered in Jacob's mind. The moment the sun rose to the moment it began to decline in the sky, his thoughts kept swirling around with the proposition that it didn't matter what he did in Purgatory or how he lived his life, God remained by his side. Everything from the CHR to having Charlotte in his life is God's blessing, but why couldn't he see it that way?

Maybe it was the fact he'd spent the better part of ten years searching for the one man who took everything away from him. Jacob realized he should have stopped looking and spent the better part of these past years focusing on what God had given him. Then there's Momma. It'd been too long since seeing her; maybe he should take a small trip to Purgatory to tell her about asking Charlotte to marry him. That was still the plan.

Not knowing what he'd find on her roof, he grabbed a few extra shingles he had back home. Tossing them into the wagon, he set off for her house. Jacob pulled out a ladder and placed it against Charlotte's cottage, then climbed the rungs with a small toolbox in hand.

"Are you going to promise me you'll be careful up there?"

Jacob gave a wry smile. "Of course. Falling couldn't be any worse than getting shot...twice!"

"That's not funny," Charlotte said, crinkling her nose.

Her scrunched-up face made Jacob laugh so hard his footing slipped, and it took a moment to regain his balance. Charlotte screamed, and Jacob laughed even harder after catching his breath.

"Stop laughing."

He couldn't help it. It came in waves. Something he hadn't done in a while, and it felt good. "Go back inside, and I'll fix your roof."

He climbed back up onto the roof and found a nice sized hole that needed attention. It took a few hours for him to get everything all patched up. The last nail was set, and he climbed down, admiring his work. The next several days brought on more projects around her place, and it made Jacob feel right at home. There was something simple and beautiful about working on a smaller spread. Sure, her cottage sat on the edge of the CHR, but he couldn't see any other buildings, men bustling around, or even his cattle. Her cottage sat in a small clearing, nestled between two sets of woods that circled her place, providing much needed protection.

It all reminded him of the Creek Ranch back in Purgatory. It wasn't a large ranch, more like a farm. Though real ranchers hated the term—Jacob sort of endeared it and considered himself a rancher, even though Creek Ranch was more of a large farm. Those were simpler days of fixing everything himself. Sure, they had a couple of hands that he paid about thirty and found, but he and his late friend, Bill, did the lion's share of the work.

Now that he was owner of the Callihan/Heller Ranch, that all changed. He owned roughly eight thousand acres, had a thousand head of cattle, and money in the bank. He could do just about anything he wanted. And the thing he loved about Charlotte was that money, status, and land didn't matter. She just wanted Jacob.

Nothing more in life did Jacob want than for Charlotte to marry him and come live at the CHR. The past month had been nice, having Charlotte by his side, tending to his care, bringing him back to full strength. On one of the several trips back to the main house, Jacob grabbed the ring which sat at in his desk drawer.

He walked up the steps to the cottage as Charlotte sipped on some tea, sitting on the front porch. He looked back at the ground-tied horse, making sure Tucker stayed put, then smiled at Charlotte as he sat down next to her.

"Jacob, thank you for everything you've done around here. I do my best, but a girl can't do it all by herself."

He smiled. "You never need to ask me to do anything. I will always take care of you." He swallowed hard. "I love you, Charlotte. I know we've talked about the future, in the past, but I hadn't said, *thank you* for everything you've done for me."

She brought the teacup to her lips and sipped on the amber liquid. "It's the least I could do. You gave me a scare. I don't know what I would have done without you, Jacob. Certainly wouldn't have been able to do the repairs around here that you've accomplished this week."

"I will always come back to you. I am a better man by having you in my life. You're the one who grounds me, holds me accountable, by telling me where I'm wrong or need to change."

"Also, I show you where you're excelling and succeeding. I remind you; you are a man who cares more for others than for himself. Jacob, you go out of your way to make sure others are taken care of. You get upset and storm around the house when someone is wronged or being taken advantage of. That's why I love you. You're a man who seeks righteousness and the right vengeance."

Jacob felt his eyes drop to the ground as he studied his boots and the lines running through each board like little rivers cutting into his heart and soul and mind. Did he deserve her? It was strange how similar Charlotte was to Sarah. How does God do these things?

"Charlotte, do you remember the other week, when Sheriff Whalen interrupted us?"

"I do."

"There was something I was going to ask you, and I never got around to asking. Though this isn't quite what I had in mind for a location."

Her cheeks blushed in the cool evening air, and Jacob knew Charlotte was well aware of what he was about to say next.

"Charlotte?"

"Yes—"

Jacob slipped off his chair and dug into the abyss of his pocket. Deja Vu. The second time he was proposing and something leapt inside his heart as a tear slipped out of his eye and snaked down his cheek. This woman sitting in front of him was a treasure, finer than the gold running through his land. He didn't need to go digging in a vein on some hill near his ranch, he had to look in front of him at a beautiful woman who captured his heart and ravished his soul.

Jacob took a deep breath and pulled up the ring. His lover, with hands on her lips and tears running down her cheeks, gasped when she saw the beautiful emerald ring he held between his fingers. A ring that once belonged to his mother.

Finally remembering he was holding his breath, Jacob exhaled and asked the question burning like fire in his heart, "Will you marry me?"

CHAPTER FIFTY-THREE

F ELIX GRANT was getting nervous. It was only a matter of time before Jacob Creek and the full weight of the United States Marshal's Service would fall on them. He chewed on the idea that Diamond Rose, or whatever name she went by, was trying to tear apart his band of outlaws. He didn't like that one bit.

Purgatory would burn. The town belonged to Gabriel Grant. Felix, being the bastard son, wanted none of it, and the time to wage war against his father for abandoning him by luring Jacob Creek into the war for a painful death would be like a little extra sugar on cake.

There was one thing lacking, men to make it happen. If someone wanted to tree a town, and make it inhabitable, you needed a wagon full of men to make it happen. There was enough money and gold from previous robberies that could get them by. Felix needed an army and when the time came, he'd put a bullet in the woman trying to take everything from him—telling him what to do.

She was like the old couple he killed all those years ago.

His knife sat on a nearby rock and visions of sliding it across Diamond's neck skittered through his mind like beetles. Oh, what joy and pleasure it'd bring him. The thought excited him. He desired to see her blood seep from her neck and trail down his arm.

He bent over and picked up his knife. The sharp tip begged for blood. A burning pain rippled up his hand as he slid the tip over his left index finger. Red blood seeped from the tiny wound and made a river down his finger. A slight laugh popped out and then he shoved the finger deep into his mouth, running it along his cheek and teeth before slipping it across his tongue. The warm copper taste filled his mouth with an unspeakable flavor. Felix sucked on the finger until he had his fill of the blood leaking from his finger.

Wiping his mouth with the bandana he pulled off his neck, Felix wrapped it around his finger to stop the bleeding. It wouldn't be long before he killed Diamond. Kidd was already working on a way to set her up and take her out.

"Felix. What are you doing standing there? I need you to go out and find some men. We can't draw out Jacob and take over the town of Purgatory without more men, and all I see is you standing here like an idiot."

Rage flashed through his mind. Whose gang was this, anyway? Sure didn't feel like his. Felix pulled his gun and eased back the hammer. "Don't ya forget whose gang this is. I run the show, I say who lives, dies, and who rides with me. Tell me what to do again and I'll end you right now."

Diamond knocked the gun from his hand. "Point that at me again and you'll be the one to die. Now, go hire me some more men. I have a small trip to make. I know someone that will draw out Jacob."

Felix exchanged glances with Kidd, who nodded. "Fine.

But these men are mine, not yours, ya hear?"

Felix picked up his gun, grabbed the reins of his horse and pulled into the saddle. "Kidd, you're with me."

They left Diamond behind and began making the rounds to several farmers who had been wronged by his father over the years, people who wouldn't care if they lived or died. Vagabonds and vagrants all were being paid fifty and found. Course they'd get a cut of any robbery pulled. But one thing certain, Felix was raising an army.

In the several days since leaving Diamond behind with the other two men he had left, he had hired an additional twenty men. Some boys who had no one left, others were ready to fight and do what they wanted. He even found a couple gun slicks near Fillmore who were all too eager to strap on their pistols and kill a few lawmen for sport.

When he returned, the look on Diamond's face said it all. *Jacob Creek and Purgatory are good as dead.*

In Felix's mind, Creek could wait, and his father would be the first to receive a bullet. After that, he'd kill Diamond and then put a bullet between Jacob's eyes.

He sat up on his horse. "Tomorrow we ride for Purgatory. We'll take the bank and tree the town. I don't want anyone left alive. That'll draw out dat marshal."

One gunslick spoke up, "What's yer beef wit'im anyway?"

"He killed my Ma."

A slight hush settled over the group of hired guns. "How are ya drawing him out?" another cowpoke said.

Diamond Rose spoke up, "I want a few bad boys to ride with me to Cedar Grove."

"What fer?" Slim Jim, a self-proclaimed gun hawk asked.

"It's time to pay a visit to someone the marshal cares about. It's time to pay a visit to an old friend."

CHAPTER FIFTY-FOUR

I T HAD BEEN four days since Diamond Rose set off for Cedar Grove, doing who knows what? She came and went at her leisure and he grew tired of that woman calling the shots. Felix chewed on his lower lip, trying to figure out what this woman he allowed into his life was up to. The men were busy gathering their things, rolling blankets, and packing their saddlebags for the journey to Purgatory. They would ride out to the mines and wait until Diamond returned with her prize, the Preacher's woman.

He scratched his rear, then pulled up into the saddle. "Boys, we're heading out to Purgatory. We'll camp at the mines near Encampment River. Questions?"

When none returned a comment, Felix took off, with Kidd and his army close behind. There was only one plan, confront his father. Rumor had it, dear old dad was holed up at the old Grant Estate. No one lived there, and no one wanted to, anyway. Felix didn't care.

"What's the plan, boss?" Kidd asked.

"About what?"

"Diamond? You going to kill her?"

Felix thought about that for a minute, then said, "I suppose I am."

No one spoke for the longest time. Several of the gun hawks were fiddling with their pistols when the Purgatory Gulch Mines rose into view.

"Boys, I want no one left alive."

Someone let out a loud *whoop* and took off toward the mines. Soon, all twenty-five followed suit. Guns blasted into the air as Felix watched several miners run toward the mine for safety. One gun hawk pulled his gun and shot one miner through the back. The man flopped to the ground, writhing in pain as he jumped off his horse and put one bullet between the man's eyes.

A young cowboy, named Phillip Jones, aimed at a couple miners and missed widely. Felix smiled at the sad attempt. He found the kid wandering around and asked if he'd like to make some quick cash. The boy told him that Jake Callihan had let him go, even better.

"Hey, Phil, try again."

Phillip aimed and fired. One miner dropped to his knees, screaming in pain.

Felix cackled. "Atta boy!" The miner begged for his life. Felix grabbed his knife. This would be fun. A slight kick to the horse and Felix was on top of the miner. He jumped off his horse and grabbed the miner by the hair, pulling back his head, then pulled the knife across the neck.

"I had it!" Phillip said. "I could've kilt him."

Felix smiled. "Okay, but ya didn't. Don't know if you have it in ya."

"Can too. I kilt my best friend. Shot 'im in the head while he slept."

Felix smiled and patted the boy on the arm, then watched as Joe Kidd took out two miners, each with a shot to the head. "See, Phillip, that's how ya do it. Fast-like."

There weren't enough for each man, so a few ganged up and took to sucker punching a few miners until they had their fill. Each man was as rotten to the core as Felix, some maybe more than he.

It was all over in a matter of minutes. Felix told the men to gather the bodies, pile them into the mining carts, and then seal them inside the mine.

Once they set the dynamite, the main entrance to the mine closed with a gigantic blast that shook the ground, frightening the horses.

"Kidd, you and the men stay here. I got me some business to attend to in Purgatory. Stay here until I return. No one leaves. If they do, kill 'em."

Felix grabbed the reins of his horse and took off toward the Grant Estate. The entire ride to his old home forced his mind to contemplate how things might have been different if Gabriel hadn't abandoned him. His father said he had plans but dropped them in favor of running from the law. God knows where he went off to. Gabriel had dropped him off at an old couple's house near town. He shivered at the times the old man tied him to a fence post and beat him. He hated his father for doing that to him and now, rumor had that his father had returned to the Grant Estate.

When he arrived several hours later, the place sat cold, dark, and rotting. Ten years of neglect caused the land to reclaim parts of the buildings. Weeds and odd-looking plants had overgrown the luxurious gardens. As he walked up the steps, Felix noticed a few trees poked up through the cracks in the foundation, arching their way toward heaven.

It was the first time since his mother's death that he'd stepped foot on the estate. He looked up and saw smoke escaping from one chimney. Dear old Dad was home. The door was ajar, and he wondered what critters lurked inside, ravaging what they left of his father's legacy.

He pulled his pistol and eased back the hammer, then pushed his way through the double-wide entrance and stepped foot into his childhood home. Light emanated from Gabriel's study and he wondered what state his father would be in. How long it had been, and what did he look like after ten years of running?

Stepping through the door, he noticed an older, grayer, and homely looking man than he remembered. Gone was the Vandyke and replaced with a long mountain-man beard that reached downward toward Gabriel's chest. His hair was greasy, long, and pulled back into a pony. A muted black coat hung from his broad shoulders and dust caked his arms. A simple bolo tie replaced his usual ascot tie. He looked different, changed by running.

The aged man, who was the former shell of Gabriel Grant, looked up.

"Hello, Father."

His eyes widened, then narrowed. "What do you want? I told you, you're not welcome in my home."

"I thought I'd pay you a visit. Been ten years. You couldn't handle me and didn't want to. Heard you were in town, and in this crap hole of a house. Small town and all."

"And you come in here, pointing a gun at me, seeing if I was the man you once remembered. What, you want me back as your father? With you terrorizing the staff and all those dead animals—" His father stood. "Well, I'm not, and you can show yourself out. I'm here gathering a few things, and then, I'm gone."

Felix watched with fascination as his father piled a few books and ledgers into a bag.

"What, you think you can start over?"

Gabriel looked up. "I already have. A lot has changed—" he eyed his son with what looked to be pity. "And you've certainly made a name for yourself, and not in the good way. I've seen the wanted posters."

Felix spit. "No different from yours. Except mine's more valuable. Isn't that what you always taught me; 'make a name for yourself, son.'"

Gabriel stopped, then walked over to Felix. "I made a mistake ten years ago. I'm just trying to atone for my sin. Can't say the same for you, my dear boy."

"You stopped being my father a long time ago."

"Still acting like a petulant child, I see. You learned nothing from me. I taught you how to be a man, own up to your mistakes, and here you are belittling yourself with petty robberies, raping women, and killing folks. You're a smart boy to pull off these without getting caught or killed—why don't you use that intellect and do something with your life?"

Heat flashed across Felix's face and his head spun light. He had every intention of pulling the trigger, so he did, except he didn't expect to miss.

In that moment, Gabriel Grant was across the room, pulling the gun away, tossing it into the fire. That's when the slap happened. An open palm slap right across Felix's face. Not once, not twice, but four times. Tiny needles poked into his skin, which he felt swell. He tried to stop the next blow, but Gabriel's fist connected with his jaw and sent him to the ground.

"Grow up, Felix. You have learned nothing from me. You're weak and pathetic. Get out of my house before I kick you out myself."

Felix spat blood, cursed, then picked himself up off the floor and left.

CHAPTER FIFTY-FIVE

T HE TOWN bustled with activity as Jake arrived back in Cedar Grove. A rancher was moving his herd through town, kicking up dust and filling the air with the moaning sound of cattle. The dusty, chalk-like air filled his lungs and dried his tongue. He smiled and reminded himself to have Freddy move the herd to the south pasture for a new view and fresh grass.

Tied to the horn of his saddle were a bunch of flowers he'd discovered just outside of town. Purple chrysanthemums, white daisies, and orange daylilies, Charlotte's favorite. Smiling to himself, he wondered what lesson she'd be busy teaching the children. The ride to town helped him clear his thoughts and allow him to relish the fact they were going to be married.

It'd been two weeks since proposing, and they'd spent nearly every waking moment together. In fact, he'd been to church for the past two weeks, and he began finding his faith in God again. It wasn't a perfect faith, and he didn't plan on preaching anytime soon, but finding the time to reconnect his heart to his faith in God felt like a good baby step. Charlotte was proud of him for stepping out in faith.

The schoolhouse sat in a small clearing just outside of town, near the giant oak tree. Its small square structure peaked high, with a bell tower fixed to the top. He could just make out the children running around, playing, and laughing.

Slim waved at Jake from across the street. *"Hola, Señor!"*

"Boy-nose diass." He tried to speak Spanish and his butchery of the language would only make his friend laugh.

"Oh, that's a good attempt there, *amigo*. It is *buenos días, señor* Jake."

Jake laughed and waved it off before heading down the street. Slim had been biting at the chance to join him on the range, to see how things worked on the ranch. Could Slim actually ride a horse? He smiled at the thought of his plump friend trying.

When he arrived at the schoolhouse, several children kicked around a ball, some read, and a couple of girls were attempting to jump a rope. He'd never seen that one before. Two boys stopped kicking the ball.

"Mr. Callihan," they said in unison.

Jake nodded. "Where's Miss Charlotte?"

Several others stopped playing as Jake dismounted, dropping the reins. One girl said, "We don't know."

Jake's heart skipped a beat, then looked around. "What do you mean, *you don't know?*"

"That's just it, sir. We don't know. Been here all morning, doing our own studies. She never showed up. She's nowhere, sir."

His mind spun for a moment, then walked into the schoolhouse. The place was empty, with no sign of Charlotte. He dropped the flowers in the middle of the dusty room. He walked back to the porch and grabbed the doorframe.

"What's your name?" he asked the girl.

"Brittney."

"Brittney, when was the last time you saw her?"

Thinking about it for a moment didn't help his heart, as it dropped to his toes. Where could Charlotte be? It was unlike her to not show up to teach school. His gaze fell onto the streets, looking for any sign of the woman he loved.

"She taught yesterday, but we've not seen her today." Brittney paused for a moment. "Mr. Callihan, did something bad happen to Miss Charlotte?"

Something bad happened. Could be, might be nothing. But what reason would she have to not tell the kids? He placed a reassuring hand on her shoulder. "I'll find her. Why don't you take over, since you look like the eldest, and help everyone finish their studies for the day?"

"Yes, sir," she said before calling everyone into the schoolhouse. "Recess is over."

Jake grabbed Tucker's reigns and swung into the saddle. Jabbing spurs into the animal's side, he shot back down the hill toward town. The slow-moving cattle blocked his access to the road, and there was nowhere for his horse to fit.

Where was Charlotte? he thought.

Jake slowed as he merged into the thickness of cattle. Images of Cory Jackson flashed through his mind. Last thing he needed was to be trampled to death. Darting his eyes left, he didn't see a way through the herd. To the right a small gap opened up and Jake pressed Tucker through the sea of beeves. The hole was closing, and he had just one shot to get onto the boardwalk. He dug his spurs into the side of his horse and the animal squealed, then shot forward. The gap narrowed. Just a few more…

Tucker shot through the gap between the rear of one cow and the horns of another. He stopped for a moment and watched as the sea of cattle moved through town, mooing. Only one problem, the Sheriff's office sat on the other side of the road, on the other side of town; the same direction the cattle headed. It might be a bit before he could head down there.

Slim stood on the boardwalk and waved him over. Several cowboys darted back inside as Jake eased Tucker down the boardwalk until he was face-to-face with Slim.

"*Señor*, what is with the horse here like this?"

Jake looked down at Tucker, then frowned. Tucker was the best horse he had ever had, and it looked funny sitting on him where people walked. He dismounted.

"Sorry. Have you seen Charlotte?"

"Not since yesterday. *Por qué?*"

"The children said she never showed to teach. You think she's at your place, visiting her sister?"

"*No.* Rachelle say Anthony about her *hermana.*"

Jake pulled his Colt out and checked the cylinder. Five bullets and one empty chamber. He never put all six into the cylinder in case the gun went off while riding. Holstering the gun, he said, "Slim. I think something bad has happened to Charlotte. It's unlike her to not show up."

"Maybe she's sick, *Señor?*"

He considered that notion. But he'd seen her the night before as they talked through ideas on when they should marry. The logistics of moving her belongings from the cottage to the ranch would be easy. He had enough men. The past several days she'd been working with the house staff in getting the place ready for her arrival after they married.

They always knew it'd be a quick engagement; being that he'd married prior, and she wasn't getting any younger for childbearing. She didn't appear to be sick. Maybe she'd been working too hard and her body said, no more work until you get some rest.

"I'm heading over to see the Sheriff. Maybe he's heard something. Then, I'm headed back out to her cottage; check in on her, make sure she's okay."

Slim took off his apron and grabbed his hat. "Let's go."

"Slim, you don't have to."

"She's my sister-in-law. I am coming too, *Señor*, Jake."

Nodding at his friend, Jake pulled into the saddle. There'd be no way of keeping Slim away on this one. "You have a pistol?"

"*Si, Señor.*"

"Good, strap it on. I'll meet you over at the sheriff's office. Don't know what to expect out at her cottage. Could be noth'n, but I have a bad feeling about this."

CHAPTER FIFTY-SIX

F ELIX GRABBED the reins of his horse and rode out to the mines. Fire raged through his body and he wished he could take the bullet back and try again, this time splitting the old man's face wide open. He fingered the hilt of his blade. Maybe a good slice across Gabriel's neck would do the trick. Slow and painful. He wouldn't decapitate the man, just enough of a cut to bleed him.

How could he be so stupid? And what did he think would happen? Did he want his father back, or did he want to see him pay for abandoning him all those years ago? When the Preacher killed his mother, he'd lost everything. Now the Preacher must pay for her murder. Mother was the one person who cared for him more than anyone else. Her rotting corpse wasn't around to stop Felix from killing his father for all the pain he's had to endure.

Several men were arguing about something by the time he arrived back at the mines. To his left he saw Joe Kidd tied up around a tree. They made eye contact, and with a finger to his lips, Felix told him to keep quiet. Two men sat on guard as Felix dismounted. Slipping the bowie knife from its sheath, Felix crept up to one man and stuck the blade deep into his neck. Carefully, he placed the dead man on the ground and tapped the second man on the shoulder.

"What?"

The look of horror filled his eyes before Felix shoved the knife's blade into the side of his temple. He had to step on the man's face to pull his knife free, then wiped the blade onto his trousers, smearing blood and brain matter like mud across them.

Cutting Kidd free, Felix asked, "What's going on, Kidd?"

"Several of the boys are deciding who's going to take ownership of the gang."

"Is that so?"

"...afraid so."

He shoved the knife back into the sheath and said, "Let's go pay them a little visit."

Felix and Kidd walked through the camp. Several hushed whispers filled the air as each hired man retreated into their tent. When they neared the campfire, the conversation regarding Felix and killing him quit when they saw the two of them.

"Don't stop on account of me, boys. If you want to run this gang, you'll have to shoot me for the position."

No one spoke or moved.

Felix swore. Pulling his gun, he fired one shot into the air. "Now, I said, if anyone wants to challenge me, do so now. I'm in no mood to deal with idiots. You are with me, or not. If not, I'll shoot ya dead right here; right now."

That's when Phillip stepped forward. "I challenge you."

He didn't give Felix time to answer. "You're a weak man, with weak vision. I've taken men twice your age and five times faster with a six-gun."

Felix grinned, "That right?"

"It is. I've killed plenty of men."

Kidd laughed. "And just last night you told me that your pal, Cory, was the first one you killed before Jake Callihan fired your sorry butt."

"I's jus making conversation, boys."

Felix cocked and opened fire.

The bullet struck Phillip in the leg and dropped him fast. He screamed against the pain and grabbed at his leg as if angry fire ants were eating him alive.

Felix dug his boot into the wound and Phillip screamed louder. He placed the gun against Phillip's temple and pulled back the hammer. "You see, I run this here gang. Not you, not Diamond, not anyone. I'm Felix Grant." Looking up, he added, "Anyone else want to challenge me?"

No one moved.

"Good." He pointed to a nearby horse. "Tie him up to the horse. Send him to Purgatory. This is an example of what happens when you cross Felix Grant."

Joe Kidd grabbed Phillip by the leg and dragged him over to a horse and tied his feet together. He then secured another rope around the horn of the saddle.

"Please! Please! Don't do this!" Phillip squealed like a pig. "I didn't mean any of it. Oh God, I'm sorry! I didn't mean to—"

"Sorry, but you get what you deserve." Then Felix slapped the hindquarters of the horse. The animal shot forward, dragging Phillip behind, bouncing and screaming all through the camp until a loud crack against a boulder silenced him. The only sound that Felix heard in the camp was the clapping of hooves to the hard mountain ground. The horse descended toward Purgatory.

CHAPTER FIFTY-SEVEN

THE CATTLE had moved through town enough for Jake to make his way to Sheriff Whalen's office. The office wasn't that big or impressive. For a small town, Cedar Grove saw little trouble, so the need for a large office didn't suit the town. Jake tied off his horse and walked into the office. His jangling spurs caught Roy's attention.

"Jake. Fancy seeing you today." He closed his journal and stood. "You okay? What happened?"

Jake breathed deep, doing everything he could to calm himself before speaking. "Have you seen Charlotte this morning? Children say she's not been there all day."

Roy checked his pocket watch. "It's eleven. That's unlike her to not show up. Quite reliable, that one is."

"I have a terrible feeling about this, Roy. I saw Charlotte last night. Came to town to surprise her with some flowers. I'm headed out to her place to check on her."

The sheriff stood, opened a drawer, grabbing Jake's silver badge, and flipped it to him. "Don't forget this."

"Thanks," he said.

Roy snatched up his hat and followed Jake out the door.

Slim arrived with a gun strapped to his waist. "I'm ready, *Señor*."

Jake stopped with one foot in the stirrup. "I'm not sure what we'll find. Keep your heads rotating."

A moment later, the three mounted and rode out of town. Each thump of Tucker's hooves matched the rhythm of his heart. They beat the ground like a Cheyenne war chant around the evening fire. His heart hammered against his chest as he feared the worst. No telling what they'd find. Maybe Charlotte was okay, maybe someone killed... *Oh God, don't let that be the case.*

Tucker and Jake led as Whalen and Slim followed close behind. It'd be a quick ride. Though she had her place on the CHR, during the week, Charlotte stayed at a small cottage just outside of town; about a half-hour ride. The sun was already hot in the sky. Heat scorched the ground, browned the grass, and he could feel Tucker's mane soaking through with sweat. No slowing down.

No one spoke or said a word as they neared the cottage. There didn't appear to be any movement. Jake pulled his Colt .45, anyway. He held up a fist, slowing Tucker to a stop at the top of the hill. Roy and Slim pulled up beside him.

"If anyone's there, they've heard us coming," Roy said, pulling his pistol.

Slim followed suit.

"What's the plan, Jake?"

Jake narrowed his eyes. His breathing stilled. His ears thumped with each heartbeat. "I don't like it." He pointed toward the cottage. "The front door is open."

His spurs dug into Tucker's side and down the hill he shot toward Charlotte's home, toward his love, toward his future.

Jake dismounted before Tucker finished his gallop. Hammer cocked back, Jake shot through the door.

As he entered, the others followed him inside. The cottage was dark. No one moved for what seemed to be an eternity. They turned the table over. Broken pottery. Books strewn across the floor. The place was in disarray. Jake's knees buckled and hit the wooden floor with a crack. The gun clattered to the floor as he dug his fists into the dust. Jake screamed, a deep groan that filled the room.

"This *can't* be happening."

"Jake…"

"This can't be *happening!* This… can't… be… happening!" he grit through teeth. Looking up, he saw Roy's pained look. "Not again, Roy. I can't lose anyone else. Not again." Tears filled his vision and burned the back of his throat.

Maybe she was never home. Maybe vandals had rummaged the place. He pulled up from the ground and checked the stove. Opening the cast-iron door, a wave of simmering heat warmed his hand. It was fairly fresh. Burned last night after he left her alone.

"I should have never left her alone."

Slim said little. He just placed a hand on Jake's arm. *"Lo siento, Señor Jake."*

"Don't worry. We'll find her. Let's head back to my office. We'll wire Cheyenne and get Tan involved. He'll want to be a part of this."

Jake stood and dusted off his pants. "Maybe she's out at the CHR. Maybe—"

Roy stood in the doorway, reading a piece of paper. "Jake," is all he said.

Taking the piece of paper from Roy's hand, he read;

"I know who you are. You're hiding behind a mask; a lie. You're

trying to live another life, but you know who you are. If you want to see Charlotte again, you will find me where it all began. The place where fire consumes everything. A place where you think you're dead but burning alive, waiting for your last judgment. I'll be waiting for you, Jacob Creek. —Diamond Rose."

Jake stared at the piece of paper, reading it over and over again. Diamond Rose? Who was that? Who had Charlotte? Why did this Diamond take her? How did she know his name was Jacob Creek?

So many questions flew through his mind like a stampeding herd of beeves. He crumpled the paper and tossed it into the oven. "Who's Diamond Rose? Ever hear of that name before, Sheriff?"

Roy shook his head. "Can't say I's rightly do. Slim?"

The Mexican shook his head. "*No lo sé, Señor.*"

Jake stood. "I think you're right, Sheriff. It's time we get Tan in on this. Someone took my Charlotte and I want her back." The shock and sadness faded and replaced by an unseen force that propelled him to walk out the door and mount his horse. "Lord, I need your help on this one." Roy and Slim removed their hats in prayer.

"I can't lose anyone else. I can't lose Charlotte. Help me, please! I ask by your everlasting mercies that you guide my hand, guard my heart, and prepare the way for us to bring justice and bring my love home. I've left you out of my heart for so long that I've forgotten how to trust you in all my ways. You said you'd prepare a table before, in-front of my enemies. Do that again. Let me see your goodness pass before me once more."

Jake holstered his gun. "And God, use this weapon and let my aim be true."

He didn't know what else to pray. "Amen."

"Amen," said the other two men.

"Boys, let's go. We're going to find this Diamond. I'm feeling that she's tied to Gabriel and Felix. Grant's grimy fingers are all over this. It's time to put an end to him once and for all."

CHAPTER FIFTY-EIGHT

THE TOWN of Purgatory sat quiet in the early morning hours as Joanna Creek made her way to the General Store for some needed supplies. It was three weeks ago when she'd placed the order and today, the train delivered her goods to the Mining Lodge.

She'd run the place for fifteen years, and it had been the last two years since she felt her strength weakening. Never calling herself an old woman, she did her best to keep up with the Joneses, as they say. But doing it alone, without the help of her son, she didn't know how much longer she could keep up the pace and run a miner's lodge.

As she stepped through the store's threshold, George Henderson stood behind the counter, helping a young woman and her daughter wrap their order.

"There ya go, Ma'am. That should about do it for ya," George said with a wide smile.

"Thank you, Mr. Henderson," said the woman as she turned to leave.

Joanna glimpsed the woman's smooth features and blond

hair poking out from underneath the bonnet. Her sparkling blue eyes caught Joanna's attention as a flash of recognition forced her to remain flat-footed at the door.

"Excuse me, Ma'am."

For the longest moment, Joanna didn't move or say anything. She just gawped, then smiled. "I'm sorry."

"It's alright. Have a nice day."

The little girl waved and smiled, then followed her mother out the door and down the street to their waiting wagon.

Joanna watched them climb aboard and head out of town before turning back to George, who seemed to have watched the entire exchange.

"You alright, Momma?"

Everyone called her Momma. It was Jacob, her son, who gave her the name. He never said Ma or Mother. It was always Momma. It stuck and the town soon caught on to using it as a term of endearment.

She looked back toward the door, then at George again. "I'm okay," she said. Or was she okay? The woman looked so much like her late daughter-in-law and the little girl, like her granddaughter. Her eyes welled, and the tears fell. It had been ten years and the wounds of their murder felt as fresh today as they did then.

God heals all wounds, it's something Joanna clung to all her life. After the death of her husband, Leonard, she trusted God for a new beginning. Didn't the Good Lord say to Paul, "*Behold, I make all things new?*" She understood the more you trust God for his provisions in your life, remain humble and meek, that you'll find strength when the storms of life rock your boat.

She sniffed a smile toward George.

George walked around the counter and pulled her into an

embrace. "Joanna. What is it? You know you can talk to me about anything." And they did. They'd sit for hours outside his store and chat the morning away before she headed back to bake for the miners.

She tugged at a handkerchief to dab at her leaking eyes. "I'm sorry. That was unexpected and un-lady like. They just looked so much like Sarah and Virginia."

He pulled her deeper into his embrace. His bear-like arms squeezed her shoulders and for just a moment everything felt right with the world. She'd be okay; she was okay.

"I can't imagine how you must feel, Joanna; losing your family, n'all. Have you heard from Jacob?"

She shook her head. It'd been a while, though she couldn't quite remember when he last visited Purgatory. Of course, she didn't blame him for staying away.

Packages; she came for those, not to reminisce about the past. "No, I haven't. But I came for that package I sent to Atlantic City for."

George snapped his fingers. "Came off the train this morning. Have it behind the counter. So, what's in the crate?" he said, heaving it onto the counter.

A smile played her lips. "Socks. Those boys out at the mines needed some, and I wanted to bless them. It gets so cold in those mines, and not having good socks to protect the feet God gave you, well, I just thought it'd be a good—"

Yelling reached their ears as several men raced down the street.

"What in Sam's name is happening out there?" George asked.

They stepped onto the boardwalk as three men tried to stop a galloping horse.

Where was the rider? That's when she noticed a man lying

motionless behind the horse. They dragged him behind a horse. Who would do such a horrible thing to another human being?

"Someone go get the doctor!" someone shouted back at them.

She lifted her dress and stepped onto the gravel. It crunched under her front-laced boots as she walked toward the wounded man.

"Momma, what's happening?"

She stopped at the sound of Missy's voice. "Ms. Cartwright, I'm not sure. Seems as if they have dragged a poor soul behind a horse."

Missy's hand flew to her lips. "That's awful."

As they walked, Joanna smiled because Missy Cartwright helped her and the miners over the past few months. She'd been away for a couple of years before returning to Purgatory. Joanna prayed for her that she'd find herself and become a strong woman of faith. Things had been quiet around town until now.

As they neared, she could tell the man was breathing shallow. His clothing was torn, and half his face caved in; exposing muscle, teeth, and his lower jaw. One of his hands hung on by a few pieces of gristle and bone. She placed her hand against her lips. "Dear God. Who would do such a thing?"

George grabbed her hand and stared. "Ladies, I don't think it'd be proper for ya to see this mess."

Missy stood there for a minute before saying, "I'll go get the doctor."

The man tried to speak. Whispered gargles escaped where his lips should have been. Joanna leaned forward before George could stop her; didn't want him to.

"*Jake...*"

She knelt next to his face. "Try again, son. The Lord will help you speak."

"*Jake Callihan. Felix Grant. Comi...ng to... k...kill...him....*"

As Missy and Doc Brown arrived, he fell limp and stopped breathing Brown checked him then shook his head. "He's dead."

Joanna stood. Who would do such a thing? Felix Grant? Jacob? The thought slammed into her like a sack of potatoes. Felix grant was coming to kill Jacob, and this man was the message of what would happen to her boy.

She grabbed George's shirt. "Grant's coming for my boy. We have to send word to Cedar Grove; warn Jacob!"

CHAPTER FIFTY-NINE

TIME SLOWED as Jake waited for Tan's arrival. It had been two days since Roy Whalen sent word to Cheyenne. Jake sat in his study, trying to focus on the finances. A piece of graphite broke off and dusted the ledger. "Dad-blamed!" Jake grabbed his knife, shaved a new tip, and started over.

As he worked, one question rattled his brain. Why was Tan taking so long to arrive? Dumb question. Two days was the max it would take to make the journey. The telegram he'd received told him to wait and not do anything stupid. Last night, he filled in Freddy, Wide-Eye, and Loretta regarding Charlotte.

Loretta prayed God would give them speed and grace. Freddy strapped on a gun, something he rarely did, and Wide-Eye said he'd do the same.

"We'll bring her home, sir. I's got me a real good iron to strap to my old hips. Won't let you down."

Jake was grateful for his friends and knew with their help and Tan's, they'd be on their way to find Charlotte.

The tip broke again, sending a dusting of graphite all over his paper and hand. He slammed it onto the desk, causing it to shatter. After shutting the ledger and filing it away, he grabbed a waste bin and cleared the broken graphite from his desk.

A knock at the door startled him as he set the can down. Filling the door width was his friend, Tan Bennington.

"Tan, thanks for coming out here."

The big man walked through the door and removed his hat. "I'm really sorry about all this, Jake. I really am. Charlotte's a good woman. I'll help you get her back."

The two men embraced. "Thanks, Tan. Means much to me that you came."

"Anything for a friend."

Jake offered him a chair, then sat behind his desk.

"I spoke with Governor Hale regarding what's been happening around these parts. He agrees that we should bring Felix in; dead or alive."

Some iron weight fell off Jake's shoulders. "That's good news. What about this Diamond Rose?"

Tan rubbed his eyes. "I've asked around. No one seems to know who she is. Been hearing the name around; real ruthless gal. Rumor has it, she rides with Felix Grant and just as cutthroat; maybe more."

That confirmed his suspicions regarding the note. But he couldn't shake the feeling that this Diamond was someone from his past—but who?

"What about the note?"

"Judging, based on what you've told me, it has something to do with your connection to this Diamond Rose."

The only person Jake could think of who might resemble Diamond was a self-proclaimed gun hawk named Ruby

Quick. She was deadly with a six-shooter. In a train robbery attempt, Jake helped Sheriff Whalen arrest her six years prior.

"Think it might be Ruby Quick?"

Tan smiled. "Haven't heard that name in a while. After staging her escape, Quick is said to be somewhere near Colorado Springs."

"But it's possible she could have returned, being that I helped put her away?"

"Possible."

Jake stood as Loretta lightly tapped on the door. "Sir, the Sheriff is in the dining room with Mr. Franklin and Mr. Jeffries. They are waiting for you."

"Thank you, Loretta."

The two men walked down the hallway toward the dining room. The burgundy carpet looked recently swept, and some of the staff nodded as he walked into the dining room. "Give us the room, please."

Sheriff Roy Whalen, Freddy, and Wide-Eye all stood near the fireplace.

"Marshal, it's good to see you again," Roy said, extending a hand.

"Sheriff." He exchanged pleasantries with the other two, then sat down next to Jake. "Freddy just filled me in on Charlotte, the note, and what it means. Told him I spoke with the Governor and I have a signed warrant for the arrest or death of Felix Grant. As for Diamond Rose, no one knows who she is. But I will say this. From what I've heard, she's dangerous and if she's the one who has Charlotte, we're in for a fight. No doubt Felix and Diamond are connected; maybe even an item and they're fix'n for a fight."

Jake leaned forward on his elbows. "Boys, we're taking the fight to Felix. The only problem, I don't know where he's at or what he's up to. I want my Charlotte back and I don't care if I go at this alone."

"Jake, you're not fast enough, especially if Felix has a crew."

Loretta walked in with Slim. "*Señor*, telegram from *tu mama*."

Jake stood and took the note from Loretta's hand.

"It's serious, Jake."

He opened it and read it out loud:

FELIX GRANT IN PURGATORY. STOP. KILLED A MAN. STOP. GUNNING FOR YOU. STOP. COME SOON HE HAS AN ARMY.

Jake's eyes widened. *Momma!* Now Felix was coming for his mother? His throat tightened, and then he read the note again. It was time to go. They had to look. Charlotte was missing, Momma was in danger, and he didn't know where to start. The room spun, and he clutched his shoulder. Pain rippled through his arm and down his spine, and then the fog disappeared.

The riddle.

You'll find me where it all began. Where what began? *Where fire consumes everything.* What did fire consume? Did it consume Jake? Diamond? Who did the fire...*the place where you're... burning alive?*

Sarah and Virginia!

This had everything to do with them.

"Charlotte's in Purgatory."

Each of the men exchanged looks.

"What do you mean?" Tan asked.

He showed Momma's telegram to the marshal. "Everything is about Purgatory. The original note said I could find Diamond Rose where it all began, where fire consumes everything. The place where you're burned alive while waiting for final judgment." He handed the note to Tan. "Purgatory. Where are you burned alive, but still live?"

"Diamond's connected somehow to Sarah and Virginia's deaths?"

Freddy's eyes widened at the prospect. "Who else was there that night?"

Jake would never forget the night they died. Gabriel Grant held him down while his family ran into the schoolhouse fire. His heart ached thinking about that night. Grant's goon burned the building to the ground. Nothing was left. Freddy was there. Momma was singing.

Like a flash of lightning, the memories, the smells, the Bible clattering next to his leg all flooded his mind. Someone else had to have been there that night, but who?

"I don't know, but everything with the Grants started in Purgatory, and that's where we're go'n. Boys, we're head'n out in the morning. Freddy, make sure we have enough for the journey. It's about a three-day ride. I need you all on this one. I will not say it's not dangerous. Even hate to say it, but if Felix has an army, some of you may die. I won't force anyone to join."

Freddy tapped his gun. "You've got mine. I've been with ya since that fateful night. Let's end this once and for all."

Wide-Eye's smile was white against his black features. "I'ma com'n too, boss."

The Sheriff and Tan nodded.

He was grateful for each man. Their willingness to help calmed his mind.

"I can't thank you all enough. Let's go bring Charlotte home."

CHAPTER SIXTY

THE NEXT MORNING Jake was up and at 'em long before anyone else. After tossing the chickens some grain, gathering eggs for Loretta, and making sure the boys mucked the horse stalls, he took Tucker out toward the lake he had shown Charlotte. The reds and oranges of the sun cascaded its light across the emerald lake. This was his favorite spot; a place to clear his head, think, and prepare for what lay ahead. The air was damp and crisp, which forced him to wrap his coat tight against his chest. He breathed deep the moist air, allowing it to calm his mind and senses. Grey clouds loomed in the distance, pelting the ground with rain. Somehow, those clouds matched his heart.

It was the calm before the storm. The dark clouds threatened to tear his soul in half again. Charlotte was missing, and his heart begged for her return. Burning heat filled his chest and rose into his throat. Jake's lip quivered as tears welled in his eyes. The dam could only take so much pressure before bursting. No one was around, and Jacob's dam broke.

Tears traced rivers down his cheeks, and he dropped to his knees. Dew from the moist grass seeped into his trousers, its cold biting against his knees. He lifted his head toward heaven and begged God to have mercy and help him find Charlotte. He tugged at Sarah's ring, which still hung around his neck; remembering how much he missed her. With his past threatening to take away everything again, Jacob Creek.

"I come on humbled knees. Your mercies are new every morning and great is your faithfulness. God, I look at this place, this land you've blessed me with, and I've done little to thank you. But now I'm at a crossroads and it's leading me back to Purgatory. I don't know what lies ahead, but I know I need you now more than ever. I've run away. I've done everything in my power to push you further from my mind. No more. I need your guiding hand to show me a path."

He can't lose everyone to the Grants. First, Gabriel took his wife and daughter and, in his anger, Moira Grant lost her life. He lived with that regret of her lost life for ten years. It was an accident, and he wished for that moment back. Life wasn't fair, and that boiled his blood. And now Felix and Diamond had Charlotte.

Jake grabbed at his Colt .45. He opened the cylinder and started loading bullets. After loading, he re-holstered and secured the hammer. "Guide my hand. Let my aim be true. Show me what I need to know so I can bring Charlotte home. I can't lose Charlotte. She's been a constant breath of fresh air in my life. I lost so much when Sarah and Virginia died. They were my world. I've let so much hate consume my waking moments and now my past has caught up with me. Paul said to forget your past and leave it behind, don't let it define you. God, I need to set my eyes on the prize. My past must die; no matter the cost."

A hand landed on his shoulder. "It's time."

Jake looked up—with tears streaming down his face—at Freddy, the one who'd been by his side since the beginning. "Franklin, thank you for everything. I can't guarantee that any of us will make it out of this alive, but I'm glad to have you by my side."

The man shifted his weight. "I know I'm not much of a pray'n man. But what you've been through, most men would have ended it a long time ago. Now, let's go get Charlotte and bring her home." They embraced and when they arrived back at the main house, the others were ready to hit the road.

Tan Bennington stopped Jake from mounting his horse. "Jake, I've got something for you." He pulled out a set of leather holsters and belt from his saddle bag. "These are yours. Picked them up in Arizona. Saw you eyeing them, so figured once you said yes to the badge, I'd give em to ya."

Jake took the deep brown belt from his friend. After removing his old belt and holster, he tried on the new set. He tied down one to his right hip and then added a cross-draw holster for his left hand. "Fits like a glove."

Tan tossed him a second Colt. "This was Marshal Drake's. Would have wanted you to have it. He respected you."

Looking at the blue casehardened gun, a matching gun to his own, Jake smiled. "Thank you. He was a good man." Jake looked at each man. Jake grabbed the horn of his saddle and said, "Let's ride."

"Bring her home," Loretta said as he mounted.

Jake nodded, then waited for Freddy, Slim, Wide-Eye, Tan, and Sheriff Whalen to mount their horses.

"I'll be gunning for you in prayer, don't forget that, Jacob."

"Thank you, Loretta. You better have fried chicken and some bear sign when I return."

She nodded, and Jake Callihan rode as hard and as fast as he could for Purgatory.

HOME IS HARDER THAN DEATH

The Lord thundered from heaven, and the Most High uttered His voice, hailstones and coals of fire. He sent out His arrows and scattered the foe, lightnings in abundance, and He vanquished them.

— KING DAVID

CHAPTER SIXTY-ONE

They stopped long enough to rest their horses, eat, and sleep. But two long days of travel forced Jake's mind to worry about what was going to happen. Sixteen years prior, Jake's father—Leonard Creek—was shot and killed over the sum of a two-thousand-dollar loan. Now facing his past, Purgatory lay ahead, begging to swallow all he had left, and Jake knew this journey would end in a bloodbath. People he cared about were putting their very lives at risk, just so he can save Charlotte.

Purgatory sat against the Encampment River and near the Purgatory Gulch mines, which lay just outside town. Each hoof pounded on the ground and his heart raced faster and faster. He fingered each Colt and ran his hand along the scabbard containing his Henry rifle. "Boys, we're not too far from the mines. I don't want to spook the miners and have someone tip off Felix that we're riding for Purgatory."

"You want to break for camp here?" Tan asked.

Jake looked around. The tall pines, rocks, and a bluff around the clearing would protect them and they could spot danger coming. The river flowed just beyond the tree line. Jake could see a small waterfall cascading over the bluff. Other than birds, cicadas, and constant swooshing of water it was quiet; peaceful.

Dismounting, Jake set up his pack near a boulder. Tan gathered some wood to start a fire while Slim fumbled around, not knowing where to put his things.

"Having issues, Slim?"

The rounded Mexican looked up. "*No Señor* Jake. I'll manage. I've been camping before."

Freddy tossed him a rolled blanket, which bounced off his belly and landed with a thump before unrolling. He turned his attention to Wide-Eye. "Hey, Wide-Eye, what are ya mak'n for dinner?"

"I've told ya, to stop calling me that. Name's Theodore or Ted." He huffed a curse under his breath before pulling a few cans of beans and beef.

"Whoa! Easy, It's just a fun name. Never seemed to bother ya before?" Freddy said.

As Jake unrolled his blanket, Wide-Eye stopped and pointed a wooden spoon in Freddy's direction. "I's told Ms. Charlotte that no one's respecting a negro like me. I'm a free man, Freddy. I gots rights just like you and no one's ask'n you to call me someth'n other than the name my Mamy gave me. Ms. Charlotte gave me her word that ya'll would be respecting me." He wiped his eyes with his sleeve, and Jake's heart broke for his friend. "I came with ya'll because she means an awful lot to me. First white woman to hug me and tell me that I's a good man, worth something more than my cooking. She said I's be a mighty fine rancher one day. Be the best black rancher in Wyoming."

When Jake met Ted, he stayed to himself, didn't communicate, and did his job without complaint. Jake was grateful for Ted and wouldn't trade him for anyone else as their cook. What he didn't know was Ted's desire and dream to own his own ranch one day. "Ted. You're more than someone of color; you're family to me. Family respects each other. It's not about the color of one's skin the defines a man's character— we're all created equal—it's about what's deep inside, given to us by hard work, our friends, how we react to life's circumstances. Just look at us. We're a good mix of ideologies, backgrounds, and yet we're all friends. I'll respect Ms. Charlotte's wishes. I'll call ya Theodore if you'd like." He grabbed a cup of coffee Tan had brewed and raised it in Ted's direction. "Besides, I couldn't do any of this without you."

They all nodded, prayed, then ate the food Theodore Jeffries had made. It wasn't any good, but Jake was glad for the sustenance. After their lunch, Jake knew he needed to head into town and speak with the town sheriff. He told Tan to stay behind, couldn't tip off anyone that they were in town.

An hour later, Jake arrived in Purgatory. A wave of recognition knotted his gut. As he crested the hill, the town's church steeple rose into view. *They'd rebuilt.* The building looked quite different from how he remembered. It was about the same size, but had an extra room attached to the left side of the building, the schoolroom. A single piece of property sat empty next to the church. The place where Sarah's school used to sit. His gut twisted as bile burned the back of his throat.

Images from ten years ago flashed through his mind. His wife was held at knife point, bloodied and bruised. Gabriel Grant gloating in his attempt to push Jake into paying off the loan he took out from the bank. It didn't matter who he owed; Gabriel Grant wanted to see Jacob burn.

He told his friend Bill to take his wife and daughter to

safety, but Virginia ran into the burning building to fetch her dolly.

Jake dismounted and stared at the empty land. Nothing was there. It was all destroyed by fire, just like his life was all those years ago.

Tears slipped down his face as he remembered Sarah racing in after their daughter. The explosion. The all-consuming fire that killed his family. Bill trying to stop them as Gabriel shot him dead.

Jake's knees weakened. How he missed them. He grabbed a fistful of gravel and squeezed tight. The pebbles bit into his skin before he released them from his grip and dusted the ground.

He picked himself up and walked over to the new church. Grateful no one was around, he walked into the building. Two rows of pews cascaded toward the front of the tiny room that ended near the cross-bearing podium. It all seemed so familiar, yet so foreign. Jake walked up the aisle and behind the podium. Something he hadn't done in years. A Bible lay on top, open to Colossians, chapter two. *"Being dead in your sins… He has made [us] alive together with Him, having forgiven you…. He has taken it out of the way, having nailed it to the cross. Having disarmed principalities and powers, He made a public spectacle of them, triumphing over them…. Let no one cheat you of your reward."*

The podium was smooth, cut from pine, and Jake wondered how much of his fallen life God had shaped. All of it? A sense of knowing that God was guiding his hand, making a spectacle of Felix Grant, causing Jake to triumph over evil. At least that's how he felt.

He closed the Bible, then focused on a single doorway which led into the secondary room. Making his way across the tiny church, he opened the door and stopped in his tracks.

Sitting in three neat rows were 20 school desks, each with a hand-held black board and a piece of chalk. A small desk sat near the front, with several primers stacked in a pile. Behind the desk was an American flag, blackboard, and a small glass case.

It wasn't the room which caused him to stop walking, it's what sat inside the glass case. His throat burned with a cry as tears flooded his eyes, blurring his vision. He walked closer to the small display case near the teacher's desk and focused on the contents. Inside sat a porcelain doll. The hair was burned, the dress frayed and browned from smoke and fire. A small crack sat on the right cheek, but otherwise the doll was in perfect condition.

He touched the case, then lifted the glass dome and set it on the desk. This was...a tear slipped down his cheek as he touched the smooth porcelain. Air sucking convulsions rocked his lungs. Jake couldn't breathe. This was the doll he gave Virginia on her eighth birthday. How did it survive the fire?

Jake hugged the doll, swaying under the grief he'd buried years ago. He let the tears drop onto the tiny blue dress as he sobbed uncontrollably. This was his baby girl's dolly. The dolly she ran to save from the fire. They never found her body; no one to bury. He didn't even know about the doll. It was all he had left of Virginia. Jake cleared his eyes and held onto the doll as if it were life itself. He kissed the doll's head. "I love you, baby girl. Daddy—" his lip quivered, "Daddy loves you. I miss you so much each day. But I have to go. I have to save someone else I care about." Kissing the doll again, Jake placed the doll back onto the stand and set the glass dome back on top, protecting its special treasure. He wiped his eyes and took a breath of air to calm his mind.

A silk-gloved hand landed on his shoulder. He reached for his gun.

"Hi, Jacob. It's been a long time."

He spun around, eyes widened, then released the gun's grip. Standing in front of Jake was his friend, Melissa Cartright.

CHAPTER SIXTY-TWO

J AKE DIDN'T MOVE for a moment. "Hello, Missy. How did you know I was in town?"

"Saw a rider come into town. Followed you to the church. But it's when I saw you holding Virginia's doll...that's when I knew." Her tanned skin blushed red as she played a slight smile. "How have you been, Jacob?"

He removed his hat and returned the smile. "Been better. Came to town looking for someone."

"I can tell. You're a marshal now?" she said, pointing to the silver five-pointed badge.

Jake tapped the star clipped to his long coat. "Got word there was some trouble, came to investigate, saw the church. A lot of painful memories."

"How about a bite of my sweet potato pie? Just whipped up some earlier today. It'll take your mind off things."

"Much obliged."

Jake extended his arm, and she tucked her arm around his. All the past emotions he had for Missy flooded his mind again. For years she'd flirted with him, and he never knew what to do with those emotions. Together, they walked out of the church and down the street. The last time he saw Missy was ten years ago, the night he left Purgatory. She wasn't happy about his leaving, begged him to stay, but he rode off into the sunset regardless of how either of them felt.

The town wasn't too dissimilar from when he left. A few new buildings, but otherwise, Purgatory remained as he left the town when setting off for Cedar Grove. They walked by the old livery stable that Freddy once ran. A large man busied himself pounding out a shoehorn. He waved, then continued to work. Several wagons were being filled near the mercantile, and Jake remembered buying the doll from his late friend, Joe. The place hadn't changed.

At the far end of the street sat the courthouse and sheriff's office, along with Momma's miner's lodge. He'll have to stop by before seeing the sheriff.

"This is it," Missy said, pointing to a new hotel and saloon establishment.

"The Lucky Diamond Saloon and Hotel?" He shook his head. "Guess more has changed than I thought. New church and new hotel. What happened to your diner?"

As they walked through the batwing doors, she said, "I tore that old place down for this one. Come on in, take a seat."

The place was clean and smacked of gambling and prostitution. Five men played cards at a nearby table, but otherwise the place was empty. Jake removed his hat and spurs and set them on a hook. Several professional card tables littered the floor, with some other gambling table he didn't know. Along the back wall sat the waist-top bar. Its brass railing shined along with its polished top. Adorning the wall behind the counter was a fancily designed mirror.

Missy disappeared behind the counter. Jake noticed a staircase sat to his right which led to the rooms upstairs, he guessed. He found a nearby table and sat down, folding his hands. A moment later, Missy returned with two plates filled with sweet potato pie. "Quite different, isn't it? Place is busy toward sundown. Right now, pretty quiet."

"Sure is. How've you been? It's been so long and I'm sorry for not coming back sooner."

Missy found her own chair and sat down. "I won't say it's been an easy ten years. I had a hard time after you left. Judge Talbert retired soon after you left and went into the gambling business, which killed him after he built this new place. I saw little in sticking around. Your Momma encouraged me to leave and go find myself. So, I did. Traveled here and there. Been to California and then came back."

"California? What's it like out there?" he said between bites.

She laughed. "Beautiful. The ocean is better than I imagined. The smell, colors, and lots of Spanish-speaking people. Could never figure out their language."

"I have a friend named, Slim. Can't ever figure what he's saying. Do my best, but he knows I mean well."

"So, what brings you to town? You never told me."

Charlotte's image flashed through his mind. He took the last bite, then he pushed the plate aside. "Momma sent me a telegram, said some strange stuff is happening." Jake leans forward. "Missy, I think Felix Grant is gunning for me. He's in town. Heard he roughed up a cowboy really good."

Her faced cringed. "Yeah. I was there with Momma. Said

Felix was coming for you. It's got everyone terrified around here. Rumor has it he has taken over the mines. Killed the miners. Momma's shaken up bad."

They killed Momma's miners. Why did he ever leave Purgatory? Momma's livelihood is now being threatened. Jake clenched his fist and slammed it onto the table. Jake feared what was coming. Felix would make his move, and Jake needed to be ready.

"When did this happen?"

"Momma noticed her miners hadn't returned home a week ago. She's beside herself. She—"

A boy interrupts Missy. "Ma, can I go out back and play with my slingshot?"

Jake's eyes widened as Missy ruffled the boy's sandy blond hair. Looking up at Missy, he noticed her hair was the same color. When did Missy have a kid? The boy's piercing blue eyes locked with Jake, and he smiled.

"Howdy."

"Elliot, this is my good friend, Jacob Creek."

"Hello, Jacob."

Jake smiled. "Please, call me Jake."

"Can I go?" he asked again of his mother.

Missy hugged her son and said, "Of course. Just be careful. Aim only at the water barrels."

"Yes'um," he said, then shot out the back door to shoot some imaginary bad guy.

She must have noticed the stupefied look on his face. "He'll be ten years old next month."

The words he wanted to say remained lodged in the back of his throat. He took a drink and swallowed hard. *Ten?* "You have a son?"

Silence enveloped them as Missy's brown eyes averted his. She said nothing for what seemed an eternity. The place had cleared, and they were the only people left inside.

His fingers ran through his hair, trying to find more words, but said again, "You have a son?"

"Stop saying that." Missy stood. "Yes, I have a son. You don't know how much I missed you these past ten years. It's been a lonely life to live. Everyone knows the boy doesn't have a father around. They call him a bastard child. He's unwanted by the community. I'm called a whore. You know how that makes me feel? I'm more than an unwashed painted dove, working here. That's what I pay the other girls for. You know what that does to a boy's confidence?"

Jake didn't know what to say. "I'm sorry, Missy. Who's the father?"

Missy pulled a handkerchief and dabbed her eyes before plopping back into her chair. She placed her head into her hands and cried. Not knowing what to do next, Jake played with his fingers, then got up and wrapped an arm around her shaking shoulders. Sarah used to say, *if you can't say anything, at least show love with actions.*

"You know how hard it's been for me, Jake? I have no one in this town. So, I run this place. It's all I have left." She looked up. "I wish you were around to help raise Elliot. He needs a good man in his life."

Jake wanted to walk away. This is not what he envisioned when riding into town. Sure, there was a possibility of running into Missy, but he didn't think the conversation would end up like this. Missy had a son, and Jacob's best guess was the boy belonged to Judge Rex Talbert.

"What do you mean?" Jacob asked.

"After the Judge died, I was free of the man who wrecked my life. But I had no man to raise your son."

Jake's heart stopped beating and he sucked air. "What are you saying, Missy?" His voice rose as he stood, hands planted on the table.

"He's your son, Jacob."

CHAPTER SIXTY-THREE

How was that even possible? Jake raced through all his interactions with Missy before leaving for Cedar Grove. Nothing came to mind how this child could be his. He never slept with Missy. Sarah would have still been alive when Missy got herself pregnant. The only logical conclusion he reached in those few seconds was the child belonged to the dead, Judge Rex Talbert.

"How on earth could the lad be my boy?"

She cried. Her sobs filled the room, and Jake was glad no one else was around. In that moment he wanted to comfort her, put his arms around her, but his arm remained rooted to the table.

"Missy, we never had relations."

She gazed at him as tears streamed down her cheeks. "Remember the days following Sarah's funeral?"

Not something he could ever forget. The cold and cloudy day. The platitudes and well-wishes. The fight with Momma before spiraling into a deep depression of drinking and sitting alone in the dark. "Yeah, I remember. They were the darkest days of my life."

She sniffed deep. "I came and visited you one of those nights at the Creek farm."

"I remember that too."

"You were so broken and hurting from your missing Sarah. We kissed that night. It was passionate, and romantic. You embraced me and held me tight. I knew it was wrong, but I couldn't help myself. I loved you, Jacob. You picked me up and led me to the bedroom. It was passionate, raw, and real. I comforted you in your darkest days. You made love to me, Jacob. We made a baby, and he's right outside playing, needing his father to embrace him."

Jake opened his mouth to speak, but only air escaped. Heat cascaded through his face and into his chest. Each heartbeat felt like a sledgehammer pounding a railroad tie. "Missy—"

"You've got to remember. It's why you left town."

"Missy, I remember the kiss. That much is true. But, it's not that I disremember us sleeping together, it never happened." Jake grabbed at his hair and finger combed it back. "I was in a dark place. The drink had me good, but I wasn't so shot in the neck that I'd forgotten something...like this. I know you took a liking to me, Missy, but the fact is, you and I never had relations. I don't know how else to put it."

Missy grabbed the plates and cleaned up the table. Jake followed her to the counter.

"I'm real sorry."

She spun around and pointed a finger at him. "You pushed me a way. I could have comforted you. I could have been your girl. But you didn't want me. That's why you left me alone in this hell-hole of a town."

Jake had no other words.

"Besides all that, I was so broken and alone that I left. Went out west to California, raised your boy by myself."

"He's not my boy, Missy." Jake had enough. He walked back toward the door to put on his spurs. Once tied, he placed his hat back onto his head. "We'll talk about this when you're less upset. I can see you're not giving up the gun on this one. I'm sorry."

Standing there with her hands to hips, Missy's eyes narrowed. "Don't leave me again, Jacob. I need you."

"I'm sorry, Missy. I really am." Then Jake walked out the door, stepping into the bright sunshine. He stood for a moment as the double doors rocked shut. As he stepped onto the gravel, his heart broke for Missy. She'd been through an awful ordeal, but to insist that the lad was his was all hogwash. This was not time to think about Missy and the boy, Jake needed answers and he came to town to get them.

He continued down the street. Several nodded or said *howdy* as he walked. It had been a long time since he'd visited Momma. And as he walked toward her lodge, he couldn't help thinking it a mistake to stay away for so long. The little boy inside was desperately trying to hide from his mistakes as a son, begging him to just walk into the Sheriff's office, talk about why he was here, and then leave town. Jake glanced up at the sheriff's sign then through the window. Nobody sat behind the desk.

"Can I help you with something, Mister?"

Jake turned around and faced what appeared to be the sheriff. "Sheriff?"

The man spit tobacco and smiled. "Not quite. I'm one of his deputies." He stuck out a hand. "Joe Kidd. What brings you to Purgatory Gulch?"

They shook hands, and Jake remembered the badge. He flipped open the flap on his trench coat. "I'm here on official business from the United States Government. Do you know where the sheriff went?"

Kidd scratched his chin. "Can't say. But I'm sure he'll be back soon. Thought he was here."

Jake tipped his hat. "Thanks. I have someone I need to see first. I'll be over at the Miner's Lodge. If you see him come in, let me know."

"Will do. Thanks for stopping by."

Stepping off the boardwalk, Jake made his way to Momma's place. Nothing had changed. The building could use a coat of fresh paint, but otherwise, her rocking chair sat on the front porch. Several planters filled with various flowers sat on the porch, and a wind chime dangled away in the soft morning breeze. His spurs spun and jangled as he stepped up onto the porch.

"I'll be right with you."

He smiled at the sound of his mother's voice. Deciding to wait, he took a seat in her rocker. The door opened and out walked his mother. Jake stood and brushed his coat flat. "Hello, Momma."

Tears filled her eyes, and she quickly set down the towel in her hands. She pulled up to her tiptoes and sandwiched his face in her hands before giving him a kiss on the lips. "Lands, my sweet dear boy."

Jake laughed. He figured she'd have this reaction. He bent and gave his short, plump mother a hug and another kiss. "I'm sorry it's been so long."

"Come in, come in. I have fresh honey oat bread and hot tea."

They walked through the door and it amazed him at how

clean the place remained. How a near seventy-year-old woman could keep up with the filth and dirt from the miners boggled his mind. But she always made sure each man had cleaned and freshened before eating or sitting on any furniture.

He found his place at the table. The place hadn't changed. The kitchen was small. A basin for water, a black kettle stove, and a tiny table. Just enough for her needs. The miners ate in another room.

"How've you been, Jacob?" She said, pouring him a cup of tea.

"I've been good. I'm sorry that such horrible circumstances have brought me to town."

Momma filled her own cup and then sliced some bread for them before sitting down. "I figured. Saw the badge right away. Good for you. But I hope you're not fooling around with one of those shakes that take up at the saloons when you're out doing whatever lawmen do."

"Momma, I've been good. Found me a good woman. She's a godly one and no, I didn't meet her at a saloon. She's a schoolteacher. Her name is Charlotte."

That made his Momma smile. "That's a very respectable name for a woman."

"She's not Sarah, but I know Sarah would like her."

Momma grabbed at his hands. "I sure miss them something terrible. I know it's been a time or two since, but it doesn't make the pain any less. And Bill. I miss his company. It's been ten years and I still think he's going to walk through that door and sweep an old lady like me off her feet."

As Jake ate the bread, it warmed his stomach, and he begged it to fill the hole that sat in the middle of his heart. Charlotte was still out there—maybe even here. "Momma,

I've got to ask you. The day you found out Felix was gunning for me, what else did he say?"

She closed her eyes as if to escape some horrible memory. "Well, I was with George—he owns the General Store—and there was some commotion on the street. Someone tied a poor boy to the back of a horse and had him dragged." A cry escaped her lips, and Momma's hand shook. Jake reached around the cups and cradled her hand in his. "He was hurt, and no one was listening to what he was trying to say. He said that Felix was coming for Jake Callihan."

"Did he say how he knew who I was?"

"No, but I knew. I'd recognize Sarah's maiden name anywhere. That's how I figured it was you the lad was referring to."

"No, no. It's fine. I'm glad you reached out. This helps me narrow our search." Jake pulled her close. "Momma, someone close to Felix took Charlotte. My Charlotte's missing. I need to know if you recognize this person's name. Do you know anyone in Purgatory that goes by the name Diamond Rose?"

Momma seemed to think for a moment then shook his head. "I don't recognize that name. I'm sure I would have; pretty much know everyone in town."

"Think really hard."

"Jacob Elliot Creek, I already told you. Now either you believe your mother, or you don't."

He kissed the top of her hand. "I'm sorry." The tea cooled to where he could drink and for the next several minutes, they talked about memories of years gone by and Momma talked about how the Lord had restored what Satan had stolen from them.

"I'm really sorry about your miners. No word from the sheriff on what happened?"

She shook her head. "Jake, the sheriff won't even put together a posse to find them. No one's been out to the mines in a week. I've heard rumors that Felix Grant has his men holed up out there."

That would be the first place to check. It was time to see the sheriff and find out what was happening.

CHAPTER SIXTY-FOUR

As Jake stepped into the sun, he smiled at Momma. "It's so good to see you again, Momma. I've missed you."

"I've been praying for you, son. God will guide your hand as long as you place your trust into his Almighty arms."

"I will. God's been showing me a lot again, and I've missed my conversations with him. That being said, please pray for me regarding Missy. I'm not sure what's happened in the past ten years, but her asserting that I'm the boy's father has me concerned."

Momma smiled and kissed his cheek. "The good Lord will give you wisdom. It's been ten years, Jacob. She's had a hard life, but she's a kind woman who cares for her son. I've watched that boy grow into a respectable lad."

He nodded and gave his mother a hug before heading down the street to see if the sheriff was back. The door to the office sat open, and Jake saw a different man sitting behind the desk. He tapped on the door as the sheriff looked up.

"Howdy. What can I do for ya?"

Jake showed off his badge. "Name's Jake Callihan, here on official government business. Looking for this man. He's wanted for several murders and robberies," he said, pointing to Felix's wanted poster. "Heard he's been in these parts."

The Sheriff stood and extended a hand. "Ben Faulkner. Got no word you'd be rid'n into town, Marshal."

"Trying to keep the noise low. If Felix and his gang of men are here, there's bound to be trouble. I'm surprised your deputy didn't mention anything."

"No, no; he hasn't said a word to me, besides, he's off running something for me." He scratched his beard for a moment. "I'm afraid there's already trouble, Marshal. Word is that Felix is up at the gold mines. Shut down the whole business. Killed those poor miners. I sent word to Encampment for help, but they had no one to spare. Guess they sent for ya, anyway."

Jake removed his hat, then sat down. Faulkner followed suit. "Not heard anything from Encampment. I'm from Cedar Grove. He hit up our bank then escaped, killing a U. S. Marshal." Jake looked at the ground for a moment. "He also has my fiancé. Got word of a woman working with him, goes by the name Diamond Rose."

The Sheriff shook his head then started rifling through some papers and notebooks. "Real sorry about your woman. Can't say that I've heard that name around. Pretty quiet around here. Town's sort of drying up. Folks headed toward Encampment to live. They get more of the trouble." He flipped through a few more pages. "Here we go," he said, pointing to an entry. "Previous sheriff wrote that a woman was accused of killing the local judge, Rex Talbert. Slit his throat, real gruesome like. She went by the name of... Diamond Rose. Know nothing else other than that."

Rex Talbert was murdered. It didn't surprise Jake. The man had it coming for years. His gambling and running prostitution, not to mention being in league with Gabriel Grant over several illegal dealings through the years. "Does it say what happened to her following the murder of the judge?"

The sheriff read for a minute. "Nope. Says she left for Sunrise after being cleared of any wrongdoing and that's the last record we have. Before my time as Sheriff. Came to town to settle down and they asked me to run once they found out I's done that 'fore coming to town. Hailed from a small outpost near Denver; real nice place, n'all."

Jake stood. "Thanks, Sheriff. I'll be in touch if things go south. May need your help in putting a posse together to apprehend Felix." They shook hands, and Jake walked out of the office.

As he mounted Tucker, a thought skittered through his mind; If someone murdered Rex Talbert, and this Diamond Rose has taken Charlotte, how was she connected to Felix Grant? Something didn't add up, and Jake was at a loss.

As he rode back toward the Encampment River to connect with Tan and his men, he couldn't help but focus on Judge Rex Talbert. The man had forced his way into Missy's life and now she was free of his grip. Following the murder, she took ownership of the establishment. Was the boy Talbert's seed? He couldn't think about it at the moment. Charlotte was missing, and he was a little closer to finding her; he knew where Felix was hiding.

The four men were busy laughing as Jake rode up. Tan stood and asked what Jake knew regarding Felix. Jake dismounted and walked through some of his events in town, leaving out a few details regarding Missy, the boy, and the doll he found.

"Seems as if Purgatory is drying up. Few folks in town. Saw a couple wagons. Seems as if most have gone north into Encampment. That could spell trouble if'n Felix is fixing to tree the town. Could spark the end of Purgatory."

"You thinking Felix will make a play for Purgatory?"

"If he hates Purgatory as much as he loathes me, then yeah, he'll make a move."

Slim dusted off as he stood. "*Señor*, what should we do?"

"I'm going to take Tan out to the mines. I want to see for myself if there's a woman riding with him. If so, maybe Charlotte's at their camp."

Freddy asked, "What do you want us to do in the meantime?"

"Ride into town, stake out shelters. If Felix is gunning for a fight, we'll need to know our way around town. I don't want to be caught unaware."

Freddy, Roy, Slim, and Ted grabbed their horses and took off toward Purgatory. Tan gave them instructions to let the Sheriff know a gun fight was coming and soon; mentioning that the sheriff and his deputies should make sure the women and children are safe and locked in their homes.

Tan and Jake rode toward the Purgatory Gulch gold mines. The mines sat nestled in the heart of the Sierra Madre mountain range. Jake heard that if you followed the range, they'd connect to the Rocky Mountains in Colorado. Though he'd heard of the mysterious mountain men that lived in the Rockies, he'd always desired to see for himself. They were ruthless yet lived off the land and tried to make peace with the locals. He only wished his guns wouldn't have to be used against Felix and his men. Bloodshed was inevitable.

"I could tell you were hesitant to say everything that happened in Purgatory. You find Gabriel?" Tan asked.

Tan could always tell when Jake held back something, especially if it included his past. "No, nothing that good. I found a dolly in the schoolhouse. It belonged to Virginia. Bought it for her on her eighth birthday."

"I'm sorry, Jake."

"I also ran into Missy. She has a boy, claims he's mine."

Tan stopped his horse. "You've not seen her in ten years, or have you been sneaking off to Purgatory for a woman behind Charlotte's back?"

Jake threw his head back and laughed. "Boy's not my seed. I think he's Talbert's. But she claims it."

They continued toward the mines, following the river until they reached the top of a bluff that overlooked the mine's entrance. The mouth looked blown shut. Several men littered the area, laughing, shouting, and shooting into the wooded area. Jake figured there had to be over a dozen men, all armed.

"Guess we found Felix's army."

Tan leaned forward for a better look. He pulled out a pair of G. & S. Merz twin-telescopes for a closer look. He handed them to Jake. "I see around twenty men. Thought I saw less." He looked at the twin-telescopes in his hand. "I've got to get me one of these. I can see things real close, better than that one-eye telescope I got. I can see with two eyes. Amazing."

Tan smiled and took them back. "Jake, I think we're out gunned on this one."

CHAPTER SIXTY-FIVE

B Y THE TIME Jake and Tan arrived back at camp, they knew a fight was coming. Hopefully, the boys could put a plan together. Unless things changed, it all would happen in town. Jake feared for those in their homes. They'd have to hunker down, so they wouldn't get shot.

The light faded as they pulled into the small clearing. Jake held up his hand as a man knelt over the fire. He had a long grey ponytail, black hat, and a long coat draped on the ground like a cape. The newcomer stood.

They dismounted and pulled their guns.

Gun trained on the man's back. "Hands up, mister," Jake said.

The ponytail man turned around and Jake eased back the hammer. "I should put a bullet between your eyes."

"Hello, Preacher. It's been a long time." Gabriel Grant's voice sounded weak, weathered with a gravel, but unmistakable. Jake came face-to-face with his family's killer. Though he was older, he had a peppered grey beard, and still chewed on a cigar.

"Be careful, Jake," Tan warned.

Jake holstered his gun and slammed his fist into Gabriel's jaw. Gabriel dropped into a pile of leaves. Gabriel rolled away from the next punch and connected his own fist to Jake's ribs.

"I've been looking for you a long time, Grant." He threw another punch that landed against Gabriel's pointed jaw.

"That's enough, Jake." Not stopping, Jake continued punching before Tan pulled him off the elder businessman.

"Get off me, Tan!"

"I said, that's enough."

Gabriel rubbed his jaw before pulling himself up into a seated position. "Quite the right hook you've got, Preacher. I'm not here to cause trouble."

"What do you want, Grant?" Tan asked, gun trained on him.

"I'll tell you what he wants. He's here to lend a hand in our slaughter, just like all those years ago."

Tan pulled out a rope and tied Gabriel's hands to a tree.

"No need for the rope, Marshal. I'm not going anywhere."

Jake picked up Gabriel's gun, then paced for a few minutes. How was he to find Charlotte and make sure Gabriel didn't get away again?

"How did you find us?" Jake asked.

Gabriel smiled. "It took little guess work. I still have a few friends in town. But it's when I saw you walk out of Momma's; kind of gave it away. Used that to my advantage, followed you out here, and waited till you showed up."

The smile that crossed Gabriel's face was enough for Jake to put a bullet between his eyes. "What's your plan, Gabriel? Show up, kill me, take back Purgatory by using your crazy son to lure me to town, just so you can have Purgatory all to yourself?"

Gabriel said little, and Jake knew that's what he wanted. "What are you planning with Felix?"

Gabriel shook his head. "I have nothing to do with my son, Preacher. I'm here to collect my affairs and leave."

Grabbing his gun, Jake armed it and put it to Gabriel's temple. "I'm going to ask you once more before I put lead in that brain of yours. What are you planning with Felix? Where's Charlotte?"

To Jake, the only question he had was, why was Gabriel here? He stood up and walked over to Tan, who stood eerily quiet. "Any idea why he shows up now?"

"Can't say, Jake. Don't know what to think. If he wanted us dead, he'd have pulled a trigger the moment we arrived. I say we hear what he has to say."

Crunching his teeth, Jake had no intention of listening to his family's killer. Not now. Never. Jake walked over to Gabriel and buried the gun into the man's skull. Gabriel grabbed at his head in pain. Jake's hand arched downward again as Tan tried to snatch the gun out of his hand. Jake spun around with a right hook, which was stopped by the marshal's large hand.

"Stay out of this, Tan."

The marshal grabbed Jake by the shirt and shoved him hard, knocking him over. Jake went to stand as Tan cocked his gun, pointing it at his head. "Jake, I will not tell you again. Stand down, that's an order."

Jake sat up. "How dare you point your iron at me?"

Saying nothing, Bennington walked over and untied Gabriel before tossing him a bandana to clean up the gash. "If you're not involved with your son, why are you here, Gabriel? After all these years of hiding, why choose now to show up? You realize the Governor has a warrant on your head. Got every right to bring you in to account for your crimes."

The bleeding seemed to slow, and Gabriel shoved the cloth into his pocket. He picked up his hat and sat back down on a rock. "Ten years is a long time to carry around guilt. I'm not the same man I was in Purgatory. I've only arrived back in town. Just fetching a few belongings before heading back out." He sighed. "Thing is, after Moira died, I lost everything. I shut down and left for Colorado. Been there ever since."

Jake's head spun. "You lost everything? What about my family?"

"I felt awful for what happened to Sarah and Virginia. Preacher, I never meant for their deaths to happen. I deal with that every day I walk this earth. What I put you and your family through was unfair, and ruthless. I was wrong. I'm sorry, Jacob. I am."

Fire raced through Jake's head. His teeth popped against the grinding. With clenched fists, he stood, walked over, then pulled Gabriel up to his feet. "You're sorry? For what, ruining my life? Killing my family? Did it ever occur to you I spared your life that day, simply because I feared I was becoming you? I didn't want that to be added to my conscience."

"I know that now. Moira's dead because of me. Your family is dead...because of me. I can't change what happened."

Jake spat in Gabriel's face as his throat burned. He shoved Gabriel harder against the tree. "Where's my Charlotte? Did you take her too?" He shoved Gabriel again and again as a deep groan filled his throat. "Where is she, you coward?"

Gabriel landed a knee to Jake's ribs then said, "I see your righteous indignation hasn't changed one bit, Preacher."

Jake released his grip. Staggering over to a fallen tree, he sat down and covered his eyes. No one said a word for what seemed an eternity. Several leaves fell from a tree and landed on his boot. As Jake studied its veins, he couldn't help but think about the deep-rooted veins of anger and resentment that lived in his heart. How do you forgive a man who took everything from you? He looked up at Gabriel, who sat with his own head in his hands, and wondered what all had happened in the past ten years.

"What happened to you, Gabriel?"

The elder businessman looked up. "I'm not proud of who I was ten years ago, left everything behind. I'm estranged from my son, who's gone on a killing rampage. I'm ashamed I raised such a brute of a boy. Told the judge to place the boy with someone who'd raise him better than I. Then, I left for Colorado.

"I didn't know what I'd find, or what I'd do. I had no money, so I lived off the land, taking what the farmers left behind to survive. Found an old mountain man named Jabez. Like me, he started with nothing, killed a man in Denver before finding religion and living off the land. So, I stayed with him until he died of typhoid three years ago."

Gabriel smiled at the memory. "Told me he prayed and asked that God would be good to him and keep him from evil. He didn't want to cause pain, not anymore. Not being someone who cared much for God or religion. After he died, I found his Bible. He had one marked passage from the first book of Chronicles. Guess someone named him after this Jabez in the Bible."

The sight of Gabriel smiling and talking kind about another man forced Jake to pause. How could a ruthless tycoon who ruined so many lives find peace, when all Jake had lived with was the guilt, shame, and anger of losing his family and hardening his heart against Gabriel? Jake stood up and walked to his saddle bag and pulled out the Bible Sarah had given him the day they were wed. He stared at the black leather for a moment—how he missed her. Jake looked up at Gabriel. After all these years looking for his family's killer, here he stood, a shell of a man. He gripped the Bible tight, then handed it to Gabriel. "What passage?"

A soft nod, and Gabriel opened the Bible to the spot he had mentioned. "Here it is. *'And Jabez called on the God of Israel, saying, oh that thou wouldst bless me indeed, and enlarge my coast, and that thine hand might be with me, and that thou wouldst keep me from evil, that it may not grieve me! And God granted him that which he requested.'*

"This passage became my life. Like the old mountain man, I didn't want to cause pain. I'd done so much of that already. I never expected for that old timer to teach me the one thing you showed me all those years ago. Anyone can find redemption. And now, I'm just trying to atone for my sins."

Tan said, "And you figured Purgatory was the place to start that redemption?"

"I suppose I am. I came to deal with my vile son. Once I knew you were in town, I came searching and—"

Four horses approached, and Jake knew the others had just returned. They dismounted and ground tied their animals. Freddy pulled out his tomahawk and walked right up to Gabriel. He raised his weapon and brought it down in a sharp arch.

"Franklin!" Jake yelled.

The blade stopped just at Gabriel's neck. Where the blade made contact, blood pooled against his shoulder.

"Put it away. He's here on his own volition."

Freddy placed the tomahawk into its sheath, then walked into the woods without a word.

CHAPTER SIXTY-SIX

J AKE FOLLOWED Freddy into the wooded area behind
camp. "Freddy, hold up." Not slowing down, Freddy
continued his push deeper into the woods. Tall pines rose
to meet the blue sky and Jake's boots crunched over pinecones,
fallen leaves, and several twigs snapped as he stopped his
friend with a hand on the shoulder.

"How can you stop me from killing the man who killed
your family...and Bill?"

"I won't argue against that sentiment. I can't stand the
sight of the man, but he might help us find Charlotte." A
conclusion he'd arrived at as Gabriel read the scriptures.

Freddy grabbed at his hair. "He killed Sarah, Jake! He
took Virginia from you."

Tears burned Jake's eyes. "Don't you think I know that? I
lost everything to that man. He took the most precious gift
that God had given me and burned them alive. He could have
stopped it all. I could have run in there and saved my family.
But he pinned me down and broke me." He shoved a finger
toward camp. "I've waited ten long years for this day, and now

I need him to find Charlotte. She's my future. I can't...no, I won't lose her too."

Freddy punched a tree before sitting at its base. "Jake, I've been with you every step of this journey. I'm not a religious man like you, but I've prayed that some god, somewhere would help you heal, find peace, and bring Gabriel to justice." He tossed a pinecone. "But when I saw him standing there, I thought of all those long years I've waited with you, so I pulled my tomahawk and was going to put an end to Gabriel Grant once and for all."

Jake plopped to the ground and patted his friend's knee. Freddy was a good man, and he had been there the past ten years—he'd given up everything to go with him to Cedar Grove. There was a steadfast quality about Freddy. He was faithful as the day was long and would take a bullet for him.

"I appreciate the gesture. But he will stand trial. I won't take that away from Sarah or Virginia. Tan knows what he's doing. I trust him." Standing, he said, "What did you and the Sheriff find in Purgatory?"

As they made their way back to camp, Freddy said, "I'm sorry, Jake. But if he makes one wrong move, I will kill him."

Jake frowned. "I can't let you do that. I understand, but I still need you. I can't bring Charlotte home without you by my side. You're my best friend, my right-hand man. I've trusted you with everything. Now I'm asking you to trust me on this. If you kill him, Tan will have no choice but to arrest you, or worse, hang you. I can't have that."

Freddy agreed. When they arrived back, they found Slim and Ted bantering about who could make the best steak and beans. Neither would concede to the other. Gabriel sat alone with his hands tied in front, while Roy and Tan talked over the fire.

"Boys," Jake said. Each conversation quieted. "I want to know what you all found in town."

Freddy started. "The town's practically deserted. I know you saw that too, Jake, but it seems far worse than before. Most folks have packed bags and are headed north toward Encampment. Several establishments have already pulled out. There's the bank, sheriff's office, general store, and the saloon. Lucky something or another. Fact is, Felix knows the town could easily be taken. Figure it'd be easy enough to make our stand at the Livery. I still own the place, have a young kid named Rowdy running the place. I told him to stay low and keep his head down."

Roy spoke up. "Went and talked with the Sheriff. Seems to be a reasonable man. Said he'd be willing to help. I noticed, and he confirmed it. Several gun hawks roaming around. My best guess, they're riding with Felix and his woman partner."

Both Tan and Jake told them what they found in the mines. Place was closed off and twenty men littered the area.

"It'll be hard going in. The place is a fortress. I think Freddy's right, we should make our stand in town," Jake said.

Twenty against six were terrible odds. Not knowing what would happen or where Felix held Charlotte worried him. The last thing Jake wanted was the good people of Purgatory being caught up in a gun fight they could avoid by clearing out of town.

"What about the folks who still live here?" Jake asked.

Roy shook his head. "Figure I'll help work on getting folks out of town before the shooting starts."

It was a good idea. He told Roy and Freddy to connect with the sheriff and get folks out of town. He needed no more blood on account of the Grants and their lust for revenge. Gabriel sat there, quiet and reserved. What would they do with him? They couldn't leave Gabriel alone, and not in a place where Felix could free him.

Maybe if they could use Gabriel to lure Felix out, he'd have time to find out who this Diamond Rose was and where they had Charlotte. Jake shoved his hands deep into pockets. He feared the worst and prayed for hope that she was still alive, but sending Gabriel out was a terrible thought. He pushed it aside.

"I know my opinion isn't worth much to you all, but I can get to Felix and end this before it begins," Gabriel said.

Jake spun on a heel. "How?"

"Let it be, Jacob. Grant is just trying to get you to free him and then he'll join his son's ranks," Freddy piped in.

Gabriel sat quietly. Jake looked at Freddy and placed a hand on his shoulder. "I want to hear what he thinks." Turning to Gabriel, "How can you help me get Charlotte back and bring your son to justice?"

"He fears me. I met the lad as I was rounding up my belongings. Told him to grow up and use that head of his for something good. He's more stubborn than I, so I threw him out. Coward, like the small impetuous offspring he is. But I can get close to him. Let me ride out to him and talk with him. He won't kill me."

Jake caught Tan's raised eyebrow. Guessed Gabriel had the same thought Jake did, and that worried him. Maybe they were more alike than he realized. What incentive would there be for Jake to untie and turn loose the man he'd hunted ten years for and now, only to lose him again?

"And what do you plan on doing, asking if Felix has Charlotte? You think he'll let you in on his little plan, after all you've done to him?"

Grant seemed to chew on that thought. "I told him years

ago that you were answerable for Moira's death. Never told my boy otherwise. He's carried his anger and offence toward you for ten years. For all he knows, I still hate you for killing Moira. Let me ride out to him. I can get close enough for him to trust me; tell him I know where you're hiding. I'll get him into Purgatory. You make your stand there."

Jake walked over and untied Gabriel. Maybe it was a mistake, but this one would be on him if it failed and Gabriel was lying. But he knew the man better than the others. Gabriel never lied, despite all the doubts. Freddy was saying something, but Jake kept his eyes locked on the older, greyer man before him. He untied the ropes from Gabriel's hands and then wrapped his own around his throat. One squeeze was all it would take to choke the life from the man who'd taken everything. He tightened his grip. Gabriel's eyes widened and his hand twitched.

Jake leaned in close and lowered his voice. "I want to kill you right now, but you listen to me; if you do anything other than bring back word of Charlotte's whereabouts or what Felix is planning, or you betray me, I will put a bullet between your eyes. Don't think for a second that I've forgiven you for what you've done. Don't think I ever will. But I'm going to reserve judgment and trust you for now."

After Jake released his grip, Gabriel coughed and collapsed to the ground, gasping for air.

Tan led a horse over to Gabriel and said, "Get on."

He did and tightened his black hat down. "Do I get my gun back?"

Jake looked at the pistol he'd taken and dumped out all but one bullet. "Use it, and make it count." Then he tossed the gun to Gabriel. And with a kick of his boot, Gabriel set off from camp toward the mines.

After Gabriel disappeared into the woods, Freddy said, "So much for telling me to not lay a finger on Grant."

Jake looked at his shaking hands. "I suppose he still crawls under my skin. Just a bit," he said, holding up his hand and pinching two fingers together.

CHAPTER SIXTY-SEVEN

MISSY CARTWRIGHT busied herself wiping down spilled beer from the counter. Today she wore her usual red and black-laced dress. Several passing men whistled her direction, which she ignored and asked what the newest customer desired. As Purgatory dried up from the locals, she relied on out-of-towners to bring in much needed business to keep the establishment going.

On this day, she wasn't expecting the man who stood at the batwing doors to come walking back into town. But there stood Gabriel Grant. The crow's feet around his eyes gave away the fact he was tired and weathered from a hard ten years of running from the law. His ponytail swished behind his head as he removed his hat and approached the counter.

"Missy, it's been a long time."

She scowled. "Not long enough."

"Now, is that any way to treat the man who gave you this job? Can't say I care for the name change from Missy's to Lucky Diamond." He glanced around the room. "Can't say there's enough luck in here to draw a man into gambling.

Don't even have any of those pretty women around. Man's got to have his way, ya know."

He slid a two-bit across the counter. "I'll have a beer."

Missy poured the drink and took the coin. "What do you want, Gabriel? My life's been better since you've left."

"Heard my boy's been in town causing a stink. Guessing most of these men are his."

"They are. And I'm just trying to keep them happy with some spirits, so they don't go causing any trouble." She continued wiping down the counter. "So, Mr. Grant, I'm going to ask you again, what do you want?"

He seemed to think about the question for a moment. It bothered her he was back in town. Notwithstanding, Jacob showing up. Seems as if the past didn't want to stay buried or gone. Gabriel sat there sipping on his beer, ignoring the question, which irritated Missy.

"Got to say, this is mighty excellent beer. Been a bit since I've had me a brew." He wiped his mustache. "I need you to get Felix a message for me. I need you to tell him to meet me out at the old cemetery. He'll know the one. Can you do that for me?"

"And why would I help you? He's hiding out at the mines. Why don't you ride out there and meet with him yourself?"

He snickered. "Don't take me for a fool, Missy. I step foot near those mines, I'm good as dead. Wouldn't surprise me if he's put a price on my head for…well, it doesn't matter why."

"I think you ran out of favors a long time ago."

Something twitched in his eye. She wasn't sure if it was anger, resentment, or something else. But what she saw chilled her to the bone. It'd been a long time since she felt like this, not since Judge Talbert knocked her around.

"How's that boy of yours? Elliot, isn't it?"

She tightened her grip around the towel. "Yes. Leave him out of this."

"I'm just asking how the lad is doing. Doesn't hurt to ask a question, now does it, Missy? 'Sides, I know Judge Talbert sired the boy, but I'm sure he's more like his momma than that deranged fat man. Heard someone killed him for ya." He threw some peanuts in his mouth and crunched down. "That true?"

She'd rather forget about the man who got her pregnant. Idiot deserved to die. "I had nothing to do with that."

A smile played against the man's lips. "Didn't say you did. Not going to say you didn't." He laughed again and swallowed the last of his beer, then slammed the mug down. "Tell you what. Do me this one favor, and we'll call it even. I won't say what I know and keep your dirty little secret. But I will say, I could have a small chat with your sheriff about who was behind the death of Judge Rex Talbert. Diamond Rose, isn't it?"

"I wouldn't know." Missy felt heat rise into her cheeks, and it took every ounce to not crawl over the counter and wipe the smug smile off Gabriel Grant's face. "What do you want me to do?"

"Tell one of his lackeys to send word that I'll be at the cemetery and for Felix to come alone. If I see anyone else, I walk, and he won't get what he wants."

"And what is that?"

"Jacob Creek."

CHAPTER SIXTY-EIGHT

JAKE WORRIED the old man wouldn't come through, but when Gabriel Grant rode back to camp, he figured the man had some sort of change. Ten years prior, Grant would have run.

"Didn't think you'd show," Jake said.

After dismounting, Gabriel took a drink from his canteen. "That little faith in my word?"

"No, I just don't trust you, that's all."

Tan asked, "So? What did you learn?"

Gabriel wiped his beard. "I'm meeting Felix out at the cemetery. Not sure when he'll show, figured I had enough time to come here and put together our next plan."

"Our next plan?" Jake asked. That was almost laughable.

"I need the Preacher to come with me. Felix needs to think that I'm still on his side. If I don't show up with you, he'll think I'm up to something. He knows I hate you enough that my only way into his camp is through you."

Jake laughed and tossed the pinecone he was holding. "Over my dead body."

Tan held up a hand. "It's not that bad of an idea. It might be the closest we can get to Felix. I'll ride out with you...Jake and I will keep out of sight. You'll tell Felix that Jake is tied up inside the schoolhouse. That's where I'll be as well."

"He's bound to have someone around. He's supposed to be coming alone, but doubt he will."

Jake shook his head. Stupidest plan he'd ever heard, and Tan was going to just go along with the man they'd hunted all these years? It's not that Jake didn't trust Gabriel, he didn't. Things could go very wrong, and Jake would be unarmed. That's a dangerous position to be put in as a gunslinger. No gun. You're dead if things go south.

All he wanted to do was put the shackles back on Grant's hands, ride for the jail, and put the man who killed his wife and daughter behind iron bars.

"How do you know he'll come?"

Gabriel smiled, and Jake knew he would not like the answer. He braced himself. "I asked Missy to send word to the mines."

It felt as if fire surged through his bones. Jake swung a fist into Gabriel's jaw. "How dare you bring Missy into this?"

Gabriel spit blood. He wiped his mouth. "I see we still have a soft spot for that woman. You realize she's the mother of Judge Talbert's bastard child?" He seemed to read Jake's facial expression, then swore. "Well I'll be. Seems as if you already knew that bit of news. We best get going. My son will show up, that much I know. Told him I was bringing you along."

"This better work, Grant. If my fiancé dies because of this idea of yours, I'll put a bullet in your brain." He looked over at Tan, who didn't correct him, so Jake figured the big man agreed with the sentiment.

Tan told the others to remain behind and to not make a move unless things went south in town. Then the three men rode back into Purgatory for Gabriel to meet with Felix.

AFTER ARRIVING, Gabriel stood by Moira's tombstone. He never saw what it looked like. The day after Moira died, he'd saddled his horse and headed for Colorado, leaving Felix and the town to figure out what to do with her body. Gave her a proper granite stone. It was fitting for a woman who he treated poorly. Now, all that was left of his former life was the estate, that sat deserted and abandoned.

Missy had better pull through. Gabriel prided himself on his wits and perception. If he were to show face at the mines, Felix would gun him down and end the conversation before it began. He stared at the single bullet that filled the chamber of his gun. One chance. One shot. It's all he had. The question he kept asking himself; where was Charlotte Jennings?

The name rang a bell, but he couldn't put a finger to where he'd heard her name before. It didn't matter. He'd do this one thing for the Preacher, atone for his sins, and head back out into the wilderness and live out his days as a ghost. It's what he'd been good at and something the man named Jabez told him, "It's better to live your life in service to others than to live a life full of regrets and missed opportunities."

He studied a scuff on his boot. Bending down, he spit and rubbed it clean. *Better.* A rustling of leaves caught his attention, and he looked up to see his son Felix walk into the clearing and toward the headstone of Moira Grant.

"I see you got my message."

Felix grinned and pulled his gun. "I have half a mind to

shoot ya where ya stand. Sending one of my own men to tell me when and where to be someplace? It's what yer always good at. Tell'n people what to do. How to think and act." He looked down at the headstone. "I figured you couldn't stay away without stopping by this place of sour memories."

"Pay your respects, boy. She deserves that much."

They stood in silence for a few minutes before Felix spoke. "So, tell me old man, what was so important you needed me alone?"

"Got word you're planning on taking down the Preacher. I want in."

Felix laughed. "You know, I was just thinking that you didn't care about him anymore. You vanished for ten years only to show up just when I'm about to squeeze the life from his veins."

"He killed your momma, boy. It's only right we avenge her death, together, as father and son." He placed a hand on Felix's arm.

Felix wrenched away and leveled his gun. "Do that again, I'll shoot ya. Not your boy anymore. But I already have a plan. Took his fiancé and now I'm biding my time before I move in on his mother and take everything he loves."

Gabriel folded his arms. "I see. Guess you just wait. But I know where he's camping out at. There are five of them. But, if we work together, we can out gun and out match them. How many men do you have?"

"Tell me where?"

Gabriel grinned. "Not before you call off your man behind me—"

Before Felix could answer, his face whitened as Gabriel spun on his heel and fired into the chest of some young gun hawk, dropping him dead.

"Never mind, I'll take care of your man for you." Gabriel grabbed at his son's throat and squeezed. "Pull a stunt like that again, I'll kill you myself."

He let go as Felix grappled for air. "I hate you!"

"Now, now. Let's not be rash. Show me what you're planning."

The boy he once knew crawled back into Felix's eyes and Gabriel smiled, knowing that he was a boy trying to fill a man's shoe. Now Gabriel had the upper hand. He knew where Jacob was, and Felix wanted that information.

CHAPTER SIXTY-NINE

J AKE FOCUSED his attention out of the schoolhouse window. Gabriel and Felix were busy talking about what to do with him, no doubt. At once, several thoughts flittered through his mind.

What could they be talking about? Was this all one giant elaborate trick, just to get even with Jake? Vengeance, perhaps?

Nothing seemed okay about this scenario. Tan stood at the teacher's desk, hand on his gun. His eyes fixed, and Jake knew the look well. He'd seen it frequently and let's just say things never worked out well for the bad guy. They always ended up in a pine box.

Virginia's doll sat beneath its glass dome. How he wished for just a moment to pick up the doll, escape out the back of the building to a life away from all of this. Jake walked up to the case and placed his hands on the dome to lift. That's when he heard the gunshot.

They both ran toward the window and peered out and saw a man lying in a pool of blood.

"One of Felix's?" Tan asked.

Jake shook his head. "Don't know. Looks like Gabriel did us a favor."

The father and son duo were arguing. Voices raised, and Jake wondered if Felix would pull the trigger and kill his old man. If that happened, Charlotte was good as dead. They'd never find her. This was his last shot at knowing where she was.

Jake caught himself holding his breath. Exhaling, he saw Felix had holstered his gun, and they began walking toward the building.

"It's time, Jake."

Tan grabbed his arms and cinched a rope around his wrists.

"Hit me."

"What?"

Jake lifted his chin. "Hit me, good and hard. Make it look as if I lost a fistfight."

His friend didn't hesitate. And it hurt. The big man's fist slammed into Jake's face. He felt the skin split near his eye.

"Again."

"I won't hit you again."

"One more time."

Tan's fist socked him across the jaw, and a loud crunch echoed through his skull. The blood ran warm in his mouth and he spit it out along with his tooth.

"Get out of here."

"We can take both Felix and Gabriel."

"I need to find Charlotte. Go! Get out of here, Tan."

Tan said he was sorry for hitting him so hard, then exited out the side door by the teacher's desk as Felix and Gabriel Grant walked through the door. It didn't take long before

Gabriel saw the bruising on Jake's face and the bloody tooth on the ground.

Then Gabriel Grant smiled. "See, I told you I had the Preacher."

Felix was practically jumping out of his skin. By the time he walked up to Jake, he was holding a large Bowie knife—tossing it back and forth. Flip, flop. It passed with ease from one hand to the next. A child-like grin crossed his face as if it were Christmas Day.

Jake swallowed hard. This was a terrible idea. Never had he seen such evil inside a man's soul than what he saw crawling beneath the surface of Felix's dark eyes.

"Howdy, Preacher. Guess this is a bad day for ya."

He held the blade to Jake's neck, and the razor edge burned into his skin. A small trickle of blood snaked down his neck and soaked into the collar. Felix's bird-like head twisted to the side, and he smiled. It wasn't a friendly smile. It was the evilest smile Jake had ever seen. Something from the pit of Hades.

"Wooeee! I kind of want to gut ya like I did that Marshall from Fillmore. S'pose you didn't know him?"

"His name was Marshal Alan Drake. You murdered him in cold blood." Jake spat more blood. Why'd he let Tan hit him again? Oh, yes, to make this look real. He eyed Gabriel, who just stood there. It was time to make a move. But the old tycoon didn't do a darn thing.

"Gabriel!" Jake was pleading, trying to not sound like he was begging. And yet he was begging. Begging to make sure his enemy wouldn't do an about-face. You know, the enemy of my enemy is my friend. Sure sounded good, but he wasn't so sure now.

Gabriel Grant did a slow walk up to Jake, knelt down, and

grabbed a hold of his shirt. In one forceful yank, he pulled Jake to his feet. Leaned in close enough for him to feel the hot tobacco breath leeching from his mouth. "I've been waiting a very long time for this day. Because of you, Moira is dead. Because of you, I'm a pariah in this town. Your worthless, self-righteous indignation is enough for me to make you suffer for all you've caused me to lose."

Jake wondered how much of this was part of the plan, or if Gabriel going to kill him. Maybe death wouldn't be so bad. He'd see Sarah and Virginia again.

"I. Hate. You. Jacob Creek." Each word its own verbal punch. And for a moment he wondered if Gabriel broke rank and was about to do the one thing he vowed all those years ago; kill Jacob Creek.

Gabriel's fist slammed down hard into Jake's chest. The wind knocked out of his lungs, and Jake collapsed, gasping for air. "This wasn't the plan."

Felix looked up. "Plan? Are you planning on sell'n me out? Kill me off? You in bed with the Preacher?"

"I may have my quarrel with you, son, but we have a common enemy in this man." Gabriel kicked Jake in the side, hard, and something snapped.

Jake screamed. The pain ricocheted like a bullet off a rock, reverberating to his skull. Grabbing at his side, he was certain a rib broke. This was the second time the tycoon broke one of his ribs. Where was Tan? This wasn't good. "Where's Charlotte?" Each word and breath sent waves of sharp pain through his body. Yep, it was a rib.

Gabriel pulled Jake up to his feet. "Felix, tell the man where his dear Charlotte is?"

Felix was giddy. Slipped the knife back into the belt.

"Don't worry. I've taken care of her. She's in a better place now."

It was like a fist slammed into his heart and it hurt more than the broken rib. Were they too late? Did Felix kill Charlotte? Hot tears flooded his eyes and dribbled down his cheeks. "What did you do?" he bit through the pain.

Felix tilted his head again, still looking ever so bird-like. "Why, I do believe..." He pulled out the ring Jake had given Charlotte, which hung on a gold chain around Felix's neck. "This used to be on her finger. But it came off real easy-like when I chopped off her dainty little fingers."

Bile rose in his throat. "What did you do?" he gritted through pain and teeth.

"Kind of like little sausages." He pulled out his knife and chopped the air. "They just plopped off with little effort. Plop, plop, plop." A sick cackling laugh ripped the air.

"Monster!"

Felix slapped Jake hard across the face. "Daddy, let's have some fun!" He snapped his fingers and four men entered the room and dragged him away.

Jake yelled back at Gabriel standing there. "I never should have trusted you. You will regret this! I am a United States Marshal," to Felix, "I'll kill you! You sonofa—"

"Shut him up!" Felix yelled.

A heavy fist slammed into his skull and everything went black.

CHAPTER SEVENTY

COLD AND DAMP.
         Water dripping.
Never stopping.
Always constant.

Thick darkness tried to pull him deeper into sleep. Desperately trying to shake it off, Jake's head throbbed with a massive headache. Whoever hit him in the head did so hard and with purpose. Having no clue how long he'd been out, one thing he pieced together, he sat in what appeared to be a cave of sorts. The continual dripping of water off his brow forced him to reposition to avoid its annoyance. He tried to move his hands, and the burn of a cord bit into his wrists. Someone tied him down. Silence surrounded him, despite the incessant dripping.

Someone would be back soon. With his hands tied behind his back, Jake had no way to defend himself if someone tortured him. He tried to feel for his gun, but found they'd removed the holster. Made sense. No way Felix or Gabriel Grant would allow him to keep his side-iron.

Why he allowed himself to get into these situations evaded

him. Tan would be looking for him or mounting a search party. He never should have trusted Gabriel to help subdue Felix and then bring Gabriel in himself, nor allowed them to escape with him in tow.

Little light shown into the cave he was in and he realized they'd taken him to the mines. He could smell a campfire burning just outside the mouth of the cave. Trying to not make a sound, he felt along the ground for anything to cut the rope securing his wrists.

His boot scraped the ground as he leaned backward, trying to finger a stone he'd felt with his fingertips. It was just a little…stretching out…reaching…he squeezed it between two knuckles, then rotated it into his fingers. It wasn't the sharpest stone, but it would work. He strained against the ropes, pulling them as tight as possible, and with his thumb and index finger he worked the stone back and forth until the rope frayed.

This was good.

One question lingered in his mind, why did they take Charlotte? Of all people, how did Felix and Gabriel know Charlotte was connected to Jake? The thought rattled around like a woodpecker pecking away at a tree, looking for grubs.

The note from Diamond Rose bothered him.

I know who you are. You're hiding behind a mask; a lie. You're trying to live another life, but you know who you are. If you want to see Charlotte again, you will find me where it all began.

He understood that to be Purgatory. Seemed right, considering this is where he found Felix. But who was Diamond?

I'll be waiting for you, Jacob Creek.

Who was waiting? Was it Diamond? Of course, it was—couldn't be Felix—but who was Diamond?

The image of Virginia's doll flooded his mind. How he missed her. He'd never see her again. Never imagined it would be possible, but if he died here, heaven awaited, with Virginia and Sarah waiting to greet him. Then there's everyone he left behind in Purgatory…

A shadow graced the cave's entrance, and Jake strained his eyes to focus on its silhouette.

"It didn't have to go this far, Jacob."

Gabriel Grant.

Jake said nothing.

"What, no snarky comeback? No screaming at me for some terrible wrong I've committed against you?"

Jake pressed against the wall for leverage to stand. He almost lost the rock. It teetered against his palm and the wall. He plopped it back into his hand and continued working on the rope.

The two men came face to face, and Jake could smell the stale tobacco on Grant's breath. "We had a deal."

A snicker. "A deal? Remember, I'm the one who sought you out. I'm the one who told you I could get close to my son. I also remember saying that you had to trust me."

Jake spit. "You're saying this is all part of the plan? What happened to apprehending Felix back at the cemetery?" He thought of Tan. "What about Bennington?"

Gabriel seemed to think about that for a moment. "I'm sure, they left him alive. My son gave me word the Marshal wouldn't be harmed…too badly."

TAN BENNINGTON RODE as fast as he could back to camp. The swelling on his face ached with each pounding of his horse's hooves. Things had gone wrong, and he reeled from thinking that Gabriel Grant had talked him into thinking they could trust him.

And maybe they still could. But one thing was certain, four bad *hombres* ambushed him after exiting out the back door of the schoolhouse. They clobbered him over the head the moment he stepped through the door.

His mistake for not being ready.

He should have been.

They overpowered him. He had tried to pull his gun, but one man pinned Tan's hand to the ground with a boot. Then they pounded his skull until everything went black.

As he approached camp, smoke filled the air from a fire as Theodore busied himself cooking something in a pot. *Sorry, Ted, we won't be eating tonight.*

"Boys, we have a problem," he said, pulling up and dismounting.

Freddy looked up from twiddling with a stick. "What's up, Marshal?"

"Jake's in trouble. The Grants have taken him."

Ted quit cooking. Slim stopped whatever he was up to and they all said, "What?"

"How'd that happen? I should have been there, Tan," Freddy hollered. He tossed the stick and stood.

"I don't need a lecture, Freddy. I know we were in over our heads, but I took the risk and—"

"It didn't pan out, did it?"

Slim asked, "So, what's our next move, *Señor?*"

"I should have taken care of Gabriel the moment I laid eyes on him. I didn't because of Jake...Now, I wish I would have put my hatchet deep into the man's neck."

"That's enough, Freddy!"

Freddy pulled his gun and aimed it at Tan.

Tan drew his own. "Freddy, I will shoot you. Now put that away and let me think."

There wasn't a choice. They had to go in, guns blazing at the Purgatory Mines. Freddy could become a problem.

"Freddy, I need you," he said. "I need all of you." He turned to Theodore and said, "Put out the fire. We're not eating tonight. Let's go get Sheriff Faulkner and ride for the mines."

———

JAKE DIDN'T QUITE KNOW what to say. Everything for ten long years has led to this moment. The only problem, they tied him up in a cave with no gun. If only he could keep cutting the rope without moving his shoulders too much.

"So, tell me. What are you planning, Gabriel? If you're going to kill me, get it over with. Let me die so I can join my family."

The rock continued its fraying, and Jake felt the warm trickle of blood soak into the rope.

Gabriel yanked his gun out and pulled back the hammer.

"Go ahead, shoot me!" Jake puffed out his chest as one strand of the rope broke free. He could move his wrist.

Gabriel moved closer and aimed the gun. His arm extended to its full length.

Who took Charlotte? Who knew about her? Who did he tell?

"You've been wanting to kill me since the day we met." Jake screamed the next, "Now, SHOOT ME!"

Gabriel screamed something unintelligible.

Diamond wrote, *I know who you are.*

A thought chambered like a fresh bullet. It rotated in the cylinder of his mind like a hammer being cocked.

I'll be waiting for you, Jacob Creek.

Another small snap of the rope and Jake, in that moment, knew who took Charlotte.

His heart sank.

"Wait!"

Gabriel pulled the trigger.

CHAPTER SEVENTY-ONE

JOANNA SAT in her rocker worried about her son. The message from the dying boy the other day bothered her. She'd never seen a bloodied man die before. They'd dragged the poor lad behind a horse. A terrible way to go. Though her husband Leonard died by Gabriel Grant's hand sixteen years prior, that wound never seemed to heal. Although she knew full well God was in control, she still couldn't get over how vile and sinful man could become.

Yet, despite all her frustrations for Jacob's lack of visits, she also understood that Purgatory held deep hurts and he was a bitter man, trying desperately to forget and leave it all behind. What her son never understood, your past always comes back if you don't deal with it properly.

She leaned back and sipped on some tea. A little honey and milk smoothed the hay-like taste and made it something enjoyable. Tears slipped from her eyes as she remembered the lives lost in Felix's attack on the Purgatory mines. She lost a lot of good friends and her home was quiet. Those left alive made their way to Encampment to take up residence. The town of Purgatory was no longer the bustling boom town it once was.

"Lord, I don't know what's happening. A lot has changed in the years since Leonard died. My son has left me. My beloved miners are dead. I'm all alone. I need wisdom on what I do next.

"Please keep my Jacob safe. I have this terrible feeling in my soul that something awful is happening. I can only pray that your will be done on earth as it is completed in heaven."

A song filled her heart, and she sang. "Amazing grace, how sweet the sound. That saved a wretch like me—"

A stiff knock at the front door cut Joanna's song short. She set down her cup to answer the door. Her eyes widened as she opened the door.

The woman before her wore man britches, a cowboy hat, and a gun in her gloved hand.

"It's you!" Joanna said.

She stepped through the door and shut it. "Hello, Momma. I hope I'm not interrupting your prayer time."

IT ALL HAPPENED SO FAST.

Only a few quick breaths are all it took to piece together who was behind the murder of Judge Talbert, Charlotte's kidnapping, and who was running the show—it certainly wasn't Felix Grant.

But when Gabriel pulled the trigger, the wall behind his neck shattered and pieces of debris peppered his shoulder and neck, that's when the final puzzle pieces fell into place.

He knew who Diamond Rose was. How had he not seen it before?

Gabriel holstered his gun. "I can't, Preacher. I've changed. I know you don't trust me, but I can't do this anymore. Jabez wouldn't want me to bed you down, and I should let bygones be bygones. It's all in the past. Moira's dead. My son's worse than I thought. I have to live with that."

Jake was flabbergasted. Words escaped him and he knew someone would race through the cave entrance soon with barking irons in hand. "We have to go."

Gabriel pulled a knife from his belt and sliced the remaining rope. "I see you've been busy," he said, referencing the bloodied wrists.

Looking each wrist over, Jake realized they weren't too bad —hurt like heck, but he'd be fine—just several minor scrapes. "Got a plan?"

Gabriel pulled his gun and handed it to Jake. "You're better with a six-shooter than me. Take it."

Two of Felix's men walked through the cave entrance.

"Howdy, boys," Jake said, and raised the gun to fire.

DIAMOND ROSE SHOVED Momma through the door of the dilapidated Grant Estate. This was the perfect place for everything to go down. It's where Moira died. It's where Gabriel lived. It's where Felix discovered his hatred for Jacob Creek.

This is where it would all end. It was so perfect, and that Jacob hadn't seen what was so obvious was even more delicious. Countless talks, hugs, and he was none the wiser.

She noticed that Momma tried to wriggle her wrists, and each time she tried, the rope would only tighten. Diamond made sure of that.

"Why are you doing this? What do I have to do with any of this?" Momma asked.

"Why, your family and the Grant family have been like a cancer to this town. Time to cut it out and kill it."

If Felix played his part right, he'd lure Jacob here, to this place, where it all began—or ended. She wasn't sure. Kinda like a big circle.

Felix could get his revenge on Jacob, and she'd get her revenge on Gabriel Grant. It was all Grant's fault. He was the one who started the whole war. If he hadn't come to Purgatory, gotten in bed with Judge Talbert, none of this would have happened. But his greed and carelessness resulted in death—the death of her late husband, Jamison. Murdered by Grant, covered up by Talbert. And Jacob was not as innocent as he claimed to be for all these years.

If it weren't for Jacob's desire for vengeance, for what Gabriel had done, he could have lived out his days in peace. It was an accident that Moira died. It wasn't his fault. Well, Diamond wasn't so sure. And look at all that had transpired. She just needed the perfect scenario. When Felix started robbing banks, it provided the perfect scenario. And that's when she approached him in Sunrise six months prior.

"Well, I'll let you two gals get acquainted. I suppose you've not met."

That's all Diamond said.

And then she left Momma alone.

CHAPTER SEVENTY-TWO

BY THE TIME the two cowboys waltzed into the cave, they didn't know what hit them until the first dropped dead to a bullet in the head. Jake said a quick prayer for shooting before being shot at, but figured God would give him grace—considering the predicament they were in. Never in his wildest dreams did he figure Gabriel Grant would keep his word. In Jake's mind, he had a knack for being dishonest in his dealings.

The second *hombre*, after watching his friend die, opened fire. They ducked for cover. Gabriel, armed only with a knife, found cover behind an old mining cart.

Jake found cover behind a support beam. He checked the gun and found four bullets remaining.

"Do you see him, Jake?"

Boots crunched as Jake listened. "I hear you breathing, Callihan. Felix will pay me well if I shoot ya dead."

Jake hunkered down. A few more steps. "That right? I don't suppose that he wants to gut me himself. Leave it to you to take care of me?"

He looked over at Gabriel, who nodded in understanding. The *hombre* was moving closer and Jake knew Gabriel could take him down.

Two more men entered the cave. One knelt down. "Hey, what's going on?"

The *hombre* hollered back, "Callihan is trapped like a rat. That old feller's with him."

A little closer.

Gabriel made his move.

Jake stood.

"There you are, cornered like a ra—" He never finished the thought. The words sounded like a rush of air as he collapsed with a knife in his back.

Jake fired toward the cave entrance as Gabriel reached for the dead man's gun. He spun and fired.

"Callihan's got a gun!" One yelled as he ran out. "Kidd! Callihan's got a gun!"

The cave filled with men.

"Grant, we've got to get out of here."

Bullets pinged off the rock and thudded into wooden beams. Jake had three bullets left. He took the closest man. His gun barked, fire illuminating the dark cave. He saw two men closing ranks on Gabriel. "To your left!"

Gabriel saw them and fired, hitting one man in the chest. He screamed in pain. "He got my belly! I'm going to die!"

The second man fired, missing Gabriel. Jake fired and took out the assailant's eye.

"You alright?"

Grant nodded. "Come on. I know a way out the back."

Jake had one shot left. Better make it count. He stuck the gun into his belt. "Show me."

TAN, Freddy, Slim, Theodore, and Sheriff Ben Faulkner arrived at the mines. Gunfire rose over the hill, and Tan knew someone had started something. Dusk was already creating shadows, which would make seeing difficult. But gunfire was both good and bad.

"Sheriff. What do you make of it?"

"My guess, someone's picked a fight they intend to lose."

Tan's thought exactly. If Jake got a gun, he wouldn't stand a chance against Felix's army of men. Yesterday, they found twenty men milling around the mines. Jake couldn't handle that many alone. Heck, it'd be hard with just the five of them without Jake.

"What do you think we should do, Marshal?" the Sheriff asked.

Tan looked at each of the men. They were good men, friends, and he'd hate to lose any of them. "First, we find Jake and Charlotte. Get Jake another gun. He's our best chance to survive this fight. I know each of you are fine men, but Jake is a gunfighter. Second, we take both Gabriel and Felix Grant alive. I want them both to stand trial. The Governor has made that abundantly clear."

They each pulled out their guns. Tan grabbed his Henry; the Sheriff, his Remington.

"Aim straight and true, boys," The Sheriff said.

Freddy pulled his Tomahawk. "Let's bring our boy home and keep Charlotte safe."

At once the three friends, one Marshal, and one Sheriff, descended the hillside into chaos. Tan found one man who pulled his gun upon first glance at the intruding party, and fired. He didn't stand a chance as his chest opened.

Several men nearing the mine entrance stopped at the sound of gunfire. They turned, ducked for cover, and opened fire at the five.

The Sheriff and Slim both fired their weapons into one man, dropping him. Gunsmoke filled the dank air as fire belched out of several guns. Tan dismounted and found cover behind a stack of crates. "Freddy, behind you!"

Freddy turned as a man came barreling down on him. He whipped his arm back and threw his tomahawk. It made a sickening thud as it landed deep in the man's shoulder. He screamed that he'd kill Freddy, but it was no use. His arm was useless.

"Thanks," he said, then joined Tan behind the crates.

Several bullets slammed into the wooden boxes before Tan realized what they were hiding behind. Not good. "Move!"

The two men ducked for cover behind a boulder as the boxes exploded in a blaze of hellfire. Dirt, wood, and other debris rained down. Looked like it killed a couple of cowboys.

"You okay?"

Freddy nodded. "That was close."

CHAPTER SEVENTY-THREE

J AKE HEARD the explosion as they exited the cave. Fire and smoke rolled up the side of the mountain, and he wondered if Tan and the boys found him. As he stood, a gun pressed into his neck.

"Hello, Preacher."

By the time Gabriel exited, he stopped at the sight of Felix holding a gun to Jake's head.

"Let him go, Felix."

Jake wasn't sure what to do. He was in a lousy position to get the gun out of his belt. One bullet left. But he couldn't kill Felix. Jake needed to know where Charlotte was.

"Where's Charlotte?" He gritted through teeth.

"Oh, the pretty lady I chopped to pieces a few days back?"

Fire raged through Jake's gut. If Felix killed Charlotte, he wouldn't need Jake alive. The outlaw's endgame was to get to Jake—make him suffer for killing Moira. He would want Jake to witness Charlotte's death, not just tell him about it.

"You're not running the show, are you Felix? You're not the gang leader," Jake said.

He heard Felix's teeth grind and pop. "I am the gang leader. I run this outfit. I kidnapped Charlotte. I killed her."

Gabriel finally spoke up. "You're just a poser, Felix. You always have been. Nothing more than a little boy trying to please his daddy. Guess what, son, I'm not impressed. You're impulsive and reckless."

Felix shoved Jake hard in the side. He gritted against the pain in his ribs. This was helpful. Getting Felix worked up would only force him to make a mistake. Throwing Jake off was the first. Now he had access to his gun.

"Felix, your father's right. Diamond's played you like a deck of cards his whole time."

He looked at Jake. Eyes wild, like a bird caught by a predator. "What are you talking about? You killed Mother! She's the only one who ever loved me," he said, aiming his gun at Jake.

"Preacher didn't kill your mother. It was my mistake that caused her death. Put down the gun, son."

"I'm not your son!" he squealed, twirling back toward his father. "Never was." Back to Jake. "What do you mean I've been played?"

Jake lifted his pistol. "Felix, put down the gun. Let's talk. No one else needs to die."

Felix aimed the gun at Gabriel again. "Tell me what you mean, Preacher. I'll shoot him dead."

Jake tossed the gun down and raised his hands. "Okay. I know you're just a pawn in all of this. The person running your outfit is Diamond Rose."

The outlaw's gun lowered. Jake got through.

"How do you know about her? You don't get to be bringing my girl into this."

"This whole time, Diamond's dusted your head with lies.

She took Charlotte. Left me a note and told me to come looking for her—not you."

His eyes widened. "She left you notes?"

"She's even claimed lives with a knife. Taken your calling card."

Gabriel kept his hands at a distance. "That's right, son. Put the gun down. Take us to Diamond Rose."

Felix's eyes darted back and forth between Gabriel and Jake. His eyes darkened and a low, guttural sound escaped his lips. He raised the gun.

Jake couldn't get to his gun.

Felix's gun barked fire and smoke!

Gabriel's eyes widened at a hole in his chest. "Jake—"

Jake dove for his gun and fired, but Felix was already down the slope and into the woods.

He set down the gun and sidled up to Gabriel. "Don't you die on me."

Gabriel Grant pulled at Jake's hands. "Go get your Charlotte back. I didn't mean for any of this. I know who took Charlotte. I'm really sorry for all of this."

"Nothing to be sorry about. You saved my life."

"I paid my price for taking your family from you.... I let... my ang...r get the best... of... me...sorry for...every—" His lip quivered as a tear escaped his eye.

"I think I know, but who took Charlotte, Gabriel?"

He pulled Jake's hand closer and whispered, "Don...t ...I made...my resti...tution with God. Find...er...at...m... p...ace, Ja...cob." Gabriel's hand slipped from his. His breathing stilled as the blood stopped pumping.

Gabriel Grant was dead.

CHAPTER SEVENTY-FOUR

J AKE SAT next to Gabriel's body for what seemed to be an eternity. He couldn't move, couldn't think. Felix was on the run, and he hadn't followed. These years came to an abrupt end. All the thoughts and vengeful desires to kill Gabriel with his bare hands seemed trivial and foolish considering the dead body lying on the ground. Sarah and Virginia's deaths were vindicated, and Jake didn't know how to feel.

His legs numbed from sitting cross-legged on the ground. The shooting subsided, and he wondered how many died in the initial explosion. Several voices echoed from the cave entrance. It almost sounded like Freddy and Tan calling out. He tried to speak, but the dry vocal cords screamed at him for attempting to reach his friends.

"Jacob!"

It was Freddy.

"Here," he managed.

His four friends and the town sheriff emerged from the cave. They looked like they'd been through quite an ordeal.

Felix had an army of men canvassing the area. *No sense sticking around much longer.*

"Jake, are you alright?" Tan asked. He noticed Gabriel's body. "Did you?"

It was an honest question, one that Jake was content to answer with, "No. Felix put him to bed."

Tan's large hand rested on his shoulder. "You okay?"

Jake nodded, then stood.

"Glad to see you got your revenge, Jake," said Freddy as he walked up, replacing his tomahawk. "Man deserved to die for all he's put you through."

"I didn't kill Grant. He saved my life. Was telling the truth all along. He was a changed man. Got right with God." Jake bowed his head. "Something I should have done a long time ago. Just...I didn't have the courage to face my demons."

"Where's Felix now?" the Sheriff asked.

Jake pointed toward the woods. "Took off after gunning down his father."

"We should go after him. I have our horses tied up at the other end of the ridge," Tan said. "It should be easy getting out of here, the dynamite took out more than half of his crew. They've all scattered by now."

"We should get going. Head back toward town. I'll get my deputy and we can fetch after Felix and what's left of his gang." The Sheriff turned to Jake. "Real sorry about your woman, in all."

Jake nodded. "Sheriff—"

"Call me Ben."

"Ben, need to tell you something about your deputy."

Ben stiffened. "Go on."

"As Grant and I were shooting our way out of the mine, I heard one of the other cowboys yell for a Kidd. Now, unless they were talking about somebody else, I reckon they were dealing with your deputy. Don't know, but makes sense to me, Sheriff."

The frail looking man bowed his head and shook it from side to side. "Guess that makes sense. Said he had some problem out of town. Figured he'd check in on some folks. We've been trying to make sense of what's happening at the mines and all those folks leaving town for Encampment. Your sheriff is helping with those evacuations." He threw his hat against the ground. "Boy's going to get himself killed. And I don't want to be the one pull'n the trigger."

Jake felt sorry for reporting the sour news, but the man had a right to know whether it was the case. The one thing he was sure about was who Diamond Rose was, and it was time to pay her a visit. After discussing the next course of action, they headed toward the horses, and he was glad that they brought him a horse.

After mounting his horse, Tan held up a gun belt. "Found this near the mine entrance. Figured you'd like to have your irons strapped down if you're going to take on Felix and this Diamond Rose."

Jake took the belt and strapped it on. He checked the guns and found them in working condition. He spun the chamber and inserted all six bullets. The one lesson his father taught him was to always leave a chamber empty, but today was different. He might need all six bullets.

It was time to head into Purgatory.

It was time to face Felix.

It was time to face the past.

If you want to see Charlotte again, you will find me where it all began.

"Ready?" he asked.

"Where are we going, Jake?" Tan asked.

"Purgatory."

Tan, Ben, Freddy, Theodore, and Slim all said they were ready. Then, with a kick, Jacob set off for Purgatory to rescue Charlotte.

CHAPTER SEVENTY-FIVE

THE TOWN of Purgatory seemed empty the day they arrived. It was a ghost town now. After these events, the town would dry up and Encampment would become the new bustling town. They even had their own police force—something new he'd heard they were trying. Part of Jake felt sorry for the town of Purgatory. He'd grown up here. So had Sarah. It's where they fell in love, brought Virginia to after he took over the church. But the town held a lot of horrible memories. Memories he'd like to stay buried and dead.

Gabriel Grant had gunned his father down in cold blood over the sum of two-thousand dollars. Then Gabriel set his sights on Jake and his family. His wife and daughter paid the ultimate price.

Passing the church, he thought about Virginia's doll. How he wanted to take it home, back to Cedar Grove with him. But first things first, finding Charlotte. He missed their conversations, the long rides through the countryside, and the enchanting picnics she'd prepare for them. He could see the

Lucky Diamond, his next stop. It was time to see an old friend.

"Boys, I want you to hole up in the Livery. Freddy, you still know that place in and out?"

"As long as they changed little, yes. We'll prepare for a fight there. Bound to see Felix show his face soon enough."

Tan spoke up. "I figure he's still got around half a dozen or more men with him, including the deputy."

Jake knew it was a matter of time before things blew up in town. He was glad they got most of the people out before the fight took to the streets and gunfire pelted like hail during a thunderstorm. After they departed for the Livery to prepare, Jake headed toward the Lucky Diamond to confront his friend. Only one thought rustled like leaves; *was Missy involved?*

He ground tied Tucker and waltzed up the steps. His spurs jangled against the rough wooden planks. He took a breath and stepped into the dank gambling room as the batwing doors flapped closed behind him. A few cowboys played what appeared to be poker at a nearby table.

Jake watched not their eyes, but their shoulders. Always watch the shoulder. A man could hide with his eyes, but the shoulder always twitched before a man reached for his gun.

"I don't want any trouble. Keep your hands on the cards, boys."

A burly looking man with a long beard that made his already fat face more round sat at the far end of the table, facing Jake. His shoulder twitched.

Jake flipped the thong off his gun and pulled. The gun barked in his hand and the man dropped backward with a heavy thud, gun still in the holster, dead hand on the hilt.

"You done an' kilt Billy!" a man with a skinny body, ruddy complexion, a pointed chin and a small mouth that twisted with a snarl, shouted. He threw back his chair and went for his gun.

Jake fired two rounds. One shattered the man's trigger finger and the other hit him square in the chest.

The other two men grappled for their hats and dropped their guns.

"Smart move, boys. Now, let me ask you a question."

"Anything, just don't bed us like ya did them," the one next to a burly and near toothless man said.

"Ya! We're just play'n cards is all."

Jake holstered his gun. "Where's Diamond Rose?"

The two looked at each other as something dark crossed their faces. One pulled his hat down and squeezed it tight against his chest. "She's not here, mister."

Jake looked around. Neither was Missy. She would have come out yelling about the gunfire. That could only mean one thing. It was a question he hated even asking. She had the motive to take out Gabriel Grant. She could have been the one to have taken Charlotte. She would remember her as the schoolteacher.

But did she know that Jake and Charlotte were together? She was upset that he abandoned her. He felt bad that she was alone, frustrated, and raising a lad all on her own. She didn't have a man to help her. Missy could have killed judge Talbert, but would she do something so evil?

He shook his head. She did not know he was seeing another woman until he came to Purgatory, looking for Charlotte.

If you want to see Charlotte again, you will find me where it all began.

Where was that?

Where did everything begin? Given Felix's involvement

and Gabriel coming out of his ghostly hiding, he figured it had everything to do with the late business tycoon.

For Jake, Gabriel confronted him at this very establishment—it was Missy's then, now it was The Lucky Diamond.

Diamond.

Rose.

If it wasn't Missy, the only other person…

The answer slammed into his chest hard and it was only then that Jake saw the two cowboys sitting there. He dismissed them with a wave, and they took off out the batwing doors. If they were Felix's men, they'd send word that Jake killed two of them.

You will find me where it all began.

Jake knew where. He should have always known. It should have been clear. Now he knew and his heart broke in half.

I'll be waiting for you…

It all began at the Grant Estate. That's where Charlotte was. That's where he was going next.

But first, he had to check in on Momma. Felix had said he was going to go after her and he needed to make sure she was protected and headed toward Encampment.

He bolted out the door as gunfire pelted the wood above his head.

CHAPTER SEVENTY-SIX

As JAKE EXITED the Lucky Diamond saloon, the awning above his head splintered with gunfire. He ducked for cover behind a water barrel. Tucker spooked the moment gunshots rang out and took off down the street. Jake pulled his .45 Colt revolver and put three more rounds into the cylinder. Gravel scraped under his boot as he tried peeking around the barrel.

Another shot popped a hole in the water barrel and a steady stream peed out. Jake hunkered down.

He pulled his leg up and unstrapped the spur tied to his boot. Using the leather straps, he tossed them into the air. Gunfire erupted again and Jake stood, located the ruddy looking man who'd just left the saloon, and using his palm he pelted him with four slugs.

Down the street he saw Tan run from the Livery Stable, firing his gun. Jake whistled and Tucker trotted up. He holstered his gun and grabbed the scattergun he'd brought. Opening the gun, he loaded two buckshots, then took toward the Livery.

He could hear gunfire and shouting. Several men encroached upon the Livery. They had pinned his friends. Freddy dashed from the building into the alleyway. He locked eyes with Jake and pointed toward where Tan had run.

Two cowboys were fast approaching Tan's location. They hadn't seen Jake yet, but by the time they did, he opened fire. The shotgun bucked hard against his shoulder while fire and smoke exploded from the first of two barrels. The man Jake shot was dead before he knew what happened. His friend whirled around, and Jake exhausted the second barrel, blowing a hole in the man's upper shoulder.

"Tan, you okay?"

The big man stood and holstered his gun. "You know I was about to get the drop on those boys, right?" he said, looking at the man who stopped writhing on the ground.

Jake smiled. "Sure, you did."

Gunfire had quieted and both Jake and Tan met up with Freddy in the alley.

"How many are left?" Jake asked.

"Not sure. Figure the two you just killed and the one I got just before leaving the Livery. Makes roughly five left."

"Six." Jake said. "Took out three of four down the street at the Lucky—" A glint of movement atop the bank caught his eye.

Slim walked out of the Livery. "*Señor,* that was *mucho divertido.*"

Jake pulled his gun. "Slim, get down!"

The man on the bank fired his rifle, and a hole formed in Slim's head. The gun slipped from his hand, and the bullets he held scattered across the ground. Every nerve in Jake's body went numb. He couldn't move as he watched his friend's knees slam into the gravel. Blood poured from the wound as he fell face first onto the ground.

A second shot rang out, hitting Freddy in the arm. He screamed in pain and ducked to the ground.

It took Jake what seemed to be an eternity to gather his composure. He turned and fired. The bullet hit the bank sign. Tan took the next shot, followed by Freddy, who was still on the ground, clutching his shoulder. They hit Felix's man, and he toppled onto the boardwalk below.

Turning back toward Slim, Jake knelt next to his friend. "I'm so sorry!"

"Jake, we've got to go. Felix's men are bound to be coming. We need to hunker down," Tan said.

"I'm not leaving Slim."

"Jacob. We have to go." Freddy rested his bloodied hand on Jake's arm. "He's gone. Nothing we can do. We'll mourn him later. Right now, we have to save Charlotte."

He continued to stare at his friend. They couldn't just leave Slim to bleed out on the street like that. The man deserved more respect. By the time they walked back into the Livery, the Sheriff and Ted Jefferies were talking about what to do next. Jake couldn't stand to lose any more of his friends. Without thinking too much, he told Ted he didn't want him to continue the fight.

Tan, Jake, and the Sheriff would take it from here. "I need you and Freddy to find Missy and her son, get them out of here. Head to Creek Ranch. Freddy knows the way. I don't want any more people I know to get shot or die. Let the law handle this."

Freddy was about to protest, but Jake stopped him. "I can't lose you. You're too valuable to me. If anything happens to me, I need you to run the CHR. You hear me?"

He nodded. "We'll find Missy."

Tan turned to Jake. "So, tell me, where are we headed?"

"We're going to Gabriel Grant's estate. That's where Felix and Diamond Rose are about to make their last stand. I don't suspect the other gun hawks will do much in town. It'll all happen there."

"Sheriff!" A voice cut through the quiet evening.

"Know who that is?"

Sheriff Ben Faulkner dusted off his pants. His boney hands holstered the gun. "It's my deputy, Joe Kidd."

"Be careful," Jake said.

"I may be old, but still fast with a six-shooter."

The four of them watched as the sheriff walked out of the Livery and into the dusty street. A man had to protect his own life at all costs. His deputy was about to make a mistake. Jake had heard rumors about Ben Faulkner's early years. He was a former gambler and gun hawk turned lawman. As a teen, Jake read some of the dime novels made about him. They all said he was fast as lightning with a gun. That's all he knew. But the old man had fire in his eyes, no denying that.

"Joe, I don't want to kill ya. But you're leaving me no choice. How'd you get messed up with these disreputable bunch of outlaws anyway?"

Kidd wasn't in the talking mood, and Jake worried the old lawman wouldn't be able to hold his own against a young man like Joe Kidd.

"I's got nothing to say to you, old man."

Jake watched the young deputy's shoulder. He could barely see in the darkening street. "I'm going out there. The sheriff is no match for Kidd."

Tan stopped him with a hand to the chest. "You know the

code. A man's got to protect his honor. Just like you did with
Dan Baley."

The big man was right. Jake didn't have to like it though.

Kidd's shoulder signaled toward his gun, and with blazing
speed, both he and the sheriff fired. Their guns sounded as
one. The fastest draw Jake had ever seen. The two men stag-
gered for a moment, and Jake wasn't sure who hit who or
who'd die.

Joe Kidd toppled backward with a thud.

"Ben," Jake said.

The old gunfighter sheriff turned, smiled, and said, "Well,
that was something. Nice to go out in a blaze of glory." His
body fell limp, spun, and he fell face first onto the street.

It was down to Tan and Jake to rescue Charlotte.

"Fool!" Freddy said. "He didn't have to die like that."

Jake agreed, but told Ted and Freddy to head out the
back. He told them Missy might be living out at the old Creek
Ranch. She always wanted to be close to Jake. That was as
close as she got before he left town all those years ago. With
that, Tan and Jake mounted their horses and took off toward
the edge of town. He had to find out if Momma made it out
or if his stubborn mother was lying low in her lodge.

CHAPTER SEVENTY-SEVEN

JOANNA SAT without saying much. The sky had darkened and the only light visible in the room was whatever the moon had provided. She knew the Lord would reunite her with Jacob and get her out of this mess. Not sure where she was, Joanna figured it was a large house and abandoned. To her recollection, and from Jacob's descriptions from years ago, it was Gabriel Grant's former estate.

The room wasn't large, but enough to hold a desk, two chairs, and a heating register. She'd never seen one of those before but figured that's what the coiled thing against the wall was. In the other chair, against the far window, sat a woman. The other woman cried. Her hair was dirty, matted, and her dress was torn. It looked as if she'd been here for a little while. Joanna tried speaking with her, but she hadn't uttered so much as a single word.

She tried again.

"Hello, I'm Joanna. Some people call me Momma." Maybe the second name might help her along.

The woman looked up. "Momma?"

Joanna didn't recognize her voice. "That's what folks around here call me."

"I know that name. My fiancé talks about his mother using that name."

That piqued her interest. "What's his name, dear?"

She cried, and Joanna wished she could untie her bound hands and place a loving arm around the poor soul and add some comfort to the dark room. She looked up and said, "His name is Jacob Callihan, ma'am. I'm sure he's looking for me right now. That awful woman took me from my home.... Why would she do this to me?" The woman sobbed again.

"There, there. It will be alright. I know who Jacob Callihan is. He's my son. And you must be Charlotte."

Charlotte looked up and sniffed at what appeared to be a smile. "You're that Momma?"

"I am, my dear. And by God's grace, my son will get us out of here." Joanna glanced over at the fireplace. Laying on the ground was a fire iron. "Now, let's see if you can help me get to that fire iron."

DISMOUNTING TUCKER, Jake bounded up the steps and into Momma's place. It was dark, no fire in the fireplace, and quiet. He ran down the hall into the kitchen to see if she was busy making her famous honey oat bread. No lantern was lit, the place was cold, Momma nowhere to be found.

"Momma, answer me if you can hear me."

Silence.

Jake nearly jumped from his skin as a hand landed on his arm. "Momma—"

It was Tan. "Sorry, Jake."

"He's gotten to her." Heat cascaded up his back and into his face. No way on earth could he lose his Momma. She meant too much to him and all these years of hardly a word washed over him. If only he'd been a better son. If only he'd been here, he could have taken out Felix and demanded to know where Charlotte was being held.

Jake caught himself from tipping by grabbing onto the table. "Let's go." He stood, walked back out, and mounted Tucker. "She's got to be at the Grant Estate. He wouldn't have taken her without having a plan."

Tan was already on his horse. "We'll get them back. You hear me, Jake? We'll get them back."

The two men kicked their horses and off they went toward Gabriel Grant's former home.

THE LAST TIME he'd been out this way was the night Moira Grant died. Jake was hell-bent on taking out Gabriel Grant. He had first stopped at Moira's second home and taken her hostage. Of course, he didn't intend to kill Gabriel, just make it seem as if he would do whatever to make Gabriel pay for killing Sarah and Virginia.

But Moira died because Jake let his anger and vengeance get inside his head. They fought over his gun that had fallen on the floor of Gabriel's study, and that's when the gun went off. It was too late, Moira laid in a pool of her own blood. That night, Jake made the choice to leave Purgatory and never look back. It was his fault that the tycoon's wife was dead. Nothing would change that. He let vengeance win out in the end. Now he was paying the price for that evening.

The evening air pebbled his skin as turned east out of

town. Tucker's hooves dug deep into the earth below and, even though he couldn't see because of the darkening sky, he could imagine dirt and dust flying behind him, creating a whirlwind dust storm. He ran his fingers across his gun belt and felt for each lead bullet jutting out from their leather restraints. Fifteen left, plus the twelve in his belt. Should be enough, not counting the five rounds still in his Henry repeating rifle.

The rise to Gabriel Grant's estate rose into view. Its dark brick was an obtrusive structure that blotted out the stars beginning their evening shine. He imagined that his wife and daughter were looking down upon him, wishing him luck and praying for his safety. Not that he believed the dead prayed, but it gave him some comfort in the brewing storm.

"I don't know what we're going to find up here, Jake. But know this, I've got your back. Have enough lead?"

"I just checked. I'm good. You?"

Tan appeared to be looking his belt and guns over, while trying not to drop them. "I'm good. There may be six or more men. Not sure how many this Diamond lady has with her either."

Jake had considered that fact. They could walk into a trap. But if Momma and Charlotte were there, he'd bring Revelation's pale horse, because death followed him. The thought made him shudder. *Time to focus.*

They had arrived. Jake held out his hand to slow Tan's approach. They both dismounted and Jake grabbed his rifle and levered a round into place.

"Let's go."

CHAPTER SEVENTY-EIGHT

EVERYTHING WAS QUIET. The only noise Jake could hear were crickets chirping their evening song. He checked his rifle again, didn't know why he'd just levered a round. They needed a plan. He wasn't sure what they were about to walk into and with the shadows of the night, it'd be even harder to make out who's who when the gunfire started.

Tan knelt next to him as they approached the horse stalls. "What are you thinking?"

"My guess is Felix will have men standing near the entrance to the home. So, best guess, we go in through the kitchen." He sat down. "Take off your spurs. We don't want to draw attention." He tugged at the leather straps and loosened his spurs. Peeling them off, he tossed them to the side.

"Ready?" Jake asked.

"Let's bring them home."

They crept forward. The only noise was the crickets and the slight crunch of gravel under their boots. Otherwise, he heard nothing, and that is what he wanted. Light filtered through the trees and Jake realized someone was in the kitchen. He held up a hand.

"I see it too."

A dark shadow passed in front of the window. They were outside. Jake sighted with his rifle. "Guess they will know we're here." And fired.

The night exploded with a clap and barrel fire lit the area. The man was no longer in front of the window. Shouting erupted and two men piled out the kitchen door.

"Who's shooting?" Silence. "Ivan's dead! Someone's out there." And then they returned fire.

Tan and Jake ducked out of the way as dirt pelted up from the ground. The quiet night turned into a shootout.

JOANNA HEARD the gunfire break out as she asked Charlotte to knock out the fire iron. Charlotte had wriggled her way over to the fireplace and flipped it off the mantle and near Joanna's chair. It took a few minutes to tip the chair over and she felt the iron bite into her wrist. Warm blood trickled out of a wound, but it was the only way to get rid of the restraints.

"I'm almost there," Joanna said.

Charlotte's eyes were wide as saucers with each gunshot. "You think that's Jake?"

"I'd bet my life on it. Jake rescues us." Snap! Success. Joanna was free from the cords binding her wrists. Now to help Charlotte get untied.

She checked her bleeding wrist. It wasn't bad, just scraped, nothing to worry about. "Come here, dear. Sit up so I can untie your cords."

Charlotte propped herself up with a shoulder and leaned

against the wall into a sitting position. Joanna felt bad for the girl. She hadn't asked for any of this, just the wrong place at the wrong time.

What bothered her the most was why their kidnapper waited until now to do something. Only the good Lord knew why this was happening and she'd do all the praying in the world to thank God if he were to get them out of this alive.

With the last of Charlotte's restraints untied, she rubbed her wrists. "Thank you, Momma. Thank you! I wasn't sure what was going to happen. I prayed God would spare my life so that I could see my Jacob again. I love him and he's out there right now risking his life for mine."

She sobbed, and Joanna wrapped her arms around her new friend. "There, there. God's got this. I've always believed the good Lord's word when it says, all things work together for the good. We have to trust him, dear. It's the only way to find true freedom and beat revenge."

Joanna stood. "Now, it's time for us to leave." She grabbed Charlotte's hand and twisted the doorknob. As she began opening the door, it flew open, throwing them back. A skinny bird-nosed man with a matted beard and pulled back pony stood there with a crooked smile.

"Now, where do you think you're going?"

JAKE TOSSED the rifle as he neared the kitchen entrance. They had dropped the two men who exited moments prior. Tan followed close behind. Jake un-holstered his Colt. No sense going in without being ready to shoot. His heart slammed against his ribs and he thought it might just pop out and land on the kitchen floor. Half expecting someone to shoot them at any moment, Jake eased back the hammer to calm his mind.

It didn't help.

Sweat dripped off his goatee as they crept forward. Movement just beyond the kitchen and into the hallway caught his eye. Jake motioned with his gun, and Tan leaned in toward the door.

The gun shot was so loud Jake almost dropped his gun. He tossed a small table and eased behind it.

Tan pressed against the far wall near where the shot came from. "You okay?"

"Fine."

Another shot and the bullet bit into the table, splintering the wood just above his head. That was close. Jake crawled on hands and knees around the table for a better angle.

The glint of a gun pierced the dark hallway. He raised his hand and squeezed the trigger as another bullet smacked the tile near his knees. He pressed behind the table again.

"I know that's you, Callihan!" the voice said.

"You realize, son, you're shooting at United States Marshals," Tan said. It wasn't a question.

Someone let out several expletives, followed by another shot. The door frame next to Tan splintered. Jake watched as the big man knelt and returned fire with two shots and their attacker screamed in pain.

"Drop your gun and we'll talk," Tan said.

Another curse.

"Guess they know we're here," Tan joked.

Jake smiled at his friend and stood, hoping to not get shot. The cooler door was open and Jake saw a bit of packing twine laying on the butcher's counter. He grabbed it. Time to tie up the bad guy.

They crept forward into the dark hallway. No one was shooting at them. That was good. The place smelled sour, almost putrid, like urine. The man had peed his pants and writhed in pain, cursing them and God. Jake took the rope and secured the man's hands. He grabbed the gun and slipped it behind his back.

"Felix will kill you both," he spat.

"Sure, he will." Tan slammed his large hand into the man's skull, knocking him out.

"Was that really necessary?"

He could just make out Tan's grin in the dim light. "Felt good."

"I'm sure." Jake stood and continued down the hall. They pressed against the wall for protection as they neared the grand staircase. A few lanterns lit the otherwise dark house and the memory of first arriving here to meet with Gabriel ten years prior flooded his mind. He confronted Grant after Felix kicked Virginia at school.

His teeth ground tight and popped as he walked down the hallway toward the home's entrance. The thought still shocked him. Gabriel saved his life. A heavy blanket of sorrow fell on his heart. He pushed the thought aside.

The grand staircase came into view and standing at the foot of the steps were Felix Grant and Momma. Jake's heart skipped a beat as Felix held a knife to her throat.

CHAPTER SEVENTY-NINE

J AKE FROZE at the sight of his mother with a knife to her throat. "This is between us, Felix, let my mother go."

Tan moved in next to Jake.

"That's far enough, Marshal Bennington. Drop your gun or I'll have my men shoot you."

On his left, two men entered the lighted landing, guns drawn and trained on Tan. Where did the bad *hombres* come from? They had just been down that way. His friend dropped the gun with a clatter and held his hands up. "What do you want, Felix?"

Gabriel Grant's son pressed the knife a little closer to Momma's throat. "Tell the Marshal to back off or I'll cut her."

Jake looked at his friend. "Go with them. I've got this."

Tan protested.

"TAN! Do it!"

He watched as they grabbed Tan and smacked him over the head and dragged his heavy body down the hall, back toward the kitchen. Jake couldn't imagine how heavy his

362

friend must be and didn't feel bad by watching them struggle against Tan's weight.

He turned back to Felix. "Okay, they're gone. Let my mother go."

Felix grinned a thin smile that rippled the hair on Jake's neck. "Tell you what, why don't I tell you a brief story while you drop your gun."

Jake tightened his jaw as he lowered his weapon to the floor but felt the bulge of the second gun in his back.

"The day my mother died. You remember her, right? Moira? I's out in the woods. Father never let me play out there, but I snuck a kitchen knife. Real sharp like. I followed a little tiny rabbit." He giggled at the memory.

"After I grabbed it, I took the kitchen knife, and I cut its head off. Seemed fitting for a tiny thing. I pictured my father when I did it."

Disgusting was the only thought Jake had. Felix had lost his mind, and he felt bad for the little boy who'd endured his father's wrath that turned him into this monster. "What's this have to do with me?"

A low growl filled the staircase and Felix's eyes went wild, like a rabid animal.

Careful, Jake.

"I's don't want no talking from you! I'll cut her real good!"

For the first time, Momma cried. The strongest woman he'd ever known. Jake's heart shattered into a thousand pieces.

Jake raised his hands a little higher.

"That's better." As Felix talked, Jake crept his hand toward his belt for quick access to his gun. "I heard the head mistress calling me to come home. Father needed to see me. When I came home, there Mother was, lying in her own blood."

"Is this what it's all about, Felix? You are getting revenge on me for your mother's death?"

Felix eased the knife away from Momma's neck. "She's dead because you killed her."

Jake kept his hand in place, avoiding any shoulder movement. "I have a story for you as well."

"I don't want to hear anything you got to say."

"I didn't kill your mother—"

"LIAR!" Distracted, Felix pointed the blade toward Jake. Something wild filled his eyes with fright.

"Your father said it best before you killed him. He shot your mother by mistake. We fought for the gun and it went off."

DIAMOND ROSE, at least that's how she referred to herself, stood in Gabriel Grant's study, then paced, and waited. She hoped Felix would take care of Jacob so that she wouldn't have to confront him. She figured that one of three men would walk through the door. Felix, Gabriel, or Jacob. What bothered her, Felix avoided the question of what happened to Gabriel after the mine incident. That could pose to be a problem. No worry though. After Felix got his revenge on the pathetic town of Purgatory, she'd kill him, ending the Grant family dynasty.

So, either way, it wouldn't matter.

"Why are you doing this to me? What did I ever do to you?"

Charlotte was starting to grate on Diamond's last nerve. She was the leverage needed to lure Jacob back to Purgatory to confront Felix. And she was using Felix to lure Gabriel out of hiding. Both worked. Now Charlotte wouldn't shut up.

She clicked her tongue. "Oh, shut up! If it weren't for Jacob, you'd already be dead. I have half a mind to slit your throat. But the good Lord knows that a Christian woman like me needs his blessing to do something so.... I don't know, permanent. I didn't want it to get this far, but Jacob needed a little push."

Tears filled Charlotte's eyes. "You think kidnapping me and Momma was going to do the trick? Jacob's already here."

"And probably dead, so I guess I don't need you any longer." Diamond raised her gun and aimed it at Charlotte's head. She would end this tonight by avenging her husband's death, and then she'd go back home. He was dead because of the Grants, and now, with all the gunfire, Jacob could be dead as well. Time to get rid of Charlotte.

"Goodbye, Charlotte. I guess all those cooking lessons won't do you any good."

Charlotte started sobbing. "*Please, Loretta, why are you doing this?*"

A single thought crashed over Loretta Lynn. This would be so much more fun. She holstered the gun and untied Charlotte. "Let's go, my dear. We must not keep your lover waiting."

As soon as she was up, Loretta pulled her gun and stuck it in Charlotte's back. "Move."

"Youlyingsonofa—" Felix suddenly turned, still holding Momma, and pointed his knife as someone just entered the hallway from Gabriel's study. "I's got this, Diamond!"

Jake pulled the gun.

"Hello, Loretta."

Jake had prayed with every ounce of his being that his gut inkling was wrong; that Loretta Lynn wasn't the mastermind behind all the death and destruction of lives over the past several months. It still made little sense. Jake thought she was a good Christian woman. One who not only loved God, had heart-to-heart conversations over the years with, but seemed incapable of such cruelty and murder.

"I have one question for you, Loretta. Why?"

She kept her gun trained on Charlotte. Jake froze but didn't lower his pistol "You of all people should know the answer to that question. The Grants. They're a cancer to this town. Just look at this place. Rotting, just like the town that's drying up."

Felix held Momma tighter. "I's thought we were in this together. You and me?"

Pointing her gun at Felix, she said, "Felix, dear, don't listen to him. We've got this. Jake doesn't stand a chance against both of us."

"She's been using you, Felix."

"Shut up!" he said and lowered the knife to Momma's stomach. "Drop the gun, Preacher, or Momma gets some lead in her belly."

He could see the pleading in both his mother and his beloved's eyes. There was no way he'd be able to take out both of them. He could try to take Felix, then reason with Loretta. Trying to understand where she was coming from. It eluded him.

"You okay?" He asked Charlotte.

She nodded through tears.

"Enough!" Loretta said. "Make a choice, Jake. It's your mother or Charlotte." She pressed the gun deeper into Charlotte's gut and pulled back the hammer.

CHAPTER EIGHTY

TAN TRIED to claw his way out of the heavy fog filling his mind. Did they have to clobber him over the head? That made twice in just a few hours. His head spun light and dizzy. If he had his gun, he'd shoot them both.

The two men, one named Guss and the other Lewis, at least that's what he figured from their conversation while they sat and played cards. Each had a drink and was dumb in the tongue from the spirits they were ingesting. Tan tried to stand by bracing himself against the clothing dryer. They hadn't noticed he was awake yet.

He felt for his gun and found the holster empty. That's right, he'd dropped it in the hallway when they took him.

Suddenly, his mind was alert. *Jake!* He left Jake to fend for himself. The two cowboys continued their cussing and drinking when Guss saw Tan stand upright. His chair flew back as he grappled for his gun, but before his fingers crawled around its grip, Tan was on him.

His fist collided with Guss' face and knocked him backward. By this time Lewis, that's who he guessed, was reaching for his gun. Tan pulled the gun from Guss' belt and fired. The man crumpled to the ground.

Guss launched toward the gun and fired. The bullet tore into Tan's shoulder and he didn't feel it leave the bone. Tan pulled the trigger and.45 caliber bullet punched into Guss' chest, forcing the man to stagger back a few feet, then collapse.

He tried lifting his arm as sharp pain exploded through his shoulder. The bullet might have lodged somewhere in the bone. His head spun light and dizzy again. He had to find the bullet and stop the bleeding somehow.

SEVERAL GUNSHOTS CAME from the kitchen's direction.

Felix grinned and laughed like a cackling crow. "Guess they took care of the Marshal."

"No one's coming for you, Jake," Loretta added.

"Jake, don't worry about me, son. I've lived a good life."

It was time to choose. How could he choose?

Momma.

Charlotte.

Tan was probably dead.

Lord, I need help.

Jake made his choice. The gun bit against his spine and he reached around, wrapped his fingers around the grip, yanked, and fired a single bullet. The gun bucked in his hand and the bullet pierced into Felix's shoulder.

Felix screamed in pain, then shoved the knife into Momma's side and she collapsed in a bloody mess. Jake turned the gun toward Loretta and pulled the trigger.

Click.

"Better luck next time," Loretta said. She pulled Charlotte down the hallway and back toward the study.

Felix went for the knife. Jake had to get Momma to safety. Dropping the gun, Jake dug his boots into the floor and launched into the air, tackling Felix to the ground. The knife slid out of reach.

"Momma, get back!"

The two rolled into the banister. Jake forced a finger into the bullet wound and Felix yelped and tried to wriggle away. He looked around to find Momma in the tangle of humanity, but was stopped by Felix's fist pounding into his jaw. Jake's teeth danced against each other.

Rolling to the side, he realized that dropping *his* first gun was a bad idea. Darting his eyes around, he found Momma was hiding behind the corner, pressing a hand to her side to stop the bleeding. She was near the front door. He mouthed to her, *"Stay there."*

Felix was on top of him again. This time, Jake felt teeth bite into his shoulder.

Jake howled as fresh blood soaked into his sleeve. Just out of finger's reach sat the gun. He kneed Felix in the groin.

Felix grabbed at his crotch, whimpering in pain.

Reaching forward, Jake's fingers wrapped around the gun's grip as a hot, piercing throb sliced through his side.

"No!" Momma screamed.

"Got you now, Preacher," Felix said, pulling the knife from Jake's side. It dripped with blood.

He had to close his eyes for a moment and shook his head, trying to clear his mind. Staggering to the side, he grabbed the banister for support. He pressed his palm against the wound. The wet smell of copper mixed with the damp dust from his clothes soured his nose. He felt his body crash to the ground.

Trying to regain some composure, his hand landed on the gun's muzzle.

He had to keep it together for Momma, for Charlotte.

Jake shook his head again and focused on one thing— keeping Momma safe and getting out of this alive. He had to stay alive long enough to stop Loretta.

"Go ahead, shoot me dead. It'll be over, I'll join my wife and daughter in heaven."

A bird-like smile crossed Felix's lips. "No problem. Happy to help."

He let Felix walk around his back and press the blade against his throat. For just a moment, Jake thought about letting Felix do the deed, slice deep, and bring all the horrible death, pain, and suffering he'd experienced these past ten years to an end.

Let the Grants win.

An image of Charlotte fluttered through his mind like a spring-time breeze. She was still in danger, Momma was still in danger, and Tan was either hurt or dead.

Felix snickered.

Momma cried somewhere near the door.

Jake's hand, still on the gun's muzzle, spun the gun and wrapped his hand around the grip. He hoped it was his fully loaded gun and not the empty one. Pressure from the blade bit into his neck. For a moment, the world stilled. Felix laughed and Jake brought his leg up and wrapped it around Felix's boot and pulled.

In an instant Felix was on the ground. Jake's knee collided against his chest.

Felix tried to shove the knife still in his hand toward Jake's throat. "Go to hell!"

"You first." Jake pressed the gun to Felix's head and pulled the trigger.

FOR A MOMENT, Jake didn't move. Felix was now dead. He deserved death for all the horrible murders he committed in the name of revenge. But all that anger Jake had built for years, searching for the man who killed his family, eluded him. In the end, it was Gabriel who saved his life, and Felix who tried to kill him.

He looked over at his weeping mother, sidled up, and held her tight. "I have you. He's dead."

"Go get Charlotte."

He felt Momma's side. The wound didn't look too deep. "Momma—"

"I'll be just fine. Just a scratch that'll heal in due time." Momma rose to kiss his cheek. "You need to go stop that horrible woman."

That horrible woman was someone he trusted with his life on many occasions. Loretta was a friend, confidant, and the one who appeared more like Momma than anyone else Jake knew. How could she be a part of this—in league with Felix Grant? It just didn't make sense.

"Momma, don't go anywhere."

The front door opened. Jake jerked around, aimed the gun…

"Whoa!"

It was Freddy.

"What are you doing here?" Jake asked, lowering the gun.

"Coming to rescue your sorry butt." Feddy looked around. "Where's the Marshal?"

"I need you to take Momma, get her out of here. I'll meet you at the Creek Ranch. I don't want her here."

"I will." He wrapped his hands around Momma and helped her stand. "Where's Tan?"

"Don't worry about him. Freddy, go!"

Momma looked at Jake and wiped her tears. "Thank you, son." She grabbed at his hands.

"I love you." Turning to Freddy, "Get Momma out of here!"

He grabbed his Colt and took off down the hallway, not knowing if Freddy would listen or not. Jake didn't care. As he ran toward the study, he prayed Loretta hadn't killed Charlotte.

CHAPTER EIGHTY-ONE

JAKE STOOD just outside the study doorway. It was time to confront Loretta, Diamond Rose, or whatever name she went by. He didn't care. She took Charlotte, and he'd find out why.

Hand on the doorknob, he turned it and pushed into the darkened room. Only a small fire cascaded light into the otherwise dingy space. The same space where he'd first encountered Gabriel Grant all those years ago.

"Hello, Jake. Guessing you took care of Felix for me. You saved me the trouble. I was planning on putting a bullet between his sorry eyes."

The woman who'd cooked and cleaned the CHR daily stood in her man britches and suspenders with a gun belt that loosely hung around her waist. Loretta had pulled her hair back like a horse's tail and a brown Stetson sat on her head.

She pressed the side of the gun to her forehead and squeezed the other side with her palm. A strange sound escaped her mouth, and something switched inside her eyes.

He looked over at Charlotte, who sat gagged and tied to a chair. "You okay?"

She nodded as tears flooded her eyes and cascaded down her rosy cheeks.

He trained his gun on Loretta and pulled back the hammer. "Why?"

While looking at Charlotte, he said, "Talk to me, Loretta. I know it was you who killed Judge Rex Talbert. Was he the one who killed your husband all those years ago?"

Loretta trained her gun on Jake. The hammer was back and ready to fire. "Remember a couple of years ago when I said there was something I had to take care of?"

Jake said he did. She came back with bloodied clothes and told him she'd killed the man who killed her husband. Jake holstered his iron. "Talk to me. We've always been good at talking, come to some sort of agreement. No one else needs to die tonight. There's been enough bloodshed."

Loretta's head snapped up. "That pig deserved his gutting. Had it coming for years. Just needed a good excuse and a moment to get away from the Ranch to take him down. Found him at the Lucky Diamond Saloon. The gal, Missy or something, who runs the establishment, gave me a key and let me into his room. The fat man busied himself with one of those skinny whores that frequent the place. I swatted her away, climbed on top of Talbert, and slit his throat.

"I couldn't get to Gabriel because you let him get away."

Disgusted, Jake had no words to express the disappointment he felt. Not just for Loretta, but for Missy. It saddened him. The two women he considered friends murdered a man.

"Gabriel Grant killed your husband." It was a statement, not a question.

She threw her hands wide. "Talbert was the next best

thing. It's because of his crooked sense of justice that Gabriel got away with my Jamison's murder. I'm giving you the big picture. When my husband and I lived here in Purgatory, Gabriel tried to buy our land. This land!"

She spun in a circle. "We were planning on raising our family here."

She convulsed as tears filled her eyes. "He wanted to leave our roots in this community. They respected my Jamison in these parts." She wiped the tears as they fell. "But Gabriel fixed his death. Came over to talk with Jamison about selling this land and next thing I knew, Grant disappeared, and my sweet Jamison was gored to death by his prized bull."

"Loretta, I'm sorry."

She laughed. "You're sorry? I thought you were my saving hope the day you showed up at the CHR to speak with Clyde Heller. Someone who understood the evil that Gabriel Grant had in his soul. Always up to no good, taking what doesn't belong to him."

If only Jake had noticed this about Loretta a few years ago, maybe he could have had Tan help with something. "What's this have to do with—"

Cutting him off, she said, "For years, Clyde investigated Gabriel Grant and his operations here in Wyoming. That's why he contacted Marshal Bennington. But when Gabriel killed Clyde, the second man I fell in love with, and my friend Moira by your hand, I just bided my time and waited until Felix was old enough to get revenge on you. You know she tried to make amends for what happened to my husband? Became a proper friend. And you took everything away from me because of your arrogance and anger toward Gabriel Grant. Because of you, Clyde is dead. Because of you, Moira is dead!"

Jake opened his mouth to speak, but no words came. He did not know all that rage was buried in Loretta's soul. Revenge was lonely and isolating.

"I'm so sorry, Loretta. But Charlotte has nothing to do with any of this. It's because of me that Gabriel Grant escaped with his life the night Moira died. It should have ended that night and maybe this...all of this wouldn't have happened. But I didn't kill Moira."

"She's dead because of you! You're hiding behind a mask; a lie. You're trying to live another life, but I know who you are, Jacob Creek."

He looked up. "I was your friend, Loretta!"

Tears formed in her eyes. "A friend? You used me, and all I was good for was waiting on you hand and foot. Do this Loretta. Do that Loretta. You know what? I was tired of it all."

Jake chose to ignore that comment. "Why kill all those people?"

"Don't you get it? Sometimes healing comes from death and chaos. Death is beautiful, and in its finite state, there's a quiet stillness that brings peace and calm to the world. Otherwise, men like that preacher I killed spread false hope that everything will be okay, as long as you trust in God."

Each word Loretta spoke came out twisted and dark.

"And you kept the girl alive because you wanted to send me a message? Well, Loretta, I got your message, and I'm sickened."

"I left her alive because men like that preacher deserve death from spreading false hope. That girl hadn't learned her lesson in life yet. Needs to grow up knowing there is nothing but pain and suffering in this world."

Jake felt sick, but he had to keep her talking. That was the goal, as she slowly lowered her gun. Maybe, just maybe, they all could walk away alive. "So, why Diamond Rose?"

She smiled again; the gun pointed at the ground. "Because my sweet Jamison always said that my eyes were like sparkly diamonds, and my skin as soft as rose petals. Seemed fitting of a way to honor my dead husband."

"That's a good way to honor him. Why don't you put down that gun and let's talk about it?"

"Stop it! I know what you're doing. You're trying to get inside my head."

"Loretta, put down the gun."

She punched her head a few times and grabbed at her face. "Shut up! It's time to learn what it truly feels like to lose someone you love."

"Loretta! I grieve for my wife and daughter every single day. You of all people should know that."

She pointed the gun at him. "You gave up!"

"How did I give up? I moved on. Now, drop your gun."

She grabbed at her face again; this time she screamed. "I can never move on from my Jamison. He died right here. This place. This property." She pointed the gun at Charlotte and decisively pulled back the hammer.

Charlotte cried harder behind the gag.

Jake's heart skipped a beat. This wasn't working. He pulled and cocked his gun. "Loretta, I won't ask again. Drop the gun!"

"I hate you!" She spun back around and fired a shot.

He didn't flinch as the bullet whizzed by his head and popped into the door frame. That was close. But the gun was away from Charlotte's direction. He could work with that. Keeping her gun trained on him was the goal.

"Loretta, it doesn't have to end this way. Put down the gun. I don't want to shoot you, but I will if you don't listen."

Her breathing came in heavy gasps, and Jake knew what was going to happen. There was nothing he could do to stop her. He leveled his gun and applied pressure to the trigger.

"Sorry, Jake. It's been a good ride."

Jake heard himself scream as Loretta put the gun to her temple and pulled the trigger.

CHAPTER EIGHTY-TWO

J AKE DIDN'T MOVE and all he could do was stare at Loretta's lifeless body bleed out on Gabriel Grant's floor. Shame it had to end this way. Loretta Lynn was a friend, confidant, and someone he trusted for years. Now, she laid twisted on the floor with a hole in her head. Charlotte was weeping, still tied to the chair, and Jake realized he hadn't untied her yet.

In two quick strides, he was behind her chair, cutting the cords that bound her wrists and ankles to the chair. The moment the gag around her mouth was out, she threw her arms around him and wept.

"Shhhh, now. It's okay. I've got you. It's over."

Her chest convulsed against his and Jake felt tears well in his own eyes and snake down his cheeks. "I thought I'd lost you. Don't know what I would have done if she would have killed you."

Charlotte pulled back and wiped the tears from her face and kissed Jake deep. They collapsed into another embrace, kissed again, and hugged tighter. He didn't want to let her go, couldn't let her out of his arms again.

"I love you so much, my dear Charlotte."

"I love you too, Jacob Creek."

She placed a hand on his side, which he'd forgotten about, but pain rippled through his abdomen. "You're hurt!"

Jake looked down at the now throbbing wound. "It's not as bad as it looks. Just a flesh wound. I reckon it'll heal right quick. More worried about Tan."

Charlotte wrinkled her nose. "If you say so," she said, then she kissed him again.

"Shall I take you home?"

She smiled. "I would love nothing better."

They embraced and kissed again. Oh, how he couldn't get enough of her kisses. She was still alive. Felix or Loretta hadn't killed her. Jake thought about the death of Sarah and Virginia that awful night. The fight with Gabriel Grant the night Moira died, and now all these years later, things came full circle. Gabriel's reign of horrors ended with Loretta's death. He killed her husband. He caused the death of Sarah and Virginia. But in the end, he came back to the man Moira always thought he was—a good man who had a good heart. She told Jake as much the night she died.

Jake smiled at the thought. "Let's go." He ushered her toward the door, and propped against the frame stood Tan Bennington. Looked like they'd shot him in his shoulder.

"I see you're looking safe, Miss Jennings," he said.

"Thank you, Mr. Bennington."

"Thought you were dead."

The big man laughed. "Can't keep a man like me down." He looked at the body.

"So, Diamond was Loretta?"

Jake shook his head. Why did it have to be Loretta?

"Where's your mother?"

Jake told him what happened, and that Freddy had taken her to Creek Ranch. It was time to leave, time to go home. It was good to see the big man alive and well.

"You take care of the shoulder yourself?"

"I did. Learned how during the war. Was a young kid back then. Enough about me, let's get out of here."

They walked out and mounted their horses. Jake pulled Charlotte up to Tucker and she rode behind him. No way would he let her ride alone. He wanted to be as close to her as possible. He prayed a prayer of thanksgiving for her safe return. And then they were off toward his old home, toward Creek Ranch.

CHAPTER EIGHTY-THREE

L IGHT STARTED filtering through the trees as they neared his childhood home. They neared a ridge that over-looked Creek Ranch as the sun pierced the night sky, chasing away the stars and washing away the evil of the previous day. He remembered the ridge well. Tugging at his neck, Jake pulled out Sarah's ring and fingered the smooth gold band as they stopped just at the top of the ridge.

"Is this the place?" Charlotte asked. Not out of curiosity, because he'd told her about this place, but to see how he was doing. At the moment, Jake wasn't sure how he felt.

Tears filled his eyes as the sharp memory reopened the wound that filled his heart for so long. He'd never see either of them again. Even after ten years of mourning their loss, it never would go away, not completely.

Jake dismounted without saying another word. He stared out at the reds and oranges that painted the sky, marking a new day. The new sunlight sparkled off the gold chain and band. He had not taken off Sarah's ring in these ten years. It was his constant reminder of all he'd lost.

Charlotte wrapped her arm around his. "It's okay."

Tears flooded his eyes and carved their own rivers down his cheeks. "I miss them so much, Charlotte." He sobbed. "It's over. They're deaths are avenged. They were my world... my everything."

Part of Jake felt wrong for speaking this way, considering Charlotte was his future, but he also knew that she understood. And she'd spent the last several years as a friend whom he fell in love with. The pain in his heart reminded him that Sarah and Virginia would always be a part of his former life. That would never change. Charlotte was his future.

Turning to face her, he said, "They will always be a part of my heart. I can't change that. But I can promise you this, you will always be my future. I love you and nothing will ever change that."

He looked out at his childhood home and smiled at the barn that still stood. His late friend Bill Erickson would be proud that the work they did still stood. How he missed him as well. He looked down at the tree in which he and Sarah carved their initials the night they were engaged. Carefully, he traced each letter with his finger as Charlotte watched on.

Jake knelt down and pulled back some moss and then dug a small hole at the base of the tree. Staring at the ring one last time, Jacob Creek buried his past. After setting the moss back in its place, he stood and realized that Tan was still there, staring at them.

"You, okay buddy?" his big friend asked.

Jake smiled, kissed Charlotte. "I'm fine. I see the lights on down below. Momma has probably started cooking something good for breakfast despite being stabbed."

Tan laughed, then circled his horse. "I'll race you!"

Laughing, both Jake and Charlotte mounted Tucker.

"Hold on tight. This horse likes to ride fast. And I'm not about to let Tan Bennington win."

He kicked his horse, and they descended the hill toward Creek Ranch.

EPILOGUE

J AKE DIDN'T WIN the race down the bluff. But it was hard
  to do that with two riders, and his side throbbed something fierce.

"Guess this fifty-year-old man still has it," Tan said.

Jake kissed Charlotte again. "Let's go inside."

When they walked through the door, Momma had
whipped up quiet the spread. The smell of his favorite, eggs,
bacon, and beet salad all sat on the table. Charlotte had her
arm tucked tight inside of his and he wasn't about to let go
of her.

Not ever again.

When they walked through the doors, everyone was there.
Freddy, Momma, and Ted.

"Miss Jennings. I's known you'd be alright. That Mister
Callihan would bring ya home safe. So glad you're okay now."

She smiled. "Thank you, Mister Jeffries."

Freddy nodded his head, saying something similar, then
worked on Tan Bennington's arm and stitched up Jake's stomach. Everything hurt his ribs, where Felix stabbed him. It all

hurt, but he could move. His mother's cooking smelled amazing.

He wanted to pour a drink to dull his body's pain, but knew that Momma wouldn't approve. After he took his seat, she came over and kissed him on the head.

"I'm so glad the Lord has kept you safe."

"How's your side, Momma?" Jake asked.

"Oh, I'll be just fine. Nothing but a scratch." She noticed the ring on Charlotte's finger. "Lands, dear, looks like I'm getting a daughter! So happy for you both."

Tan and Freddy held up their glasses and cheered in agreement. Trying to be happy about everything seemed hard to do after so much bloodshed. Slim, Purgatory's sheriff, Loretta! How she got messed up in all of this eluded his thinking. Then there was the case of Missy. Funny, he just realized she was not here. This was where he figured she'd be, considering everything.

"Freddy, was anyone here when you and Momma arrived?" Jake had to know.

Freddy shook his head. "Sorry, the place was dark." He reached into his pocket and pulled out a piece of paper. "Found this on the table. It's for you, Jake."

Jake took the paper from his friend and read while everyone else waited to find out what it said.

My dearest Jacob,

First, I want to apologize for ambushing you regarding the birth of Elliot. I know he's not your son, but I was scared, and when I saw you ride into town, I figured things might be different between us. Knowing that you have someone else waiting for you to rescue her, I left Purgatory to start a new life, away from the pain this place has caused, what I know, and what I've done.

After I learned I was pregnant with Elliot, I knew Rex Talbert was the father. It made me sick. When a woman came in having a score to settle, I let her into his room. It was wrong. I know that now. Please forgive me. Revenge is a medicine that is served ice cold. I will regret that decision all the days of my life.

I don't fault you for walking out how you did a few days ago, and understand I pressed a little too hard, trying to make you believe Elliot was your offspring. You take care of that woman of yours and I hope you find whatever it is you're looking for in this life. Inside this box, you will find something that I know you will want.

God bless you, dear Jacob. I love you. Always have.

Love,

Melissa K. Cartright.

Jake looked up from the note. *What box?* He didn't have to even ask. Freddy picked up something off his chair, and with a smile, handed it to him. Peeling off the lid, he found something wrapped in some fancy white paper. He unrolled the paper and into his hand fell a porcelain doll. Its slightly burned dress and singed hair reminded him of all he'd lost. A small crack ran across the right cheek of the doll like the one in his heart, but he knew what it was. This was Virginia's dolly. The same dolly sitting in the schoolhouse in Purgatory.

Heat cascaded up his throat before burning the back of his eyes as hot tears flooded his vision, then dropped onto the doll's blue dress. This was Virginia's dolly. He looked around the silent room. Everyone was watching him, but for just a moment, just for that second, they all disappeared and standing next to him was Virginia.

He knew she wasn't real, wasn't standing there. But there she was, holding his hand, smiling, laughing and begging him to take her to the creek that ran along the property to be baptized. The memory swallowed him until he could almost feel the water rushing around his waist. Taking her hand in his, he asked, "Are you ready?"

"Yes!" she giggled, then twirled in the water.

Then he lowered her into the water.

The memory faded, along with Virginia. Jake stared at her dolly. This is the only physical memory he had left, something that would be a constant reminder of what he had and how blessed he was to have had her in his life.

"Jacob?"

Charlotte's soft voice pulled him to the present. "This was Virginia's. I bought it for her on her eighth birthday." A tear rolled down his cheek."Missy left it for me."

"Oh, Jacob," was all Charlotte could say. Tears also filled her eyes.

"Well, now..." Momma's voice cracked and Jake wasn't sure if it was from pain or the doll. "...this food's going to get cold if we don't eat."

Jake kissed the doll and gently placed her back in the box. As he did, he found another note stuffed inside the hem of the doll's dress. Jake unfolded the paper and his heart skipped a beat.

"What is it, Jacob?" Charlotte asked.

"It's a... a note from..." Tears filled his eyes again and Jacob Creek collapsed into a waiting chair. He handed the note to Momma, who gasped with a hand to her lips.

"Is it true?"

Jake shook his head.

"Come on now," Freddy started. "Don't keep us waiting, read the note."

Momma handed the note back to Jake. He glanced at the words again and read.

"To my dearest, Daddy,

I am at a loss for words which cannot fully express how much I miss you. I don't know if this letter will ever find you, but I want you to know that I'm okay. Don't come looking for me, because I fear for your life. If you ever find this, know that I love you more than mere words can say. I miss you and I'm so very sorry about running into that fire. Can you ever forgive me for what happened to Mother? If God has his way, and it's safe for me to do so, we'll find each other again.

Your dearest daughter,

Virginia."

TO BE CONCLUDED IN...

|| THE REDEMPTION OF JACOB CREEK ||

SIGN UP AT JBSISAM.COM
TO RECEIVE UPDATES!

ABOUT THE AUTHOR

JASON (J. B.) SISAM is a professional blogger, pastor, and author. He helps writers and leaders stay motivated with clear thinking so that they are equipped with tools to find their voice, write their God-story, and succeed in their family, business, and life. He creates believable characters that connect with the heart and delivers stories that resonate with truth. Jason lives in Minneapolis with his wife, Kari and their two children, Amelia and Aaron. Learn more at JasonSisam.com.

Follow me on all the social channels: @jbsisam

www.ingramcontent.com/pod-product-compliance
Lightning Source LLC
Chambersburg PA
CBHW030546260626
47157CB00006B/2211